PRAISE FOR THE ROM

INCEPT
"Brilliantly plotted original story, combining the historical with the futuristic. It's a real edge-of-the-seat read, genuinely hard to put down." – Sue Cook

CARINA
"This is a fabulous thriller that cracks along at a great pace and just doesn't let up from start to finish." – Discovering Diamonds Reviews

PERFIDITAS
"Alison Morton has built a fascinating, exotic world! Carina's a bright, sassy detective with a winning dry sense of humour. The plot is pretty snappy too!" – Simon Scarrow

SUCCESSIO
"I thoroughly enjoyed this classy thriller, the third in Morton's epic series set in Roma Nova." – Caroline Sanderson in *The Bookseller*

AURELIA
"AURELIA explores a 1960s that is at once familiar and utterly different – a brilliant page turner that will keep you gripped from first page to last." – Russell Whitfield

INSURRECTIO
"INSURRECTIO – a taut, fast-paced thriller. I enjoyed it enormously. Rome, guns and rebellion. Darkly gripping stuff." – Conn Iggulden

RETALIO
"RETALIO is a terrific concept engendering passion, love and loyalty. I actually cheered aloud." – J J Marsh

ROMA NOVA EXTRA
"One of the reasons I am enthralled with the Roma Nova series is the concept of the whole thing." – Helen Hollick, Vine Voice

THE ROMA NOVA THRILLERS
The Carina Mitela adventures
INCEPTIO
CARINA (novella)
PERFIDITAS
SUCCESSIO

The Aurelia Mitela adventures
AURELIA
NEXUS (novella)
INSURRECTIO
RETALIO

ROMA NOVA EXTRA (Short stories)

―――――

ABOUT THE AUTHOR
A 'Roman nut' since age eleven, Alison Morton has
clambered over much of the remainder of Roman Europe.

Armed with an MA in history, six years' military service and a love
of thrillers, she explores via her Roma Nova novels the 'what if'
idea of a modern Roman society run by strong women.

Alison lives in France with her husband, cultivates
a Roman herb garden and drinks wine.

Find out more at alison-morton.com, follow her on Twitter
@alison_morton and Facebook (AlisonMortonAuthor)

·JULIA PRIMA·

ALISON MORTON

PULCHERIA
PRESS

ISBN 9791097310349 (ebook)
ISBN 9791097310356 (paperback)

DRAMATIS PERSONAE

Bacausus household at Virunum, Roman Noricum
Julia Bacausa – Daughter of local ruler
Asella – Julia's body servant
Prince Bacausus – Julia's father and local ruler
Suria (deceased) – Julia's mother, a tribeswoman
Daria – Housekeeper
Patulus – Head cook at palace
Aegius – Fresco painter and more
Cuso – Aegius's grandson
Musius – Former soldier, Bacausus's security chief

Roman authorities at Virunum
Lucius Apulius – Tribune, Virunum detachment Legio I Noricorum
Opsius – Commander, Virunum detachment, Apulius's superior
P. Vindius Clemens – Governor (*praeses*), Noricum Mediterraneum

Others at Virunum
Deodatus – Julia's ex-husband
Bishop Eligius – Deodatus's uncle
Gylfi – Amber trader from the north
Quietus – Businessman
Paula – Quietus's chatterbox daughter
Priscilla – Quietus's thoughtful daughter

Laurinus Turcilus – Bacausus's cousin
Talusia – Alamanna shaman

On the journey
Serandius – Julia's host in Santicum
Verina – Serandius's wife
Melissa – Hostess in Caporetum
Florus – Innkeeper at Fons Timavi
Crispus – Florus's son
Victorina – Hostess in Tergeste
Simonides – Obnoxious customs officer
Siro – A tribesman
Therasia – Innkeeper in Ancona
Mermelus – Therasia's brother-in-law, stable owner
Fulminius – Stable owner in Nuceria
Cordus and his ancient father – Innkeepers at Vicus Martis
Leonius Mercator (Leo) – Stable owner, Porta Flaminia
Clarita – Leo's wife

In Rome
Quintus Apulius – Lucius's father
Constantia of the Flavii – Lucius's mother
Pia Afra – Innkeeper
Valeria Polia – Baths acquaintance
Gaius Mitelus – Lucius's comrade
Maelia Mitela – Gaius's sister
Honoria Mitela – Matriarch
Lucilla – Pastrycook at Domus Apulia
Diacu – Alamanna slave

Historical figures
Count Theodosius – A senior imperial military leader
Flavius Theodosius – Son of Count Theodosius, later emperor
Theodosius I – AD 379-395
Dulcitius – Dux Britanniarum, military leader
Valentinian I – Emperor AD 364-375
Gratian – Son of Valentinian, later emperor of the Western Roman
Empire AD 367-383

Julia's journey – *Noricum and Italia annonaria*

TEURNIA

VIRUNUM

SALOCA

SANTICUM

MECLARIA

TARVISIUM

PLETIUM

CAPORETUM

EMONA

PONS SONTI

FONS TIMAVI

AQUILEIA

PUCINUM

VALLICULA

TERGESTE

(c) Alison Morton 2022

VIRUNUM

ROMA

Julia's journey – *Italia suburbicaria*

VIRUNUM

ROMA

ANCONA

AUXIMUM

SEPTEMPEDA

PROLAQUEUM

NUCERIA

FORUM FLAMINII

MEVANIA

VICUS MARTIS

CARSULAE

NARNI

OCRICULUM

MARE ADRIATICUM

ARCH OF DIVINE CONSTANTINE

PONS MULVIUS

ROMA

(c) Alison Morton 2022

Julia's Rome

Showing relevant bridges, gates and streets

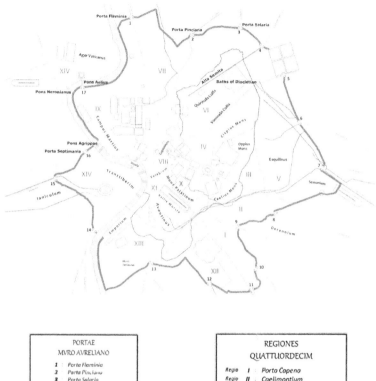

Based on Map of Rome, made by S.B. Platner for his book The Topography and Monuments of Ancient Rome, 1911

PROLOGUE

Danuvius River, AD 369

The tips of the oars paddle the water softly at each stroke. Rain obscures our passage as we cross the fast-flowing river. In the dark night, the only things I see are the steersman's eyes in his blurred face. He's swinging his head round, wary for any shouts of discovery. The two rowers hunch against the rain. But it's often like this whenever I take trade goods across. Anything to avoid paying taxes to those Roman bastards.

At last, a light shows on the far bank and our small boat struggles against the current to head for it. On the narrow stony shore, I hoist my pack onto my shoulder and jump out, then hand over a leather purse with the balance of the passage money. The steersman nods, then grunts and slips the purse into his belt pouch. He'll discover it's copper, not the silver I promised. But I'll be gone by then, never to return. He turns and heads back to the water. I scramble up the bank through trees so similar to those surrounding my old village. And the rain falls as heavy as it did that night when the Romans came.

I won't ever forget it. I was twelve. A warm day fading into evening, the smell of blood and already decaying horseflesh, cries of wounded and dying warriors, carrion crows circling in the dark clouds above the battlefield. Above all, the implacable faces of those Roman bastards – metal creatures who stood unmoving in straight lines waiting for their commander.

My grandfather stood, his feet in mud, his shoulders drooping. His son, my uncle Ittu, twenty-one summers and the only one of his male children left alive, his eyes gleaming dark, wrapped his arm round his father's shoulders. My mother, my grandfather's eldest child, grasped her father's hand, and stared down the line of Romans as their commander approached, not in fear but in defiance. Her shoulders were rigid. The breeze caught her hair, shades of burnt brown. She ignored me then as she always had for the whole of my twelve-year boyhood.

Two hands came to rest on my shoulders, old hands, wrinkled. I smelt her before she whispered, 'Not a word, Siro. Whatever happens. Just know you will always be in my heart.'

I shrugged off her hands.

'As you say, Great-Aunt.'

She always believed in me – too gullible for her own good. Even when I'd strangled her best-laying hens just for the fun of hearing them croak as they died. I'd sworn all innocent-faced that another boy had done it. He'd got a right good beating. I'd hidden behind his house and laughed until I was nearly sick.

The Roman commander, a tall man with red hair tied back, had stridden up to my grandfather and demanded surrender. I didn't know any Latin then, but it was obvious what he was saying. I shivered. Great-Aunt had told me they would take us all away to the slave market to be separated and sold. Men would do unspeakable things to us. She pressed a hand into my shoulder bone, but I wriggled out of her grip. I didn't need her, the old fool. I'd survive.

Grandfather knelt. Teutates! My warrior grandfather, still in his mail shirt kneeling before this... this Roman. Great-Aunt gripped my shoulder again as I tried to move forward. Grandfather ignored me most of the time – he was hard and fierce – but sometimes he patted me on the head when my mother wasn't looking.

The Roman stopped talking. He was staring at my mother. She was staring back. Her eyes half closed, then widened. She tipped her chin up. Nobody spoke. Silence dropped as if the sky truly had fallen on our heads. They all watched her, then him and back to her. Only the sound of rain dripping off the trees and far distant moans of the dying interrupted the stillness.

After many moments, the Roman gestured to Grandfather who stood up, then he pointed to my mother. My uncle stepped forward, his face angry, but Grandfather thrust out his arm to stop him. He talked to the Roman again in Latin. The Roman replied and waved his arm slowly in a wide circular movement as if to include what was left of the tribe. Grandfather shrugged but his eyes seemed to send a questioning look to my mother. The Roman then stretched out his hand to my mother. She glanced at Grandfather and nodded. She whispered something to my uncle. Her eyes were blazing as if she had caught a prey and was going for the kill. I'll say this – she hunted as well as any man. The Roman turned and she and Grandfather followed him between the two lines of Roman soldiers. Her body servant, Asella, the one they said was a witch, pushed out of the crowd and trotted after her.

Two of the Roman soldiers bound my grandfather's hands.

I didn't care if I never saw my mother again. Others in the tribe who did talk to me told me she couldn't bear to look at me from the day I was born.

It started to rain heavily and my nose dripped. I wiped it on my tunic sleeve.

As all the other Romans marched off, the tribespeople didn't move. They were like trees rooted in the ruins of their fields. They let the rain wash over them and the mud and blood under their feet seeped between their toes. At last, slowly they seemed to wake up. Several looked at my uncle; they started gabbling at him, some growled and shook their fists in the Romans' direction. Great-Aunt sobbed, then let out a breath.

'What is it? Where have Grandfather and my mother gone?' I asked. Nobody replied. I shouted out my question. My uncle glared at me.

'Oh, it's you, the little bastard. Well, your grandfather has gone into captivity. He was prepared for that. But the Roman has taken my sister as the price for releasing the rest of us.'

'No, Ittu,' Great-Aunt said. 'He was no Roman. He was of the Norici.'

'The same thing,' he replied bitterly.

'Your sister went willingly. I saw the look in her eyes – she wanted that Roman.'

My uncle Ittu looked at Great-Aunt then rubbed the back of his neck.

'Speaking truthfully, I don't think you're wrong, Aunt.'

'And agreeing to go with him she's saved us all from the slave-market,' Great-Aunt said. 'She was never happy or even content after…' She glanced quickly at me, then looked back at my uncle.

'Agreed,' he said and stared down at me. He jabbed his finger at me. 'You, you're the reason for my sister's unhappiness. Now I've lost her. Keep out of my sight. Always.'

'Hush, Ittu, he can't help it. He didn't ask to be born,' Great-Aunt replied.

'No, and my sister didn't ask to be raped at fourteen.'

I stared at him, then at Great-Aunt. She looked away, her face grey in the bad light. So that was why my mother hated me. Well, I could hate back. She'd abandoned me when I was born and she'd abandoned me again. I spat on the ground. I vowed then, child that I was, that she would learn, and so would that fake Roman, even if it took my whole life.

I'd tried it before, seven years ago, and nearly succeeded. But I'd barely escaped. Now, with another seven summers behind me and gold in my pocket mostly from fools not able to keep hands on their own money, I stared down the track leading to Noricum, ready again to keep that vow.

PART I

VIRUNUM

1

Virunum, Roman Noricum AD 370

What an arrogant bastard! Gone, of course. Taken his pleasure and left. I stretched out and took a deep, deep breath and smiled. But it had not only been *his* pleasure. I pulled the linen sheet up over my legs, stomach and breasts. I was still warm, a tiny film of moisture shone on my skin, but a cool wind funnelled through the tiny window along with the last sunlight, now orange. I closed my eyes. His had been brown, not nearly black like Deodatus's, but brown like a peat pool. I wanted to dive again into that pool, naked as I was, and never leave.

I drew my hands up over my head, arching my back. Gods, this bed was hard. The lumps in the thin mattress were digging into my back. How strange that I hadn't noticed that before.

My robe lay in a heap by the end of the bed; I only hoped it hadn't been torn as he'd pulled it off me. It was an old coarse-weave one, perfect for inspecting the household inventory, poking in corners of the kitchen cupboards to see what the housekeeper had forgotten was there. Daria was good, but she always opted for the easy life, directing the slaves to use the same tableware all the time.

Only hours before, at the back of the cupboard, I'd spotted the fine Gaulish redware set my father had brought back after the battle at Argentoratum, but pieces were missing. I'd told Daria to replace them from that Gaul in the market, but she'd pursed her lips and said she wouldn't demean herself by going shopping in the market like a slave. She would send one of the kitchen servants out to find and command the Gaul to bring his wares to the palace for inspection. Gods, nothing like a snobbish freedwoman! I'd flounced out, completely forgetting what I was wearing, or not wearing.

I'd marched out through the kitchen gardens round to the entrance portico, past the porter who opened his mouth and looked like a surprised chicken, grabbed one of the servants' hooded mantles off the row of pegs and stepped into the street. The steps and sloping path down the hill from our *domus* to the forum was easy and five minutes later I was in the thick of stalls, shops and deafening street cries.

'*Domina*! *Domina* Julia. Wait.' Asella, the body servant I'd inherited from my mother, was flapping behind me, but I didn't stop.

Weaving between ambulant hawkers with trays suspended from their necks, I nearly tripped over a pile of metal vessels and tools. Why they had to cover half the street with their goods, I didn't know. One hot-food trader stirred the contents of a large cauldron suspended over a fire and steaming in the chill, partly tempered by the spring sun. Next to him, a pie and sausage man who wiped his nose on his sleeve. Ugh. More permanent stalls were set up under awnings strung between stakes in the ground. Towards the centre, shops had disgorged onto the pavement and even into the street. The bread and vegetable vendors displaying their produce on wooden tables were more circumspect. At least I didn't have to make a detour round them like the dratted shoe seller who had set out wooden benches for his customers and marked out his place of sale with curtains hung between columns.

And did they all have to shout so loudly and wave their arms about so much? Along with the chickens squawking, mules braying and children shrieking, my head was fit to burst. At last, it quietened as I reached the crafts and household goods area. Fine pottery, leather and beadwork; one tribesman with curly blond hair and a friendly smile was selling beautifully worked fibula brooches and belt buckles. At last, I found the Gaul in front of a small glassware shop at the end of the row. The leather cover of the cart behind him was half drawn up to display stacks of redware, bedded in wooden frames lined with straw, but on the table in front of him were the best.

The redware was beautiful; exquisite figures chased one another on the widest part of one serving bowl, another showed a hunting scene with hare and hounds that my father would love. I stayed silent, picking up each piece, examining it slowly and putting it back. He shuffled behind his counter watching intently. Did he think I was going to steal it?

When I stopped and looked him direct in the eye, his face was expressionless. But I decided I would take the two serving dishes, a dozen of the cups and half that number of small bowls and plates. In the end, I relieved the Gaul's agony, gave the order and told him to deliver them to the service area of the palace.

'And who are you to give me orders?' He looked me up and down. 'I'll deal with your steward. You run back and get him.' He flicked his hand at me.

'How dare you! Do you know who I am?'

'No, but I know more than to go on a fool's errand started by some kitchen wench.' He wiped his hand on his checked tunic and turned towards a newcomer – the new Roman officer. A tall man, he must have been several years older than me, possibly in his late twenties. His face tight with anger above his red neck scarf and scale armour shirt. His boots were dusty as were his breeches. He walked a little wide as if chafed from being on his horse all day. He stopped, set one hand on his belt, the other on the pommel of his short sword. He glanced at the Gaul, then turned his gaze on me. Brown eyes, reflecting the pale light. Something twisted inside me, immobilised my breath, then settled in my core. Perhaps a meeting of something familiar, a recognition. He didn't move, just stared at me. I returned the stare. I couldn't find a word to say. Heat crept up my neck and into my face. Venus Suleviae. He must have thought I was half-witted.

Eventually, he moved, pointing at the Gaul.

'Is this man cheating you?'

'What business is it of yours?' It was out before I could think.

'None,' he said, frowning. He looked at me again, then turned away.

Oh, gods, I had behaved like a true barbarian and was ashamed. And he was walking away from me. I had to stop him.

'Wait, Roman.'

He walked on, ignoring me.

Please, Great Mother, make him stop.

'I said wait!' I cried after him.

He walked on. I knew I'd been rude, but he could at least stop and let me apologise. He didn't need to be so uncivil, even for a soldier. I hastened after him, determined to make him hear me. Nobody turns his back and walks away from me.

When I caught up with him, I seized his arm. He instantly grabbed his sword pommel. The gladius was halfway out of the scabbard by the time he saw it was me. He released it, then looked at my hand on his forearm as if it were a viper about to bite.

'How dare you touch me!' He looked at me as if I were the meanest drudge. 'Remove your hand or I'll have you whipped.'

'You can't,' I retorted. 'You have no right.'

'We'll see about that.' He went to raise his hand – to summon some of his men, I supposed – then he let his hand drop. His eyes gleamed and he looked down his Roman nose. I caught my breath and tipped my chin up at him. I knew my face was flushed – I could feel the heat – but I was going to teach him a lesson. When he found out who he'd insulted he'd be broken and sent back to Rome in disgrace. I opened my mouth to tell him exactly what his fate was going to be, but as he prised my fingers off his arm they tingled. The rough skin on his hand chafed my softer one. My fingers were jammed together but I hardly noticed. Before I could protest, he grabbed my wrist and pulled me to him. Gods, he was strong. His arm slid round the back of my waist, and he crushed me against his body. Solid, unyielding. He smelt of horse, a day's sweat and pine resin. His eyes narrowed then gleamed again. His breath shortened.

I should have struggled, but I didn't want to. His other hand gripped my buttock. I stared into his eyes. I was lost.

He pulled me round the corner of the row of shops where he pushed me against the wall and hitched up the hem of my tunic. I gasped as he slid his hand between my thighs. No, it shouldn't be this mechanical. But warmth flowed through me. I didn't want him to stop. Dazed at myself, I could say nothing. My mind was shocked at what I was doing. Or allowing to be done. His fingers touched my mons. I gasped and drew back.

'You refuse me, a Roman officer?' His voice was tight, the hollows of his eyes dark with desire. My body knew exactly what it wanted. I arched my back and he pulled me closer again. I shook my head, closed my eyes and parted my lips.

'*Domina*!' Gods, Asella's voice. The curtain moved on its rings and her veiled head appeared round the edge. 'Oh, thank Belestis,' she said and stepped into the tiny room. There was only just enough space for the bed, a narrow side table and a stool in the corner – a typical *caupona* upstairs room for an hour or two's hire. Asella looked at me, searching my face. Hers wore a frown. After a few heartbeats, she bent down and picked up my old robe from the floor and handed it to me. I swung my legs off the bed, stood, slipped it on and adjusted the leather belt. Next, she draped the old mantle round my shoulders.

'You can take that look off your face, Asella,' I said. 'And keep your tongue inside your mouth. It's nobody's business but mine, so I don't want to hear even a hint of a word of a whisper of a rumour.'

She glanced at the floor, then back up at me, her face cleared of any expression. She'd been my nurse originally, so she fussed – a habit she'd never lost especially since my mother had died when I was just sixteen.

'You cannot believe I would lower myself so, *domina*, but—'

'Yes?'

'Your father will have the man executed for this insult.'

'No. I will not be telling him,' I retorted. 'And he will not find out any other way. He knows that since the divorce I choose my own way.' In truth, my father would either storm into the Roman camp and kill the Roman with his bare hands or he would give me a cynical look, sigh and go back to his book and his cup of wine.

Gylfi had been the only one since my divorce. A tall, blond-haired giant from the Northern Sea, he'd arrived in Virunum with another half-dozen amber traders and their armed escort. In his role as a good client, old Quietus, the town's unofficial businessmen's representative and general busybody, had been calling on my father to make his morning *salutatio*. He'd brought Gylfi to the palace atrium as one of a group of traders. The northerners, most of whom spoke Latin with an accent, had laid stones and jewellery out on trays lined with soft dark cloths. Gylfi had placed his necklaces, brooches and earrings on the table and stood back as the older men started talking about their treasures, holding up lengths of fiery amber and trying to convince us all that each drop carried the sun's gold within it.

'Thank you, gentlemen,' Father said after five minutes and stood. 'But talk to my daughter and the steward. The women will know what they want.' He beckoned Quietus. 'A moment of your time, Quietus.' He led the businessman off to his *tablinum* and waved the other clients away. Two of them stayed to look at the amber; the younger tried not to look over-interested, but his eyes gleamed.

Asella and Daria clustered round the trays with the female house servants. Even the steward looked interested, for a gift I supposed, or a bribe. I glanced at Gylfi, who caught my look. I smiled at him. He half bowed in my direction, then looked back at the chattering group. As the others drifted away with their trinkets, I approached the table. The chief trader bowed and gave me a wide smile. Then I saw it. A heavy rope of amber and gold; polished oval stones with worked gold collars in between each one. The yellow and orange colours twisted and turned inside the semi-transparent stones, blazing yet contained. I touched them. Warm and smooth, yet full of fiery promise.

'It's yours, my lady. Only a woman with hair as red as flames should wear it.'

I jumped at his deep voice so near behind me. My heart started beating harder and I turned. The grey eyes, like the hard stone of the north. No, with a tone of blue as the Northern Sea is said to be. I swallowed hard. He lifted the necklace and placed it over my head and settled it on my neck. His hands brushed the skin on my neck and sent warmth into the core of my body.

I invited him to share wine when the others departed. That evening, he shared my bed. He'd stayed for three months but when we'd parted, I'd had no regrets, only a fond memory of the man who had restored a little of my faith in myself as a woman who could be loved. Or perhaps he'd been content to take an opportunity when it had presented itself.

Now Asella knelt down and retrieved my boots from under the bed. She wrinkled her nose, probably at the overcooked food smell percolating through the floorboards. I hadn't noticed before. As she stood up, she stopped, one ankle boot in her hand. She was staring at the rickety little table by the bed. Three gold *solidi* coins, neatly stacked, glinted in the rays of the evening sun falling through the window.

The Roman had paid me like a whore. A vast amount, as for a superior one, but a whore nevertheless.

I strode back into my father's house with Asella fussing behind me. I pulled off the mantle and thrust it at her as I stalked through the entrance portico into the inner courtyard, then the atrium. Our home was a strange mixture of grand Roman *domus* and suburban villa set on the lower slopes of the hill leading up to the old hill settlement deserted at the time of Claudius. Apparently my great-great-grandfather had pulled his original hillside palace down and built this sprawling complex in the traditional Roman style. He was the last of the house of Bacausus to spend so lavishly, mostly the money from wool and Norican steel.

Slaves were lighting the lamps on the tall stands as the light was fading from the *oculus* in the atrium roof. The delicate birds and flowers on the painted panels were merging into the darkening green background.

'Julia?'

'Father.'

He scoured my face with his direct gaze.

'Are you well?'

'Yes, thank you,' I said and gave him a quick smile.

'Where are you rushing off to?'

Very little escaped him which was one of the reasons why he still commanded his territory despite the Roman presence. Or perhaps it was his height and breadth and the gold band he wore on hair that was shot with grey now, but still thick and deep red, just touching his shoulders. Except on formal occasions, he still dressed like the Celt he was with generations of rulers behind him, but he was more Roman in his thoughts than he realised. Nevertheless, he did not tyrannise me.

'I must visit the bathhouse before eating,' I said, brushing the skirt of my robe with my fingers. He looked me up and down.

'Yes, you seem a little dusty and dishevelled. I hope your flushed skin doesn't mean you're coming down with a fever.'

2

I broke the surface of the water, took a breath and raised my hands to squeeze the excess out of my hair. Asella waited on the warm flagstones by the pool ready to wrap me in a linen cloth. Her face was passive and she looked at the far wall as she patted my body. She caught my hair up in a smaller cloth as I lay on the massage couch. She dripped warm oil onto the skin of my spine and her fingers kneaded it with more vigour than usual. The cinnamon and styrax scents grew and filled the room, warm yet not overpowering. But Asella hadn't said a word since we'd entered the bathhouse.

'Asella?'

'*Domina*?'

'Are you sulking?'

'It isn't my place to sulk.'

Oh, gods, she was mightily offended. When somebody has bandaged your grazed knee weeping with blood, wiped the snot from your five-year-old nose and held you when you wept at your first disappointment in love, it's the work of a Titan to order them around. I'd been abrupt with her. She was a slave, but I could never see her merely as such. When she scraped my body with the silver *strigil*, pressing especially hard over the backs of my thighs, I felt her disapproval with every stroke. After she'd finished, she wiped my skin with another linen cloth and still said nothing. She would not meet my eyes.

To Hades with her. She wasn't my mother. In my chamber Asella silently braided my hair. When she went to fetch my inner dress, she held two up and merely said, 'Which one?' I pointed to the cotton and silk mix one. It would be soft against my skin and the long sleeves would keep my lower arms warm; it was still March if only by two days. I couldn't bear it by the time she was fastening the belt round my waist over the wool *stola*.

'Asella!'

'*Domina*?'

'Please stop being so cold. I apologise if I was discourteous to you, but my actions are my own. You must understand that. And accept it.'

She didn't reply immediately, but fastened the clip on my belt, then stood back and looked me up and down as if to admire her handiwork. Eventually, she brought her gaze up.

'I will speak plainly. I won't throw my promise to your dying mother in your face. That would be a simpleton's trick. But think about cheapening yourself with the Romans.'

'But *we* are Romans, citizens for generations.'

'The Italians will always see us as provincials, Celtic peasants, however illustrious your father's service and the gods know how many of his ancestors have aped their ways.'

'You are too harsh, Asella.'

'I did not mean to be disrespectful to your father, *domina*. Prince Bacausus is a good man who treated my mistress well.' Her eyes softened. She'd accompanied my mother when she'd left her tribe to marry the young warrior prince my father had been. Father had been fighting against the tribes raiding across the Danuvius as part of the Legio II Italica based at Lauriacum. He'd led his men across the river into tribal territory and captured the local chieftain himself.

Asella said he'd stood as proud as the Christians' Lucifer and demanded the chieftain's surrender. If he gave himself up, the tribespeople would be spared. Given the overwhelming number of Romans armed to the hilt, the chieftain acquiesced and was led away as a captive. Then my father saw the chieftain's daughter, Suria, defiant and trembling with rage at her father's fate. Asella said sourly that he might have won the fight against the father, but it was at that moment he surrendered to the daughter. He said she had to be part of the surrender bargain and held out his hand. The daughter – who would become my mother – had stared at him long and hard, but stepped forward. She knew her refusal would mean disaster for the tribe. Asella told me that my mother had gone very willingly and had never regretted her decision, but she became homesick from time to time and would ride all the way up to the Danuvius River and watch across it for hours.

I remember Asella nursing my mother when she was dying. The *medicus* from the military camp had given her poppy seed draught to relieve the pain but shook his head when my father raised his eyebrow in question. I watched my father's shoulders slump as he turned and trudged back to his *tablinum* and drew the curtain across to forbid any possible visitors.

Asella's cousin had appeared at our door the next day without warning. Her face looked like any other tribeswoman's, but she wore a boldly patterned dress with bells and fringes at the edges of an overtunic. The fibula holding her cloak at the shoulder was silver, but with fantastic and frightening animal shapes and the gold torc round her neck the most intricately twisted that I'd ever seen. Her belt looked like metal skulls linked together and a pouch hung from it on the right side. The most normal thing was her hair, dark and gathered at the back with ring-headed pins sticking out. She fixed me with dark grey eyes buried deep in her face. I felt she was reading my soul, then she ignored me as she greeted Asella who bowed to her and called her Talusia. They'd disappeared down the corridor together towards my mother's room, leaving me alone, feeling a mere bystander.

Only when my father threatened to slice the cousin in half if he wasn't permitted to see his wife did she let him, and me, into my mother's room. Her poor face, so thin, her skin stretched across her cheekbones. I had fallen to my knees by her bed, ignoring the herbal smells from the brazier, the tribeswoman crooning and the other people in the room, and I took her hand. Warm tears ran down my face. I was supposed to be an adult at sixteen, but at that moment I was a tiny child desperate for her mother to never leave her. She turned her head slowly and looked at me.

'Julia,' she'd said softly. This thin croak wasn't her voice. Hers should be assured, positive and warm. But it *was* her hand, even though it felt like skin with only bones and sinews underneath. 'I'm so sorry to leave you. I wanted to see you with a good man and strong children.' Her fingers curled round mine as if she tried to grip them, but her touch had no strength.

'*Matir*,' I said, my throat parched. 'Don't tire yourself.'

'My Julia, listen. When you find a man who pleases you, marry him in the way of my people. And please your father and marry as the Romans, but not as their new god.' Her eyes glowed for a moment. 'Promise me!'

'I promise, but—'

Her eyes fluttered as she searched my face.

'I hope I have been a good mother to you,' she whispered, then sighed and looked up at the ceiling. After a minute she turned back to me. 'Now, farewell. Let me speak to your father. He is a noble and courageous man, and kind. Honour him.'

The last sight I had of my mother alive was of my father kissing her mouth in the Roman way to take her breath, her essence, into him. Then he'd stroked her forehead and run his fingers over her eyes to close them.

I finished my meal with a honey-flavoured pastry and picked at the bowl of nuts left on the table. I signalled the slave to set down the bowl of perfumed water and towels and leave us. Father sent me a questioning look, but said nothing. His face was difficult to read even in the good light provided by all the lamps. To be truthful, I was unsure where to start, but I took a deep breath.

'Father, when you saw Mother for the first time, what made you want to take her with you?' My words tumbled out as fast as I could speak them. I looked down at the nearly empty table, not daring to meet his eyes. He said nothing for several minutes. As the seconds passed, I was sure the heat I felt crawling over my skin wasn't from the braziers.

'What a strange question,' he said eventually. 'Why do you ask that now?'

'No reason,' I said too quickly. Curse it. He would know I was being devious. I yawned, pretending indifference and stretched out my hand to take an almond. He grasped my wrist.

'Yes, you have a reason. You are always direct, Julia, and unafraid. Now you are trying to hide something.' He scrutinised me with a hard stare which softened as he released my wrist. 'Am I such a harsh parent?'

'No, no, of course not. I – I was thinking of her. I apologise if I have intruded.'

'You haven't.' He slumped on his couch. 'I miss her sorely, too, even after five years. I always will.' He rinsed his hands in the bowl and dried them. 'I suppose when your brother died, I should have remarried to provide another son, an heir to my domain, but I've never met another woman I wanted to share my life with.' He snorted. 'I've bedded a few, but take into my house? No. Suria was my woman and I want no other to take her place.' He smiled at me. 'Nor can I see you giving up the keys.'

Gods, no. I couldn't imagine some snooty woman trying to tell me what to do or trying to run the household.

'You should see the look on your face, Julia!' He laughed and raised his cup to me. 'You may have my red hair and height, but inside you are very like her. Now tell me why you asked.'

'I wondered if it was a matter of war and power or whether it was something inside you?'

'Gods, you take no prisoners, do you, Julia?'

I said nothing, but waited. Inside, I was trembling with having crossed a barrier of some kind. Was it right for a child to ask a parent such a question? But I knew it was vital to know. Had he experienced the same feeling of connection I'd had with the Roman officer?

'It was something instinctive,' he said. 'A decision of the moment. I had a perfect right to take the whole tribe and sell them for profit. That's the price of defeat when rebelling against Rome.' His fingers clenched round his cup. 'But truth to tell, when I saw her, it was as if there was a cord linking us together. I didn't know anything about her. All I saw was a magnificent woman, fierce and vibrant. No shrinking girl. I knew she was to be part of my life. She knew it too, although it took her a year before she would admit it to me.'

'Did she try to run away?'

'No, never. She never really understood the Roman way. She was a passionate, headstrong woman with a nature like Mercury, but completely and fiercely loyal to me. Once, she discovered one of my ironmasters was slicing the profits, and she attacked him verbally and physically with a *pugio* I'd given her to defend herself if need be. The poor man lost two fingers and his face was never the same. He left soon after.'

'I remember her shouting at the Roman commander's painted wife who said she'd brought me up as a savage. The woman's daughter had stolen my doll and wouldn't return it. She ran around taunting me. So I slapped her and took it back.'

My father laughed.

'My Suria's daughter to the life! I didn't know about that. She never had a high opinion of the Italian women, saying they were useless except as ornaments and bedmates. Harsh, but many of them from the peninsula were unused to the practicalities of frontier life.' He reached over and tipped my chin up so I was obliged to look him direct in the face. 'If we are baring our souls to each other, Julia, I think she would have been very much against your marriage with Deodatus.'

I pulled my lips in. 'Nobody regrets it more than I do, Father. I saw a handsome cultivated man, the nephew of the bishop. I had no idea what a shrivelled soul there was inside.' I looked into the red and orange flames of the brazier. 'Nor did he seem to come to my bed with any passion.'

My father laid his hand over mine and pressed it for a moment. He gave me a sad smile.

'Well, whatever the bishop says, you've divorced him,' he said. 'Both in your mother's tradition and in Roman law. And that's an end to it. If that oily young bastard comes sneaking round here again mouthing his Christian inanities, I'll beat him to a pulp with my own hands.'

'Don't. You're only upsetting yourself. Deodatus will never accept the divorce, especially as I consented to go through their baptism ceremony after we were married. Gods! Now I see that ceremony was the stupidest thing I ever did.'

'No, not quite the stupidest,' he replied and raised his eyebrows.

The heat ran up my neck into my face. 'That was a cruel thing to say, Father.'

'Yes, but true.'

I bowed my head. 'I only did it to try to make the marriage work.'

'I know, child.'

'And you can't afford to fall out with Bishop Eligius.'

'Ha, my daughter the politician!' He shrugged. 'We go to his religious service every Sunday in his draughty *ecclesia*. That should be enough for him.'

'He's content to let things be as they are. He's not entirely sure he can challenge you openly. When I lived with Deodatus as his wife, *he* used to say in his smug way that the bishop had influence even in Rome.' I laid my hand on my father's. 'I would rather live into old age by myself than go back to Deodatus. But I will never do anything to endanger you, Father, nor your authority over our people.'

'You're a good girl, Julia, but it would break my heart if you sacrificed yourself like that. Of course, I will keep you safe from that excuse for a man. You need never fear on that account. But what happens if you find a man who pleases you enough that you want to risk another marriage? What then?'

3

A week later, I was vaguely aware of Daria asking me something about food but I didn't catch her words. The kitchen windows were open and the birds singing such a sweet song as the sun burst from the horizon that I was distracted. I loved the bright, almost white light that fell on the snow on the mountains in the distance and then seemed to roll across the valley to settle on the red tile roofs of the town below. It always seemed a miracle that it happened every day.

'So shall I see if the fish merchant can supply a fresh batch of oysters for this special dinner tonight?' Daria said with an impatient tone.

'What? Oh, yes, of course. My father has asked the governor and the camp prefect, so everything must be of the best.'

'Well, I'll try but the deliveries from Aquileia have not been as reliable as they used to be. I don't want to open the barrel and find a stinking mess.' She sniffed through her pointed nose that I'd always thought didn't belong to the rest of her fleshy face.

'Well, at least we'll have a full set of decent plates and bowls now,' I said.

'That Gaul was grumpiness itself, but I admit his redware was very fine although a pretty price. He was moaning about the road through Raetia being dangerous these days with tribes rampaging along the roads and he'd have to go through Italia and come up through Istria another time, if he came at all.'

'Nonsense!' I said. 'From Augusta Raurica the *limitanei* protect the frontier and after that the road is safe. He was just trying to extort a higher price. I hope you resisted it, Daria.'

'Of course, *domina*.'

One of the slave girls was rinsing and wiping each piece of redware as we spoke. She glanced up at me, then quickly looked back down at her work with a red face. Patulus, the head cook, scowled in her direction. He was harsh, but a genius with the roast meat my father loved. He cast round at his three assistants who kept their heads down grinding, slicing and chopping food. Another leant into the brick arch above the semi-concealed fire with a long-handled shovel and slid out two loaves of bread and a batch of spelt rolls. After depositing them on a rack, he leant back and wiped his forehead with his sleeve and took a deep breath.

It *was* warm in here with the heat of the two hearths and I was wearing two long-sleeved tunics, the outer one wool. I quickly approved the rest of the menu and agreed Daria's plan of decorations, then left her to it. I shivered as I passed into the corridor, then across the atrium where Father would receive our guests.

A tall, well-built man with thick protruding eyebrows and salt and pepper hair was holding his lower lip between his teeth as he brushed tiny strokes of paint onto one of the wall frescoes. A child was standing at his side holding a tray of vibrant reds, yellow, green, black and precious blue. His narrow shoulders drooped with tiredness and boredom. I knew the six-year-old Cuso would much rather be out with the horses than working with his grandfather.

'Aegius,' I said softly, not wishing to startle him. He didn't hear me. I coughed.

'Grandad,' hissed Cuso. '*Domina*'s here.' He tugged on the hem of Aegius's tunic.

'What?' The man's eyes were unfocused as he turned, probably strained at working closely on the wall. I looked up at the new paint, hardly discernible in colour from the old. He'd painted the originals nearly twenty-five years ago; glorious hunting scenes in the forest, the snow-fringed mountains, gardens full of pines, box hedges and roses, and the gods themselves at play. Here and there were interspersed some strange scenes that I couldn't fathom out.

Perhaps they were symbolic or supernatural. But they were exquisitely drawn and painted, one even decorated with gold.

'I don't wish to disturb you, Aegius, but I think it's perfect now. You've been working all week on the walls. You must be exhausted.'

'The day won't come when I'm too tired to paint, *domina*. And I keep seeing little bits that need patching up.'

'I can't fault your dedication, Aegius, but I think you must stop now so it will dry for this evening.'

'Humph.'

'It's early still. Go and rest before lunch, then take Cuso out in the spring sunshine.' I hoped he would find a warm spot in the garden and sit and drink a cup of wine. Perhaps one of his cronies from the gardens would find him.

'The boy has his lessons to learn or he'll get a whipping from the schoolmaster,' Aegius grumbled. 'And I have paint to mix in my workshop.' But he bent down, rinsed his brushes in a pot, then rolled them up in a linen pouch. He nodded and turned, shoulders hunched above his broad back as if I'd ordered him into eternal exile. Cuso picked up the dirty water pot and followed his grandfather. The boy glanced back and gave me a cheeky grin. I frowned at him for his lack of respect, then relented and grinned back.

According to Daria, Aegius had arrived twenty-five years ago riding a mule with a small saddlebag and carrying a satchel of brushes and dry paint powder on his back. He'd offered to paint the frescoes for a ludicrously small sum and had been here ever since. Nobody had ever found out where he came from; he spoke Latin with an Italian accent and Greek with an Athenian one. That was it. But his work was superb, glowing with rich colours, and animated. I studied the one of Venus, delicate even in her erotic pose. It could have decorated the emperor's palace in Constantinople but, of course, they all thought only of saints now and wouldn't contemplate such unholy, yet human, images. I sighed and carried on down the corridor.

In the semicircular dining room that Father had ordered to be refurbished last year, I stood back against the wall and watched two male house servants draping the curving *stibadium* couch in red cloth to cover the three-quarter ring of solid masonry. It was more intimate than the old-fashioned separate three-couch arrangement. At least everybody could hear what everybody else was saying and the servants could serve Patulus's choice efforts onto the table in the middle so it was within easy reach of all the diners. Daria entered from the other side, waving her hands at two girls struggling with a pile of long cushions, their faces red and tendrils of hair sticking to sweating skin. They dropped the cushions as soon as they reached the *stibadium*.

'Oof!' one said and pushed her dark hair back. 'That lot's bloody heavy.'

'Don't rest there, my girl,' Daria retorted. 'There's a second layer to fetch.'

'Oh, Pluto. Do their noble arses need so much pampering? We manage without even one cushion.'

'That's enough,' Daria snapped. 'Hard work killed nobody. Think yourself lucky you're fed, housed indoors and kept safe. Out there, especially on the farms in the north, or up in Lauriacum, you wouldn't last longer than the frost on a spring morning.'

'S'true,' piped up the blonde girl. 'My friend at the governor's palace said the Alamanni had raided right down the Druna valley to Ovilava last week and killed nearly twenty people – farmers and shepherds mostly.'

All three slaves and Daria stared at the younger girl and said nothing for a few heartbeats.

'Well,' Daria said crisply, 'I'm sure the governor will order a retaliatory raid and punish those barbarians. They'll soon learn not to tangle with Rome.' She turned and spotted me in the shadow. I shook my head. She turned back to the girls. 'Enough gossiping. Go and fetch the other cushions. That's all you have to concern yourself with. Now, or you'll feel my hand.'

Heads bowed and muttering to themselves, they trotted off to the door. Daria waited until they'd left the room before she turned to me.

'Ovilava isn't that far, *domina*. Could we be in danger here?'

I was about to snap back with a positive answer but hesitated for a couple of breaths.

'The mountains lie between us and the route is not easy for a single file of horsemen, let alone a full raiding party. And it would take several days to reach us.' I laid my fingers on her arms. 'Father says the signal fires would reach us quickly enough for the local detachments from Legio Noricorum and the Italica to mount a rapid counter-attack. And they know the passes and valleys. As ever, the mountains will protect us. Never forget that, Daria.'

Red and orange blended into blue as the sun set behind the mountains across the valley from Virunum when the governor and his party arrived. Lyre music and soft singing from the hired musicians drifted into the atrium as we waited to welcome them. Aegius's retouched walls shone in the flames from sconces flickering with a strong yellow light.

'Here they come,' Father whispered, but I'd heard the clatter of military sandals and even the governor's softer ones before they turned the corner. Apart from the thin gold circlet on his head and heavy gold torc around his neck, Father was formal old Roman in dress, his only-brought-out-for-holidays toga over a long tunic with the edge embroidered in blue and purple. I didn't know whether he wore it to reinforce his Roman-ness or as an ironic gesture. I was wearing Gylfi's amber to give me strength and my red silk robe and deep yellow *palla*. Asella said I looked as if I were on fire.

Publius Vindius Clemens, the governor, was a solid, snub-nosed man swathed in a *pallium* too big for him, but he wore a determined expression under his short grey hair. Father said his family originally came from Flavia Solva to the east of Virunum, but his grandfather had moved to Mediolanum where Clemens had been born. His accent seemed very Italian to me. But whether he still thought of himself as Norican or not, now he was the *praeses*, representing the emperor.

'Ha, prince, salutations,' Clemens said in a gravelly voice and gave a shallow bow. Father returned the same gesture.

'Welcome, *praeses*, as ever, to my home. I trust you continue to be in good health?'

'Passable, thank you, Bacausus. I shall be pleased when it warms up.' He gave me a smile. 'Lady Julia. You're looking well.' Before I had time to answer, he turned and beckoned the local military commander forward. 'I know Opsius needs no introduction, but he has a new second. Young feller recently arrived from Britannia.' He gestured to the younger man standing slightly behind Opsius and who was rooted to the spot and deaf, it seemed. He was staring at me. As well he might.

His uniform was immaculate – polished and pristine – his brown hair cut short and shining with health, but his face had flushed and his eyes widened. Seeing his horrified expression gave me not a little pleasure. Should I pretend to faint and declare him my violator? I stared back with a knowing little smile. He didn't move. Opsius frowned at him.

'Come forward, Apulius,' he said. 'You're not in the wilds of Britannia now.'

So that was his name. I glanced at my father who gave the young Roman a puzzled look.

'I apologise, sir,' Apulius said at last, stepping forward. 'I was overcome with the beauty of the paintings and splendid mosaics.'

What a liar! But a smooth one.

'Lucius Apulius, tribune, of Rome, lately on Count Theodosius's staff in Britannia,' he continued, then drew himself up and brought his fist across his chest in salute.

'Welcome, young man,' my father replied. 'May I present my daughter, Julia Bacausa?'

He bowed but stiffly, then stared at me again as if he were an unbearded boy of fifteen. In the light from the sconces he looked paler now. Perhaps it was shock. That was a pleasing thought. But as I stared back, I was confused. Part of me wanted to reassure him, even protect him; the other half wanted to knock him to the ground and stamp on his face. He had made me lose control of myself. No, he had made me lose my mind in the deep waters of his eyes.

Father coughed which broke my trance. He beckoned me to his side as we walked past Aegius's beautiful frescoes towards the dining room. Clemens talked about some local dispute to my father as I tried to compose my thoughts and feelings. Apulius and Opsius trailed behind, the older man muttering something to the younger that I couldn't hear. Just inside the dining room door, Father stopped and raised both hands halfway.

'May the goddess Noreia and Jupiter Arubianus bless our meal together,' he said. He glanced at Clemens and the two soldiers. 'And

Christos, of course,' he added. But Apulius looked away with a sour look on his face.

At the rounded end of the dining room we went up the three shallow steps. Father directed Clemens to the place of honour with the most luxurious cushions to the right of the curving *stibadium* couch – *in dextro cornu* – where he would face out to get the best view of the entertainment. I lay next to him, then Father and Opsius which left Apulius at the left end, the inferior placing where he would face the wall. Well and good. Then the theatre of the formal meal began. We would show Lucius Apulius, tribune of Rome, that we were as civilised, if not more so, than in Rome, and as sophisticated as in Constantinople.

Daria had set out displays of silver, glass and fine redware on sideboards along both walls and Father's *phalerae*, helmet and sword with its jewelled scabbard on a table beyond them. In the sconces, the flames burnt evenly giving out a strong yellow light and silver candelabra hung with lamps spread a sweet almond scent through the room. The musicians played soothing, almost featureless melodies.

Slaves came forward to take our sandals and the military men's boots and brought us water and towels to clean our hands. A flurry of kitchen slaves flitted in from behind heavy crimson and gold-edged curtains and laid out over a dozen dishes for the *gustatio* on the polished semicircular table which followed the interior line of the *stibadium*. I winced internally when Clemens added a spoonful of salt to the oysters. They were perfectly fresh and delicately seasoned by Patulus's team. At least he didn't drench them in stinking garum. I took an egg and some asparagus, the first of the new season. The shoots were small, but the pride of our gardener who covered the beds in straw, then in oil cloth at night as if they were favoured children. But my father loved asparagus.

Father signalled to Daria who was standing just inside the velvet curtain and she flicked her fingers backward. Father's secretary and one of the younger girls came forward and read a comedy while we ate in silence. The senior military man, Opsius, looked bored; perhaps it was too subtle for him. But Apulius smiled and then chuckled at a particularly witty line. He only sipped his *mulsum* twice while he ate his appetiser. So, although the honey and wine drink was well diluted, he was abstemious.

He watched me as the servants cleared the table and brought small bowls of scented water and towels for our fingers, but I glared at him then turned away and talked to Father. Who did Apulius think he was? It was bad enough that the *stibadium* meant our heads were close, but it didn't mean I had to fawn over him.

'Julia? Are you well?' Father murmured to me.

'Yes, merely a little tired.'

He said nothing more but held my gaze for a few seconds before resuming his discussion with Clemens and Opsius while the slaves brought in the next course. As a group of singers and dancers came forward with colourful costumes and tiny cymbals, the slaves carved delicate pieces from the suckling pig and young chickens and presented squares of brown trout from our river. Clemens nodded in reply to my father but concentrated on the cheese-filled savoury parcels which I knew he savoured. He'd taken to our local specialities quickly or maybe his distant Norican blood recognised them instinctively.

I watched Apulius from under my eyelashes. He took a few pieces of the chicken in cinnamon and fennel sauce, but more of the vegetables and pulses. As the slaves brought in the pastries, nuts and fruit, my father raised an eyebrow at one dish.

'Why did we have *puls* on the table, Julia?'

'Father?' I said, assuming an innocent expression. 'It's a traditional dish. I thought our military guests would find such food familiar and comforting.'

It wasn't the bland grain pottage soldiers ate on campaign; I *had* asked the cook to add herbs and salt with a little chopped onion. Nevertheless, it wasn't the sort of thing you put on the table when the governor was invited. I dropped my eyes under my father's gaze. To cover my embarrassment, I reached for one of the plum pastries and a handful of nuts.

'I see,' he said in a stern tone.

Out of the corner of my eye I saw Apulius shift his body and gaze at me. The heat crept up my neck into my face. Curse it! There was no mistaking the warmth in his eyes then a flash of anger. Father turned to him and smiled.

'Have you settled into our town, Apulius? It must be quite a change from serving with Theodosius in Britannia.'

'I have my billet and my duties, sir,' he replied. 'I hope to see some proper action soon, though.'

'You young men always want to kill other young men.' Father sighed. 'Argentoratum with Julian thirteen years ago was enough for me.'

'You fought against Emperor Julian?'

I gasped but Father burst out laughing. 'You really *do* think we're barbarians!'

I glared at Apulius. Next to me, Opsius, the military commander, jerked upright. *Praeses* Clemens frowned into his wine cup. Even the lyre player and singers stopped. Only a muted spitting from the brazier broke the silence.

'Apologise this instant, Apulius,' Opsius growled at him after a few seconds. 'You're talking out of your arse.' Opsius glanced at me. 'Begging your pardon, noble lady.'

I nodded graciously, then fixed the hardest stare I could muster on Apulius.

'Prince Bacausus served in the emperor's *palatini*,' Opsius added.

Apulius swallowed so hard he almost choked. Well he might. Father's regiment was one of the most elite in the army, with a fearsome combat reputation. He still maintained good relations with some of the other officers there as well as with the two local units. Offending him may have sealed this upstart's career. Serve him right.

Apulius coughed, then stood and beckoned to the slave to fetch his boots. He nodded to his commander, then bowed to the governor and my father.

'Please forgive my error, prince,' he said. 'I was crass. I beg your leave to withdraw.'

'Well said, young man,' Father replied, his eyes assessing him. 'At least you have the balls to apologise when you're wrong.' He flicked his fingers at Apulius. 'Go and get some fresh air. Julia will show you the garden.'

I couldn't believe my father had said that. He wanted me to be polite and play the good hostess after that gross insult. More than that, I couldn't feel calm in the Roman's presence.

'But, Father—'

'Do as I bid you, Julia.' Then he resumed his conversation with the governor.

I had no choice; my father had – unusually – played the *paterfamilias* who expected immediate obedience. I wouldn't shame him in front of these damned Romans. He started talking about Emperor Valentinian's campaigns and the wisdom of taking his nine-year-old son Gratian with him when they crossed the Rhine into Alamanni territory and whether the negotiations with the Burgundians would come to anything.

I slid to the end of my couch and stuck my feet out for Asella to fasten my sandals. I was damned to Tartarus if I was going to be gracious to this young boor. But as we crossed to the door leading to the private gardens, I noticed his face was pale and his face set hard. A sheen had broken out on his forehead.

Asella draped a shawl across my stiff shoulders and arms even though the weather was mild for the season. She kept five steps behind me as I led Apulius outside. Not bothering to see if he was following me, I strode across the paved terrace, then down two steps onto a gravel path lined with box hedges. I ignored the stones getting into my sandals as I stamped along the path. Nor did I take much notice of the beauty of the fruit trees just coming into blossom or their light scent. I was too angry.

I strode up a path lined both sides with tall columns of evergreens which ran parallel to the avenue leading from the rear courtyard of the villa section to the front entrance gates. Halfway along, a small area opened out into a circular area. I stopped and turned round.

'Thank you, Asella. You may go.' I waved her away.

'*Domina*?'

'Go!'

I watched until she was out of earshot, then spun round to Apulius and struck him hard in the face. He staggered back, almost crashing into one of the stone benches.

'That is for being a snotty Roman and treating me like a whore, but mostly for daring to insult my father this evening.' I took a deep breath. 'You are ignorant and uncultured. The sooner you crawl back to your village in rural Latium among the pigs and weaving women the better.'

His hand rubbed his face. And his lips tightened. Even in the falling light his eyes brimmed with anger.

'Why didn't you tell me who you were?' he snapped. He took a step towards me, but I stood my ground. I wasn't one of his tame city women.

'Why should I?' I shot back. 'I pick where I want.' I looked at him with narrowed eyes. 'And I decided you were what I wanted at that precise moment.'

'But I forced you.'

I laughed in his face.

'Ha! You think I couldn't have disabled you? What a spoilt boy you are. You'll find we Noricans are a great deal tougher than you think.' I looked him up and down. 'Nevertheless, you performed well enough.' My heart was thudding. He looked ready to murder me.

'You're shameless. You behaved like a prostitute.'

How dared he! Something inside me, an evil *genus* pushed me on.

'What, did you think you were the first?' I retorted. Oh gods, now I *did* sound like a shameless whore. But aside from Gylfi, I'd never had the least inclination for any man. Until now. I wanted to fight this man and bed him at the same time.

I raised my right hand to strike him again, but he grabbed my wrist in mid-air and with his other hand seized my other wrist. He pulled both to the back of my waist and squashed them together in one hand. Gods, his grip was hard. He circled my waist with his free arm and pulled me in tight. His chain mail shirt scratched my flesh and my shawl slipped to the ground. I trembled, but not from the cold. I felt as if I were on fire but caught in a vice. He stared at me, a hard look, then his eyes became liquid, like dissolving peat.

He bent over and brushed the base of my throat with his lips. A ripple of warmth ran through my whole body. Then he kissed my lips, gently at first, then with determination. He locked his arm harder round my waist and my back arched in response. Juno. I shuddered. I wanted him, but not like this. I could not submit so easily again. I flexed my knee under my robe and drove it hard into his groin.

'You little bitch,' he croaked, doubling over. I gasped as still holding one of my wrists he pulled me down with him. He pinned me under him, his body weight stopped me escaping. But I didn't want to. He took some quick breaths to recover. I laughed, mostly from nervousness. Then I stared into his eyes. Fear stared back. What was he afraid of? Me, or the consequences of what he had done?

Even though my shawl was no protection from the chilly ground, we stayed like that for several moments. As I searched his face, he calmed. I felt that tug of recognition again. A settling, as if everything else in my life had led to this man and this moment. Now I was in the right place in the world. And thought I saw the same in his eyes.

Both of us should have stopped at that moment, but my nipples hardened against the silk of my robe and I gasped as desire flowed through me. I wanted this man again, and now.

I let him guide my wrists over my head. Exposed, but relaxed I relished his nearness, his warm breath and his male scent. He was breathing hard by now and running his fingers down my neck onto my breast. I shuddered with desire flowing through me. He hesitated. I looked up at him and smiled.

'Do it, if you have any strength in your cock.'

My legs curled up each side of his body inviting him in.

Oh gods, oh gods, what had I done? How could I behave like that? Again. We'd lain contented, united, breathless, gazing into each other's eyes. A cool breeze curled round us. Night had fallen.

'Julia,' he whispered at last. He ran his finger over my cheek, down my neck. It was almost unbearable. He kissed my forehead, drew back and opened his mouth to say something, but a voice interrupted him

'*Domina*, where are you? *Domina*, please, you must come. Your father is calling for you.' Asella, and with an urgent voice. Apulius stood up and extended his hand to me. I brushed down my robe, bent and recuperated my shawl which I shook out. He took it and draped it round my shoulders, resting his hands there as he bent to whisper in my ear.

'I shall speak to your father.'

'No!'

'Why not? I want you as my wife. I don't have unlimited wealth, but my family is prosperous with properties near Rome and Naples, enough to keep you comfortable.'

'It's not that simple. You see—'

'Oh, thank Juno,' Asella ran from round the corner of the alley of trees. 'I've been looking for you everywhere, *domina*. Your father—'

'Yes?' I stretched every nerve to keep my voice calm despite the warmth flowing through my body. Asella glanced from me to Apulius and back again. Her lips tightened. She was no fool.

'I think, tribune, your commander needs you.' She took on the aspect of a terrifying *materfamilias* in the mode of Antonia Minor. Apulius gave me one last look then marched off towards the lights casting yellow glows out of the back windows.

'How dare you dismiss a guest like that, Asella?' I said. 'And a senior Roman. He could insist on you being punished for such insolence.'

'Oh, please, *domina*, don't attempt to bluster at me. Remember I was wiping your infant arse not that long ago. How can you have let him have you again? And in the garden where any snivelling slave could trip over you.' All the fierceness of generations of tribeswomen accused me along with her.

'It's none of your business. You have no right to criticise me.'

Asella seized my hand.

'Julia, you are as my daughter. No, if you were, I'd have whipped you more to make you behave.' She took a cloth out of her waist pouch and wiped my face. 'You should have more respect for yourself.'

'I—'

She gave my hand a firm shake.

'Deodatus was a pathetic specimen, a non-man. The failure was his. Never yours.' She gripped my hand tighter. 'You are a striking and passionate young woman and surrounded by people who love you. Child, you don't need to prove yourself by luring any man you fancy to your bed or a scrabble in the bushes.' The moonlight was reflected in her eyes and her face was as white as any tribal priestess's as those same eyes bored into mine. She held up her hand to my face. I shivered in the breeze funnelling up between the trees as she spoke in almost a commanding voice. 'Now go indoors and make your peace with your father and see to your guests.'

I stumbled back to the house, guided by the lanterns along the path and the patio. I felt confused as if my mind had been invaded by a mountain fog, but I managed to say farewell to our guests in a conventional way. Apulius gave me a long look as he stood with Opsius, the commander, then bowed and left. I stared after him, watching the red-brown lights in his hair highlighted by the torch the slave carried before him. I only looked away when I felt my father's eyes on me and we were alone.

4

'Julia,' Father said peremptorily. 'Into my *tablinum*. Now.'

He knew. Oh, gods, he knew. Juno save me. As it was early April, the tall shutters were closed on the garden side and a thick wool curtain pulled across the glazed window. He pointed towards the folded door and I quickly opened the hinged panelling and pulled it across the opening into the atrium.

'Let's start with the easy question. What *were* you thinking putting that *puls* stew on the table before the governor?'

'I thought it would make the new officer comfortable if he was offered some familiar food.'

'Oh, please! Field rations are perfectly adequate on campaign, but this young man is, or was, a senior tribune on Count Theodosius's staff. Do you think it was the sort of thing the count would have on his table? I was embarrassed in front of the governor. Even Opsius, who is a rough old soldier, was put out.'

I looked down.

'Well?'

'It was a misjudgement. I apologise.' I glanced up. 'And it wasn't the harsh field version. The cook had flavoured it subtly with herbs and added other ingredients. Romans are supposed to eat it all the time!'

'Not young aristocrats from old senatorial families with influence.'

'Is he so precious, then?'

'Probably not, but these are not easy times and I need every bit of support that I can garner. And I don't mind if it comes from Constantinople, Mediolanum or Rome. The Christ believers are growing in influence and power every day.'

'Then I'm sorry, Father, but I don't think you need to worry about Apulius.'

'What do you mean?'

I tried to keep my look as steady as possible. In the light from the three scattered oil lamps he couldn't possibly see the growing red in my face from the warmth creeping into it.

He frowned, then took another sip from his wine.

'Are you telling me he's another Gylfi?' he said after a few moments. 'I know that young northerner didn't stay here for three months just to refurbish your mother's jewellery.' He sighed. 'I'm not an idiot, Julia. You're too old to whip and you're no dainty virgin, but—'

'I am fully aware of that,' I said with bitterness in my heart.

'All I ask is not to make an open scandal and not to bring any bastards into my house.'

'You know I wouldn't do either.'

He sighed.

'Yes, I do know.'

'This is different,' I said.

'It always is.'

'Truly.' How could I explain my feeling for Apulius? I didn't know myself.

What a liar you are, Julia. You know exactly how you feel.

'I want you to keep it completely decorous. This Roman is probably a follower of Christos like the other two who were here tonight. Anything beyond smiling and hand touching would be reported instantly by Opsius's spies and probably to the bishop. Anything to undermine me and mine.'

Too late, Father. But only Asella knows.

'Does Opsius have spies here, then?' I whispered.

'He must have. We'd be naive to think otherwise.' He glanced at me. 'Come, come, Julia, don't looked so shocked. We all do it to each other.'

'Oh. Do you know who—'

'I have my suspicions.'

'Not… not Asella?'

'I don't think so. Why?'

I shrugged, but I felt sick in my stomach.

'I suppose you share all your women's secrets with her.' He snorted. 'No, I think she's safe. She was devoted to your mother and has a healthy contempt for all Romans, especially Italians.'

'I shall watch for anybody acting suspiciously and tell you immediately.'

'No, don't change anything you do or look as if you're watching or they will know you have discovered them. Go about your day as usual. But now you are aware.'

I escaped to my room, shaken by what Father had said. Could it be Daria who ran the *domus*, or Aegius who seemed completely loyal, if taciturn, as he created the miracles on our walls? Or perhaps it was Patulus, the cook?

Just after daybreak the next day, Asella brought me a dish with the spelt bread I loved with some olives, mountain cheese and chopped chicken from last night's meal. I swallowed several gulps of watered wine before eating; I had woken with such a dry mouth.

She pushed open the shutters and the sunlight streamed in, white and weak, but rising above the wooded hills to the east. The faint shimmer of mountains in the far distance was white from the light reflecting in the snow. I shivered at the cool breeze and pulled my woollen shawl across my shoulders. Warm and light, it was fine wool from Tarentum, dyed a deep green and edged with a red and yellow pattern. Asella grumbled it was too good to be used casually as a wrap in the bedroom. It had been the one gift from Deodatus that I had kept from the marriage, but I wasn't going to give it a special place or wear it in public.

I splashed water over my face and wiped off the excess with a small rough linen towel. Asella brushed out the tangles in my hair as my mind wandered trying to make sense of last night. Not Father's revelation about spies, although I should not have been surprised. I glanced up at Asella, but she was out of my line of sight. She'd been my mother's slave and mine since my earliest memory. Surely not her? She plaited and twisted my hair up, fixing it with plain pins. Today was a day of setting the household back into order and restoring its natural state after the disruption of yesterday evening. A simple warm underdress and tunic over would be sufficient.

Daria's staff would be busy with clearing and washing, then thoroughly cleaning the dining room and flinging open all the shutters to air it. I strolled through the atrium and towards the vestibule. I had to ensure the porter refused any callers. Any. Until I'd corralled my thoughts about Apulius, I couldn't face him.

I looked out through the peristyle across the wide terrace to the two lines of trees in the far garden. I could just see where the hedge bulged halfway along. Inside that private circle I had lost myself last night. For all his words, did Apulius really intend to speak to Father? If he did, he'd find out the truth about me and walk out of my life. I caught my breath. I could not let that happen.

'Your head is now lying in the sand and blood spurting from your neck, *domina*,' Musius barked at me. I was panting hard, wooden sword in my right hand, my left clutched to the side of my neck where he'd smacked his weapon against it. Gods, that stung. Sweat poured down my back and the April wind blew over me making me shiver.

The old soldier grinned at me. Bastard.

'You were doing well until you took your eye off my sword. Distracted by another sort of sword, were you?' He smirked.

'You go too far, Musius,' I snapped back.

'Sorry, I'm sure.' His face lost its dirty humour. 'If, no, *when* those barbarians pour over the Danuvius, you'd better be paying attention then.'

I wiped my forearm across my forehead and shivered again. I was only wearing a light sleeveless tunic, *bracae* and boots. Usually I enjoyed these training sessions; they were so much more challenging than genteel ball throwing and trotting around the outer garden track. That was all Deodatus had allowed me to do. He was disgusted when I wanted to continue training to fight with weapons. I explained I'd done it from childhood in the tradition of my mother's people. Living in a province on the northern edge of the empire, we were always aware of the barbarians to the north.

'Proper Roman ladies need have no fear,' he'd pronounced in his most sanctimonious voice. 'Our noble military will defend you.' A military he'd refused to join as a Roman gentlemen. He thought it an occupation fit only for slaves and foreigners, but I would lay money that he'd scuttle behind their blades if he thought he was in danger. The old Romans had counted it a core civic duty to enrol in the armies and only citizens could join. Now they paid riff-raff to join. Officers like Apulius must despair.

Apulius.

No.

I picked up my wooden training sword.

'Let us go another round,' I ordered.

'Sure you're up to it?' Musius looked at me with a face full of scepticism.

'Completely,' I said and thrust forward.

Father emerged from his *tablinum* at the sixth hour and we ate companionably but in silence. Patulus, or more likely one of the assistant cooks, had warmed some vegetables to accompany the bread, salads, olives, cheese and fruit. Father took a slice of the ham smoked over the winter. He didn't care what the Italians thought – he enjoyed his meat. He leant over and wiped his hands on his linen napkin.

'I've received an invitation from Quietus to a poetry evening in three days' time,' he said. 'Strange. I would have thought his wife would have sent it to *you*.' He shrugged. 'That's a new man for you.'

'Perhaps he's not yet versed in the social niceties, Father. But I think he means well.'

'Oh, aye. He's a fussy little beggar but pleasant enough. Do you want to go?'

I hesitated. Quietus would have invited all the *illustres,* landowners and worthies from the surrounding areas to ensure a good audience before approaching Father. Assuredly, he would have invited Eligius, the Christian bishop who didn't despise 'civilised' entertainment like poetry even if it contained pagan subjects. And that meant Deodatus would come with him. I wasn't afraid of my former husband. Life was just easier if I didn't have to meet him. Every time I encountered him, I couldn't help remembering the disaster of our wedding night. All I'd felt was embarrassment for him as his performance had been dismally lacking. Unlike…

Stop it, Julia!

But I couldn't avoid Deodatus forever. And if I could try to think only of his cultured side, perhaps, one day, I could even forget the intimate failures between us. He might even give up his stubborn refusal to give me a Christian bill of divorce, always presuming such a thing existed. Not that I cared, but Father did, politically. Oh, gods, why was life so complicated?

'Yes, I'd like to go.' I pulled my shoulders back and looked up at Father.

'You don't have to, but Quietus is a good contact who I need to keep happy as his wagons are essential for our steel.'

Father need not have worried as each consignment of Norican weapons left Virunum with a full military escort, but I made no comment. Men liked to think these business 'encounters' important.

'No, I would like to hear the latest and it's a good opportunity to meet friends.' Even if several 'friends' had stopped speaking to me after I'd broken with Deodatus and left his house. Still, they would be curious, especially if Deodatus attempted to speak to me. I took Father's hand. 'I will always do my duty and support you, Father, whatever happens.'

'You're a good girl, Julia.' He sighed. 'I only wish you could settle.'

I withdrew my hand from his and glanced at him.

'I would like to invite another to come as our guest. It would show you and the Roman authorities are very close.'

'The governor won't come – he's too busy – and you surely don't think that old tough Opsius would?' His eyebrows shot up.

'No, I was thinking of Lucius Apulius, his new second in

command,' I replied. 'He's from a senatorial family, I understand. He should be literate at least. It would also introduce him to people here.'

'Is that the only reason?'

'Of course.'

5

'Will you please stand still, *domina*?' Asella nagged. 'I'll never get this belt fastened if you keep wriggling to look in the mirror.'

Her hands slid over my waist and secured the white silk robe. At least it was relieved by a red and yellow embroidery at the neck. The blood-red cabochon ruby on my gold belt clasp shone out like a malevolent eye. So be it. I stroked it for luck. Asella clipped matching bracelets at the lower edge of the long sleeves of my underdress and hung red rubies from my ears. She draped a white wool *palla* over one of my shoulders, then stepped back.

'You'll do,' she said, 'but I hope nobody thinks you're going to your bridal.'

'Oh, gods, Asella. Surely not!'

'You could wear the blue *palla* instead – a good match for your colouring. Or do you want to present yourself as pure for anybody special?' She cocked an eyebrow.

'Hold your tongue and fetch my shoes,' I snapped back.

The moon was waning, but there was enough light to see as our carriage made its way down the hill past the forum to Quietus's house. Next to the driver who had a long stick under his seat, one of Father's ex-legionaries sat nursing a cudgel on his lap, but we had never been attacked even at night. Once, a counting clerk dismissed for siphoning off Father's profits had lobbed a stone at him but he'd quickly been set on by others in the street. I thought it was because they respected and loved my father who often intervened on their behalf with the governor or the quaestor, even Opsius. But Father gave me a cynical look and said it was more because they had good employment in the iron sheds, a well-run market and assured money each week. More important in his eyes was the food ration he doled out to each household.

'I don't call it bribery, Julia, but let's say it helps oil the wheels of everyday life.'

I hadn't replied, but I realised the official Romans let him rule here because they didn't have to do the work themselves, or pay for it. As long as Noricum continued to supply weapons from its expert workshops and ore-rich ground, pay its taxes and order was maintained, they weren't going to lift any more fingers than they needed to. They had plenty to keep themselves occupied with further north on the Danuvius frontier.

At Quietus's house, which occupied half an *insula* block near the *basilica*, flames from torches in towering sconces each side of the doors shone on the faces of two red-tunicked slaves dressed up as guards. Another came forward to give his hand to Father as he stepped out of the carriage, but was waved away. Father turned and helped me out. As we walked the long passage to the atrium, the rumble of voices grew into a cacophony as the fine society of Virunum tried to out-shout itself. I winced. Father glanced at me, then shrugged. We paused on the threshold and waited.

Quietus spotted us and hurried over.

'Welcome, prince, and Lady Julia.' He beamed at us and looked as if he'd captured a fine prize. 'We are truly honoured.' He snapped his fingers and a slave appeared with a tray of cups. 'Your guest, the tribune Apulius, has just arrived. Let me lead you to him.'

Quietus waddled ahead of us to a small group consisting of three young men and two women, one of which was his eldest daughter, Paula. She was fluttering her eyelashes at Apulius. Her freckles were looking particularly prominent this evening and her wishy-washy blue eyes were a stark contrast to his warm brown ones. Apulius gave her a polite smile, then turned as we approached. He held my eyes for several moments and I caught my breath. Thank the gods, my father held his hand out in greeting and broke the moment.

'Well, young man, have you a strong liking for poetry?'

I could hear the irony in Father's voice and prayed Apulius wouldn't react.

'As much as anybody who holds himself literate, sir.'

'Ha! Very diplomatic. Are you going to read something?'

'Only if they are desperate and the wine is flowing well.'

Father thumped him on the shoulder and said, 'Good man!' then disappeared into the crowd, greeting people with a smile or a nod as he moved through.

'Are you reading, Julia?' Paula asked before I could even greet Apulius.

'No, I've come to listen to the latest. I believe we might hear Ausonius's *Mosella*.'

'The one going on about the dreary river in Germania? I hope not.' The edges of Paula's mouth dropped.

'I hear it's quite lyrical,' I replied.

'Oh, Julia, *you* must read. We need something to cheer us up after that.' She turned to Apulius and trilled, 'Julia Bacausa writes some very witty verse.' Her delicate face creased. 'I don't always understand some of the jokes that others say are there in the words, but it sounds very clever.'

Oh, gods. Why did Paula witter on like this? She considered herself to be my best friend; I didn't and wouldn't ever. She turned to Apulius again. Our little community had few incomers so for Paula he was fresh meat. I did feel sympathy for her, if truth be told. She'd been brought up as if she were a daughter of an *illustris* with tutors and an impoverished 'lady companion' from an old Roman *equites* family to guide her socially, but with a father like Quietus not even a middle-ranking aristocrat would look at her. But her doting and ambitious father wouldn't settle for another mere merchant for his daughter. Caught in the middle, Paula had nowhere to go. At least tonight she could enjoy herself flirting with Apulius.

But Quietus ushered us to the seating in his dining hall and beckoned Paula to his side. She almost dragged Apulius with her into the middle seats of the semicircle. Father and I settled on the left side of the semicircle and I smiled as I watched Apulius replying to Paula's chatter, but not starting any conversation with her. I turned to ask Father what he thought might be recited tonight when I froze at the sight of two men entering, then sitting at the far end. Oh, gods. Deodatus and his uncle. With the Galilean cross on a chain round his neck, his rich robe and hand stroking his grey and black beard, Eligius seemed completely at his ease and nodded graciously to several of the people who came up to him, bowed and exchanged a few words with him. Deodatus looked sulky.

'Ignore them,' whispered my father. 'I do if I can nowadays.'

'Suppose he speaks to me?'

'Humph. He can try. He hasn't attempted to come to the palace since I threw him out last time with a flea in his ear.'

Father had used some extremely coarse language in the end when Deodatus had started giving a speech about women's duty to submit to their husbands. I'd been hiding behind a curtain and nearly laughed aloud. I'd peeped round the edge and seen Deodatus's face go puce. Once, I would have felt sorry for him, but he had been so uncaring and cold to me. But he still persisted in the idea that he had a moral hold on me. Father had disillusioned him in robust terms. And yet…

Quietus stood and introduced the first speaker and the buzz of chatter died. A middle-aged man whom I vaguely recognised unrolled an old scroll and spouted one of Ovid's love poems. His face was flushed and he shifted from one foot to another and looked all the time at his much younger wife. She beamed at him and I suspected she must have pushed him to read. The bishop's face was expressionless; but he raised one eyebrow at a particularly sensuous reference. The reader glanced at the bishop, finished quickly and handed the scroll to Quietus who swapped it for another. He paused, drew himself up and curled his shoulders back. Ovid again, but from *Metamorphoses*. Several of the audience snorted or even laughed at the way the poet poked fun at the Greek gods. His irreverence had helped lead to the displacement of the Greek gods and replacement with Roman ones. The speaker was greeted with a round of applause when he finished and nodded at his neighbours, smiling. as he settled back in his seat.

A young woman, around eighteen stood. Priscilla, Paula's sister. Quiet and studious, she never gave herself airs or pushed herself forward into conversation. Clad in a modest blue *dalmatica* with only one embroidered stripe down the centre, she stood holding her codex and waited for people to quieten. She opened the book and as she read, every single voice stopped and every eye was on her, even Apulius's when I glanced at him. He caught my look and held it for several heartbeats, then turned his attention back to Priscilla.

Her voice was full of passion as she read Ausonius's love poem to Bissula, the poet's slave whom he loved and later freed. Her journey from captive German to a Roman's beloved, her vibrant golden hair and blue eyes, Ausonius's love for his barbarian whom he declared outshone all the girls in Rome played out in front of us. My throat ached and a tear ran down my cheek as I felt Ausonius's heart swell with adoration for his dearest love. And I wasn't the only one. Even Father sniffed. When she finished, Priscilla gave a gulp, almost a sob. Quietus and Paula's eyes widened in astonishment as they looked at her, as if they didn't know their own daughter and sister. I stood and embraced her.

'Such pleasure, Priscilla. I shall never forget this,' I whispered as the audience recovered and applauded her.

She nodded and didn't seem capable of saying a further word. She sat quietly for the rest of the evening. To my disappointment, nobody recited Ausonius's *Mosella,* but Father's eyes sparkled when one of his former tentmates in the Legio II Italica gave a long, rousing passage from Vergilius's *Aeneid.* Some of Horace's odes were spoken by one of the *decuriones* from the town council; he matched the poet's urbane, witty manner with his own.

Unfortunately, the whole tone of the evening was depressed by one of the bishop's keen followers reading a panegyric about a Christian nobody had ever heard of martyred by Emperor Diocletian. I hid a yawn behind my hand and played with my bracelets. Apulius fixed his gaze on the back wall with a stony expression on his face. I was sure then he didn't follow the Christos. Thank the gods.

Sure that every single stone was in its place in my bracelets, I looked up and caught him watching me. He didn't smile, but he wasn't frowning either. Those eyes. Maybe it was being surrounded by the flow of words or Ausonius's love poem, but I felt a warmth from him that wasn't anything to do with lust. It seemed to envelop me, almost to protect me. I knew I would be safe with him. I could trust him.

Father nudged me. I broke away from Apulius's gaze. I was being fanciful.

'Look out,' Father muttered and glanced across the room. I followed his glance. At the far end of the seating, Deodatus stood, then strutted to the front of the room. I frowned and fidgeted in my seat. Father reached out and took my hand in both of his. Several people glanced at us, then back at Deodatus. He bowed first to his uncle who smiled back and nodded as if to give his nephew permission to begin.

He read the first few lines, pausing a little too dramatically here and there. It was a short pompous reflection on Roman domestic virtues. After acknowledging some desultory applause from the audience, he looked directly at me and launched into one of Tibullus's elegiac love poems about his love, Delia. This was so unlike anything he'd ever read when we'd been married. Hearing his cold, awkward voice reciting emotions alien to him, I didn't know whether to laugh or be sorry for him. The poet described his tempestuous love for an unattainable and unfaithful woman of dubious social standing, to whom he figuratively enslaves himself.

But all pity for him fled as he fixed his gaze on me and continued with lines which complained about how fickle and luxury-loving she was and how she deceived her husband. He would forgive her if she left and came to be with him, Tibullus, where she belonged.

I heard a few gasps and murmurs from the other guests. I sat up rigid in my seat staring at him. I felt the heat rising up through my entire body. How could he embarrass me like this? How dared he address me in such terms? I wanted to strike him to the ground, but I couldn't move. My hands trembled and Father pressed the one he was holding.

'Steady!' my father whispered. 'Don't react.'

Others started calling out to him to stop and sit down. Even Quietus protested, but Deodatus ploughed on. After another minute, he stopped. The audience fell silent. He rolled up his scroll, then stretched his hand out to me. I fixed my gaze on his white hand

48

with its polished nails, remembering its flabby touch on my skin, and shivered in revulsion.

'Come, wife. Now!' he commanded, advancing towards me.

Father was on his feet and stepped in front of me, towering over Deodatus. He was so close he was almost touching the younger man's robe. I couldn't see my father's face, but the cords on the back of his neck stood out and his shoulders were flexed back.

'How dare you importune my daughter!' he thundered. His words resounded round the room. 'She divorced you. Twice. That is final.' His shoulders rose and fell as he took a deep breath. 'Now leave this room while you still live.'

I moved half a step to the right. Deodatus looked as if he'd been blasted by a mountain storm. He stumbled backwards. His eyes were narrowed and his pale skin even whiter than usual. The bishop was by his side almost instantly.

'Now, prince,' the bishop said in his most mellow voice, 'let us not quarrel in front of friends.'

'Keep out of this, Eligius,' Father growled, not turning his head away from Deodatus. 'Except you can take your young whelp home and keep him out of my sight forever.'

'Once he has his wife by his side, his companion under God, I'm sure that will be his pleasure,' Bishop Eligius said in a soft, oily, voice.

Father turned his fierce gaze on the bishop.

'I have no quarrel with you, Eligius, but I will not tolerate this kind of behaviour or the continuation of a private quarrel in public.'

The bishop merely smiled back but said nothing. Nobody else said a word. Some of the other male guests stood, but one or two women grasped their husbands' hands pulling them back down to the seats and out of the conflict.

Father crossed his arms. His gold armlets reflected the flames of the wall torches. He waited. The audience watched, mesmerised as if this was another performance. After several minutes, Father turned, took my hand and nodded to Quietus who now stood up along with many of the male guests including Apulius.

Quietus looked at Eligius, the rest of the audience, even Apulius, but eventually dragged his gaze back to Father. Quietus shifted his weight from one foot to the other and his fingers, heavy with rings, plucked at the embroidery on his robe.

'Now, prince, I'm sure we'll all be better for sitting down to compose ourselves,' he said in a hurried and nervous voice. 'Please—'

'No,' Father growled. 'Thank you, Quietus,' he added as an afterthought. 'The air here has turned rancid. I'll bid you good evening.'

He shot Deodatus such a caustic look that my former husband should have been destroyed on the spot and left only a small damp residue on Quietus's veined marble floor. Father turned and made his way towards the door with me in his wake. I was breathing calmly again and lifted my head in the air and pulled my shoulders back. I was damned to Tartarus if I was going to let the Virunum busybodies see I was at all disconcerted by Deodatus's ridiculous antics. But I blinked hard to stop any tears escaping.

Two feet in front of the doorway, Father stopped. The tall wooden doors were closed. Two men wearing chain mail shirts over their tunics and breeches, and helmets, blocked the way with crossed staves. They appeared to be military.

'Get out of my way,' Father ordered and flicked his fingers at them. His voice would have made even barbarians' stomachs turn liquid. One man flinched, the other looked down, then glanced towards the bishop. I turned just in time to see Eligius give a tiny shake of his head. I saw a smile on his face, nearly hidden by his beard. I gasped. Eligius had planned this expressly to humiliate my father.

Nobody moved. My father ruled here but Eligius was the coming man according to some. But no supposedly pious man should play such a trick. I opened my lips to protest but stopped as I saw Apulius advancing towards us. He had arrived earlier in full uniform, presumably straight from duty. Now his hand rested on the grip of an antique gladius. It looked ceremonial, matching his polished mail shirt. He walked slowly but deliberately, full of confidence as if the power of a whole Roman field army was behind him. The guests parted like sheep. He stopped and bowed to Father.

'Allow me to escort you, prince,' he said. He narrowed his eyes.

'Thank you, tribune,' was all Father said.

Apulius stepped in front of him and gave the two men a sneer as only a patrician could, straight down his Roman nose. They hesitated for a second, shrank back.

'Open the door, or I'll have you flogged,' he said in the coldest voice I could remember hearing for a long time.

6

'*Will* you stop pacing and sit down?' Father scowled at me.

'How dared he? How *dared* he humiliate us like that?'

'If you don't calm down, that red hair of yours will burst into flames and consume you.'

'I wish I was Taranis. I'd incinerate both of them with lightning bolts.'

'Julia, we have a guest. Come. Sit. Pour us some wine.'

'Wine? I want to throw it at that little prick.'

'Julia! Your mouth.'

I stopped. 'I apologise, Father. And to you, tribune.' I glanced at Apulius. His face was impassive. I took several long breaths. I took the jug of wine that the servants had left and mixed it with water and handed Apulius a cup and a tight smile. I did the same for Father.

'Well, that was a trap I hadn't foreseen,' Father said. 'I am duly warned.' He raised his cup to Apulius. 'My thanks, young man.'

'It was unconscionable, sir,' he replied. 'A man supposed to be religious, playing a trick like that.'

My exact thoughts.

'Ha! Unfortunately, a sign of changing times,' Father said. 'The power of the traditional rulers is fading. That of the Christians is rising.' He set his cup down on the tripod table beside him. 'When I fought at Emperor Julian's side, I hoped he'd redress the balance. But Fortuna intervened at Samarra and he died.'

'Sir? I thought you worshipped with the Galileans – I mean, Christians.'

'Do I know you well enough to answer that?' Father said half to himself. 'It's politics, tribune,' he added in his normal voice. 'My people once ruled in Virunum by right before the Romans had ever heard of it. Now Noricum is divided into two Roman provinces and they allow me to rule in my little fiefdom. But they've planted this damn bishop here.' He waved his hand. 'Not exactly planted. Eligius's family come from Teurnia just up the valley, so he knows everything and everybody here. Julia and I go to his church once a week in order to keep the peace. It was working until his bloody nephew appeared on the scene.'

I was watching Apulius for his reaction while Father talked. When he stopped, I looked down at the mosaic floor, my eyes not really seeing the fine detail. I wished with all my heart and for the thousandth time that Deodatus would quietly vanish into the bowels of the earth.

When I looked up, I saw Apulius was studying me. His eyes were full of curiosity. Perhaps he was wondering how I had married Deodatus in the first place. His gaze stayed on my face for some moments, and I saw a warmth turn his eyes darker. Or perhaps I was imagining things. But he sat up straight and talked politely to my father without addressing me. He seemed withdrawn, almost a stranger, which was laughable considering our previous encounters. What on earth could he be thinking behind that slightly stern but impassive face?

After a few minutes, he finished his wine, stood and bowed to Father. I walked with them both to the vestibule. I couldn't let Apulius leave without a word. I brought my eyes up to his.

'Thank you,' I whispered.

'Do you want anything special this time for when the tribune comes to dinner this evening?' Daria waited respectfully enough for my answer, but I saw the tiny upturned movement at the edges of her lips.

'No,' I said. 'Father expressly stated we were to eat as we usually do. If Lucius Apulius joins us, then he will have to take pot luck.' I looked at her. 'We don't exactly eat poorly.'

'No, *domina*,' she said. 'There's some pork left and Patulus will conjure up something clever with the vegetables.'

'Conjure? I hope not.' If there was anything we didn't want even a hint of in this household it was a whiff of witchcraft. Eligius would have a field day. And I still didn't have a clue who could be a spy and who was innocent.

'I didn't mean anything by it, *domina*.' She frowned at me.

'No, of course not. I'm sorry, Daria. I'm a little tense this morning.'

She smiled and glided off in the direction of the kitchen. To be truthful, I was anxious this morning that my monthly courses hadn't started. I was always irregular, though. Asella said it was probably the hard training; my mother had been the same. But bearing a child in my uncertain state between marriage and divorce was unthinkable; aborting it made me shudder, but what else would I do? And Apulius was probably here only temporarily. Like any other soldier, he could be posted anywhere else in the empire at short notice.

Father was wealthy enough to give me a tempting *arrhae,* a wedding gift to take into any marriage, and the Bacausi had been kings in Noreia before the Romans had even traded here hundreds of years ago, but Apulius came from a snooty senatorial Italian family. They would see no advantage in such an alliance. What was I thinking?

Apulius had said he would speak to Father, but perhaps that was just words. Gods! But even if Apulius wanted to, if I attempted to marry here and now, Eligius would raise such a scandal, Father's position and reputation with the mostly Christian imperial system could be damaged irreparably.

No, this was not to be, however much I yearned for it. But how could I endure a whole evening in Apulius's company without thinking about what might have been? A stab of pain ran up from my toe. I'd stamped my foot so hard on the marble floor, I'd broken my sandal strap and stubbed my toe on a column base when I'd nearly run into one of the tall columns in the atrium. I was letting my mind wander and acting ridiculously. What on earth would my mother have said at such feeble behaviour? I took a deep breath and marched on to the small dining room to check on preparations.

The evening light was fading as slaves cleared the last of the food and brought in some bowls of nuts and fruit, and a fresh jug of water to mix with the remaining wine. Apulius and Father were relaxing happily on cushions on the dining couch; I had elected to sit in a chair. The two men had been talking military strategy which was mildly boring. I'm sure Father didn't mean to exclude me, but he was clearly enjoying talking to somebody intelligent from the practical soldiering world. I nibbled a dried apricot.

'So tell me, Lucius,' my father said, 'why *did* you leave Britannia? Theodosius must have spotted your abilities and given you your own command. He's no idiot.'

Apulius looked down into his wine cup. He frowned and then shifted his weight on the couch. He didn't speak for a minute or so. When he looked up his face was a picture of misery.

'No, prince, he's not an idiot, just a man in the circle of power and a political realist. When I was dismissed from his staff, he told me I was a fool. And I probably am.' His voice dropped, but I heard the bitterness in it.

'How so, young man?' my father asked gently. He glanced round. 'What you say will go no further than Julia and me.' He glanced at me. 'Or would you prefer to talk man to man?'

I glared at Father, but perhaps he thought Apulius had been enmeshed in a scandal with a woman and was too prudish to talk in front of me. I kept completely still and waited.

'No, sir, I wasn't caught sleeping with the legate's wife or daughter,' he said and gave a little smile. 'It was more serious than that. I'd become a religious embarrassment.'

I refilled our cups and waited. The charcoal in the braziers crackled in the silence. Apulius raised his cup to his lips, set it down purposefully, then began.

'I sailed to Britannia with Count Theodosius's staff eighteen months ago, eager as any young officer to reimpose Roman rule after the barbarian conspiracy. We'd smashed the predatory bands who'd looted their way across the colony and restored property to the traumatised inhabitants, less our cut, of course. Gods, their pale faces and pathetic thanks, their hands touching us and words praising us made us feel like noble heroes of old.'

'In their eyes, that must have been what you were,' Father said, and raised his cup to Apulius. 'Theodosius likes success from what I hear. Surely you should have been set?'

'Indeed, sir. My promotion came quickly. The count promised my own new command in the west and I couldn't wait to set off. But that damned Dulcitius, appointed by the count to be the new *dux Britanniarum*, strode into the staff tent and reminded them all at the top of his voice that I was a pagan, as he called it, and had no place among good Christians. So despite serving the emperor for six years to the utmost of my ability, and completely loyally, I was out.'

'What happened next?' I asked, barely above a whisper. Father made no sound, but kept his gaze fixed on Apulius.

'I lost my senior tribune's rank and any status and privileges attached to it. In the week it took to arrange my posting here to the Legio I Noricorum, my colleagues drifted away, little by little. Conversations about the campaign – the thing that bound us together – stopped when I was near. Pity, embarrassment, even fear of contamination. I was no longer in the outer circle let alone the inner one. Because of my record, I was graciously permitted to stay in the army, but reduced to serving in the auxiliary detachment of a *limitanei* unit. Posted to a place I'd hardly heard of.' His voice was harsh and he looked into his cup, then took a hearty swig.

'Yes, we are a little out of the way,' Father said. 'Opsius is a sound man, a good camp prefect, but unimaginative. I think that's why he's heading a low-level auxiliary troop in the middle of nowhere.'

Apulius looked away. I wanted to stretch out my hand to comfort him for Fortuna's hard blow, but he seemed untouchable in his anger. Father gestured him to continue.

'Count Theodosius called me into the staff tent the morning I left and asked me if I wouldn't reconsider. He said it was a small thing to have to do – half an hour a week chanting a few prayers along with the other officers and men. When I thought about it, it occurred to me that I'd only seen him at his prayers in the company of others. Perhaps he was a less enthusiastic Christian than he appeared to be in public. To my amazement he told me I had the potential to become a great leader of men, certainly a legate, and perhaps even aspire to the purple. I did wonder at that moment whether I should give in. I was throwing away my first independent command, a giant step in my career and the chance to make my mark.' He looked up at us, his face harsh in the flickering of the flames.

Father gave a deep sigh. 'What a waste, and for a few words and prayers.'

'But I couldn't, sir. I couldn't be such a hypocrite.'

'No, not you, Lucius, but Theodosius. Well, I expect he's right. Things are changing and the Christian hard-line believers are cementing their hold on the empire. If that boy prig Gratian takes over after Valentinian, we may find ourselves in a much harder place.' He took a handful of nuts and chewed on them. 'As far as I'm concerned, you're safe here. Whatever ambitions Eligius has here, I still rule. I have no idea what the Roman governor believes – he leaves the day-to-day administration to me. With the incursions to the north and Valentinian's strengthening of the *limes*, he's more in the north at Lauriacum or Ovilava than here.'

'That was the excuse for sending me down to Virunum – to bolster the auxiliary detachment here as part of the emperor's new strategy. But aside from training the new men assigned here, all I've done is bring in a few local hotheads and suspected Alamanni spies.'

'Vital work, though,' my father said. I think he was trying to be kind. Apulius said nothing.

'What happened to those two guards from the poetry evening?' I asked, mainly to distract Apulius from his sombre mood. 'I suppose they must have been Christians to have acted like they did.'

'Ha!' Apulius snorted. 'They'll be cleaning latrines for a week, then they're joining the Lauriacum troops and patrolling the Danuvius border. Let's see if they're so brave when facing the Alamanni.'

'I don't know the young officers there now, but I knew the Legio I Noricorum commander when we were thin-stripers at Argentoratum. Let me know if you want me to put in a word.'

'Thank you, sir,' Apulius replied, 'but I've already written a dispatch to the tribune there, with my recommendations.' He gave a little smile; not a particularly nice one. He set his cup down and rose. 'Well, if you will excuse me, sir, I shall say farewell. I'm duty officer tonight.'

'Go with the gods, young man,' Father replied, but stayed in his chair. 'Julia will see you out.'

I pulled my shawl close as we walked through the courtyard to the front gate. The very last light of the day had disappeared in the west and the moon crescent was riding high in the sky over the hills. Below us were a scatter of bobbing lights as people hurried home along the streets before the night creatures came out. The watchmen would only patrol the *decumanus maximus* and the *cardo* crossing it, then find a safe nook somewhere, probably in a warm tavern.

Apulius turned to me. Even in the light of the flames in the sconces I could see his eyes full of a warm glow.

'Thank you for welcoming me to your house.' He looked away. 'I want to apologise again for how I treated you with such a lack of respect that first time in the market. I wish I could take it back.'

'I—' I swallowed hard. I put my hand out to touch his forearm. He drew his arm away before my fingers touched his skin. 'Well,' I continued, 'you'll no doubt think I really am a whore, but I regret nothing. Nor the time in the garden.' I tipped my head up at him, then spun round to retreat to the house.

An iron grip on my upper arm. His warm fingers almost encircled it.

'Wait!'

'What?' I did not attempt to pull away. It would give him too much satisfaction. I gave him my best impression of an icicle.

'I only wanted to make amends.' His eyes reminded me of a wounded animal's. 'I cannot pretend that those two times weren't the most momentous of my life.'

'You mean the best fuck you've ever had?'

He winced, then smiled and released my arm.

'You thrust straight to the vulnerable spot, don't you, Julia?'

'It must be my rough provincial upbringing,' I retorted.

He laughed, then became serious once more.

'I don't think that's so. You are a very intelligent and gracious woman when you are with others.'

'Look, Lucius Apulius, I would stop if I were you. You are digging yourself further into one of your beloved military trenches with every word you say.'

He shrugged.

'Perhaps, but I speak directly.' He looked at my face steadily. 'As do you.'

I felt that tug of recognition again. This was no lazy son of aristocracy, nor a blustering Italian. He was a man of determination and decision. A chill breeze started up and the torch flames crackled and flickered as we stood there. But I did not feel cold.

'If you are not unwilling,' he said, 'I would like to court you in a more traditional manner. Perhaps we could start again.'

7
_____

A week later, Father and I received an invitation from Lucius Apulius to be his guests at his unit's games. I wasn't at all sure we should go. When Lucius found out the truth about how I was only half divorced – and some busybody would delight in telling him all the details – he might distance himself. He wouldn't care about the Christian annulment, but without it, even if we married purely under Roman law, I could imagine the damage we would inflict on Father's position.

To Hades with them all. I wrote back accepting Lucius's invitation.

The old amphitheatre up on the hill had closed over fifty years ago for gladiatorial games. Constantine had been persuaded that the altars and reliefs dedicated to Nemesis and the sacred nature of the games were too pagan. More importantly, Rome had stopped payment for its upkeep and refurbishment. Father sent a mason there to make essential repairs now and again. Nevertheless, weeds grew at the base of the *balteus*, the balustrade running round the edge.

The entrance to *porta libitinensis*, the death door where the dead animals, criminals and gladiators had been dispatched, was now blocked up at the end. I'd walked round there once and ventured a few steps inside the arch, shivering in the chill of the old stone and brickwork moist and green with mould. Several somethings had flapped wings slowly and loudly and the noise bounced from one wall to the next. I was convinced Libitina, the goddess of death, corpses and funerals was still present. I'd hurried out back into the sunshine.

Today, Lucius Apulius greeted us and accompanied us to seats at the other end, the *porta sanavivaria* through which gladiators and animals used to enter ready for battle. If they were lucky enough to survive the content, they'd exited through the same doorway. At least these days I wasn't relegated to the back as my ancestresses had been. Whatever the changes going on now compared to the golden days of Rome hundreds of years ago, there were sometimes advantages to living in modern times.

Lucius's slave wore a sullen expression and stood to one side with an armful of additional cushions as we settled.

'Take no notice of Ascus – he's always this cheerful.' But he beckoned to the slave who then dropped his load into the stone seats. Lucius instructed him to find himself a perch at the back, then took my hand and guided me to my seat. His grip was sure, but not intimate, but I still felt flustered. Then I glanced along the curve of the front row and spotted my ex-husband with his uncle.

'Please don't be concerned,' Lucius said. 'Opsius felt as senior officer he was obliged to invite Bishop Eligius and, of course, the nephew, but I made sure we'd be sitting apart from them as far away as we could.'

'I just ignore him when I can,' my father said gruffly. 'Best way. I'm surprised he accepted, though.'

'So was Opsius, sir. But as you can see, there's a fair crowd here.' He swung his arm round to indicate the hundreds of spectators.

'Well, I suppose the politician in Eligius wouldn't miss a chance to show that he's omnipresent like their god. We don't get many free public events these days, young man, so people are taking advantage of it. So are the pie hawkers.' He raised an eyebrow at the men walking up and down the steps at the ends of the rows and sporting trays of oily pastries and shouting out the virtues of their delicacies. 'In truth, we haven't seen troops here in any numbers for decades, so it's a novelty.' He snorted. 'No doubt there'll be a few Alamanni spies taking notice of any tactics.'

'I've told my men to look out for any suspicious characters, sir.'

'The Alamanni don't look that different from us these days, Lucius,' Father replied. 'We underestimate them at our peril.'

Apulius shifted in his seat as if uncomfortable at that thought and turned to talk to me.

'If you look carefully, you can still see Nemesis's sanctuary at the eastern apex,' he said, pointing to the crumbling altar and faded reliefs. 'Closed now, of course.'

'The old gods are important to you, aren't they, Lucius?' I searched his face.

'I couldn't be a Roman without them.'

'But what does it mean to be Roman now?' I gestured at the men warming up with practice fights below in the sand, at the audience in a mixture of cloaks and ornate robes in the front rows, then at those sitting further back on the curved benches, a good proportion of them tribespeople in native dress and with long hair.

Lucius shrugged.

'We're living in times of transition,' he said. 'Even Roman troops wear breeches and consist of mixed native levies including a sprinkling of Goths.' He gave a wry smile. 'But the Noricans in my unit are tough and loyal-hearted.' He glanced up at the hills beyond the amphitheatre. 'Maybe it's the pure air that makes them so strong and all the clambering up and down mountains,' he said chuckling, then became solemn. 'It's a good country, one where any man would be content to settle. I certainly would.' He gave me such a warm look that I had to turn away. At that moment, I was certain that he was serious about wanting to stay and live with me here as my husband. I wished with all my heart and soul it could be so. But it was impossible. I blinked back a tear.

Trumpets sounded, and the games began. I leant forward to watch carefully. Perhaps I would learn a new trick or move I could try out on Musius in our training session and throw *him* onto the sand. But then I spotted the old soldier laughing and bantering with his cronies, all drinking. Hades.

As they circled round each other, I studied the moves the pairs of soldiers made. The sunlight reflected off their bladed swords and they seemed to be genuinely competitive as they slashed and jabbed, but I sensed a slight holding back. They were dismounted auxiliaries and I knew Lucius had been training them hard. Despite his efforts, I didn't think he'd ever transform our local boys into classical legionaries. Musius called out something in a raucous tone using words I'd never heard. I'd bet *solidi* they were indecent. Apulius frowned in his direction. On the amphitheatre sand, the young soldier nearest us flinched. He glanced sideways in Musius's direction for an instant. His opponent lunged forward and slashed. A red line sprang out along the youngster's upper arm and he uttered a noise between a cry and a grunt.

'Oh.' I winced. I couldn't help it.

'It's only a scratch,' Lucius said and enclosed my hand in his two. He pressed lightly.

'But it could have been you.'

'Would you care?' He looked at me intently.

I placed my other hand on top of his and pressed it. 'Of course.' We stayed like that for a time. Our eyes could find nothing else to look at but each other.

Another trumpet blast interrupted us as the one-to-one bouts finished. The troops lined up in front of Opsius and my father and saluted more or less in unison. The young lad with the wounded arm looked crestfallen as he marched out, but he held himself bravely.

'Anyway, I wouldn't have taken notice of that old tough's obscene catcall,' Lucius said. He nodded in the youngster's direction as he trudged through the *porta sanavivaria*. 'He'll take more care in the future.'

'That's harsh.'

He shrugged. 'That's what training's about. He can do a week's training against a static pole. That should concentrate his mind.'

'You're a hard taskmaster, Lucius.'

'No, I just want them to have skills and instincts to be able to keep themselves alive. And to be single-minded. The barbarians won't be at all accommodating when they pour over the Danuvius.'

'Is that likely?'

'Maybe not today, but one day, I can assure you.'

After athletics competitions and a display of archery skills on the ground and horseback, the games ended with the presentation of prizes – mostly purses of coins – then a general procession. Lucius escorted us to the gate, then left to accompany the other soldiers back to the camp. I was disappointed he didn't come back to the house with us, but Father said that after the baths there would very likely be a heavy evening of hard drinking and betting and it would look strange if Apulius wasn't there for at least part of the evening with his men.

'In a way, he's still finding his feet here,' Father said. 'He's an Italian aristocrat – they're mostly Norican hillmen with a few Pannonians and Goths thrown in. Opsius is a good sort, but he's an Illyrian. Apulius must look like an exotic being to them. Best he try to integrate a bit.'

The next morning, I tried out a manoeuvre on Musius that I'd seen in the amphitheatre. We'd been striking and feinting for about ten minutes. I'd fended off several attacks with both shield and wooden sword. My shield was lighter than the standard one used by the military, round and with a good Noricum steel boss from one of Father's workshops. Musius had taught me to use it as a weapon, not just as a protection.

As we circled, I lunged forward, jerked back as he came to parry, then slipped in underneath. Straight in his chest. He staggered back and caught his breath.

'Bugger me,' he said, panting. 'That's a crafty move.' His throat spasmed as he swallowed hard and rubbed his ribs. 'If you're going to hit me like that, *domina,* I shall have to wear my mail shirt.' He brought his wooden sword up in salute. I grinned at him.

The sound of hands clapping behind me.

'*Macte!*' Lucius Apulius's voice was warm with praise. A tingle crossed my shoulders at the sound. But I kept my eyes on Musius, and my mind. If I turned, or even glanced sideways, he'd seek his revenge. I carried on moving, balancing my weight on the balls of my toes. I jabbed, trying to tempt Musius to attack. But he wouldn't.

'I think we'll leave it there for today,' he said and brought his sword down to his side. 'You'll want to speak to your guest, *domina.*' He winked. Cheeky bastard. He winced as he picked up his overtunic from the ground. Had I really hurt him that much? My wooden sword still in my hand, I watched him until he was several steps down the path on the way back through the gardens.

Lucius chuckled. 'Yes, best not to trust an old lag like that if he's training you seriously. No doubt he pulls surprises from time to time.'

'He does,' I said. 'But he says that's all part of the training. Father trusts him completely.' I glanced at Lucius who was looking at me intently. Gods, I must look a fright. I could feel tendrils of hair sticking to the edges of my forehead and temples. I picked up a linen cloth from the nearby stone bench and wiped my face.

'Is it usual for ladies here to practise such hard exercise?' he said.

'Italian *ladies* wouldn't know one end of a kitchen knife from the other let alone a fighting blade. And they scream if somebody runs past them fast.' I shrugged. 'Some of them practise ball games and gymnastic exercises, but I don't know any other in Virunum who trains as I do. Many ordinary *women* here, though, know how to use a dagger. We live in a frontier province. Father has instructed Musius to provide all free members of the household with a blade and give them a measure of rudimentary instruction.'

'But why do *you* do this?' He pointed to the wooden practice swords and shields.

'Because I enjoy it.' I dropped down onto the bench. 'My father was a soldier. My mother came from the tribes where women went into battle alongside their men. She started with me from the age of five. Mostly with a stick.' I rubbed the stone of the bench with the tip of my finger and loosened some surface grains. 'And with my brother until he died.'

'I'm sorry. How old was he?' Lucius sat down beside me and put his arm around me. I leant against him.

'Nearly eleven. He was two years younger than me. It was quite sudden. One day he was healthy and the next crying in agony. My mother and Asella were beside themselves as they took care of him. The following day, he just went to sleep and never woke. Marcus was cremated in the old Roman way. *Matir* stopped talking, shredded her clothes and wailed for a day and a night. After that she rode up to the river for three days.

Asella said she performed sacrifices for the dead and some of her kin came across the river to be with her, including her bother Ittu. But I have always wondered if *Matir* crossed the river looking for an answer. Asella refused to say anything at the time, telling me to mind my lessons and not poke my nose into adults' affairs. Apparently, Father went and collected her on the morning of the fourth day and brought her home. I can't recall much of that time, but I remember her looking ill and drifting around the house saying little. Poor *Matir*.'

Lucius held me to him and I felt my eyes fill. I sniffed and blinked but wouldn't let the tears run.

'Were you close to your mother?'

I nodded. 'She was very proud of her people, but she loved my father. It's funny, but the Italians all thought she was a wild savage from a dark forest in the bowels of the earth, but from what she told me, her town was paved, had stone buildings with shops, smithies and meeting places. The laws were agreed and enforced and the leaders were usually literate. People wore similar tunics to us here in the Roman Empire.' I looked down at my legs. 'Well, with breeches, of course. They weren't stupid Romans who went around with their arses only half covered.'

He burst out laughing.

'But as you know, Julia, I wear them. Particularly for riding a horse.'

His eyes shone with such warmth I knew he was remembering the first time we had met just after he'd come back from a fruitless patrol in the hills. But this man holding me so gently was not the arrogant Roman wanting a quick trick with a tart. I laid my hand on his thigh, on those breeches. The flesh under them was warm to my touch. He caught his breath, bent and brushed my lips with his. But then he drew back and released me. He stood and looked away. But when he looked back at me, his eyes were dark. I could see he burned for me as I burned for him.

'I will not take advantage of you,' he said to the line of trees. The muscles in his neck stood out in taut lines.

'Oh, for Juno's sake, Lucius, can't you see what's in front of your face?' I jumped up. My fingers had curled into fists.

'I said I would speak to your father when the moment was right. Until then, I will not touch you.' He turned towards the back courtyard. I grabbed his arm.

'Don't you dare run away from me. If you won't fuck me, then fight me.'

He looked aghast. I'd been coarse, but he knew I spoke my mind. And he was no prissy boy. But why in Hades had I said that? He was a military tribune, battle-hardened, in peak physical condition and half Musius's age. Stupid, stupid, stupid. I closed my eyes for a second but opened them to see a grim look on his face.

'Do you think you have enough breath to go another round?' His voice couldn't have been colder. He unclipped his cloak and took his time folding it neatly on the bench, then crossed his arms and waited.

I hesitated. I would be lying on the ground in less time than it took to say I hadn't meant it. Or maybe that was his intention. I half closed my eyes, squinting against the sun's light, and searched his face. He raised one eyebrow as if mocking me. I could *not* withdraw my challenge now. Teutates and Belestis save me. It would be quick though.

I wiped my hand on my breeches' outside leg and grasped my wooden sword. Thank the gods it wasn't one of our own steel blades. I lifted my shield up and braced myself. My throat was so dry I could hardly breathe.

He said nothing. The only sound I heard was the chattering and fluttering of small birds. The only smell came from herbs in the ornamental beds warming up in the sunshine. But I smelt my own fear.

He lifted one of the practice swords and swung it at me in one movement, point in full jab. I sidestepped and flung my shield up to deflect it. But the wooden sword grazed my upper arm. He frowned. Had he expected me to stand still and be skewered like a farmyard pig? I pivoted on my heel and ran at him, sword horizontal to return the favour. He thrust his free arm out. He had no shield. Arrogant. I struck him in his stomach and ran back. His face hardened and his eyes narrowed into points of brown stone. We circled. His right arm flashed out. I ducked, raised my shield but the sword caught my neck. Even the rounded end of the wooden sword stung. As I sprang back, I blinked hard and took another breath which seared my throat. He was going to pay for that.

Holding my shield forward, I ran full pelt at him, shrieking as best I could. I didn't care if he jabbed at me again. I just wanted to fell him. I rammed him with my full body weight, pushing my shield boss into his face. The next second, I was on my back, squinting up at the sun, and pinned down on the ground. His arm was across my throat as hard as a band of steel, his body sitting on mine. I coughed and the pressure increased. My heart pounded. His eyes bore into mine. My head began to swim.

'Please…' I gasped.

Instantly, the pressure relaxed. He knelt back on his heels, wiped his forehead then sprang up. I rubbed my throat and took a few shallow breaths. He bent down and with his arm around my shoulders lifted me to my feet. He looked stricken as he drew his arms back.

'I apologise,' he said. 'I didn't mean to hurt you. Is it bad?'

'You nearly strangled me!'

'I'm so sorry. It was instinct, training…'

I grabbed another breath. I was bruised, but not nearly as badly as I made out.

'Instinct! You were pushing me to the bank of the Styx!'

'You were fighting me like some damned barbarian. Like an Alamanna.'

'Ha!'

'We give them no quarter. They torture any prisoners in hideous ways. Any who survive are crippled for life and pray daily for death, so we fight to kill or die ourselves.' He looked at me gravely. 'I will never let you provoke me into fighting you ever again.'

'Don't be so damned pompous. You didn't exactly refuse. Besides, "never" is a dangerous word.'

With that, I picked up my wooden sword and shield and marched back to the house.

8

He didn't come and eat with us for the rest of the week, but he did send me a letter the next day. He hoped I wasn't permanently damaged after our 'sword practice'. I smiled wryly at that and ran my hand over my throat. I would forgive him anything. How your judgement changed when you were in love. With the letter was a leather bag containing a bracelet made from multiple woven gold textured strands twisting around each other. It was exquisite. I kissed it and slipped it on my wrist, vowing never to take it off. He further wrote that he would be away for a few days on a joint patrol up near the Danuvius frontier.

He finished by saying he hoped I would accept the bracelet as a symbol of his love for me which he swore would last forever. I folded the letter and put it in my waist pouch and made my way to the back of the house into the garden and out up the hill. I was so overcome that I could hardly gather my thoughts together. As I looked across the valley beyond Virunum, the pulse from my heart sang through my entire body. Oh, Lucius, you know you have my love into eternity.

I had to sit through another of Eligius's sermons on Sunday about how the Christos favoured faithful marriage and family life. Not that their son of God had experienced such a life unless the stories about Miriam of Magdala were true.

Father pressed my hand in sympathy as I fidgeted on the hard bench while Eligius droned on. We only went to their primitive little *ecclesia* out of political expediency so that the Christians, specifically Eligius, couldn't have a reason to say we, especially Father, weren't complying with the official religion. Father's motivation for a peaceful and secure life for himself and his people governed everything he did.

The following morning, I approached Aegius, the fresco painter. He was in his studio, more of a workshop on the south wing of the villa section to the side of the inner courtyard. The wall was covered in small tools held in neat rows like a legionary order of battle. He wore a leather apron over his tunic and was shaving tiny curls of powder off a solid block of colour into a small pot. He looked up and smiled, then his face fell back into a more solemn expression. He stood and wiped his hands on a cloth on the bench.

'*Domina*?'

'Good morning, Aegius. I wonder if you would do me a favour.'

'Of course. Something to make or paint?'

'No. I want you to accompany me somewhere. As protection.'

'Me?' He shot me a puzzled look. 'I'm no bodyguard. And I'm too old.'

'I'm not a fool, Aegius. You didn't get a muscled body from painting pictures. And I know you train with Musius.'

'I like to keep healthy, *domina*.'

I didn't comment further but I'd seen his reflexes when he dropped something; it rarely reached the ground. When I was a little girl, I thought this was normal for all men. Certainly, my father was the same. And now I'd seen it was so with Apulius.

I would bet a hundred, no, a thousand gold *solidi* that Aegius had been a fighting soldier. Was he a deserter? I'd never seen any sign of punishment on him. He'd married one of the estate worker's daughters who'd died giving birth to his own daughter, but he never remarried. His daughter kept house for him in two rooms next to his workshop. Nothing was known about her husband if she had one, but the grandchild, Cuso, was a delightful imp and now Aegius's apprentice.

'What I really want from you, Aegius, is your steadfastness and your intelligence. I also need you to hold your tongue. Musius wouldn't know how.'

He looked at me steadily, one eyebrow slightly raised. I waited.

'Very well,' he said. 'Now?'

'If you would,' I replied. 'Fetch yourself a sword and a light mail shirt from the steward's store.'

'Are we expecting serious trouble on this mysterious errand of yours?'

'I hope not, but I want to have somebody at my side who will not be intimidated or leave me.'

'Ah.'

Asella and I waited under the main gate arch, in the shadow. She twitched on her feet, looking this way and that. I pulled my cloak tighter, then let a breath out. This next hour would be humiliating, but I had to do it.

Aegius returned duly armed in the legionary fashion, no helmet but with a *pugio* dagger on his other side. He rested his hand on the hilt of his *spatha* sword.

'I've brought my own.'

I nodded, now sure he'd been under arms as a younger man.

We set off on foot down the hill towards the centre of the town. As I stood at the top of the flight of steps that ran down from our villa wall to the first housing blocks of the town, I glanced back up the hill toward the military *castrum*. Lucius was still away on his patrol in the north. I would be so glad when he returned – we had so much to talk about. I sniffed in the chill morning air and pulled my back up straight. But whether a future with him was possible or unattainable for Father's political reasons, I had to disentangle my status for my own sake.

The house I was looking for was on the *decumanus maximus* which ran the whole length of the town out onto the Via Claudia military road heading to the north to Ovilava and Castra Regina on the *limes*. As I emerged onto the *decumanus maximus* opposite the house, I looked across the wide gravelled street, rutted but with occasional stone slabs to cross without becoming mired in rubbish and filthy water. It looked innocent enough but when I glanced up at the lintel over the door and saw the chi-rho, my heart hammered. That round sign sculpted into the stone was the symbol of my enduring embarrassment.

Asella frowned at me, but I took no notice. Aegius humphed, but I ignored that. I needed to gather up my courage.

'Come,' I commanded. 'We are here now and must continue.' The door swung open before I knocked. As I suspected, the porter had spotted us approaching. I knew him from old. He watched everything and everybody rather too efficiently, as I remembered.

'*Salve*, Lady Julia,' he murmured. He attempted to close the door immediately after me, but Asella was too quick and slipped in. Aegius just pushed the porter to one side.

'I must protest, Lady Julia,' the porter said. 'You do not need an armed escort in your own home.'

'Insolence!' I snapped. 'This is *not* my home. Now go about your business and announce me to Eligius.' The porter gave me a sullen look. '*Immediately*!' We waited in the vestibule as he slinked away. This place had been where I had lived for a few months with Deodatus as his wife, but it was never my home. There was no heating, or light beyond one dismal flame from an oil lamp on a small shelf that smelt rancid. Even the stone walls seemed to exude dampness. I shivered.

'My dear Julia. Welcome home.' Eligius moved towards me, smiling, and with his hands held out in greeting. Mine stayed by my side. He glanced at Asella and nodded, still smiling. She returned a stony look. 'Your guard may return to your father's house and your woman can go and prepare your chamber. Come.' He half turned, obviously expecting me to follow him. I did not move. 'Julia?'

'Bishop Eligius, I have come to talk to you and then I will return to my home, my father's house. My presence here is only for that.'

'Oh? Well, it's always pleasant to talk. Your servants may wait here while we talk privately.'

'No, they will remain with me,' I said.

Aegius took a step nearer me.

'Really, we do not need such people present while we discuss family matters.' He waved his fingers at them in dismissal.

'I wish them to stay,' I said, trying to keep calm. He couldn't know my stomach was tying itself in writhing knots. 'And what we are about to discuss is known by at least half of Virunum.'

He frowned, then turned. We followed him into the atrium, an area I had always liked for its spaciousness and its intimate corners and niches. When Deodatus had been at his interminable prayers, I had sat and read – usually a classical work with as many pagan gods and goddesses in the story as possible.

'Shall we sit?' Eligius extended his arm towards a group of stools with colourful embroidered cushions. They were new since my time.

'No, thank you. My request to you is short.'

'Very well.' His eyes took on a hard quality.

'Deodatus and I were, and are, incompatible. I only agreed to be baptised under the Christos ritual to please Deodatus, but that was *after* we were married. It did not improve our marriage. I divorced him under Roman law and in the tradition of my mother's people. Those were the ways in which we married. I was thus twice divorced. I have come today to ask you to give me a writ of annulment from your religious community.' I took another breath. 'I do not need it as I am legally divorced, but it would clarify my status.'

Eligius didn't move but looked at me gravely. I nipped the inside of my cheek with my teeth and forced myself to stay statue still. I was determined he would have to speak first.

'Oh, Julia, I am so distressed for you,' he said at last. 'God sees man and wife as one being which cannot be split. My nephew is a pious Christian and you are his baptised wife.' He shrugged. 'It is impossible.'

'But I wish to marry again and it is only out of courtesy that I ask you for this writ.' Whether Apulius wanted to marry me was another question, but I would not let this inflexible priest know that.

Eligius shook his head slowly and with a tight, sanctimonious smile. He sighed theatrically. He was enjoying this too much.

'It's the young Roman commander, isn't it? Opsius's deputy. No. You cannot marry him. Marriage is for life, Julia. You would be committing spiritual adultery. More than that, he is a pagan, so your eternal soul would be in danger.'

'I don't believe that, or in your hell,' I cried out.

'Be careful, Julia. Your Roman soldier lost his career for not adhering to the true faith of Christos.'

How did Eligius know that? Father had mentioned the bishop was very well connected. Now I realised that this knowledge was proof of how well.

'Do you wish to lose everything for practising pagan rituals?' Eligius continued. 'Or your father to be in danger of execution for worshipping up at the old shrine of Mars Latobius on the hill? He knows it's strictly forbidden.'

'You cannot threaten me like that!'

'I am not threatening, Julia,' Eligius said softly. 'I merely wish to save your soul from the peril it stands in.'

'No, I think you want to exert your power over my father and me.'

His eyes narrowed. He looked away and then back at me.

'I think you and your father need to consider the growing strength of Christ's message here and the influence of his representatives on earth. My correspondents in Rome and Mediolanum – two vastly more sophisticated places – would support me on my stance as would my superior in Aquileia. And they have the ear of Emperor Valentinian.'

I trudged back up the hill, with Asella supporting me, her hand under my elbow as we navigated the path and steps. Back inside the *domus*, I thanked Aegius. He said nothing but saluted me before turning towards his own quarters. Asella brought me to my room where I shed my cloak and my dignity and burst into bitter sobs.

In the bathhouse, I sank into the water to let the warmth comfort me. But neither that nor Asella's massage made any difference. At least the face I would present to Father would be less puffy and more composed. No Lucius, of course. I hadn't seen him for days. Five to be precise. After my bruising encounter with Eligius, I wasn't sure I could face him. As Father and I ate our evening meal, I was finding it unbearable.

I picked at some vegetables without taking in exactly what they were, merely tasting the tart herbs on them. Father hadn't mentioned any visit by Lucius to ask about marrying me, but what good would it have done? I was caught in Bishop Eligius's trap. He refused to consider giving me a Christian annulment and I would not upset my father's position or safety or bring any scandal by trying to marry again without it. Many of the townspeople had become followers of the Christos. They would be outraged and call me an adulteress. Eligius must see that I was never going to return to his wretched nephew as his wife. If our marriage could be annulled, then Deodatus could contract with somebody else, a Galilean, who would make him a better wife and possibly give him children. Men liked to think of continuing their family line and name. Whether Deodatus was capable was another question.

'Julia? Have you lost the power of speech? You usually have so much to say.'

'Oh, I hope you don't think I chatter on like a songbird at dawn, Father.'

'No, child, but you seem to be in another world, an unhappy one. What's troubling you?'

'Nothing in particular,' I lied and gave him a smile. 'I'm a little tired. Asella's massage was rather vigorous.'

'Yes, and I'm Gaius Julius Caesar. Tell me.'

I confessed everything, babbling every detail except the intimacies between Lucius and me. But my father was no fool. When I'd finished, I felt tears running down my cheeks. I seized my linen napkin and wiped them away.

'You've left a smear of olive oil on your nose,' my father said without humour. 'You were very unwise to go to Eligius. What on earth were you thinking?'

'I had to try,' I muttered.

'Surely you must have known you wouldn't get him to change his mind?'

'I thought if I appealed to his heart he would have had compassion on me.'

'He has no heart, only a thirst for power. I'm only relieved you were alert enough to take Asella and Aegius with you.'

'After the fiasco at the poetry evening, I didn't want to be abducted and forced to remain in that house.'

'Be assured, Julia, you would not have remained long there.'

'Yes, but Eligius would have won in your quarrel if he incited you to remove me forcibly from his so-called protection.'

'Ha! My daughter the strategist. You're not wrong.' He took a long swallow of his wine. 'I'd like to go and thrust his words back down his bloody throat. But I can't go against him – he's becoming too powerful. Emperor Valentinian is reasonably tolerant but he likes to keep in with the religious hierarchy. It's all about politics, curse it.' He got to his feet and walked over to the side table, picked at a dish of nuts and walked back to me. 'Eligius and his Galilean cult already have bishops at Celeia to the south-east, Teurnia west of here, north at Lauriacum and in the far west at Aguntum. And they're digging in. You must remember that Christos rabble-rouser who whipped up a mob and tried to attack the statues near the baths in the town? Thank the gods for Opsius's quick response. But the Christos followers' power is growing fast.'

'But most people don't believe in it, surely?'

'I don't ask these days. But Eligius's church, small as it is, is packed each Sunday with people like us who are playing it safe. As I said, it's all politics.'

I ate my honey cake in silence and made a note to ask Daria to pass on my compliments to the beekeeper. It was superb this year with a true alpine tang. But I was avoiding my father's eyes.

'You didn't actually marry under the Christian rite,' he said and sighed. 'But Eligius will insist until his dying day that you're a Christian wife.'

'I only agreed to the baptism for Deodatus's sake. It was making him unhappy that his wife was technically a pagan.' I looked down at my hands. 'He refused to share my bed until I gave in.' I looked up at him. 'Father, I only wanted to make my marriage work, but—'

'I know.'

The servants came in and removed the empty plates. I waved to them to take the bowls of leftovers, everything. I waited until the last one closed the door. I couldn't blame my father for appearing to adapt. He was responsible for thousands of Noricans, people our family had ruled for hundreds of years, even before the Romans. He dealt well with the Roman governor and military, having their respect as one of a previous emperor's commanders. And he kept a firm hand on any discontent while judging genuine grievances.

Only Eligius and his crew threatened to upset this balance. And my life.

'I do understand, Father, truly I do,' I began.

'Yes, you're no fool, Julia.' He sighed. 'I'm so sorry, but you' re still in the same position.'

'It didn't really matter until I met Lucius. All I want to do is share my life with him. I know he loves our mountains and would be happy to settle down here. Is there nobody in Rome we could appeal to?'

'The Senate is stuffed with old men tutting over minutiae of legal texts. However, many are faithful to the traditional gods. The trouble is that it has little power compared to even Julian's day. However, I think they would support you. You have to remember, though, that it could take months, even years and even then it could be ignored by the Christian leaders. Eligius and his cronies are only looking for an excuse to mobilise and assert their power over the state. And we know they would use any way available to do that.'

'Could I appeal to the emperor?' I looked at Father, almost aghast at my own temerity.

'I may be a prince here, Julia, but to Valentinian, I'm a provincial nobody. If he thought it would keep the peace, he wouldn't hesitate to put in a new governor here, depose me and exile us to some damned island in the middle of nowhere, if we were lucky. He's said to have a brutal temper.' He looked at me steadily. 'I'm still responsible for you while you are in my house and protected as part of my *familia*. I want you to be happy, Julia, but I cannot sacrifice the safety and welfare of thousands of people, their families and their livelihoods. You are a Bacausus, a descendant of strong rulers. You know we must sacrifice our personal wishes if we have to make such a choice.' He studied the far wall for a long moment. 'I think you know the best you can hope for is contentment.'

An invisible iron claw grasped my heart.

'You can't marry Lucius Apulius and settle down with him here. Or anybody else, for that matter.'

9

The next morning, I rose too tired to train with Musius. I stabbed my
bread in olive oil at the breakfast table instead and drank a beaker of
mulsum. Father wasn't there. I waited in the atrium, pretending to
read or sew with Asella. The hours dragged by. I was desperate to
see Lucius and kept trying to imagine schemes to circumnavigate
Eligius's refusal. I dreamt of killing him, holding him or Deodatus to
ransom, writing an annulment myself and holding a dagger to
Eligius's throat and forcing him to sign it. I expelled a deep breath as
I realised none of these ideas was practical. All or any of them
would lead to would be my trial and execution and Father's ruin.

At the fourth hour, I saw the porter walk by escorting one of the
Norican auxiliaries to Father's *tablinum*. I half rose to follow, but
Asella grabbed my arm and shook her head. It wasn't uncommon
for Opsius to send messages to Father. It could have been about
anything. I sighed and sat down again. Shivering, I pulled my *palla*
round my shoulders, set my elbows on my knees and rested my
head between my cupped hands.

Shortly after the soldier left, Father sent me to see Priscilla,
Quietus's daughter, about some poems. I protested, saying a servant
could go, but he insisted. Codices were too important to hand to a
mere servant, especially his newest one with decorated front and
back boards. Father had replaced nearly three-quarters of his scrolls
with codices, but although easier to read as they could be opened at

any part of the work, they were heavier to carry because of their wood boards. He also gave me a sealed note for Quietus which he told me to give him as soon as I arrived.

Priscilla invited me to stay and eat *prandium* with them. Quietus insisted, so I gave in. If Apulius called at our *domus* – if he wanted to see me – but found I wasn't there, perhaps he would leave a message and call again. The lunch was very refined, with tiny morsels of songbird, beautifully cooked, and seasoned vegetables, fine ground white bread with a delicate crust, *savillum* cheese dessert dripping with honey and every sauce imaginable.

'It's only a few bits and pieces, Lady Julia,' Quietus oozed as he sat down with us. 'I expect you keep a far better table at home.' He laughed in a way that sounded false, but although a little condescending, he was friendly enough. Priscilla's sister, Paula, giggled. But then she tittered at all her father's remarks that he obviously thought were witty. She continued to pick daintily at the bowls of food with her fingers in an affected way.

'Not at all, noble Quietus,' I replied. 'This is far richer than our simple spelt bread, cheese and fruit. A feast in fact.' He gave me a sharp look, then glanced at the door again. He was doing that every so often, so I concluded he was expecting a visitor soon. We ate on in silence.

I eventually made my excuses and rushed back home with a cloth bag of codices that Quietus insisted Father had asked to borrow. Father had an excellent library. Why on earth did he need anything from Quietus?

I knew something was wrong the instant Aegius stepped out in front of me as I walked through the entrance archway. The sun was behind him, but I could see the solemn expression on his face, then a fleeting look of sorrow in his eyes.

'What is it, Aegius?' I stared at him. He just stood there. I clutched the base of my throat with my free hand. 'Not my father?' He was only in his forty-sixth year and full of vigour.

'No, *domina*. The prince is well. But you must be strong.'

Gods, what had happened? Then a grey dread crept over me. 'Tell me,' I whispered.

'First, you must promise to keep your dignity and remember who you are.'

'What do you mean?' I searched his face but saw no answer there. 'In the name of Pluto, what are you not telling me?'

'The young tribune has gone. Your father has forbidden him to step across the threshold of this *domus* or speak to you outside.'

The bag of books fell from my hand as I covered my ears. No. I hadn't heard right. I shook my head to clear it. I looked up at Aegius again, but his face was stern. I took a deep breath, then thrust out my arm to shove him aside and run inside.

'No.' His hand caught my wrist in an iron grip.

'How dare you! Release me immediately.'

'No, *domina*, I will not until you have composed yourself.'

I pulled against his grip, but I couldn't get free.

'Peace, Lady Julia. Listen to me. Your father did this with stone in his soul. But I saw him wipe his eyes briefly as the young man trudged out through the atrium. The prince glared at me like a recruit who'd deserted. At that point, I thought it wise to bow and withdraw.'

I stopped struggling. Ever since Father's words last night, I had to acknowledge in my mind this might happen, but my heart had dreaded it. But why hadn't Lucius come to see me, at least to say farewell?

'You can let me go, Aegius. I am ready to go in.' My voice broke. I swallowed hard but set my shoulders back and my chin up. Aegius handed me the bag of codices, now dirty, but I didn't care. I didn't care about anything now that my heart had been ripped out. Whatever they said, I would go out every day and hope to see Lucius Apulius somewhere. I would sit by the approach to the military camp and watch. I had to speak to him.

I avoided my father as much as possible over the next few days, eating in silence when I had to take my meals with him and answering with a simple yes or no when I had to reply to a question. He put his hand out to take mine after one meal, but I turned away and marched down the corridor, anger bursting out of me. I spent most of my days in the town trying to spot Lucius. I walked up and down, but mostly I sat by the bookseller's shop, holding a codex in my hand.

As I fidgeted for the thousandth time with woven gold bracelet Lucius had given me, I tried again to work out why I hadn't seen him. After the barbarian raids around Ovilava, patrols rode out almost every day. In the late afternoon on the fourth day, I'd had enough. I signalled Asella to pack up my stool and the sunshade

My back ached, I couldn't stop yawning and I couldn't pretend to be interested any longer in the book I'd tried to read for the twentieth time.

The market was closing. Shopkeepers had cleared their pots, tools and cloths from the pavement in front of their premises, fruit and vegetable sellers were packing unsold leftovers into baskets which they loaded onto handcarts. Exhausted women whose feet probably hurt after standing all day behind stalls fending off thieving children and time-wasting browsers were sitting waiting for their men to finish. Then they would go home, feed them and their children and fall into bed only to wake again at sunrise tomorrow and trudge back to the market. The few chickens left hanging on the butcher's stand were smelling so much after a day in the open that I wanted to retch. I didn't usually notice it, but today they stank. He plucked them off their hooks and stuffed them in a bag. He'd probably sell them to the pie shop opposite as exclusive choice birds. Even the blond brooch seller who usually stayed to the bitter end had gone.

'Lady Julia?' I looked up to see the old bookseller outside whose shop I had stationed myself. He was unpinning his list of books for sale from the side post of the door. He glanced at Asella. 'Would you like me to send my boy with you to escort you home?'

'Oh, no, thank you, Laurus.'

I thought I saw sympathy in his eyes. Juno, half the town probably knew I pined for Lucius. I couldn't bear the old man's sympathy and looked away, glancing one last time towards the route that led to the military *castrum*. A cloud of dust and the noise of horses. It grew louder and a good dozen mounted auxiliaries thundered towards us, causing the stallholders to run out to retrieve their remaining goods from the road at double speed. Then the troop halted. Their leader nudged his horse on and came to a halt by me. The pulse in my heart echoed in my neck, my ears and down through my stomach. Lucius Apulius stared down at me. Lines round his eyes that hadn't been there before, his face unshaven, his expression dull like a man who had lost purpose. Then his eyes grew warm. The light in them sparked for a moment, then faded. He looked away, swallowed so the bulge in this throat bounced hard, then his gaze came back to me. I raised my hand to touch his.

'Don't leave me,' I whispered.

'Julia,' he croaked. Then the horses of his men closed up behind him and pushed him on.

I waited still as a forum statue until every trace of them had disappeared back into dust. As we stumbled home, I felt tears fall down my face. I didn't care. My heart was broken and nothing mattered any longer.

I went back the next day and the following four days, but saw no trace of him. Patrols went past me. The old commander, Opsius, led one. He saw me and looked away quickly as if embarrassed. That was odd; Opsius rarely stirred out of his office. I ran after him, but the patrol had picked up speed and left me standing in the middle of the road. When I reached home that evening, Father called me into his *tablinum*.

'You cannot continue to make yourself a laughing stock. You're acting like something out of a Greek tragedy.'

'I don't care,' I replied, only wanting to go to my room and my bed.

'*I* do. I will not have you parade yourself on the streets of Virunum. Every spotty youth will laugh at you, even if they aren't already.'

'I've had some offers already,' I said bitterly. I didn't tell him about how one Christian woman had spat on my sandals, or the drunk who asked if I was missing a good swiving and said he would oblige.

Father stood stock still, his face turning red.

'Then I forbid you to leave this house unless I am with you.' His voice grated. 'I've let you have far more freedom than other fathers do as I thought you had intelligence as well as strength of character. I've obviously been wrong.'

His face was stern, his mouth a tight straight line.

'Go to your room. I don't want you in my sight for the rest of today.'

'I don't care what you do,' I retorted. 'My life is over now.'

'Don't be so damned dramatic.' He waved a piece of parchment in my face. 'It's pointless hanging around the street like a two-*follis* whore. This came from Opsius this afternoon. Lucius Apulius has been stripped of his army commission and sent back to Rome. He's been forbidden to leave Latium for the rest of his days.'

10

I lay on my bed for two days and nights. Asella made me drink weak wine and water and Patulus sent up delicacies from the kitchen, but I didn't feel hungry. In truth, I didn't feel anything, just tired into my bones. I huddled under my blankets at night, black despair oozed round my mind. When I woke each day, I was surprised I had slept. Perhaps Asella was putting something in the *mulsum*. I didn't care.

'Come now, *domina*,' Asella said on the morning of the third day. Gods, she was using that bracing tone she'd aimed at me when I was ten years old. 'You cannot lie in bed like a sulky adolescent. Your father has need of you.'

'I'm not speaking to him,' I mumbled from under the bedding.

'Oh, please!' She shook my shoulder.

I turned and glared at her. She frowned back.

'It's the last day of Floralia and people will be expecting you.'

I groaned and closed my eyes. It was nothing like the riotous festivals of centuries ago or even a hundred years ago – the Christians had seen to that. But Father used an old altar in a field corner for people who brought offerings of wheat ears and flowers, especially lupins which represented fertility.

After reciting a few prayers, some to Flora, others to Ceres, Father would offer wine and beer to everybody, and the slaves would set out pastries and meats on trestle tables and everybody would get drunk. Then the huntsmen would release hares and everybody would chase goats in some kind of lingering memory of the great Roman fertility festival. I'd read Ovid's description. Gods, our little mountain ceremony was tame by the sound of his description.

Of course, Deodatus had tried to forbid me to take part when we'd been married. Eligius gave his tight smile at the following Sunday service every year and with a mock-sorrowful expression offered the whole congregation blanket forgiveness. He followed it with an exhortation to pray for their souls and to turn away from pagan licentiousness.

'Come along, now,' Asella persisted. 'You must have a proper breakfast and get ready. I've made a floral wreath for your hair.'

Gods! She wasn't going to give up. I sat up and blinked. I gave her my most severe frown, but she merely shrugged in reply. She turned and rinsed a cloth in a bowl of scented water and wiped my frown away along with the salt traces of my tears.

I stood almost inanimate as she dressed me in a yellow short-sleeved gown. I didn't even protest when she draped Deodatus's green *palla* over my shoulders. I felt like a narcissus. She wound the wreath of columbine, yarrow and thyme into my hair and added a few gentian flowers.

I could hear the voices of my father and other people assembling downstairs; they would be local farmers, both owners and tenants. I sighed. If I didn't take part in this day, it would look negligent. All I wanted to do was flee to my bed and hide. But I knew I couldn't shirk it.

'Now, lift your chin and walk like the prince's daughter.' Asella stood back to look at her work.

'You don't need to remind me of my duty,' I snapped at her.

She beamed at me and said, 'Better!'

I put my hand out to take hers.

'I'm sorry. I shouldn't have been so bad tempered.'

'*Domina*, I do understand, but now you must pull your backbone up and put the tribune behind you. That is finished.'

I nodded, unable to speak. A tear slid down my cheek as I followed her downstairs.

. . .

Father held my hand firmly as we processed up the slope in the direction of the abandoned town on the hill. I didn't pull away from him despite my anger at him. It would have spoilt the celebratory holiday mood. The altar in the fields was only a mile away, so it was a pleasant country stroll. Although being out in the clear mountain air under a bright blue sky did nothing to soothe my broken heart, I relished the sun warming my face and arms, and the light mountain breeze refreshing us as we climbed.

Chanting and hymns to Flora and Ceres rose from the trail of people following us, along with some shouting and laughing. I glanced back. There must have been over three hundred people behind us. At the field edge, we stopped under a small cluster of lime trees shielded by a crescent of pines.

After some shuffling, the crowd settled down as Father intoned some prayers followed by three children laying dried wheat ears and white alpine flowers on the stone altar. I laid my own yellow and purple ones next. Soon the altar was covered in colour. People split up into groups to exchange greetings and gossip. A flock of birds flew overhead, circled over us for a few seconds, then raced towards the mountains across the valley.

'A good omen, I'd say,' murmured Aegius who had come to stand by me.

'I didn't realise you went along with omens,' I replied. He always seemed so practical and grounded. His face didn't show any emotion, either, although his eyes followed his grandson who was playing a tag game with his friends.

'Never hurts to keep in with the gods and their messages.'

I went to reply but was interrupted by Daria and her own flock of servants who were setting out the food and drink. She handed me a cup of wine and Aegius a larger one of beer frothing over the edge.

'I've only brought small beer and watered wine, but the prince said we had to offer generous amounts.' She raised her eyes to the heavens.

'Well, that's what Floralia is, Daria. Everybody letting go a little.'

'Yes, and counting the babies next winter,' she grumped.

I laughed. Her eyes gleamed.

'I'm so pleased to see you recovered from your, er, illness, *domina*.'

'I don't think I'll ever recover, to be truthful, Daria, but we must carry on with our lives.'

She laid a hand on my forearm, an intimate gesture for a servant, even such a senior one.

'It will ease, my dear. Truly.'

I stared at her. I realised I had never given a thought to her own family situation.

'Oh, Daria, I'm so sorry.'

'It was a very long time ago,' she said slowly. 'But now I have other friends and my *familia* here with the prince and you,' she added in a much brisker tone. She glanced at the tables. 'Oh, those silly girls. All they want to do is giggle and flirt with the men. Excuse me, *domina*.' With that, she hurried off.

Aegius followed her with his eyes, watching as she chivvied the slaves to hand out the food. His daughter, quieter and efficient, came up to Daria's side and helped her direct them. I glanced up at Aegius whose expression had become warmer and his features softer as he smiled. It hit me between the eyes. He cared for Daria. Why on earth hadn't I realised that before? I must have kept looking at him. He smiled down at me, then took another swallow of his beer.

'Have you never thought of marrying Daria?' I said. 'Father would give you his blessing.'

'With respect, *domina*, that's none of your business.' His tone was soft, but his smile had vanished.

'Oh. I only wanted to help.' I rubbed the string of polished agates round my neck with the tips of my fingers. He was right; they were both free citizens.

'Perhaps you would do better conducting your own affairs more wisely than intervening in other people's,' he continued and gave me a measured look.

I turned my back on him and, batting insects away, I stalked towards the edge of the pines. How dare the painter consider himself permitted to comment on my behaviour? Who in Hades was he? An itinerant who had found himself a comfortable perch with few restrictions for over two decades. I would have Father turn him out.

I looked over the valley, my beautiful valley with fresh green as far as I could see. The river sparkled in the distance, and the paved road running like a grey line along the valley bottom was reflected in the sunlight. I crossed my arms. I took a deep breath in of spring air. Aegius was right, damn him to Hades. And he'd supported me loyally in my confrontation with the bishop. I returned to the increasingly noisy crowd around the food tables and found him chatting to Musius.

'May I have a private word with you, Aegius?' I asked.

He bowed and smiled as if he hadn't said those brutal words only minutes before. He pressed Musius on the shoulder with his free hand then turned and walked a few steps with me.

I stopped and looked at the hills, not wishing to meet his gaze. 'You are right. I shouldn't interfere in people's private affairs.'

'And I apologise to you, *domina*, for my harsh words. You've had a bad time recently and I did not intend to add to your hurt.'

'I'm really very grateful for your support, Aegius.'

'My pleasure.' He narrowed his eyes as he looked at me. 'The Christos followers are pernicious and their behaviour towards you is unpardonable. I know what the bitterness of an opportunity snatched away from you feels like. You can rarely remedy it. If you ever need me to act for you again – in any circumstances – do not hesitate to call upon me.'

I was so surprised at his personal revelation that I couldn't reply.

He looked up and searched the crowd over on the other side of the clearing and let his gaze rest on the figure of my father. 'I mean it. Even if others do not need to know about it,' he added softly. 'Sometimes, it's best to arrange things quietly.'

Later in the afternoon, the huntsmen, miraculously reasonably sober, released hares from wicker cages and the men staggered after them. The youngest of Patulus's kitchen assistants tripped over one of the hares and fell into a cowpat which caused the younger slaves to fall into hysterical laughter. None of the men, even Musius, caught a single hare. The poor animals, shut up for so long, shot out of their captivity like Parthian arrows. They were too clever and fast for the men who chased around in noisy circles after them. As the defeated men wandered back to the tables, their red faces shone with sweat. Aegius and my father had declined to join in, but both watched and smiled.

The goats were a different game, a children's one. Cuso, Aegius's grandson, was fast and caught one quickly. He threw a rope round the beast's neck and tugged him towards a girl hiding behind her mother's skirts. She was one of the farmers' daughters, also around six or seven. She gave a shy smile and darted out a hand to receive the loose end of the rope. Cuso beamed at her then his face went bright red. He turned and fled in the confusion of being a child who wanted to act the man. After a few steps, he turned and gave the girl a wave, but she was talking to the goat and patting its nose. I laughed. I felt a surge of warmth for the day, the people and the freshness of the meadows stretching in front of me. I would be so content if only Lucius Apulius was here to share it with me.

11

The cousin arrived a few days later for a long stay. I only found out he was there when I entered the atrium that evening, and he was in the middle of greeting my father. I'd been sick the morning after Floralia and felt hot, so I concluded I'd eaten something that had been tainted. I'd rested in my room with Asella fussing about and giving me strange looks and must have missed Father sending out the invitation.

His name was Laurinus Turcilus and there was nothing intrinsically wrong with him. He was tall, well built with chestnut-brown hair. He smiled, relaxed in the baths with my father and ate with elegance. He could read and write Latin and Greek well enough and had some knowledge of the poets. He was no mountain man and hadn't even served in the local auxiliaries. He smelt of horse sometimes and sweat always. His skin was soft and pale, and he seemed to be everywhere.

I knew what Father was up to but when Turcilus leant in close to me every time we walked in the gardens or I showed him some of Father's war memorabilia or gifts of silverware, I'd had enough. I marched into Father's *tablinum* when I knew Turcilus was in the town. My father looked up at me, then away. He laid his stylus carefully on his desk.

'This will stop now,' I said in the hardest voice I could muster. 'If

I have to bear his warm breath and sweaty clothes near me once more, I shall scream.'

'What on earth is the matter? Has Laurinus been impolite or offensive?' He frowned.

'No, of course not. He's *too* respectful, in a way.'

'Great gods, girl, would you prefer he jump you?' He raised both eyebrows.

I folded my thumbs into my palms. How to begin? My father had always been my beloved parent and ally until now.

'I know you mean well, Father, but Laurinus Turcilus will never have my respect nor affection.'

'What's wrong with him, Julia? He is a fine man, a cousin, so would keep property in the family, and he has no time for the Christos followers. He is perfectly happy to accept you as divorced and would marry you tomorrow.' He sighed. 'You are nearly twenty-one and still not settled. And I need grandsons to carry on my line.'

'I am fully aware of that, Father,' I said in my coldest voice. 'But perhaps after my mother's death you should have remarried to produce another son. Now you want me to mate with another cold fish to turn out a Bacausus heir.' I shot him an angry look. 'No, I will not.'

'Enough!' He slammed his fist hard on the inlaid table. One sliver of wood bounced out in a perfect arc and landed on the tiled floor. 'I have indulged you too much. You will go now with Laurinus Turcilus to his estate near Emona. You will stay there for a few years then after you have borne a child or perhaps two, when the eldest is of age you will all return and settle here. Perhaps I'll make one of them my heir if they live up to my expectations.'

I fixed my eyes on him. My gut clenched as if Musius had driven his practice sword right through it. Then I relaxed.

'But you know I can't marry anybody,' I said. 'Eligius forbids it and it would damage you greatly politically.'

'Which is why you will go to Emona and be married from there. His grandmother, my aunt, will make all the arrangements, quietly and discreetly. Eligius may hear of it after a few months, but it will be too late for even him to do anything about it.'

My fingers curled up into my palms.

'No. I will not.'

'I'm sorry, Julia, but there has to be an end to it. You are my beloved daughter and I must make provision for you.'

'I am content to stay here.'

'I am not. Sit down.'

It would have been petulant to refuse, so I perched on the stool opposite and sat up as stiff-backed as I could. He looked around as if he was trying to find his words, which was unusual.

'I've let you have your own way for far too long,' he continued. 'Now you must face reality.' He glanced at me, then back to his fingers. 'You must understand that I'm doing this for your sake. Do you not understand why?' He shot a glance at me, half worried, half bullish.

'You think I will forget Lucius once I'm away from here and busy with my new life.'

'After a while, you will forget your romantic affair and see the advantages of being a settled married woman. And when you and Laurinus return, you will be back among your own people.'

'But you cannot expect me to marry a man for whom I have no affection? Not again? And not *you*, Father?'

'We cannot always please ourselves, Julia.'

'But *you* did.'

'Enough.' He waved his hand as if batting away any argument.

'Then if I must be married, I will travel to Rome and marry Lucius.'

'Out of the question. It's far too dangerous a journey. I forbid it. How certain is it that Lucius would marry you? His old-fashioned family may not accept you or may have already arranged a marriage for him for all we know.'

'He wouldn't. He loves me.'

'Pah! No, it's decided. I signed contracts with Laurinus Turcilus this morning. You were married *sine manu* as I was damned if I was going to let that whelp Deodatus have control over even one *solidus* of my *familia*'s property. Given the circumstances,' he said drily, 'that was the right decision. And you are still under my legal guardianship. Now you will obey me.'

I stared at him. My father was exerting his family power as if he were a stiff-necked Roman from hundreds of years ago.

'And what about the bishop? And Deodatus?' I retorted. Gods, for a few instants, I contemplated returning to Deodatus, just to spite my father. But that thought passed as quickly as it had sprung up.

'Eligius will have moved on to greater things, I'm sure, by the time you return. I know he has the bishopric of Aquileia in his sights. And his damned misery of a nephew will go with him. Good riddance.'

I was too angry to shout and scream. Outside Father's *tablinum*, I was assaulted by the sour smell of nausea rising from my stomach into my throat. My body itself was revolted by the whole idea of marrying Laurinus Turcilus. I took a deep breath then strode through the atrium towards my room at the back of the villa section. At the end of the corridor, beyond my father's favourite Greek vase balanced on the side table by my bedroom door, there was a door to the outside. I glanced at it and wondered. I'd never thought about it before, but it could be a possible escape route. When the household was settled for the night, I would check if there was a latch along with any concealed bolts.

In my haste, I tripped on the loose mosaic stones in the corridor. They skittered away. I must remember to ask Daria to have the workmen fix them. I stopped. No. It was no longer my responsibility. I gulped. To Hades with them all!

Despite the sun, the shadows cast by the columns in the peristyle seemed darker than they should have been. A grey cloud was forming overhead and I smelt rain in the air. But nothing resembled the greyness in my soul. I slumped against the wall and brought my hands up to my face. How could Father do this to me? He had the right as *paterfamilias* which he'd retained even when I married Deodatus but I'd never dreamt he would use it.

A cough interrupted my thoughts. Musius. His face didn't show a scrap of the usual cocky attitude. Nor his confident chest-out relaxed stance. He couldn't look me in the eye. He just stood there. What was the matter with him?

'*Domina*.' He bowed his head.

'Yes?'

'Your father…'

'Well?'

'He has assigned me to see to your personal safety until you arrive at your betrothed husband's house.'

'What?' I glared at him until he looked away. I swallowed and then took in a deep breath. 'You mean, he has set you on to guard me so that I don't run away.'

'These are difficult times, *domina*,' he mumbled. 'He is only concerned that you arrive safely in Emona.' I was sure that even he didn't believe the lie he was speaking.

'Then you can get out of my sight until we leave,' I said coldly and pushed open the door of my room. An instant after I slammed it hard behind me, I heard the noise in the corridor outside of smashing pottery. The end of Father's treasured vase.

But this wasn't the end of the treachery. Asella was bending over my clothes chest and laying out my gowns and cloaks, *dalmaticae* and underdresses on my bed. My jewellery box was open and its contents divided into two mounds. One was small and supplemented by a pile of gold *solidi*. The other, she was wrapping in soft cloths. Her sewing kit lay open on the small table under the window.

'What are you doing, Asella?'

'*Domina*.' She shot me a furtive look. 'Your father said I should…'

I stamped my foot and raised my hand. Gods, I had become a child. No, they had reduced me to a child – a plaything to be handed around.

'My father? It seems everybody in this *domus* knows what's happening to me, but nobody has had the courtesy to tell me, let alone ask me.'

'He only means it for the best, *domina*.'

'In the same way he dismissed the man I love and want to spend my life with?'

'That young man is in a perilous place. He's been thrown out of the army and sent back to Rome. He cannot move from there under pain of death, Musius says.'

'Musius! What does he know? And how? Has my father been gossiping with him?' I grabbed Asella's arm and shook it.

'No, of course not, *domina*. Your father doesn't gossip or listen to idle talk. Musius has his own sources through his old army tentmates.'

'Ha!' Then it struck me. I wondered if Musius not only received information but sent it back. Was *he* the spy in our household? I watched Asella as she worked methodically packing my travelling trunk. I dropped down onto a stool by the window, tired of all this arguing. When would I see the tile roofs of Virunum, the spelt fields, the drifts of smoke from the metalworks? I wrinkled my nose – even their smell. In the distance, the column of the Ara Norica rose high to reach the gods. By the time I returned, I expected Eligius would have had it demolished in his Christos zeal.

'I suppose I must do as my father commands, but why can't I have a last summer here in the valley?' I said without turning my head.

'Because you will be too—' I turned slowly as Asella gasped. Her eyes were wide.

'Too what?'

She shook her head and bundled the blue gown in her hands into a ball and thrust it in the trunk.

'Asella?' I stood and went over to her.

She pulled her lips together and shook her head again so violently a pin dropped from her hair.

'Tell me, Asella. Now.'

She threw a glance at me like a goat tethered in a mountain pasture waiting for a wolf to attack it. A tear escaped from her eye.

'He made me tell. Your father. He questioned me gently at first recalling the years with your mother who said I should always obey him. Then he threatened to turn me out on the spot.' She looked at me with pleading in her eyes. 'I am over fifty years old, *domina*. I would die very quickly out there.'

'But *what* did he want to know?' I started to tremble as a thought swirled in my mind and started to become solid. It couldn't be...

'He asked me about your courses.'

'Gods.' I took a deep breath. 'But I'm always irregular – you know that.'

'But you've never been nearly seven weeks late.' She looked at me steadily. 'He will not insist on you aborting it – be grateful for that – but he will not let you carry a child and remain unmarried.'

She spoke other words and she took my hand in hers, clutching it tightly, but her voice seemed to fade away so I could no longer hear her. My father, my beloved father, hadn't even discussed this with me. He'd pulled on his authority as the head of family. He'd reminded me of my family duty, he'd promised me I could return after a few years of virtual servitude as Laurinus Turcilus's wife, but he'd never questioned me about my courses or situation. How could he deceive me like this? I touched my stomach. Was there really a little person in there, half mine and half Lucius's? I smiled at the thought of it. Our child, a son perhaps, with his father's beautiful peat-brown eyes.

I would never forgive my father for this. I would be forced to go with Turcilus, but I would use him to raise my child. And when that child reached his fourteenth year and could wield a sword, I would divorce Turcilus and return to Virunum. Then my father had better watch out for his throne.

PART II

THE JOURNEY

12

Musius cupped his hands for me to mount my horse, my own Snowfoot. I pushed down on them, watching him strain as I swung my other leg up and settled into my saddle. I didn't bother to thank him. He had dogged every step I'd taken and had accompanied Asella and me when I made some last purchases in the town – silver cups and bowls for my father's aunt and sets of pins and some brooches for my new household staff.

Virunum was a metalworking town with artisans known across the empire after all and still the chief town of Noricum. Emona was little more than a grand village.

We'd travel there on the long lowland route via Santicum as the old imperial route over the high mountain had fallen into disrepair. Rumour said there were wild men living up there now, having thrown off Rome's authority completely. Slow with the wagons, we'd be perfect prey for them. Not even Belestis would be able to cast her protective life-giving force over us despite her altars up there, as men had abandoned worshipping her. I shook my head to clear it. At least I'd have a few more days of freedom.

Laurinus Turcilus was all compliance, smiling at my father, at me, at the world. His betrothal ring on my finger was heavy, but not merely from the weight of the gold. The dull green stone seemed to sulk in its setting. I wriggled in the saddle, settling my thighs between the front and back horns each side. The saddle had been made especially for me of soft leather padded with felt. Beneath, for the comfort of the horse's back as much as for my own ease was the thick fur of a mountain bear. The whole was held in place by a leather girth, cinched tight.

Combined with my leather breeches, boots and thick woollen cloak and my hair in a single braid down my back and dagger in my waist belt, Asella said I looked like a wild mountain woman rather than a prince's daughter. She wanted me to ride in the wagon because of my 'delicate condition'. I didn't answer her. Riding at a steady rhythmic pace on the back of a strong mount like Snowfoot and held securely in my saddle was infinitely preferable to being jolted around in a *raeda* carriage with my trunks and bundles.

Father came down the steps to the back courtyard as we were ready to depart. He smiled and nodded at Turcilus, gave him his hand then exchanged a few words with Musius. He nodded at Aegius whom he was sending with me, but didn't address any word to him. Father had commissioned Aegis to paint murals for me at my new house in Emona, subject to Laurinus's consent. He also knew that I liked and respected Aegis and he knew the painter would watch over me while I was settling into my new life. Eventually, Father came and stood by my horse.

'Well, daughter, I wish you a safe journey. You are travelling on main roads under the escort of your betrothed husband and the bodyguard specially selected by Musius.'

I merely nodded, pulled my lips tight together and said nothing.

'Julia, at least give me a word of farewell.'

'Farewell,' I muttered, not looking at him. Did he not realise how betrayed I felt? He reached for my hand. I let it go limp in his.

'Don't let us part like this,' he said. 'I only want you to be safe and contented.' He looked at my stomach. 'Turcilus is an honourable man, perhaps not your choice but he will look after you.'

'As you say, Father.'

'Very well,' he sighed.

The horse fidgeted, anxious to move. I steadied her and turned to my father.

'You should have trusted me. You should have given me a choice. I will return, or my child will, and there will be a reckoning. Farewell, Father.'

I nudged the horse's ribs with the heels of my boots throwing my weight down through my spine and buttocks, giving Snowfoot a clear signal to spring from a standstill into a canter, and headed towards the exit gate, passed through the arch and left my home.

The first night we camped by the great lake with its shimmering green-blue water. After one look at the peeling door and patched up walls of the way station *mansio* at Saloca, even Turcilus had sniffed and opted to camp in a field nearby upwind of the *mansio*'s stinking latrines. At least our own camp beds wouldn't host bedbugs or fleas, he commented. The horses would enjoy fresh, lush grass and avoid the risk of eating old hay gone mouldy in a dirty stable.

Aegius and Musius went fishing and we sat on the strand eating the crisp skinned white fish grilled on an open fire. Turcilus retired early to his tent and Musius settled down with some of the men to throw dice. Aegius sat and drew patterns in the sand with a fine stick, silent and pensive.

'Walk with me, Aegius, if you would,' I said. 'Sitting down again after a day on horseback has stiffened my muscles.'

'Of course, *domina*.' He sprang up and extended a hand to me which I took gratefully.

'It's so peaceful here and the air is so pure. I shall be sorry to leave it for Emona.'

'I understand Laurinus Turcilus's villa is in the south-west of the city itself, so facing the countryside.'

'It's not the city I'm dreading, but my captivity there.'

'I don't understand. Your life there will be very similar to before. You will enjoy all the comfort of wealthy circumstances with your husband and move in cultured and fashionable circles. The daughter of the ruler of Virunum will be welcome everywhere.'

'Oh, Aegius, I'm sure you're right, but I don't want it.' I looked across the lake. 'I don't mean to sound like a spoilt child, but there is only one man I wish to spend my life with, but that's impossible.'

'Is it? Truly?'

'What do you mean?' I looked at him sharply, but the moonlight was dim; only a hunter's moon tonight. 'My father sent Lucius away and said the military had stripped him of his commission and banished him back to Rome, the other side of Italia. I haven't had a word from him.'

'But you wrote to him?'

'Of course, but he hasn't replied.'

'Are you sure?'

'Yes, of course. No letter has come from him. Nothing.'

'Have you never thought they may have been intercepted?'

'What? Nobody would dare!'

'If your father ordered it…'

'Oh, gods, no.'

We walked on in silence. Although the water was lapping gently at this end of the strand and insects murmured in the night air, I wasn't at all calmed. I was choking with fury, so much so that I couldn't speak. That my father would stop my letters was too much. One or two could become lost, but I had written almost every day.

'From what I gather, Apulius *was* sent home in disgrace,' Aegius said after a few more steps. 'The rumour was that the bishop had pulled some strings with his church contacts in Rome to put pressure on the army to have the tribune recalled.' He shrugged. 'But I can't say for certain.'

I stopped and caught Aegius's arm.

'Aegius, do you think he could still be in Rome?'

'Well, if he's confined to Latium, then yes. You could write to him from Emona. You'd have to be careful how you found a messenger, but it should be easier than in your father's house. In Emona, you would be the mistress.'

'But I would be married by then. No, I must go to Rome now. I must know.'

'I don't think Laurinus Turcilus would agree to that.'

'No, of course he wouldn't. I must take the chance I have now. My horse is strong and I could ride south to the coast and follow the road to Italia.'

'*Domina*, that's impossible. You cannot travel alone. There are bandits everywhere and a lone woman would be especially vulnerable. You would never reach Rome alive.'

I opened my mouth to answer, but suddenly he swept his arm up and pointed to a line of three bright stars. With his other hand, he touched my arm and pressed his fingers into my flesh.

'… and that is the story of the huntsman,' he said in a loud voice. 'The birds transformed into stars shining forever. I even painted the scene once for a commission in Neapolis.' He smiled at me, but narrowed his eyes and shot a look sideways. A warning look. I half turned and saw Musius barely a few steps away. He was frowning. Had he heard our talk about Apulius?

'*Domina*,' Musius said in a harsh voice. 'I have come to escort you back to the campsite.'

'There is no need. I am perfectly safe with Aegius.'

Musius snorted and shot Aegius a hostile look.

'I would hardly call an old painter a safe escort in such open country. Bandits rove everywhere.'

'I'm sure they do, but we are not far from the tents and there are ten men in our party. Even the foolhardiest of bandits wouldn't attack us.' I stared him out.

'But—'

'Enough. I will return when I wish.'

'We have a long day ahead of us tomorrow,' Aegius said. 'Perhaps Musius is right that we should return. We all need our rest for our journey.' His eyes gleamed and I thought I saw the hint of a smile on his lips. But Musius had already started plodding back to the tents.

The next day, we started at daybreak and continued along the road west until we came upon the course of the Dravus River which would lead to Santicum. Only the occasional public courier interrupted us and Musius's men shoved other traffic to the side to clear the way for us. He didn't seem inclined to ask first and his men, many of them unfamiliar to me as they were not from our household, were enthusiastic in obeying him. Musius must have hired them specifically or perhaps they came from Turcilus's household. Some were tall, others short. All of them were armed and wore cloaks with hoods which they kept on most of the time. I could hardly tell one from another. But they were well behaved and kept themselves to themselves whenever we stopped.

We made reasonable progress, but the *raeda* carriage with Asella and the luggage held us back at ox pace. My back and legs ached miserably by the time we reached the necropolis outside Santicum.

We passed by individual tombs on the approach road and eventually reached the bridge across Dravus.

A fussy little customs official attempted to insist on inspecting our entire baggage train and charging duty on every single thing we carried. Musius told him in no uncertain terms that as we were still in Noricum he could go and whistle. In any case, the prince's household was exempt. The two military guards leaning against the bridge parapet grinned when Musius asked the official if he could swim. After a tense silence the official worked it out and decided to step aside allowing us to enter the main town.

We were received by Serandius, an acquaintance of Father's who couldn't stop saying how honoured he was to receive the prince's daughter. His wife, Verina, seemed practical enough though, as she beckoned a servant to hand us refreshing drinks. Asella was still supervising unloading my travelling trunk, but Verina led me to a chamber, helped me shed my travelling clothes, gave me a loose robe and escorted me to a bathhouse at the back of their house.

'It's natural, Lady Julia, and warm.' She smiled as I looked at the bubbling water. I slid into the pool, only too grateful for the relief.

I blinked as I woke suddenly. The sunlight was streaming into the room and onto my face. Asella was opening the shutters. I sat up quickly. It must be late.

'Rest, *domina*.' She turned and smiled. 'We're not travelling today.' She brought a tray to me with cheese, bread and olives. I sniffed at the pale liquid in the jug. Mountain beer, but sweet. 'Laurinus Turcilus asked me to let you know that he's accepted our host's invitation to stay for another day to break our journey.'

I nodded as I chewed on the bread and drank the cool liquid. Turcilus might not have been exciting or even attractive – to me at least – but he was considerate. As I dressed, Asella inspected my night robe and the bed linen, pretending to tidy them. She thought she was being subtle, but I spotted her mouth turning down at the corners. I brushed my hand over my stomach. I knew already she wouldn't find any bloodstains. So far, I had experienced only a little of the nausea some women felt when expecting a child, but tiredness seemed to be creeping up on me earlier and earlier in the day.

When I went through to the main part of the house I found Turcilus in the atrium reading old-fashioned scrolls with his hosts. They stood when they noticed me.

'Julia.' Turcilus smiled at me. 'Are you well rested?'

'I am, thank you, and I appreciate the break in our journey.' I turned to our host and smiled at him. 'The warm springs are so soothing. What an advantage you have here.'

'The public baths have a similar pool, although it does sometimes leak.' He looked away. 'Unfortunately, the council hasn't allocated any budget for maintenance this year. Or last year.'

'Really? Then something must be done,' I said. 'Keeping people healthy and clean is of the utmost importance, surely. Who are the *aediles* this year?'

'None were elected, and nobody volunteered.' He looked embarrassed, then looked up. 'Nobody wants to stand as the expense of funding public works is crippling. I've suggested a contributory fund, but only half the wealthier citizens paid their allocation.'

'Isn't it their duty?' I said.

'Things are not always as well ordered as in Virunum, Julia,' Turcilus said, almost chiding. 'I hope you will not find Emona too disappointing in that respect. It's considered to be a civilised town, part of Italia home province after all.' I murmured something polite. 'If you are at leisure,' he continued, 'will you join me for a walk in the town?'

I studied his face. He looked perfectly serious, for once not smiling in his irritating way. That intrigued me. Either he had something to say to me in private or he was trying to make a connection with me.

'Yes, I would enjoy that,' I said.

Santicum wasn't that large a town and Serandius's house lay only ten minutes from the forum. The valley was flat and green, young wheat and oats in the fields and the mountains a good distance away. I bought some pins and a pair of lambskin gloves in the market. They were beautiful, covered in red embroidery.

'I lost one of mine last night when we camped by the lake,' I said in order to find some conversation not related to our awkward situation. But in vain. Turcilus directed me to a chipped stone bench underneath the large portico in front of a temple. Pleasant as the spring sun was, it was a relief to find shade from its glare.

'Julia, I need to talk to you about our marriage.'

'Surely, there will be plenty of time—'

'No. Listen to me.' He laid his finger on my mouth. I did everything not to flinch. 'You must understand something,' he continued. 'I cannot pretend to be a husband as you would expect.' He stared out across the forum. 'Has it never occurred to you why I am not married? I am forty-nine. In truth, I have no inclination to bed any woman. I will not elaborate – it could lead to unpleasantness for us both – but I trust you understand what I am saying. When your father explained your circumstances—' he looked down at my stomach '—I was happy to comply with his wishes. I can offer you a home, give your child a family name but there it stops. But I will make this clear. I will not tolerate any scandal, so you must not think you are free to take lovers. If you did, I would take the child and divorce you, as is my right under the law.'

His voice wasn't cold, just flat, devoid of any feeling. I shivered. To him I was a business arrangement, a direct alliance with the ruling house of Bacausus. But I felt his determination to set out my future life with him on a very specific path, whatever ideas of my own I might have. There wouldn't be an ounce of passion, not even a husband's dutiful bedding even if I could reconcile myself to him. I was alone. Completely alone.

After a minute or so, he rose and held out his hand to me. I was incapable of speech. I didn't know whether to be angry, relieved or fearful of my solitary future. I glanced at him as we walked back. His skin was pink and shiny, his hair plastered across his skull. He didn't give me another look until we reached Serandius's house.

'I will leave you to rest now,' he said as we made our way through the vestibule. He nodded, then went back to the chair he had occupied opposite our host, picked up a scroll and resumed his reading.

13

I walked in the gardens with Asella in the afternoon; to be accurate, I marched around and she trotted along to keep up. I gave her short answers to her many questions. In the end, I snapped.

'Oh, peace, Asella. Please stop plaguing me.' In Virunum, I would have confided in her. Not now. But she looked stricken at my outburst. 'I have something on my mind and must work out how to resolve it.'

'It's Laurinus Turcilus, isn't it?'

'His offer of marriage is not as straightforward as it seems.'

'Oh.'

'He sets harsh conditions.' I shook my head. 'I don't want to talk about it. I must think.' But trying to find a way out of the trap that had closed on me was only giving me a headache. And Aegius stamping on my idea of fleeing south into Italia by myself had made me melancholic.

'*Domina*, I am truly sorry about speaking to your father about your courses, but when he threatened to have the porter set me outside at that very moment in the cold wind and said it was forever, I—' She looked about to burst into tears and wrapped her arms tightly around her body.

'He wouldn't have done it, Asella,' I said gently and laid my hand on her arm. 'You are too strong a link back to my mother.'

'That's no comfort at all.' Her eyes blazed for a moment, then she calmed. She seized my hand. 'Tell me how I can make amends. I will not be so weak another time.'

I drew her into an embrace.

'You are never weak, Asella. Like all women, we are subject to the whims of others. If we are to survive, we can only make the best of the situation we find ourselves in.'

I couldn't bear to stay in the same room as Turcilus after our meal in the late afternoon, so I fetched my *palla*, draped it round my shoulders and retreated to the garden again, this time for a last walk. We'd be up at dawn for the next stage of our journey tomorrow. I bent down and rubbed the leaves of a large rosemary plant and inhaled the sharp, exotic scent. Ah, Lucius, if only it was the sun-warmed one of your gardens in Rome. You described it so well that if I closed my eyes, I could visualise it. At the thought I would never see it, a tear slid down my cheek and I bowed my head.

'*Domina?*'

A figure rose from a stone bench tucked into a recess; Aegius with a stick of charcoal and a sheet of vellum pinned to a thin tablet of wood in his hands. He was sketching one of Serandius's fine statues standing in a small open circular temple.

'It's only a copy, you know, but a good one,' he said pointing at the marble goddess. He turned to me. 'Knowing the fake from the real is the trick.'

'For me the difference is glaringly obvious,' I said. 'And I'm not talking about the statue.' I couldn't keep the bitterness out of my tone.

'But are you prepared to do something about it?'

I jerked my head up.

'What do you mean?'

'There is a way through your problem, but it's risky and the path is hard.'

'I would do anything.' I fingered the gold bracelet Lucius had given me just before he was banished.

'Very noble and courageous, *domina*, but you might not feel that way when you are exhausted beyond the possible and the tips of your fingers are near to dropping off from cold.'

'Go on.'

'If you truly wish to see your tribune again, you could run now and take the short cut from here through the mountains to the coast, then catch a ship to Italia.' He proposed this momentous plan in a matter-of-fact voice, all the time keeping his eyes on the vellum and carrying on with his sketch.

'But we didn't use the old imperial route from Virunum to Emona that passed through the mountains because of the bandits and the disrepair – hence this longer journey.'

'I didn't say it would be easy – just possible. It was Turcilus who objected to the original mountain route. I presumed his delicate body didn't like the idea of a bit of climbing and hard riding. Also, the carriage with your belongings wouldn't have hacked it. You, on the other hand, were brought up in the mountains. Even so, nobody would suspect you would go that route.'

I didn't say a word. I marched up to the end of the path and at the end, I swivelled round and walked back to him, but slowly. It would be the final rupture with my father, I would be ostracised if I was caught. Turcilus would repudiate me, and my child, if allowed to survive to term, would be born a bastard and probably exposed. I could not let that happen to my and Lucius's child. But I wasn't even sure Lucius Apulius would be there at the end of my journey.

'One thing, *domina*,' he said.

'Yes?'

'You have to bring Asella.'

I stopped and stared at him.

'How long have you been a comedian, Aegius?'

'You cannot arrive in Rome, accompanied by an unrelated man, without a woman with you.'

'Do you know how old she is? She'd never survive in the mountains.'

'We have good mounts and plenty of warm clothing and boots. Asella was bred in a tough world before she came south with your mother. She may have lived a softer life since then, but she is strong.' He cocked an eyebrow. 'Do you doubt it?'

'She's a fussy and irritating woman at times, but dear to me. I would never forgive myself if she came to harm. Perhaps this is too wild a plan.'

He shrugged, then carried on with his sketching.

I perched on the stone bench beside him.

'Why do you want to help me?' I said. 'And now? Two nights ago, by the lake before Musius interrupted us, you seemed to think such a thing was too dangerous.'

His hand stopped, but he still studied his drawing.

'A long time ago, I failed to pursue my dream, my passion.' He looked at me. 'I've regretted it ever since. Oh, I've been content enough. I had a satisfactory career as a fighting man and gathered enough to make myself comfortable. One day, after a particularly heavy night of drinking with my tentmates, I realised I'd turned into a soulless machine. I left the next morning and made my way north, eventually arriving in Virunum.'

'Ah, I thought you'd been in the legions.'

'Is it so obvious?'

'No, just your rapid reaction in catching your paintbrushes that fell and your confidence when you went with me to see Eligius. Your weapons and armour seemed to become a natural part of you.'

'Ha! Not so closed-eyed as I thought.' He smiled. 'I think Musius suspects but hasn't broached the subject.'

'Did they pursue you when you, er, left?'

'At first, but they gave up after a few months – too many other things to do, like killing barbarians.'

'But if you come with me to Rome, won't you be in danger?'

'After all this time? I expect my name was written down on a list by some bureaucrat, but it's probably turned to dust by now if the mites haven't eaten it.' He sighed and after several heartbeats said, 'I have at last admitted to myself that I have unfinished business in Rome. Family business. Accompanying you would be a good excuse to myself.' He shut his eyes for an instant, then opened them to gaze in the distance.

'Gods, Aegius, this is such a weighty decision for both of us. I feel the Fates flapping round my head and taunting me.'

'So is it a case of *anerrhíphthō kúbos*?' A ripple of mockery ran through his voice under the soft tones as he suggested I roll a die to decide.

'Don't quote Plutarch at me, Aegius.' I brought my hands to either side of my head where a headache was growing. 'I'm not going to decide my future on a game. Nor am I the Divine Julius on the bank of the Rubicon gambling whether to invade Rome.' After a few moments, I let my hands fall to my sides and drew myself up straight. I had no choice in my heart. 'Yes, we go.'

'So, decision made – *iacta alea est.*'

I rolled my eyes at him. But yes, as with the Romans of old, the die was indeed cast. 'How would we go?'

'Turcilus wants to reach Meclaria by tomorrow early afternoon. He has some business there, apparently. Impossible to get there by that time with the luggage cart plodding along at ox speed, so it would be perfectly natural for each of us to pack a saddle bag with a few essentials and for Asella to ride one of the spare horses. The cart would probably catch up by the end of the day, ready for the next stretch. So, you can insist on riding ahead with Turcilus and feign great interest in what he's saying.'

'Of course. You may be sure I will play my part.' I held out my hand towards him. He laid down his charcoal stick, wiped his hand with a rag, then accepted mine. 'Thank you, Aegius. I cannot convey my feelings of gratitude enough.'

'You and Asella must rest tomorrow afternoon – you'll need your sleep because in the evening after *cena* we leave for the high mountains.'

Meclaria was indeed an easy ride. Set in a wide valley, the town was compact, surrounded by forested hills and snow-capped mountains. Oddly, Turcilus insisted on staying at a *hospitium*, not with his business friend in the town itself. From the outside, the place had clean walls, a strong looking gate and a welcoming porter. He swept the gate open easily without it making the least groan and Turcilus, Aegius, Asella, three of the men escorting us and I trotted into the courtyard to be met by grooms eager to take the reins of our horses. A man in a calf-length tunic and with curling hair oiled in the Greek fashion smiled graciously at Turcilus.

'Welcome, noble sir. The decurion has asked us to make you comfortable to the best of our poor ability.'

I searched round. Everything looked tidy, freshly painted or polished. Pots of spring flowers lined the entrance to the inn building. There, a woman bowed and came forward with a bowl of scented water and thick towels for us to wash our hands. And even in the vestibule, the walls were painted with country scenes. There was no sign of the innkeeper's 'poor ability'. These were rich man's lodgings.

An older woman, dark-haired, sturdy and neat as any councillor's wife, bustled up to us as we entered and addressed herself to me.

'Welcome, Lady Julia. I am Zena. Please follow me.' I glanced at Turcilus, but he was occupied talking to the innkeeper. Zena led us to a small room furnished with a carved bed and red and blue woven coverings, a chest, a chair and a table inlaid with marble. Linens, a bowl, a water jug and a dish of combs and pins lay on a stand. She pointed towards a curtain in the sidewall. 'Your maid can sleep in this alcove. She can collect water for you from the kitchen between the first and second hours.' She smiled at me. 'We will serve *cena* in three hours, but I will send a girl with some bread and fruit for your comfort in the meantime. Please ask her if you need anything else.' She gave a slight bow, hardly inclining her head, turned and swept out.

'Well,' Asella sniffed. 'She's full of herself.' She pulled back the curtain to the alcove to reveal a low bed with a thin mattress and a single blanket. The only other things in the windowless space were a three-legged stool jammed into the corner and a single peg on the wall above it for hanging clothes. 'Good thing I won't need it for long,' she said in a caustic tone. She rubbed her back. It must be aching from the ride. That stretch had only lasted a few hours. I hoped in my heart that she'd be able to stand the long days in the saddle that would follow.

'Peace, Asella,' I said. 'We'll go and bathe, then rest as Aegius recommends.'

Although I'd changed from my tunic and breeches into a respectable if creased *dalmatica* and warm underdress and wore a gold necklet and earrings, I probably didn't look like what anybody expected a prince's daughter should look like. Still, the service at table was impeccable and the food delicate and tasty. The luggage cart hadn't caught up by the time we sat down to eat. I prayed it would rumble into the courtyard soon. I wasn't particularly worried about my clothes and household goods – I could buy new ones – but we needed to have the inn settled down for the night before Aegius, Asella and I could leave.

We'd eaten the last course and the slaves were setting lamps around the room and starting to close the shutters when I heard the familiar loud bellowing of the oxen and the thundering crunch of wheels across the courtyard outside. I saw Asella hurry across from the kitchen along with Aegius as they helped unload my travelling trunk.

'There, Julia, you need not have worried.' Turcilus gave me a superior smile. 'Your dresses and trinkets are safe now.' I looked at him. Did he think I was such a superficial creature? The best of my trinkets, as he called my jewellery, were already safe, sown into the inside of Asella's and my cloaks along with a supply of gold *solidi*. Despite our armed escort, Father had insisted we hide the highest value items and enough gold to survive in case the wagons were stolen – not an unusual occurrence these days, he warned us. But I made an effort to give Turcilus a smile in return to look compliant. And I think he genuinely wished to reassure me, almost as one does a child.

'You are all consideration, Laurinus,' I said, and looked down, then up at him. I meant it as part of my play-acting, but he looked startled, then gave me a warm smile, a genuine one. Perhaps, after all, there was some possibility of making a connection with him. Was I making the right decision to leave the safety and security of life with him to chase my wild dream?

14

'Mm…?' Something was moving my shoulder. No, a hand was shaking it. I turned onto my back. My clothes pulled. Sleeping in breeches was not the most comfortable thing.

'*Domina.*' Asella's voice was hardly more than a breath. 'Time to leave your bed.' I sat up and rubbed my eyes. Only the white of moonlight piercing the gaps in the shutters gave any light in the room. I bent down and pulled on my boots. We bundled up my bedclothes into a long shape as if somebody was still there. I draped my cloak around my shoulders and fastened it with my mother's fibula.

Asella was already dressed in breeches, tunic, leather overtunic and her cloak. She beckoned towards the window where she'd placed the stool from her alcove. Then slowly she eased the shutter catch up. We both let a long breath out as it slid open with only the faintest sound as metal brushed against wood.

I took her outstretched hand, stepped up onto the stool and swung one leg over the sill. No noise. I searched round the courtyard. Nobody. Even the watchdog was asleep in the far corner. I swung my other leg out and eased myself onto the soft earth of a flower bed, then caught my foot in a shrub. Really, these Greeks were obsessed with their plants and flowers. I turned and gave a hand to Asella. She passed me the bundles of spare clothes we'd packed earlier – a long tunic, a pair of sandals, two shorter long-sleeved tunics each and underclothes. I'd squeezed a small toiletries roll in. We would have no space for anything else. Asella had slung a satchel across her shoulder. We slid the shutters back inch by inch but they went smoothly with just a soft swishing noise.

'Aegius will have the horses outside the rear gate,' Asella whispered. We crept along the side of the building staying close to the walls. As we passed some of the closed shutters, we could hear snoring. Asella placed her hand over her mouth, but her shoulders trembled as she suppressed a laugh. We edged along the stable wall. A horse whinnied. Then one of the oxen bellowed. We froze. Asella looked terrified.

'Count slowly to ten in your head,' I whispered directly in her ear. 'It's a calming trick Lucius taught me.' She nodded and took a long breath. I grasped her hand and step by step we reached the stable corner and turned round it. Opposite us, the studs on the rear gate hinges reflected the moonlight. The latch lifted and my heart started to beat faster. A figure stepped round the edge of the door.

Aegius. Thank the gods.

Our three horses waited outside, loosely tethered by the reins with the bits and anything else that might jingle bound by rags to deaden careless sounds.

'Place your hand over the muzzle of your animals, ladies, to stem any snorting,' Aegius whispered. We walked the horses away from the back of the *hospitium,* leading them down a path to the edge of the trees. With our saddlebags back and front, they might possibly be taken for pack animals; they were mountain horses after all. Aegius turned abruptly onto a pressed earth street which eventually ceded to gravel. Each sound echoed in the silence despite Aegius having wrapped the horses' hooves in sacking to muffle their noise on the road. I was sure we'd be challenged, but there wasn't a soul to be seen.

After walking a good hundred paces from the *hospitium,* we stopped and quickly removed all the rags. We checked the saddle girths were tight, mounted and rode on in silence, not daring to make a single sound. As the *hospitium* was outside the town walls, at least we didn't have to negotiate town gates with surly guards wanting their cut. The countryside was flat, a valley between more distant mountains and woods a good distance away. Nevertheless,

Aegius watched with narrowed eyes up and down the road. Then we started climbing. I couldn't help shivering. It wasn't with the cold, but with excitement. And not a little anxiety about the road ahead.

The road deteriorated as we rode along the river that Aegius called the Gila Parva. By the time we reached Tarvisium an hour to the south, the river was a mountain stream, the stones of the rocky bed white in the moonlight. There was no guard to be seen on the bridge but we crossed slowly, watching for any challenge or even ambush.

'Probably local Taurisci tribesmen acting as guard for the bridge rather than *limitanei* from the militia. Lazy buggers probably hunkered down in a scrubby *caupona* somewhere,' Aegius said and searched round. 'If there is such a thing here.' But there were only a handful of small stone buildings, some with trade signs hanging from beams above shuttered frontages around an open *basilica* with empty animal pens in a large, uncovered space to the side. Further along the road were wooden houses, some round like tribespeople's houses, then barns and huts. 'Let's press on.'

The road became more gravel and less paving. Somebody had made an effort to fill in the gaps left by missing blocks with smaller stones but it soon gave way to more of an earthed road with a gravelled surface and it climbed between high mountains covered in trees almost to the summits. Silence and darkness seemed to engulf us as we rode among trees. I pulled the collar of my cloak tighter. As the river widened in a small lake, I glanced up to the left and saw five jagged peaks in a row thousands of feet above us. They looked like giant teeth ready to devour us. I turned to look at Asella. Her cloak hood was drawn up over her head, but I could make out the pale face and sunken shining eyes.

'Aegius, we must stop and rest soon. Asella is exhausted.'

I thought he hadn't heard me, but a few paces on he stopped in a bend in the lake where there was a narrow beach. He looked from Asella to me and back again.

'There's a small settlement a few miles ahead. It's nothing to get excited about, but we may find a shepherd's hut, or better, a barn or an abandoned roundhouse to shelter in.' He glanced up at the sky. 'But we can only rest for a few hours. We must carry on at dawn.'

Fortuna was smiling on us. We found a barn – space for the horses and dry ground for us out of the cold wind.

'I wouldn't drink that water,' Aegius said, pointing at a bucket on the ground. 'If you ladies would unsaddle the horses, I'll fetch fresh water for them from the river. It's too risky to take them down there on such a badly lit night.'

'Our bottles are empty,' Asella said. 'What are we supposed to do?'

'You didn't leave any as a reserve?' Aegius's eyebrows went up. 'You should never empty your bottle completely until you have a new source.'

Asella glared at him despite her exhaustion.

'Here, Asella,' I said quickly. 'Take from mine.' I thrust the leather bottle at her. She gulped it down. 'But leave me some in the bottom!'

After she gave me my flask back, she looked round. 'I suppose we'll have to go outside behind the barn to relieve ourselves. I wish we were back at the inn with their posh marble latrines. At least there you wouldn't get a gorse bush up your backside.'

I had hardly closed my eyes, it seemed, when Aegius shook my shoulder. I blinked hard. My eyes prickled. I pulled the blanket back over my body against the cold.

'Come, *domina*, we must take advantage of the day.' He tore a piece off from a loaf and cut a large lump from a round mountain cheese. It was sharp, tangy and had been dipped in salt. I felt even thirstier afterwards. Asella was crouching in the corner on her blanket, munching on hers. 'Give me your water bottles,' Aegius continued. 'I'll fill them from the river now I can see to climb down the bank. Keep your knives handy.'

Two minutes after he'd closed the door and we were back in semi-darkness, it was flung open. A tall, thickset figure waved a pitchfork in our direction with the tines shining in the growing light.

I leapt up.

'Who the hell are you?' he snarled. 'Beggars, I'll be bound.' He spoke in the mountain dialect. I gripped my knife harder and moved my hand to my side to hide it.

'No, travellers,' I replied, 'seeking shelter for a few dark hours of the night. We have merely rested here and will be on our way shortly. We have caused no harm and will pay for the hay the horses have eaten.'

He looked us up and down.

'The old one can get out now.' He reached down to Asella and went to grab her arm. She bit his hand.

'You old bitch,' he shouted as blood seeped from the side of his palm. He shoved her back then swung the pitchfork above her, pulled back ready to strike. I jumped forward and grabbed the handle.

'Stop! Leave her alone.' He swung round to face me. Even in this light, I saw the over-warm glow in them. He ran his tongue over his bottom lip.

'I'll take the horses in payment and you.' He leered at me.

'Don't be ridiculous,' I said.

He tore his pitchfork from my grasp and jabbed it at Asella.

'You, stay in your corner. You,' he said to me, 'get on the floor on your back.'

'No.'

He dropped his pitchfork and shoved me against the back of the barn with his forearm. He was a strong man. I felt the force of his muscles hard against my chest. But a second later, when I rammed my knee in his balls as hard as I could, his eyes bulged in surprise. His mouth let out a strangled groan. He must have felt the searing pain spread up from his crotch. As he bent over, I brought the tip of my knife up and dug it into the his skin on his neck just below his ear lobe.

'One more movement from you and your life's blood will flow out onto the hay you care so much about. Now take three steps backwards, very slowly.'

He hesitated, so I jabbed hard enough to release a trickle of blood. He would sense it running down the side of his neck, so he would know I was in earnest. He backed off, his gaze flitting between the tip of my knife and my face.

'Now kneel,' I commanded and pushed the knife a little further through the top layer of skin. His knees sagged and he dropped to the ground.

'Is all well here?' Aegius stood in the doorway. He frowned and searched round.

'Yes,' I replied without taking my eyes off the kneeling figure. 'We were exchanging greetings with our host here who owns this barn. I was thanking him and he dropped something. You find him looking for it, searching in the dirt on the ground.'

Aegius smirked.

'Is that the official story? Would you like me to finish off the conversation for you?'

'No, I think we will just pay him with our absence.'

In the end, after we'd bound and gagged him, I dropped a few coins by the door for the hay. Aegius glanced back after we'd ridden a hundred paces, then turned to me.

'You should have let me dispose of him, *domina*. He won't forget us. If anybody comes seeking us, he'll be able to give a good description.'

'Do you think it likely?' I nudged Snowfoot's side with my heel and she moved forward.

'Turcilus is not stupid. He will conclude one of two things. You will either have gone back to your father in Virunum or you will have made for the coast and the road to Rome.'

'Diana save me! He will come on us within a day.'

'No, if he discounts you returning to Virunum, I think he'll assume you'll have gone west on the easier route through Statio Plorucensis and joined the Via Iulia Augusta from Iulium Carnicum that runs down through Tricesimum to Aquileia. He's an urbanite who dislikes the mountains, so our cut through route won't occur to him. Don't forget he's travelling at ox pace, and I doubt he'd want to be parted from your marriage property. Your *arrhae* isn't just a few tables and chairs but a significant portion of your father's treasure. So even if he went ahead with just horses, that western route would take several more days to complete than ours.' He nodded towards Asella, ambling along ahead. 'If we get on with it.'

'But he could catch us anywhere on the road into Italia proper. It could take weeks. The more days we travel, the more chance he has.' It was impossible. I shook my head, wondering if we could continue to outrun him as we rode all the way to Rome.

'Not if we take a ship to somewhere in the Picenum *diocesis* on the east coast of Italia, then ride a route through the Apennines to Rome. There are countless ways.'

'A ship? You mentioned that before, but how safe would that be?' I was happy on the river – I could see both sides – or even a lake which had edges. But a ship on the open sea, subject to Neptune's whims? I shivered.

'Nothing in life is safe, *domina*. But going that way, we'd cut travel time by many days compared to by road and once we reach Italia, they'd never find us.'

We rode on past a spectacular lake, its dark blue water mirroring the mountains surrounding it. Even though it was late spring, the lower edge of the snow stretched halfway down from the peaks. The track, for that was what it had become, bent back on itself as we climbed, but was still wide enough to accommodate two horses or a small carriage. To my surprise, there were occasional cobbled parts. When the road straightened out again on a high alp, my curiosity couldn't be restrained.

'Aegius, how do you know which way we should go? You seem very sure.'

He smiled to himself.

'Are you sure you want to know, *domina*?'

'Is it something difficult to talk about or ignoble?'

'Ha! Of course, it's ignoble. This road was built as an imperial route for the *cursus publicus* hundreds of years ago. The engineers cursed and the gangs building it – mostly military – were said to have turned the air bluer than that lake down there. But it meant the imperial messengers could send messages from Aquileia and thus Rome, by the fastest route possible.'

'But now?'

'Oh, it belongs to the smugglers now, and criminals fleeing one way or another. There are no longer innocent travellers to prey on – ones that are carrying enough gold or other things to make it worth the effort – so the marauders usually leave the few travellers alone. Smugglers get upset if some chancer attacks them and upsetting them tends to end fatally.'

I glanced up nervously at the stunted trees each side of the road.

'Don't worry, *domina*. They won't worry us. I give them too much trade.'

I was aghast. I stared at Aegius and fingered the hilt of my knife.

'You're a smuggler?' Was he going to betray me? Hand me over to his fellow criminals for ransom?

He laughed.

'Of course not, but I know some of them. How do you think I get my paint? Gold and ultramarine, oh, and murex purple, aren't exactly easy to get now.' He shrugged. 'The merchants refuse to come north until the summer and even then some of the pigments are not good quality.'

'Does my father know you do this?'

'Prince Bacausus is a realist. Besides, I've done a few favours for him this way.'

I didn't reply but rode on in silence. We were climbing again almost at the level of the mountain tops now. At the summit of one of the highest hills, we found small pillars each side of the road and a simple temple at the side. Flecks of silica reflected in the sunlight. I dismounted and helped Asella down and led her to a stone bench flanking the temple. Inside, there was an altar with an inscription to the goddess Belestis. The air round us was light and pure; her blessing and protection was on us. I drew in a breath, then went to gather some tiny yellow and purple flowers nodding in the breeze and just starting to bloom in the grass behind the shrine.

I returned to the temple and Asella stood and we shared the flowers and grasses as we laid them on the altar.

'May the goddess extend her protection all the way to our destination,' Asella said. Then she raised her hands in the air and started chanting in my mother's Alemannic language. A few minutes later she gave a sigh, dropped her hands, then whispered some words to herself. She stared at me for a few moments as if she were seeing something in the distance. Her eyes were glazed. She took a deep breath, then seemed to come back into herself.

'Well, we'd better drink our water, then mount up,' she said in her normal voice and pointed towards Aegius sitting on a rock at the edge of the road. He was searching into the distance with half-closed eyes. 'Or he'll start grumbling at us again.'

15

The two-width track narrowed to one and a half and sometimes one as we passed along a steep-sided valley south of the pass. Two hours later it widened out to the valley of a river Aegius told us was the Aesontius. It was scattered with occasional huts and barns among meadows bright with spring grass. In the distance to the left, a young lad was moving a dozen cattle along a track. The road was even and in places paved so we were able to make good speed. We continued descending and even Asella got her breath back. But by now, Turcilus would be searching for us, so I urged her on. The horses had carried us well but needed rest and water. A much more kindly farmer than the one from last night let us use his own barn and his wife brought us bread, a platter heaped with smoked meat and weak mountain ale for our midday meal. I took two slices of the meat which almost melted in my mouth, but then hesitated.

'Eat, child,' Asella said in a soft voice and loaded more slices onto my bread. 'You must nourish the little one.'

I checked the wife was too far away to hear.

'I can't eat all this,' I whispered. 'These people are poor. This is probably a week's food.'

'Aegius will more than compensate them and with good silver coin from Virunum,' she replied. 'Which will also buy their silence.'

Aegius glanced round but the farmer and his wife were nowhere to be seen.

'We're near the edge of the Venetia and Histria home province of Italia,' he said. 'So as we ride south we must be careful not to attract attention from any nosy centurion in charge of his first patrol.' He glanced at Asella. 'I suggest we assume the identity of a family. I'll be Tullius Ferrantius, painter and artist. Asella can be my wife, Serena, and you, *domina,* our daughter, Placida.'

'Placida?'

He grinned.

'I'm sure you can play the role to perfection, Daughter.'

Although I could see the snow-capped peaks, the mountains seemed to retreat as we passed through the village of Pletium. The wide flat valley was bursting with spring planting arranged in neat fields which stretched to the foot of steeply rising hills. Fruit trees in small plots next to farmhouses were in full flower. I took in a deep breath. The scent of birch and pines hit me. This was so like home.

A tear ran down my cheek. I sniffed and turned away. I was leaving all that behind. Was I really doing the right thing?

'We're approaching Caporetum,' Aegius said several hours later as we descended the Aesontius River valley. Thank the gods; hot food, a proper bed and a good night's rest. My thighs were aching and my backside was numb from the hours in the saddle. Even my fingers were sore from holding and rubbing the leather of the reins for so long. I turned back to look at Asella who didn't say a word but just moved her head slowly from side to side as she clung on to her horse's mane. We'd left the truly high mountains and the rough tracks behind us and were entering hill country now.

'I suppose baths would be too much to expect,' I said to Aegius.

'In a hill village of twenty houses?' Aegius look at me as if I had lost my wits. 'Unless you want to be a guest of the camp prefect there, but then our escape could be at an end.'

'Why?'

'These may be difficult times, *domina,* but news still travels very fast and your disappearance will not have gone unnoticed. This town is also a customs post for entry into Italia. Travellers from

Noricum rarely get asked for an exit pass these days as the authorities can't be bothered as long as you don't look like a barbarian, but the customs will want their cut.'

'But we're always exempt.'

'You're no longer travelling as Julia Bacausa, daughter of a prince of Noricum, but Placida, daughter of Tullius Ferrantius, painter and artist.' He winked. 'That's me, if you remember. So we pay our dues and pass as ordinary and of no interest to anybody.'

Leaving the main road, we climbed up the hill along a winding track. The daylight was only just starting to fade, but we were tired after a long day riding and suffering from a lack of sleep.

A cool wind blew round us as we reached the top of the hill. It was becoming colder by the minute and I pulled my cloak tighter around my neck and shoulders. At the town gate we were, of course, stopped. A guard pointed at our saddlebags.

'Right, off those horses. Open your bags, and be sharp about it,' he growled. His small eyes were too close to his nose, his breath smelt of onions and his helmet and mail shirt were rusty. Hardly a soldier of Rome. What a contrast to Lucius Apulius.

'Of course, legate,' Aegius said in a compliant voice and swung down. He gestured to Asella and me to do the same.

'You trying to be funny?' the guard said.

'Not at all, sir,' Aegius said, even more obsequiously.

A junior officer, a *circitor* from his belt badges, broke off his conversation with another guard and ambled over from the gate. He was less slovenly, but started picking through our spare tunics, my toiletries roll and footwear. He took one of the smoked sausages and some dried fruit we'd bought on the way when we were resting the horses and tucked it away in his pouch. He looked at me, daring me to protest.

He ignored Asella's satchel; perhaps it was the look she gave him. Then he fingered my fur-lined wool cloak and raised an eyebrow as he felt the quality of the cloth. I could see the acquisitive look in his face and nearly choked. The best pieces of my jewellery and a fair amount of gold *solidi* were sewn into it thanks to Asella.

'That's my daughter's only cloak, sir,' Aegius intervened. 'A gift from my patroness at the imperial court. I'm on my way to paint her new walls. She'd be very upset if my daughter didn't turn up in it and think we'd spurned her gift.'

Aegius looked steadily at the *circitor*, who eventually dropped his eyes. Aegius dropped a couple of silver coins into the *circitor*'s hand and we were passed through. Once out of earshot, I breathed out with relief. Asella and I hoisted our weary bodies back into the saddle and nudged our exhausted animals to follow Aegius's horse.

'Look out for lamps above the doors of the private houses,' he said. 'It'll show lodgings are offered. We should see them, as the dusk is nearly on us. I doubt there'd be even a half-respectable inn in this place. If it does exist, it'll be full of the military from the local camp letting off steam and chasing the barmaids.'

Asella and I nodded and said nothing. We were both too tired and the cold breeze was freezing our faces. The fifth house along showed a light, but Aegius said it was too near the nosy soldiers at the gate. Fifty paces further on, we came upon a stone-built rectangular house set back from the road with a high gate. The flame in the lantern by the door latch flickered wildly. Aegius dismounted and knocked on the door. A woman with greying hair and dressed in a long-sleeved brown tunic answered.

'Yes?'

'I see you have your light on. I'm seeking a place to sleep for my wife and daughter. And a hot meal. We can pay in silver.'

The woman looked him up and down, then stepped forward and inspected Asella and me.

'Well, you don't smell, and you look respectable. I suppose your horses aren't stolen?' She sniffed and peered at them.

'Bought with money from working, I assure you.'

'Wait here. I'll open the gate to the courtyard.' She reached up and unhooked the lamp by the door which she slammed shut. We heard a bolt shot inside. I sighed. Were we to be locked out on the street? But then the courtyard gate juddered open, and we rode in.

Our hostess, Melissa, showed us to a room with two wide low-platform beds with thick mattresses and a linen sheet on each.

'They're stuffed with wool. I air them every day, so there shouldn't be any bugs,' she said. She looked us up and down. 'You've got cloaks to cover you, so you'll be warm enough. Supper will be in the other room.' She turned to Aegius and pointed at a large bowl on a table at the side under which was a leather-lined wood bucket. 'Your daughter can fetch water for washing from the barrel in the courtyard.' With that, she left us.

'Well!' I said. 'She's very direct.' I looked longingly at the bed, but my stomach was grumbling with hunger. Asella dropped her bags down on one of the beds.

'I'll go and get the water. You rest, *domina*.'

'No, we'll go together. It would look strange if I didn't, after the hostess's comment. I'm supposed to be a dutiful daughter.'

Aegius made a noise between a snort and a laugh.

'I'll come with you and go and check the horses. If the stable lad is as efficient as his mistress, they'll be well looked after. But I need to make sure.'

Outside, the stable at the other side of the courtyard was outlined in the pink and lemon dusk light. The cold breeze had turned into a freezing wind. Aegius vanished into one of the stalls. With stiff fingers we poured water into our leather bucket. I wondered if I'd ever be warm again.

After a quick breakfast of bread, olive oil and weak ale, we set off again. Melissa's goat stew last night had revived our spirits but had done nothing for our aching muscles. I longed for a warm bath. Whether she was aware of doing it or not, Asella gave me such a reproachful look. A strong sense of guilt crept over me. How could I have imposed this journey on her? Nevertheless, she wrapped her cloak round her, pulled on her hood and tipped her chin forward.

We passed out of the town gates with only a surly expression and a brief nod from the guards. They were too busy rubbing their hands and cursing at the chill that enveloped them. Slowly, we picked our way down the hill to the road. I glanced back as we turned the last bend. I never wanted to return to this grim, grey place again.

'Now the valley is wider and the road better, we should make good progress, *domina*,' Aegius said. He pointed to the left of the sun. 'We go south-east following the valley of the Aesontius, heading for

126

Pons Sonti. That way we avoid Forum Iulii where we'd risk running into a load of questions.'

He was right about the road, and the countryside seemed to fly past. After a while, the steep wooded hills closed in again, but the road was still wide enough for two horses to ride side by side. Aegius rode ahead while Asella and I rode together. We leant back slightly, allowing our mounts to pick their own way, our hips swaying to their sure-footed rhythm.

We stopped to rest the horses every two hours; no fool pushes animals even when fleeing. Who knew when we might be forced to push hard? Then we would have to call on the horses' deep reserves. When the sun reached midday, we stopped where the horses could drink and graze and we could eat the dried meat and fruit Melissa had sold us.

'If we continue at this pace we'll reach the sea this evening,' Aegius said in between chewing.

'The sea?' I stared at him. 'But we are still surrounded by mountains.' I looked up at the dark green trees covering everything to the horizon. 'Or at least very steep hills.'

'Nevertheless, we will.'

'Are you sure?'

He snorted.

'Have I led you astray yet?' He tipped his leather water bottle up and took a long swallow. 'If you and Asella wish to relieve yourselves, I suggest you do it now.' He glanced up at the sun. 'Then we can get on.'

After another two hours, paved sections became more common. And there was more traffic, mostly farm wagons and the occasional merchant with a trail of mules and well-armed men. The air became warmer as we descended into a hamlet which, as we progressed, became a village. At the bridge itself, we rode past the guards and stayed on our side of the river.

'That bridge leads to the Aquileia road – not the one we want to follow,' Aegius said. I shuddered. Not if it took me into the arms of a furious Turcilus. 'We'll get through here, then give the horses a rest before the final push,' he said.

. . .

127

We were back in the hills again and winding along tracks in single file. Some were lined with low stone walls which suggested animals to me, but I saw none. Small farmhouses clustered together with round huts were the only sign of life. We then passed through interminable woods, but less oppressive than the dark mountain forests. Light shone through between the fresh green leaves and the air seemed clearer. We emerged from a wood that was sparser than before – more shrubs than trees – and suddenly we were looking over a wide open plain with low hills in the distance.

'Where are we, Aegius?' I pulled my horse up and was unable to take my eyes off the soft countryside full of small fields, fruit trees, and patches of vines. The sun was starting to descend which flooded the whole scene with yellow light. And there was another smell – tangy, salt.

'Within throwing distance of the sea. Well, possibly a little further, but only a mile or so.'

'Hopefully near somewhere civilised,' Asella muttered, but I caught her looking round at the countryside before us with great interest.

'Fons Timavi is a small place, but we should find lodgings there. There's a small Christian church where the river flows out of the earth. It attracts the gullible who think it's a miracle. The priests don't mention to those fools that people have been worshipping Diomedes, Hercules and Saturn let alone the river's own god, Temavus, there for hundreds of years. Oh no, they claim it purely for the Christos.' His voice didn't carry the usual light satirical tone but a bitter one, and he slumped in the saddle. Asella and I exchanged glances. Who *was* Aegius? He was a gifted artist – that was obvious – he knew about horses and I'd found out that he'd been in the legions, but his voice now betrayed another hurt.

'What do you mean, Aegius?' I said. 'Has the Christos—'

'Let's get on,' he snapped. He pulled himself up into his usual erect position and dug his heel into his horse's flank. Startled and grunting its displeasure, the poor animal leapt forward, head tossing and tail swishing, into a fast canter. But I was determined to find out what had wounded Aegius so badly that his strong, genial shell had been pierced, even for that moment.

16

Aegius was right; there were plenty of lodgings to choose from, but they all had the circular symbol with crossed lines of the followers of Christos carved into the door lintels. We rode on.

At last, we found a large two-storey house, isolated and unusually, with windows to the street. All the shutters were closed, but we could see a dim light leaking where one pair had not been fully closed, but left latched. I glanced at the lintel. Nothing. The wall plaster was cracked in places and even missing here and there; shards lay on the earth in front of the building. A tarnished metal plate engraved with a list of prices hung on the gate post.

'What do you think?' I said in a low voice.

'It's an inn and it should be open.' Aegius jerked his head back along the road we'd come along. 'The rest of the town is full of trippers.'

'Perhaps somebody has died and they're closed for mourning.'

'No cypress branches hanging outside, nor any mourning gifts on the steps.'

The horses' heads were drooping. They were as tired as we were, if not more so, and daylight was starting to fade. Aegius dismounted and knocked lightly, but nobody answered. After a few more breaths, more firmly.

'Hello, the house,' he shouted.

I dismounted and stepped up to the double entrance door.

'We are weary travellers and mean you no harm,' I shouted. 'We've been in the saddle for over eight hours. Let us in, please, in Juno's name!'

Nothing. We waited for a few minutes, then Aegius shrugged and pointed at the horses.

'Looks like camping under the trees, then.'

I shivered. It wasn't cold as in the mountains, but we would have to keep watch in turns, in case of roaming brigands. Well, it would more likely be poor people or runaway slaves scavenging for something to eat. But they could be just as dangerous. I touched the base of my throat, praying it would be unsliced by the morning. This was the last house in the village, so we had no option but to find somewhere under the trees. Aegius cupped his hands and I'd placed my foot in them to mount my poor horse when the door at the front of the house creaked.

'Who are you?' a hesitant voice said through a tiny gap. A second, older voice behind it whispered something I couldn't make out.

'Tullius Ferrantius, painter and artist on my way to Rome,' Aegius lied smoothly. 'With my wife Serena and daughter Placida.' He glanced at me and I nodded. 'Now that Nox is casting her shadow over us at this end of the day, we are seeking shelter.' I caught my breath. If they were Christos followers, they'd curse us for invoking the traditional gods and slam the door in our faces.

The door opened a little further. The face of a young man appeared.

'You call on the old gods, but how do we know you are not followers of the Christos come to attack us again?' he said. Even in the fading light, I could see the muscles in his face were tight. He watched Aegius intently.

'You can't know that,' Aegius said. 'I could swear by all the gods you care to name, but you may still not believe me. But we passed by other possibilities and came to your house because your lintel didn't display their symbol.'

'Please trust us,' I said. 'Our horses are desperate for rest and water and my m…mother is bone tired.' Gods, I nearly called Asella my maid. The other voice whispered hurriedly. The young man turned and talked to the other person, then back to us.

'Very well. My father says to trust you. Enter.'

The gate swung back and we led the horses into a large courtyard surrounded by stables and tall outbuildings. A small forge with no fire lay to the side of a block of stables. The young man turned out to be scarcely more than fifteen or sixteen. The other figure was an older man, probably in his late thirties or early forties, bearded, but with grey hair above a much younger looking face. When he turned to talk to the younger man, dark red bruising showed around the base of his neck. At his side, he carried a stick.

'Follow me,' the older man rasped and leant on the stick. 'My name's Florus of the Aurelii, by the way. That's Crispus, my son,' he said, pointing at the younger man.

'Thank you for believing us, Florus.' I looked around. 'You have large accommodation here.'

'Yes. In the old days, my parents' time, it was a thriving inn. We're only a short distance from the mouth of the Timavus, so the place was always bustling with pilgrims bringing prayers and sacrifices to Hercules or one of the other gods. Now, things have changed.' He frowned, then nodded in the direction of the corner of the courtyard. 'Crispus and I live quietly over in the steward's house. It has a back door opening onto a track leading up to the woods – a safe escape route in case they come back again.'

He looked and sounded desperate. Why was he so afraid?

Inside, the main room with a large hearth was flanked on one side by a kitchen, the other by two curtained-off areas, possibly for sleeping, and a third with shelving and a desk with a stack of wax tablets. Above were more shelves full of books – shelves and shelves of them – almost as many as Father's in Virunum – but mostly scrolls with only the odd codex book. Aegius's eyes widened at the sight, but he quickly brought his gaze back to Florus and smiled. But I could tell his mind was thinking of something other than acting as a grateful guest.

The *puls* young Crispus served in olive wood bowls was delicious, flavoured with herbs and onions and full of cured ham pieces. He apologised for its simplicity, but we reassured him it was like gods' ambrosia to us. Florus poured and mixed a refreshing white wine, smooth and light. As we raised our cups to him, he smiled.

'Apparently, even the great Pliny mentioned our Pucinum in his *Naturalis Historia* hundreds of years ago. They still export it from Tergeste in shiploads. This is one of the last amphorae from my brother's vineyard. We lost him in the riot that destroyed the temple by the mouth of the Timavus.'

'What happened?' I asked. Florus closed his eyes for a moment and winced as he swallowed hard. I stretched my hand out. 'Please don't tell us if it's too painful.'

'My family lived side by side with the Christos followers for years, each secretly despising the other, but staying polite and civilised. We'd had the inn here since the time of my grandfather's grandfather. It was still flourishing when I was a child, but when I was a little younger than Crispus, a new priest came to the town, a firebrand who egged his flock on to smash down the temple to Timavus and build an *ecclesia* on the site to their god. The temple was beautiful with marble columns just redecorated with leaf patterns and wonderful wall paintings showing the gods hunting, Hercules with the lion, and feasting. They were so vivid. I went there the day after the refurbishment was complete. I could imagine myself in those scenes, as part of them.' He raised his hand briefly in the air. 'Gone, all gone.'

Aegius made a strange noise, a cross between a grunt and a cry. Then he leant forward and clasped the man's hand hard.

'But the spirits behind them haven't,' he said and looked steadily at Florus without blinking.

'Hopefully not,' Florus replied. 'I also hope the painter who did the renovation never finds out that his beautiful work has been destroyed. It would break his heart.'

'Yes, it would,' Aegius replied, his face sombre. 'If he hadn't suffered anything else at the time.'

What in Mercury's name did Aegius mean by that?

'The ugly little thing they've put there now – their *ecclesia* – looks like a peasant's hut,' Florus continued. 'They came mob-handed with tools and carts, singing their hymns. My father ordered the shutters closed and the gate locked. We were well known as traditionalists. They did stop outside, and their priest shouted to us to repent.' He snorted. 'My father leant out of the top window and told him to go and f—' He broke off. 'Oh, apologies, ladies.'

His face reddened. Crispus laid his hand on his father's shoulder. Florus covered it with his own and smiled at his son.

'Things started to go downhill after that. Our trade dropped off. Now there's hardly anything.'

'Have they hurt you since? Your neck…' I said, looking at the dark bruising at the base of his throat.

'That? One of my ex-colleagues in the guild grabbed me when I had to go into the town the other day to buy some provisions. He tried to shake what he insisted were the devils out of me and told me he was saving my eternal soul by doing so.' He slumped on the bench. 'I don't know what's going to be here for Crispus. Perhaps he'd better convert to them, or pretend to. At least he'd have a chance in life then.'

'I can't do that, Father. That would be betraying you and Grandfather.'

Florus looked at his son.

'Sometimes you have to give in and compromise, Crispus. It's too late for me, but you should think about it.'

Florus showed us to a good-sized room with a large bed, a pile of mattresses and shelves from floor to ceiling crammed with jugs, bowls, stacks of linen and kitchen crockery. He pointed to a heap of blankets neatly folded on top of a large wooden chest.

'We salvaged the bedding from the inn to stop it becoming damp and going mouldy. Help yourselves. The well in the courtyard still works – the water comes from the hill behind us.' He gave a sad smile. 'You have plenty of jugs and bowls to choose from for washing and as you can see, any amount of linen to dry yourselves with.' He turned and left us without another word.

'Poor, poor man,' I said. 'And curse those who persecute him because he prays another way.'

Asella looked at me and nodded.

'The world has become a crueller place,' she said. Her eyes shone with anger in a face that looked grey in the light of the oil lamps

Florus had left us. But I didn't think she was trembling because of that. She must have been at the end of her strength.

'Hush, Asella. Don't agitate yourself,' I said. 'You should rest.' I scarcely had the energy to stand up myself and my legs ached as if they were being dragged down to the underworld by the fiends of Tartarus himself. I grasped her shoulders. 'Calm yourself and help me arrange some of these mattresses.'

'I will leave you ladies for a few moments and check the horses.' Aegius turned towards to the door. 'Don't worry if I'm a little while. Just sleep.'

He'd said nothing since we'd come into the room and now his voice was tight, controlled, even as if he was suppressing a powerful emotion. Nor did he meet my eyes as he left.

I woke suddenly. It was pitch black, so we were still in the night. Somebody entered the room. My heart pounded. I reached out slowly under the sheet and grasped my knife in my right hand. Asella was next to me, snoring lightly. I opened my eyes halfway. I couldn't see anything, but I felt somebody moving around. As my eyes adjusted, I could make out faint light round the edges of the shutters – moonlight – and I could also make out a tall shape. Slowly and carefully, I started to slide my feet off the bed and pulled back the sheet.

'It's me!' A whisper. Aegius. I slumped back on the bed and took a deep breath. Then the anger came.

'What in Hades do you mean by sneaking around in the night?' I hissed at him.

'Shh,' he whispered back. 'Asella is still asleep. Leave her to rest but put your boots and cloak on if you want to have an argument with me.'

In the kitchen, he stoked the banked fire back into life and set a small pot on to heat water, then lit two lamps with a taper from the fire. He moved about purposefully, almost studiously, without saying another word. When the water bubbled, he poured it into two beakers and added honey and a dash of wine to each. We sat at the table on opposite benches.

'I apologise for disturbing you, *domina*. I meant only to make sure you were both still safe.'

'We are behind a locked entrance door to the house and behind locked and barred gates in the courtyard. I think that would be considered safe.'

He looked down at his drink.

'You went outside, didn't you?' I said. 'Not just to the stables to check the horses, but into the street.'

'I locked the gate behind me.'

'I'm sure you did, but where did you go?' The dawn light was starting to show through the slats in the kitchen window shutters and I could clearly see the distant look in Aegius's eyes. Then it struck me who the painter of Florus's story was. It was obvious now. I must have been so tired last night that my head had been full of wool, or Mercury had been playing a trick on me to dull my senses. 'Ah, you went to see where the temple had been.'

'I had to see it for myself. Florus isn't the sort to lie, but I couldn't think of sleeping without knowing. *She* said they wouldn't leave it alone.' He raised his cup to his mouth but set it down again before drinking. He was hunched over the table and clasping the beaker with both hands. Tough, jokey Aegius had vanished. This man was in agony.

'Tell me,' I said. 'Who was she?'

'Stella. She was the daughter of the town's leading decurion, one of the few of the *curiales* class who could afford to hold the office. He was full of himself, a pal of the Bishop in Aquileia, but a Christian out of pragmatism. Anyway, Stella came to watch me work as I painted the temple as part of the refurbishment and we started to talk, sometimes nearly until the light faded. I was sleeping in the temple so I could get up at sunrise and capture the early light. I hardly went into the town, only to buy food and an occasional cup of wine. After four weeks, I knew I wanted to share my life with Stella. And I thought she felt the same. But she was a true believer in Christos and assumed I would convert. I just couldn't do it.' Aegius's eyes were full of misery. 'I would have let her keep her religion and I would keep to mine, but it wasn't enough for her. She wept as she turned away that last evening. I only saw her one more time when she ran to warn me the new priest was whipping people up against so-called idolatry.'

'But who had commissioned you to paint the temple? I would have thought that these days nobody who had money would have funded such a job.'

He laughed. Another of those short harsh barks.

'Irony of ironies, it was her father's brother – Stella's uncle. The two brothers were fierce rivals – both wanted to become chief councilman. At the time, there was still a significant number of traditional religion followers, enough to vote the uncle in. Florus's father was probably among them. But when that new priest arrived not long after I'd finished my work, the uncle converted. Of course, he fell on his knees and repented having commissioned "pagan" images.' Aegius snorted. 'I urged Stella to come away with me, but she shook her head and said she couldn't imperil her immortal soul.'

He took a long drink of the now lukewarm liquid in his beaker, then sighed.

'She told me to go the very next day. She couldn't have borne it if they came for me, she said. She knew that if they couldn't make me convert, they'd kill me. So I left and went north through the mountains and ended up in Virunum.'

'Oh, Aegius. I am so sorry. Did you ever see her again?'

'No. I don't know if she's still alive.'

'Don't you want to find out?'

'No,' he said abruptly and stood up. 'That door is closed.'

17

I roused Asella and after a breakfast of bread and olives, we crossed the courtyard to the stables to check that none of the horses had sores from the girths or metal bits. We'd been riding for several days now. Aegius lifted the hooves of his and Asella's mounts while I examined Snowfoot's. Happily, all was well.

We led our horses out of the courtyard just as the sun broke the horizon and bade farewell to Florus. He and Aegius clasped arms in the traditional way and Florus muttered something about hoping that Aegius had found everything he needed. I knew Aegius paid him well over the usual rate, but I couldn't help fearing for him as we waved to the forlorn figure leaning on his stick and standing in the open gate. In Virunum, we'd managed to live with the Christos followers despite Eligius's machinations towards me personally, but these two had suffered directly.

Crispus accompanied us, riding with Asella who looked none too pleased about it, but she stopped grumbling after a few minutes. It was only for an hour at worst, I reminded her. Early as it was, the air was warm and as we rode along the narrow coastal path, we were surrounded by the smell of pines, juniper and small oaks. Scents rose from scrub around us that I couldn't identify. To our right, the Mare Adriaticum was a stunning blue, concealing the gods knew what in their cobalt depths. To the left, the hill rose steeply. But I hardly had time to think about any of it as I had to pay attention to the narrow path which was uneven and strewn with loose stones. At any moment, one of the horses could stumble and fall, damaging knees, or at worst, dislodging a rider and damaging us.

Crispus had explained that this was a more discreet route than using the usual road. That one was straighter and paved, but was used by the military and what was left of the public post between Aquileia and Tergeste. None of us wanted nosy patrols asking us our business. But when I steered my horse round another interminable boulder, I wondered whether the risk of using that main road really had been too high.

After only a few miles, we descended a winding track to a cove sheltering behind a headland. Fishing vessels bobbed about, some setting off one after another like a trail of ducklings after their mother.

'Welcome to Castellum Pucinum.' Crispus grinned as only an adolescent can in his brighter moments. 'There,' he pointed to a long open boat tied up to the end of the longest jetty. 'That's the *actuariolum*. It runs from here down to Vallicula and then Tergeste. They can only take five or six passengers, but it's quick.' He looked up and squinted at a pennant flapping on a tall building. 'They'll probably put the sail up as well – there's a good breeze today.'

'What's that building?' I thought I'd seen a figure in a helmet at the top.

'It's a watchtower,' Aegius said. He shaded his eyes with his hand. 'From here, it looks as if it has a functioning signal stand for flags. Move along. We need to be out of its sightline.' We rode on until we came to shelter under a clump of trees. 'Mind you,' he continued, 'it's a gamble whether or not the other end could read them properly, but let's not risk it.'

Crispus dismounted, then wove deftly round barrels and bales on the narrow wharf, and finally trotted out to the passenger boat at the end. He waved at the shipmaster and talked to him animatedly. We stayed concealed under the trees.

'Do you really think Turcilus will have spread news about me this far?' I said.

'Never underestimate a blow to an inadequate man's pride, *domina*. The poorer the specimen, the greater the perceived injury.'

'That sounds almost philosophical, Aegius.'

'No, just experience.' He cast around watching everything and everybody.

I kept my eyes on Crispus. Eventually, he stopped talking and dropped something in the sailor's hand.

Aegius slid off his horse and started unbuckling his saddlebags.

'Right, I think Crispus has done the deal. If you would gather your things, ladies, we'll take to the water.'

With two banks of six rowers, there was little room for Aegius, Asella and me, but we huddled together on one of the two benches just in front of the steersman. As Crispus had predicted, the shipmaster had ordered a small sail to be raised and it fluttered noisily above us, pulling on its ropes. Crispus himself waved energetically from the wharf. We could just see him holding the reins of our three horses. I'd brushed away a tear as I'd left Snowfoot on the wharf and wound my arms around her warm neck for the last time. I'd cared for her since she was a foal and then been completely confident riding her over any terrain. She'd listened steadfastly to my confidences in her gentle way. The gods knew what she'd made of them. Now she would be living with strangers.

'What do you think Florus will do with the horses?' I asked Aegius as the *actuariolum* swayed with the rowers' strokes.

'I told him to sell two of them and keep one for himself.'

'I hope that's Snowfoot.'

'I'm sure he'll make a wise choice,' he replied. Which was not a comforting answer.

Asella grabbed my arm as we sailed round the headland and the shallow boat entered the open sea. Her face was grim and her fingers gripped my flesh as if they were a hawk's claws.

'Peace, Asella. Loosen your grip.'

'We're going to drown on this… this barge,' she said in a wavering voice.

The steersman behind us laughed, but as it rocked with the waves as well as each stroke the oarsmen made, I could completely understand her fear.

'I thought you wanted to see the sea,' I replied.

'I did. I have. Now I know I prefer my forests.'

I eased her fingers from my forearm, then put my whole arm round her shoulders and hugged her.

'It's only for an hour or two, and look, we're keeping to the coastline.' I pointed to the second headland in the distance jutting out into the water. 'There's Tergeste.'

'What happens there?'

'We board another vessel.'

Asella groaned.

'A much bigger one, and one that takes us to Italia proper.'

When the *actuariolum* put into Vallicula, Aegius told us to cover our heads with scarves and not meet anybody's eyes.

'There's only room for one or two more at a pinch,' he continued but lowered his voice. 'We'll have to stop talking if anybody new gets on.'

'Why?'

'Because Vallicula is full of elite Romans getting bored in richly decorated villas or dropping into one of the several spas to have their backs rubbed. In between strolling around the gardens, they sometimes come into the town to see if anybody interesting has arrived. Fresh meat, you know. We have to look as uninteresting as possible.'

'How do you know all this?'

'Trust me. I know.'

Gods, Aegius could be so damned superior sometimes, given he was just a painter. But I was starting to doubt that.

'Anyway, we don't want to learn that some smart-arse signalled from that tower in Pucinum and sent any suspicions about us to Vallicula for transmission on to Tergeste.'

'Why on earth would they have done that?'

He looked at the steersman, then the rowers and spoke in barely above a whisper.

'Because I think we're being followed.'

I gasped.

'Surely not Turc—'

Aegius grabbed my arm.

'Stop. No names,' he hissed. 'I don't think so. I'm pretty sure they were hanging around when I went to look for any remains of the temple at Fons Timavi. Possibly before.'

'They? Are there more than one?'

'I don't know. I also don't know why he or they haven't pounced.'

Nobody joined us at Vallicula, but some amphorae and a bale were unloaded there into the care of a middle-aged man with grey and black curls and a Greek beard who was fussing around insisting the shipmaster sign his list. The sailor thrust a similar laced pair of tablets at the man, who promptly opened them, counted the amphorae with deliberation and signed in the wax. The man bowed his head very slowly and gave a smug smile. The shipmaster stalked back onto the boat, making it wobble so wildly that Asella groaned and I grabbed the side. The shipmaster grumbled about 'bloody Greeks' all the way to Tergeste, which turned out to be only fifteen minutes away.

The city of Tergeste stretched up the side of a hill that rose steadily from the harbour. As we came closer, the walls with their many watchtowers looked impressive. Below them was a theatre building with a large square and a tall column. We sailed past and landed on a beach a short distance from the wharves. The sailors shipped their oars and several bent down and fished leather water bottles from under their bench and drank deeply.

Aegius nodded to the shipmaster, then jumped down into a few inches of water.

'Hand me down the bags, daughter,' he said giving me a sharp look. Asella slung the band of her satchel across her upper body – Juno knew what was in it that was so precious – then helped me pass the bags down. Soon they lay in a heap on the beach. I hesitated. 'Come along, Placida. Move your arse,' Aegius shouted. I was about to shout back at him, but something stopped me. I sensed I was being watched. I climbed onto the edge of the boat and slithered into the shallow water which was surprisingly warm. Aegius went to help Asella down, carrying her above the water to the beach as a good husband would.

'Right, cover your heads and don't say a word, either of you,' he said as we walked up to the city gate. 'Let's hope they're too busy checking foreigners to look at a humble artist and his womenfolk.'

We passed easily through the gate, which was nothing special, just simple, solid construction decorated with pilasters and a vegetable motif under the arch. Aegius pointed right and we turned into a square, then down a side street full of small shops. Further on was a tall building with a plaque on the front – *Good lodgings, reasonable rates.*

'That remains to be seen,' Asella sniffed.

'Let's at least look,' Aegius said.

He rang, a porter opened the gate promptly and we entered a courtyard populated by every size of pot full of burgeoning plants. The rooms turned out to be simple, clean and relatively spacious. The landlady, who introduced herself as Victorina, was friendly as she showed us to our room. When she'd closed the door, I turned to Aegius.

'How are our funds?' I waved my hand around. 'This room can't be cheap.'

'Actually, it *is* surprisingly reasonable.' He sighed. 'Ah, money… Your father took me aside and gave me a purse before we left – for miscellaneous expenses on your behalf, he called it. I wondered at the time what he meant, but I felt he was giving me a commission of some sort, almost imposing responsibility on me. Perhaps he knew his daughter well.' He smiled as if remembering. 'But yes, we'll be about halfway through our money once we've paid the ship to Italia. If we're careful, it should be enough to complete our journey.'

'How careful?'

He shifted his weight from one foot to another.

'Careful.'

'Aegius, you must take some of my *solidi*, or better, some of my jewellery, and sell it. We're in one of the biggest cities in the empire. There must be traders from the east looking for fine work. You know yourself some of it is unique and all of it is of the highest craftsmanship. My amber and gold collar alone would pay for the rest of the journey.'

He didn't answer at first. I would be sad to see the amber go as it reminded me of three months with Gylfi, but I could hardly wear it in Rome if I ever managed to find Lucius.

'No, *domina*. I will not take your jewellery – it's your personal property, part of your marriage *arrhae* if we manage to reach Rome.'

'Well, at least take some of my gold *solidi*.'

'Only if we get desperate. And we're not at that point yet.'

'But—'

'No. We'll manage.'

He went out shortly after that to enquire about sailings to the Italian coast, he said, but I wondered if he wanted to get away from us for an hour or two and find the company of other men.

Victorina gave us some fish and bread with olive oil to eat. When we'd scooped the last of the oil up with the bread, she offered us a bowl of fresh pears and figs. I sent Asella to rest afterwards.

I would have loved to have looked round the harbour and the town, but Aegius had impressed on us how important it was to stay out of sight. It would have been stupid to ignore his advice. The thought of Turcilus catching us just as we were about to take ship to Italia made me shiver. A bubble of sour air rose through my chest into my throat. To throw off the queasy feeling, I sat quietly by Victorina's window from which I could watch the soothing ripples of the dark blue sea and feel the warmth in the air folding round my head and shoulders. The perpetual shouting, slamming, crashing of pots and cursing found in any city were no less present, but the salt breeze disguised some of the smell of rotting rubbish and the contents of chamber pots lazily emptied onto the street instead of the public latrine.

Sitting still with nothing to do, I had time to reflect. I'd offered to help with any household task I could, but Victorina said there was nothing. I found that strange, as there was always something to do in most houses, but I could hardly insist. After a while, she brought me a pile of wool to wind. Asella joined me after an hour, bringing another pile and we sat silently, our arms and hands moving rhythmically.

The afternoon wore on and it must have been near the tenth hour of the day when a loud, irregular thump on the street gate disturbed the quiet of the early evening. I hadn't noticed it had become so late. My stomach grumbled as if it knew better.

'What in Hades is going on down there?' Asella put down her ball of wool and leant out of the window. 'Oh, Great Mother! It's Aegius and he's staggering around.'

'What?' I jumped up. 'Is he injured?'

'No, he looks pissed.'

'Oh, for the gods' sake.' I couldn't believe he'd left us here with nothing to do but become more and more anxious about him and then turn up the worse for wear after an afternoon's drinking. And he'd suspected we were being followed so he'd also left us defenceless against possible abduction. I spun round and took a step towards the door, ready to rush down the narrow stairs and give him my exact opinion.

'Stop!' Asella shot out her arm in front of my waist and pressed me back. 'Remember you're the dutiful daughter – Placida. Leave it to me. I'll go and play the typical wife and bring him up here.'

She was right, of course, but it didn't stop me walking from one side of the room to the other and back again several times. A seagull alighted on the window frame and twisted its head from side to side. I flicked my fingers at it, but its screech as it flapped its wings and flew off didn't rival Asella's down in the courtyard. Heavy footsteps on the stairs were followed by a torrent of speech from an aggrieved sounding Asella. The door opened and Aegius stumbled in.

'Where in Hades—?'

'Drink,' he said.

'Yes, I see that.'

'Give me some water, for pity's sake.'

He dropped down onto the stool near the window, treading on one of the abandoned balls of wool, then cursing, kicked it away. Asella poured him a beaker of water which he downed in one swallow. He held it out for more. After two more, he let out a sigh, then stood.

'I apologise, *domina*, for coming to you in this state.' His voice wasn't slurred, but his words weren't quite as crisp as usual.

'Where have you been? Apart from in a rough *caupona*, getting drunk.'

'Rough, yes, but profitable.'

'What do you mean?'

He threw his waist pouch on the side table. It thumped, then clinked. It was bulging.

'Where did you get that?' I said.

'I made a few wagers and threw a few dice.' He hiccoughed and stretched his beaker out to Asella for a refill of yet more water.

'Gambling?' I was aghast. It wasn't always or even often enforced but if the *aediles* were in a grumpy mood they could impose a heavy fine up to four times the winnings. 'Are you mad? If you'd been caught, apart from wrecking our finances and you being thrown in prison, it could have exposed all of us.'

He gave me a look bordering on the insolent; it was almost a sneer.

'With the greatest of respect, *domina*, that was very unlikely. In your sheltered life, the servants would have made sure they hid it from you. But even your father bet on the races and wasn't averse to a late-night game of twelves.'

'Gods, Aegius, whatever the gains, you took an enormous risk with our money, our freedom and our lives.'

He looked straight at me, then swept his arm in an open gesture to include the whole room.

'And we're not taking a risk with this whole escapade?'

I had to look away. I had no answer.

18

I thought I'd never get to sleep with Aegius snoring on the other side of the room. Even Asella by my side was restless. But I must have dozed off as the next thing I was aware of was Asella pinning back the shutters and the early morning sun breaking across the Mare Adriaticum.

'Come, *domina*, Aurora has already risen and so must you.' She turned and gave me an impatient look, then pointed across the room to the single bed. 'Aegius has gone already to check the sailing time.'

'Do we have a ship, then?' I asked, rubbing my eyes.

'Surprisingly, yes.'

'But—'

'I know. I was equally taken aback. I went downstairs to order our breakfast and met Aegius with his bathing kit under his arm and water dripping from his hair. He was returning from the baths and whistling far too cheerily.'

She started folding our things and shoving them into the saddlebags we were still using as luggage. 'You have time to wash, dress and eat some breakfast, then we must go to the harbour.' She looked up. 'Aegius is still downstairs filling his boots.'

In the dining room, I found the erstwhile drunk eating heartily and smiling and chatting to the landlady, Victorina, as she set steaming *puls* porridge, bread and olives on the table. He started to rise as I entered, but almost instantly remembered he was supposed to be my father.

Luckily, Victorina had her back to us at that particular moment. She set a beaker down in front of me. When she turned away, I sniffed it; acidic wine with water. I added a spoonful of honey to it. She returned with an egg in a small dish and a bowl of figs. When she had gone, I leant towards Aegius.

'I see you've recovered.'

'I have, thank you, *domina*.' He glanced at me then looked down at his bowl of *puls*. 'I apologise if I was discourteous to you last night, but I was not completely myself.'

'No, you weren't, but tell me what happened.'

'I went to investigate a passage for the three of us and succeeded. The ship sails for Ancona mid morning today.'

'That's wonderful!'

'Lucky more like. I thought we might have been forced to wait for several days or risk sailing into Ravenna where we could run into all kinds of trouble. I mean, there are only a few scruffy navy patrol boats there these days, not the fleet of the imperials. The main fleet is based in Constantinople. Still, they throw their weight around if they feel like it, checking every new arrival in depth, especially when they're trying hard not to put out and chase pirates.' He shrugged. 'But even now Tergeste is still a great city of the empire and Ancona is still one of Italia's premier ports, so merchants still need to trade. According one of the dockside workers, a ship sails the route at least three times a week, especially now the main sailing season has started up.'

I leapt up.

'Then we must get down there immediately in case they go early.'

'No, you have plenty of time to finish your breakfast. They're nowhere near halfway loading their cargo.' He glanced towards the kitchen and then the stairs, but there was nobody. 'My winnings were considerable last night, so it's a good thing we're leaving today,' he said in a low voice. 'There was one young man, well, in his thirties, that seemed particularly upset at losing and I don't relish his knife in my throat.'

'You weren't cheating?'

'For Mars' sake, *domina*! What kind of question is that?' He looked genuinely offended.

'I was only teasing.'

'He was a bad loser, but although he shrugged and seemed to take it reasonably well, he had a vicious look in his eye.'

I was eating the last of the bread as Asella came down the stairs. She raised her eyebrows as she sat down beside me and planted her elbows on the table.

'What are you two up to? Plotting to overthrow the empire?'

'Hush, Asella,' I said. 'You never know who's listening.'

'It was a joke. Not a moment too soon by the look of your faces.'

Aegius slid two leather pouches over the table under each of his hands.

'Take one each and put it somewhere in your bags. Better, split it up with some in your waist pouch and some wrapped in your clothes.' He focused his eyes on each of us in turn. 'I won a considerable amount last night, even though I had to stand the whole bar a celebratory drink. Nevertheless, it will enable us to travel on in comfort and pay for the best horses and accommodation. If one of us has an accident or is robbed, we'll still have more than enough.'

'Is that likely?' I said.

'We must be prepared for every eventuality.' He looked at Asella. 'I mentioned it as a suspicion to the *domina* the other day, but now I must put you on your guard too, Asella. I think somebody is tracking us.'

Asella gasped. She covered her mouth with her hand.

'Not the master or Laurinus Turcilus?'

'No. I think they would have declared themselves. I drank a lot last night, but I was still capable of taking some evasive measures on my way back here.' He stood. 'We'd better get going. The sooner we're on that ship, the better.'

Down on the quay, the shipmaster confirmed our passage to Ancona. A light naval escort would be joining us to Pola, returning to its home base. The *oneraria* would sail around the sixth hour; we were only at the third. He didn't have a full passenger load today, he said, so there was plenty of space to pitch a shelter on the deck: premium places available for a small fee. Aegius nodded and ushered us away, back along the wharf towards shops under a row of arches in front of a warehouse.

'Although we have cloaks and blankets, we'd do well to buy a mattress each, even a thin one. The ship's deck is a hard place. Also, something to make a shelter in case it rains.'

'Can we not hire one of the cabins?' I said.

'They'll belong to the shipmaster and the owner. I reckon they might have two more for VIPs, but a painter and his family aren't likely to afford that. We'd look out of place if we even asked. And looking out of place is something we've tried to avoid so far. No, we'll have to bear it. It's only for two days.' He grinned. 'You can always doze during the day, Daughter. If you're not looking after your seasick mother.'

I raised my eyebrows at him, but he just laughed. It was so infectious that I joined in.

We returned to the ship an hour before sailing laden down with rolled up bedding, a small leather tent, a bowl for washing, bread, fruit, smoked fish, cheese, olives, a small bottle of olive oil, and four jars of prepared *posca* to drink. 'Perfect for a sea voyage,' the shopkeeper said as he smiled when charging us an outrageous amount for the vinegary wine. Aegius protested and the shopkeeper reluctantly added another spoonful of honey to each bottle before sealing them. Aegius made him give us three beakers and eating bowls to make up for the price.

'It's not a feast but we'll survive on this for two days,' was all he said as we walked back to the ship. I knew nothing about ships; it looked to me like a very large floating bathtub. The enormous sail flapped noisily in the breeze. Asella looked terrified and clutched my arm. Gulls shrieking round our heads did nothing to diminish our anxiety.

'You!'

We turned to find a short, neat man holding a wax tablet and stylus and wearing an officious expression on his face. A boy beside him clutched another half-dozen tablets in his arms and fidgeted.

An armed soldier stood behind the man and looked thoroughly bored.

'Yes?' Aegius said.

'Exit pass. You cannot sail without the governor's permission.'

Oh gods! I clutched Asella's hand.

'Who are you?' Aegius said, looking down his nose.

'Marcilius Simonides. I am the imperial customs officer. You must show me your pass.'

'Oh, must I?' Aegius said, crossing his arms.

The little man frowned. His face became redder.

'You will not board this ship unless you do. I insist.'

I thought he was going to stamp his foot. For an instant, I had an instinctive urge to laugh, but almost as quickly I realised it was no laughing matter. The soldier would back the clerk up and we could be hauled off to the court or even arrested. Then Turcilus would arrive. I blinked hard. Several people on the dock and the shipmaster were edging closer to listen.

'Insist away,' Aegius said, and smirked.

Why in Hades was he being so relaxed about this? He looked at me then stopped smiling. Perhaps he realised his little game with the customs official didn't seem like a game to me. We were supposed to be being discreet. Aegius opened his waist pouch and drew out a piece of parchment folded in four. He opened it and I saw a heavy wax seal in one corner. He held it up in front of him, but as the official went to take it, Aegius drew back, his fingers clutching the document top and bottom. The clerk leant forward and squinted at it.

'Humph,' he said. 'That seems to be in order.' He looked crestfallen.

'Oh, good,' Aegius said genially. 'So pleased the empress's invitation and the governor's countersignature and seal satisfy you.'

The customs official made a last-minute attempt to recover his dignity.

'Why are you going to Ancona, then, if the invitation is to Mediolanum?' He seemed petulant and suspicious at the same time. I held my breath. Would Aegius's lies be found out?

'It's none of your business,' Aegius retorted. 'But if you really must know, it's to collect some special pigments. I can't arrive at the imperial court without the materials to do my job.' He turned to Asella and me and pointed to the ship. 'On you get, women. Don't dilly-dally now.'

I bit back my reply. Aegius was enjoying his role as paterfamilias a little too much. But I sent up a silent prayer of thanks to Juno, and to Mars, Aegius's favourite, for sending us such a clever and competent guide.

Neptune smiled on us as we sailed down the coast south of Tergeste. To be sure, we needed our cloaks round us early morning and evening – it was still May for a few days yet and the breeze was hearty – but the sun shone and clouds gathered over us only once. We sailed down the coast of Italia as if on a holiday. I remember Lucius telling me about his grandmother's villa by the sea and how pleasant and fresh it was.

The only discordant note was when a group of passengers started chanting prayers to Christos as the ship left harbour. It went on forever. The shipmaster looked on with half-closed eyes and a curl to his lip, but he himself hadn't made any sacrifice to the gods before leaving. Perhaps he'd felt it was too conspicuous in this day and age.

Walking in his confident way, Aegius led us to a place on the deck up against the wall of the cabins.

'Right, let's make ourselves comfortable for the night before anybody else gets ideas about our spot. I've paid for it so we might as well take advantage of it.' Under his direction, we fastened our leather tent to three of the row of rings spaced along the side of the cabin exterior.

'That's convenient,' I said.

'They're really for securing open cargo or animals, but handy for making a shelter,' Aegius replied. 'Not quite home from home, but it will serve us well enough tonight.'

He left us with our new possessions and instructions to lay things out in a certain way, then swanned off to talk to the shipmaster, the *gubernator*, he called him.

'Men!' I hissed to Asella. She smiled.

'I know, *Placida*,' she replied, emphasising my false name and giving me a strong look. Then she glanced around. There were about twenty other passengers on the wide deck. Added to that were the crew and, below, several hundred amphorae of wine, bales of cloth and spices from the east, all relying on the mere finger's width of wood planking to arrive safely. She leant close to me so she could whisper into my ear. 'We have to be discreet. We have no idea who any of these people are. So, keep to your role as dutiful daughter. We'll be polite and friendly, but stay together rather than chatter with the other women.'

'I never saw you as an idle chatterer, Asella.' I laughed.

She smiled at me.

After an hour, Aegius came back and squatted down by us.

'All well?'

'Yes,' I replied. The deck was hard, the mattresses thin and we were on a cold food diet and living among noisy strangers who smelt as if they didn't often wash, but over the past week I had hardened up. My privileged life with servants, endless changes of clothes, well-prepared food and, blessing of blessings, baths, had ended. I'd thought I was a tough mountain girl, but that had been an illusion. Without Aegius, Asella and I didn't have the skills or knowledge to have made this journey. We would have fared very poorly.

He smiled and his eyes twinkled.

'Well done, *domina*. I know it's been hard for you, but we'll come through it.'

'I have one question, though,' I said. 'How on earth did you get that invitation letter and even more the local governor's countersignature and seal?'

I knew perfectly well from Virunum that getting an interview with a governor's secretary was hard enough, let alone the man himself. And that invitation to Mediolanum…

Aegius gave a broader smile and winked.

'I'm a painter, *domina*, and have many artistic skills.'

I shouldn't have let my mouth hang open even for the second it did, aghast at the idea of such a forgery. Then I burst out laughing. The talking around us stopped. Several other passengers stared at us. We'd been whispering, but my laugh was unrestrained. An unshaven man with brown and grey hair, about Aegius's age, ambled over to us.

'Want to share the joke, love?'

His eyes assessed us, then came back to me. He was measuring us, me in particular. I pulled my *palla* over my head.

'No, sir, just a silly family joke,' I mumbled, looking down at the deck.

'We all have families, dearie. Don't be shy.'

Two other men joined him. They hooked their thumbs in their belts and looked down at Asella and me still sitting on the hard wooden planks. I felt vulnerable, threatened, yet I had to maintain my role. But through the fabric of my skirt, I felt for my knife tucked in my boot. Aegius stood and smiled pleasantly at the man.

'Just a silly girl, my daughter. And my wife's not a lot better.' He held out his hand. 'Tullius Ferrantius, painter. And you are?'

'Carpus, out of Tergeste.'

'And what do you do, Carpus?'

'This and that.'

'Well, I apologise for my womenfolk if their noise has upset you and your friends.'

'P'raps they might like to say sorry in a more friendly way.'

I stopped breathing for a moment. Asella took my hand and pressed it.

'I don't think so, no,' Aegius said and crossed his arms.

'Pretending to be a tough nut, eh?' Carpus said. 'Look at this, boys, artist trying to look big.' He glanced at Aegius's arms. 'Your fingers won't be much use to you if they were all broken up, now, would they?'

I knew Aegius was ex-military and still fit, but his hand shot out so fast I hardly saw it. Within one breath, Carpus was sprawled on the deck, blood streaming over his face. One of his companions was bent over clutching his stomach. The other one backed away.

'When an ex-centurion says no, lads, it's always best to heed him,' Aegius said in a conversational tone. 'Now bugger off. If I see any of you near my women again, it'll be the last thing you ever do.'

· · ·

In the evening, Asella and I took our new bowl and queued at the galley for hot water. The other women eyed us suspiciously. Nobody spoke to us but we weren't unhappy at that. Aegius gave us privacy while we washed in the little tent he erected on our portion of the deck. After a while, the flap opened and he poked his head in.

'May I?'

'Of course,' I said. I handed him a small bowl with bread, cheese and some of the dried fish seasoned with olive oil. We ate in silence. After Asella had handed out beakers of *posca* and we'd all taken a good swallow, Aegius spoke in a whisper.

'We'll be putting into Pola at the southern point of the peninsula tomorrow in the late morning. This *oneraria* will meet up with others at Pola and then cross to Ancona with one, possibly two of the scruffy naval ships.'

'Why escort ships?' I asked.

'Because of pirates.'

'Here? But the navy *milites* won't check the civilian passengers, will they?'

'You seem more worried about them than the pirates, Daughter.'

'I'm not frightened of anybody!'

'Hush, not so loud,' Asella hissed.

'The *milites* will only take you off the ship and send you back to Virunum or to Turcilus,' Aegius said. 'The pirates will rape you then sell you in the Eastern slave markets. Red hair is very sought after there.'

'Gods.' I stared at him in horror.

'Exactly. Now, some of our fellow passengers may get off in Pola, but I expect the rest of them will rush to the side and gawk at the port as we go in. You should stay here. Perhaps Asella – sorry, *Serena* – can pretend to be recovering from seasickness. We don't want any sharp-eyed nosy lookout on the quay spotting you two.'

'And where will you be?' I asked. 'If they see you, they'll assume we're not far away.'

'I'll be hiding behind the cabin block, watching.'

'Watching who?'

'Everybody.'

'You suspect the person who may be following us is on this boat?'

'Possibly, or they may get on here.'

'Look, Aegius, you were sure Turcilus wasn't following us, but who else would be?'

'A very good question, *domina*. One we want the answer to sooner rather than later.'

19

Approaching the port of Pola, we sailed between two long arms of tree-covered land, each with a watchtower and signal station at the far seaward end on the headland. The ship sailed on between two small islands and rounded a larger one as we approached the town itself. Our naval escort left us here and made for the small military dock on the bigger island. Apart from a Roman officer coming on board our *oneraria* in Tergeste and examining the shipmaster's documents, they had ignored the passengers.

Across the dark blue water, I could see walls, high gates and rising above them all the biggest amphitheatre I had ever seen. Not that I had seen many, but this one imposed itself on the skyline.

'Beautiful, isn't it?' Aegius stood at my side at the ship's rail.

'It's magnificent!'

'But full of blood, despite its former pretty name of Pietas Iulia. Emperor Julian's brother, Gallus, was murdered here sixteen years ago by that bastard eunuch Eusebius. The old emperor Constantius – another true bastard and paranoid with it – sentenced Gallus for treason. I reckon it was jealousy. Anyway, Constantius changed his mind, but Eusebius went ahead with Gallus's execution anyway. Still, Eusebius got it when Julian became Augustus.' Aegius made a slicing action across his throat.

I drew back. Pola wasn't quite as magnificent now.

'Time to retreat,' Aegius whispered in my ear. 'Your mother is still unwell, Placida,' he said in a normal voice. 'You should tend to her.'

'Yes, Father,' I said, acting the compliant daughter. I knelt by Asella's mattress and took her hand. I poured a beaker of *posca* and held it to her lips, but I watched Aegius out of the corner of my eye.

'Careful, or you'll tip it all over me.' Asella's voice reproached me.

'Sorry.' I repositioned the cup and smiled at Asella.

When I looked up again, Aegius had vanished. From our place by the cabins, I could see the gangplank and the crew carrying bales of cargo down it. After a few minutes, they disappeared from my sight behind the ship's rail. Carpus threw a surly look back as he and two of his companions stepped off. A portly woman and a tall thin youth with greasy hair, accompanied by a man dressed in a long robe and blue cloak, followed.

Two men strode up the gangplank and dropped small bales on the deck. Both carried satchels with straps slung diagonally across their chests. Then the two crewmen reappeared with more bales on their shoulders followed by a boy carrying a stack of wood that hid most of him except for his head and lower legs. He tottered towards the galley. I heard a large thunk, presumably the boy dropping his load. The cook shouted and the boy ran back to the gangplank and sped down it.

Just as they were pulling on the ropes to lift the gangplank up, somebody shouted at them to wait. They released the ropes, and a blond man in his thirties ran up the gangplank, huffing and puffing.

'My thanks, shipmaster,' he said when he'd caught his breath. The crewman, who wasn't in reality the shipmaster, nodded, then turned away helping his fellow to stow the gangplank. The late arrival looked round, smiling all the time, paused his eyes on us, then moved on.

I spotted Aegius leaning on the outer cabin wall, arms crossed and studying the man who was a good height, and well built, but nothing as solidly muscled as Aegius. The man's blond hair waved in the breeze. He bent down to pick up his bale and, nodding once at Asella and me, he walked to the other side of the ship. He stopped at the now empty place previously occupied by the merchant family who had just left.

Asella started coughing and grasped my arm. Was she still pretending to be ill? We'd only just got underway and were for the moment protected by the long arms of Pola's natural harbour. No, her face was agitated, not pallid with seasickness, feigned or real.

'What's the matter?' I said and offered her the drink again.

'Noth…nothing.' She pushed my arm away and swallowed her breath.

'Something's upset you. Tell me.'

'That man, the one who just got on,' she whispered. Her voice was so soft I had to bend down almost touching her face with my own.

'What about him?' I glanced over at him. He looked like anybody else. With that light hair and moustache, short tunic and breeches, he must be a tribesman of some kind, but his belt with square panels and his leather sandals were obviously Roman.

'I thought I'd seen a ghost.'

'I knew you were in touch with the spiritual world, Asella, but do you really think so?'

'No, you don't understand. He looks like a grown-up version of a child I knew.'

'What child?'

She shook her head and gave me a furtive look, almost as if she was frightened.

'Nobody. I'm going to sleep now.'

I shook her arm, but she closed her eyes and took no notice. What in Hades was that about?

I left her dozing on her mattress in the shade of the cabin wall. Once we were away from the dockside at Pola, I went to the ship's rail to look at our new sailing companions. Our *oneraria* had been joined by two other merchantmen and a naval ship, larger than the previous one.

'Red sail, and look at that standard in the bow,' Aegius said. 'They must be carrying a bigwig of some sort.'

'As long as they don't interfere with us, I don't mind if it's the emperor himself,' I retorted.

Aegius threw his head back and gave a bellow laugh.

We ate most of the rest of our food that evening, leaving some cheese and olives for the morning. The bread had gone hard despite Asella having wrapped it in a damp cloth.

'You'll eat it if you're hungry enough,' Asella replied tartly to my protestations. I'd been worried about her after her upset earlier, but she seemed to have recovered her composure by the time the light was fading. She glanced once more at the blond man, then settled down to sleep by my side.

'I'm going for a walk round,' Aegius said. I nodded. He was probably going to dice with somebody. Despite his almost heroic qualities, Aegius had the typical man's love of gambling. But it had proved so useful in Tergeste when he'd won so much silver.

It was still warm and I watched the stars through the gap at the end of the tent as I lay on my thin mattress. What was Lucius doing at this very moment in Rome? Perhaps he was out dicing as well or going to dinner with a friend, laughing about his time in the barbarian mountains. A tear rolled down my cheek. I closed my eyes and saw him in my mind on that very last morning as he looked down from his horse in the middle of Virunum. Gods, would I ever get to Rome and find him again? Would he still want me if I did?

The ship's motion was soothing and I yawned, lulled by the soft rhythm of the waves. My eyelids became heavy and closed. I took a deep breath and started to drift off to sleep. Then I felt a prickling running over my skin. Somebody was watching me. That was absurd. How could anybody watch me through the sides of a leather tent? There was nobody in the gap that I could see. I'd been used to being looked at as the prince's daughter in Virunum, but this was different. Gods, I hoped there wasn't going to be a repeat of Carpus and his roughnecks or that disgusting farmer in the mountains.

A plank on the deck creaked. I tried my best not to jump. Perhaps it was pure animal instinct, but I felt a threat, a predator nearby. Something scuffed on the deck the other side of the leather tent. Probably a shoe or boot. I grasped my knife.

'Lost your way in the dark, young man?' Aegius's voice.

I threw off my cloak and scrambled up onto my knees. Through the narrow gap in the tent, I could see Aegius's face and arms illuminated by a lantern in his hand. It also lit up the face of the blond tribesman standing next to him. I relaxed my shoulders, which had rolled up in tension, and the muscles eased in my whole body. I gazed up at the young man who appeared contrite.

'I apologise. Please accept my assurances that I meant no harm. The moon is only a poor crescent tonight and I lost my way.' He bowed, then turned and walked to the other side of the boat.

Aegius watched until the man had sat down and started laying his cloak out on the deck, then he pulled the flap back fully, entered the tent and crouched down beside me.

'Are you well, Daughter?' Aegius asked me in a voice louder than necessary.

'Yes, thank you, Father,' I replied, shaking my head. Aegius frowned at me. 'Are you coming to sleep now?' I widened my eyes at him.

'Yes, I think that would be best.' He unrolled his mattress next to mine, lay down and pulled his cloak over his body. He turned so he was facing me. I felt no discomfort from him lying so close. He glanced round. 'Now what in Hades was going on?' he whispered. His breath smelt of wine.

'Nothing actually happened,' I whispered back. 'But I felt a sense of threat. The gods know why, as that man seems agreeable with a friendly manner.' I pulled my cloak tighter. 'Though Asella was very disturbed when she saw him board earlier, but she wouldn't say why.'

'Hm. Well, let's go to sleep now. But I'll be keeping an eye on him until we reach Ancona.'

The tent was flapping noisily in the wind as I woke the next morning. Asella was fidgeting and murmuring in her sleep. Her cloak had slipped, so I pulled it up over her shoulder. Aegius was nowhere to be seen. I stretched. What I would have given for slipping under the warm water of a bath. Perhaps they had good ones in Ancona. I pulled on my breeches and boots, belted my tunic and searched for the bowl to go and get some hot water from the galley. At least our faces and hands would be clean. But it was missing. Damn, had somebody filched it in the night? Our small bowls, spoons and beakers were still there in the string bag hanging from one of the hooks.

The tent flap opened and a bowl of steaming water slid in followed by Aegius crawling in. None of us could stand properly; it must have been particularly awkward for him.

'I'll leave you ladies to wash.' He glanced at Asella. 'Is she all right?'

'A bit restless. I think she's been dreaming, but I expect she'll wake up now the crew are tramping around.'

He let the tent flap fall without saying another word. I shook Asella's shoulder. She didn't stir.

'Wake up, Asella. It's our last few hours at sea. We need to get our breakfast and pack up our things.'

She turned, gasped and blinked at me.

'You are unharmed?' Her eyes were full of fear.

'Yes, of course. Why do you ask?'

She grabbed my hand.

'I had the most dreadful dream, *domina*,' she said in a low voice. 'You were in mortal danger with an evil force stalking you.'

'I'm hale and hearty as you see, although I could do with a night in a comfortable bed and a bath.'

'Be careful when we land. I will make an amulet for you, to protect you, and visit the nearest shrine to the Mother.'

'Peace, Asella, we have a strong protector in Aegius and we're not without our own resources. All will be well once we are in Italia.'

20

I stood at the rail two hours later and marvelled. Even this far out, Ancona gleamed. Aegius said it was the gilded bronze figures on Trajan's Arch, or maybe the *pharos* fire on the headland. As we approached the end of our sea voyage, I was rather wistful. Now we would be back on a hard trail across mountains riding for many hours each day.

The wharf was crowded with merchant ships, small boats and at one end two naval patrol boats. I'd combed out then replaited my hair, coiled it round my head and pushed my travelling cap over the top. I was eager to see everything and was certain that dressed as I was, I would be taken for a young man. At the ship's rail I crossed my arms and leant on them. Mixed with the salt tang were smells of animal dung, oil and unwashed humanity which made me feel nauseous. Towering above the wharf was the arch built by Trajan. On top were bronze statues of the old emperor himself on horseback, his wife Plotina and sister Marciana, Aegius informed me. He didn't know who the other horseman was.

Away from the wharf stretched shipyards, but many of the berths were empty and their timbers rotting.

'Not the navy yard of previous times,' Aegius said. 'But it's still an important port as an entry to Italia proper.' He pointed to the steep hill behind the port. 'That's the Temple of Venus Euplea, the patron of seafarers. She doesn't seem to be very effective against the pirates though. Maybe the temple the Christos followers have built next to it is putting her off.'

We'd packed up our tent, mattresses and eating and drinking vessels, and stood ready to disembark. We dodged in between the porters unloading the cargo and stepped onto the wharf into the noise and smell.

'Move!' A furious driver of an enormous four-wheel cart was thundering straight towards us.

'Quick! Run for the colonnade,' Aegius cried out.

We raced across the stone wharf and gained the shelter of a colonnade in front of a row of red-tile roofed buildings.

'Pluto take that driver!' I said dropping my bags and catching my breath. 'Is there no harbour master here to control such maniacs?'

'He'll crash into somebody's cargo bales making them fall into the sea, then you'll see him shout,' Aegius said. Just as he finished, a patrol came into view bearing down on the offending driver and his cart. 'Come on, ladies, let's get away from here in case there's a fight.'

Aegius led us towards the grand arch at the end of the wharf and into the town. The streets were narrow, lined with multiple-storey apartment blocks, most with enclosed wooden balconies hanging over the street almost touching those on the other side. Even in the afternoon sunshine the street was dark. We walked on gravel with some paving here and there, but all covered in piles of rubbish. People rushed past, some with bales on a yoke slung across their shoulders, others pushing handcarts or carrying canvas bags bulging with goods. And everywhere stank of dirt, unwashed people and urine.

'Gods, Aegius, is all the town like this?'

'No, *domina*, but we wanted to disappear. Rough as it is round here, we should be able to shake off anybody following us. Don't worry, we'll find somewhere to stay at least half reasonable.'

We turned into another street lined with equally tall *insulae*, but far fewer rickety balconies; some even had plants in containers on them. The street rose gradually with more paving and steps. Five minutes later, we came across an open door through which we could see a small courtyard. A plaque on the wall proclaimed the marvellous benefits of the establishment and prices. The murals on the street showed trees and animals, with amphorae and bunches of grapes dotted around.

Aegius ran his eyes over them.

'Not very well executed, but at least they're not erotic. The innkeeper may be a follower of Christos. They tend not to have explicit decorations.'

'Will we be safe?' I said.

'It looks clean enough and I can't smell anything rotting.' He gave Asella and me a serious look. 'If it *is* run by Galileans, you will have to be careful not to mention any of the true gods. We can put up with it for a night or two. It may be a good disguise for us. Just follow their lead if they start any of their rituals.'

Inside, the courtyard was small with only two stalls for horses, now empty, and a few pots of plants just coming into bloom. Walls with regular windows rose on three sides giving shade to most of it. A woman came down two steps of an entrance doorway. She was covered neck to ankle and down to her wrists in a plain beige linen dress drawn in at the waist with a simple leather belt. Apart from a pair of sandals on her feet, the only other thing she wore was a fixed smile which looked as if it had been pinned onto her face.

'*Salve*,' she said. 'Welcome in the Christos' name. You are seeking accommodation?' Her voice carried a note of surprise.

'We are indeed, *domina*,' Aegius said. 'I am seeking somewhere respectable for my wife and daughter.'

'There are no mistresses or ladies here,' the woman replied sharply. 'We are all equal in this house.'

'Ah, of course. Forgive me. Whom do I have the pleasure of addressing?'

'Therasia. And you are?'

'Tullius Ferrantius, painter and artist.' Aegius waved his hand towards us. 'My wife, Serena, and daughter, Placida.'

She looked us up and down, pausing on our breeches and boots.

'You are travelling far?'

'To painting commissions in Spoletium and Asculum.'

'I see.' She pursed her lips.

'Nothing unbecoming, I assure you, or I would not bring my family.'

Gods, Aegius was working hard to convince this prim woman we were acceptable. I would have bid her good day and found somewhere else, but he was right. Nobody could think of looking for us in such a house.

She showed us to a simple room with a bed large enough for two. The covered chamber pot in the corner didn't smell and the chair and row of pegs on the wall looked sturdy enough. On a little triangular table in the corner were two candle holders.

'I'll bring you a mattress for your daughter on the floor,' Therasia said. 'We eat at the tenth hour. You may join us, if you wish. I will add it to your bill.'

'Thank you, Therasia,' I said. She looked at me, then glanced at Aegius and back to me. 'One last thing,' I added. 'Where are the nearest baths?'

'I thought she was going to eat you when you thanked her,' Asella said as we walked back from the baths an hour later. Luckily, we'd been in time for the women's session even though part of the facilities were closed.

'She looked at me as if I needed permission from Aegius to speak,' I said. 'And after all that "we're all equal" talk!'

'Well, it's only for a night or two, *domina*.'

'I know, Asella. But isn't it glorious to be clean? It wasn't like the warm springs at Santicum, but then…' I shrugged. 'That was a different world and I'm glad to have left it.' I smiled at Asella. 'But the water here was so clean and inviting.'

'Let's hope the dinner is the same,' she replied.

We'd both changed into simple tunics to go to the baths as it was a warm evening, and it made a welcome change from our travelling clothes. Even if you paid a bath slave to watch your clothes, you couldn't be certain somebody hadn't stolen them when you went to get dressed afterwards. Losing a tunic would be embarrassing, but nothing as disastrous as losing my cloak with my jewellery and gold *solidi*.

Back in our room, we found Aegius dozing on the bed. He sat up as we entered.

'Better?'

'Much,' I replied. 'I feel relaxed enough to go to sleep now. Unfortunately, my stomach doesn't agree.'

Aegius laughed. Even Asella smiled.

In Therasia's kitchen where *cena* was served, we met her son who said little, and two other travellers who didn't stop talking. The food was laid out – the smell of freshly baked bread was tantalising – but Aegius frowned at me as I lifted my hand to take a portion. Therasia was looking at me, her lips tight. I brought my hand back to my lap.

'We thank our Lord Jesus Christos for this simple meal and ask his blessing on our house,' she intoned. Then followed several minutes of more prayers. *When* would she finish? As soon as she had, she gestured to us to start. Aegius took the loaf and broke off pieces for Asella and me. After that, we helped ourselves to *puls*, vegetables and inevitably fish. Aegius made conversation when he could with the two men and laughed politely at their dreadfully weak jokes, but Asella and I said little.

At the end, we rose together and retreated to the corridor.

'You two go back to the bedroom and rest,' Aegius said in a low voice. 'I'm going out with the pair of jokers.'

'What? Why? They look like idiots,' I said, looking out of the door to the courtyard where the two travellers were still laughing and waving to Aegius to join them.

'Agreed, but they'll give me cover while I find out where to get horses for our ride to R— our destination. I'll try and steer them to the baths first,' he said. 'I might find a contact there.'

To be truthful, I was exhausted and Asella looked no better. On the ship, I had relaxed, knowing nobody would be following us and Aegius would only have a small area to patrol in order to protect us. That blond man had given me a scare, but that was only for a few moments. And he had gone. But back on land, we were in the open. Anybody could find us.

I woke to the sound of clattering and shouting. Daylight leaked around the edge of the window. I eased myself out of the bed, careful not to tread on Aegius sleeping on the mattress on the floor, and opened the shutters. A man standing by the closed entrance gate – the porter, I presumed – was shouting at a girl in a ragged tunic who was throwing his harsh words back at him in a shrill tone and brandishing her broom at him. She dipped down, seized her bucket and lobbed it at him. He ducked and it hit the door. Therasia came rushing out looking furious. She glanced in my direction, flushed, then crisply commanded the two servants to be silent and get back to their duties. The man tilted his head up at the girl who stuck her tongue out at him. That earned her a slap from Therasia. Then all three turned their backs to each other and went about their business.

'What's going on?' Asella yawned loudly.

'Nothing special. Servants quarrelling,' I replied. But I felt sorry for Therasia who had looked mortified.

At breakfast, she placed eggs, *puls,* olive oil with fragrant herbs and bread on the table and filled cups with watered wine. She hovered around, bringing fresh fruit and a bowl of nuts as soon as we had finished the rest. I'd been hungry again – Asella said it was the babe growing inside me – but even I felt full after such a good breakfast.

'I must apologise for the disturbance this morning,' Therasia said, her cheeks pink again. 'This is an orderly house used to giving our guests peace and tranquillity.'

'Please don't concern yourself, Therasia,' Aegius said and gave her a warm smile.

'Both have been reprimanded.' She sighed. 'They've all been unruly since I freed them.' She looked up. 'If you stay another night, there will be no charge.'

Aegius placed the core of his apple in his empty bowl.

'We may have to take up your kind offer as I couldn't find any contact for reliable horses or even mules for our onward journey. I'll go out this morning and have another try.'

'Ah, I may be able to help you,' Therasia said seeming to cheer up. 'My brother-in-law runs a stable on the southern edge of town. He's fond of the bottle, but my sister keeps him in line.' She turned and shouted. 'Bolcus!'

A boy around ten or eleven, dark-haired and skinny, ran in through the back door and came to a halt by our table.

'Fetch me a tablet and my stylus.'

He was back within seconds. She opened it and started scratching her message. Once finished, she snapped the two halves together and fastened the string.

'Take this to Mermelus, but also tell my sister you have delivered an urgent message for me.'

The boy nodded and vanished.

'He's very reliable,' Therasia said. 'We'll probably have an answer within an hour or so. He'll hang around by Mermelus's side and wait, doing his best to look like a starving mongrel. My sister will feed him and then he'll ask for more when he gets back. Boys.' She sighed.

Therasia proved correct. She must have had enough force of personality to exert effective influence on her brother-in-law. Just after an hour and a half, the boy was back, grinning and mounted on a horse far too big for him. With him were two other riders, each leading two further horses. Therasia stood in the courtyard, her arms across her chest and her eyes gleaming.

'Not bad, Mermelus,' she said.

'Humph,' the first adult rider behind Bolcus said. 'Well, sister-in-law, I hope these guests of yours treat my horses properly. I will expect them to be in Fulminius's stables in Nuceria for us to collect in seven days. I also expect them to be sound of foot, no saddle sores, no loss of condition. Nuceria's as far as I'm willing to let them go.' He glanced at us.

'Don't agitate yourself, horsemaster,' Aegius said and went forward to greet the largest horse. 'We're used to riding all over the empire, and caring for our mounts. No rider gets very far if he doesn't.' Aegius handed over a small purse of coins. 'I will leave the rest with your sister-in-law for when the horses return.'

What was Aegius thinking of? Therasia could give her relation the balance immediately we'd left. On second thoughts, Therasia was the upright kind and probably wouldn't.

21

Ruthless as ever, Aegius told us to abandon the tent and present it to Therasia.

'But we paid good money for that,' I said.

He shrugged.

'We have no way of carrying it, what with everything else.' He glanced at the saddlebags full of our clothes, the eating bowls and beakers and the provisions Therasia had given us. Our mattresses were tightly rolled and strapped to the back of the saddles Mermelus had provided and our blankets underneath them. The sun was already high in the sky but we had to wear our cloaks as there was nowhere to pack them. Perhaps it would be cooler in the hills.

Mermelus handed Aegius a tablet for his contact Fulminius in Nuceria with a gruff comment that we should get reasonable mounts from him for our onward journey. As we left, Therasia give us a brief wave, then turned back to her door and disappeared.

We left the town and started to climb. We hadn't gone far when I stopped and turned. The sea had disappeared from view. Now we were back in hills, although they didn't rise and fall dramatically like the mountains at home. But the road was good and, to my surprise, busy. We passed merchants leading pack animals and accompanied by guards who gave us looks full of suspicion as we overtook them. Peasants on mules with wicker baskets of vegetables and bottles of something – wine or oil – looked sullen as we went by.

'It's the horses,' Aegius said. 'They're strong, even though they're a bit short of breath. I'm pretty sure they're ex-cavalry mounts. The saddles certainly are.'

'Will people think they're stolen, then?' I replied.

'No, not at all. Mermelus obviously has some kind of, let's call it, an arrangement with the local cavalry commander. It's just that horses usually mean officialdom and therefore trouble.'

'What do you mean?' I'd always ridden a horse, almost always Snowfoot.

'Most people travel by mule, or carriage or wagon or on foot. Horses are for the well off, but *they* normally travel with cartloads of luggage, like Turcilus when we left Virunum. Only imperial or official messengers use horses with light luggage.'

'Do we look out of place then?'

'If we keep to ourselves and don't make too many stops or start gossiping to people,' – he glanced back at Asella – 'we should pass through unremarked.'

We stopped that night at Auximum in a clean but unimpressive inn, but it was gated with a heavy iron bar across the inside. After what Aegius had said about the horses, I was relieved they were so secure. The next morning, we rose at daybreak and set off early. I still worried about Turcilus and urged Aegius to press on.

'We'll go as far as the horses allow us, *domina*. If we ride steadily on with regular stops on the way, we should make Septempeda by nightfall.'

'How do you know this road and these stops, Aegius?'

'I've marched along enough of them when I was younger and ridden along many of the rest as a courier. We always carried a list of the stops along the way – the official ones – and a line sketch with distances. I can remember a fair bit of them now we're here in Italia.' He waved his arm in an expansive gesture. 'This one's a branch of the Via Flaminia. When we get to Nuceria, we join the main one which leads straight to Rome.'

Rome, where Lucius was. Aegius didn't say any more, so we rode on in silence. After an hour out of Auximum and the rolling hill country, the road flattened out onto a plateau, but ever since we'd left Ancona, I'd noticed how fertile the land was. Some farms had been abandoned – roofs had fallen in and weeds and wild shrubs covered what must have once been fields. Others looked busy with fields showing fresh sprouts of new spelt and grass. Fruit trees everywhere were in blossom. If the Apulius farm in Latium was anything like this, they were indeed blessed.

By the time we stopped in a village before midday, the sun was high, and we sheltered under a large fig tree. Aegius took the horses to the river while Asella and I bought dried sausage, apples and bread in the market. I'd left a sweaty cheese offered by a woman with filthy nails – too many flies alighting on it.

When Aegius returned, he ate his share of the food in silence, just grunting now and then between mouthfuls in reply to Asella's chattering. After he'd brushed crumbs from his tunic, he took himself off in the direction of the *caupona* behind the market that I'd spotted earlier. Asella and I had hurried past it when shopping for food as it was full of drunks shouting. I suppose Aegius wanted to fortify himself with some bad wine before moving on. He was a mystery; talented artist, ex-soldier, as I'd learnt now, ex-official courier. But still a man who liked going for a drink.

When he came back he was carrying a long, thin cloth bag. He set it down on the ground then fished out his sword scabbard from his pack and attached it on the other side of his belt from his *pugio*. He drew the sword blade out and examined it, twisted his forearm and jabbed the air.

'Is something wrong?' I asked.

'Yes and no.' He bent down and scooped up the cloth bag.

'Here.' He thrust it at me. 'It's only a short sword, like an old legionary gladius, but you know how to handle one.'

I gave him a steady look.

'Am I likely to need to?'

'Perhaps. From the gossip in the tavern, I heard that the roads in the hills, especially the wooded ones in the steeper valleys, have suffered bandit attacks.'

I opened the bag and hefted the short sword. It was no heavier than the ones I'd used in Virunum in my training, but it was made more roughly. I could still see hammer marks. It looked sharp enough though. I attached the scabbard to my belt. I heard a gurgling sound behind me. Asella's eyes were wide as eggs in a pan.

'You will not be asked to fight, Asella,' Aegius said. 'Just use your knife to defend yourself and make sure the horses don't run off if the *domina* and I are busy.'

'That was heartless,' I said to Aegius as we rode on side by side with Asella trailing behind.

He shrugged.

'I'm being realistic. If we're lucky, she won't panic if she has something definite to do like look after the horses.' He grinned. 'If we're truly lucky, she'll cast one of her spells at any attackers.'

'What? You don't really believe she's a witch?'

'I've seen her look a bit funny at people and they go off as meek as lambs and do what she says, and she *does* know a great deal about herbs and healing.'

'That doesn't make her a witch.' Then I recalled how she'd been able to subdue me after I'd been in the garden with Lucius and the times she'd calmed fights between the servants. I said nothing as we rode on. We climbed steadily, then the road evened out onto a plateau as the sun progressed into the late afternoon. Although we kept a sharp watch on the woods either side of the road and I felt on edge every time the branches loomed over us, nothing happened.

As the sun started to dip, I caught sight of a town sprawled over one of the countless hills slightly to the north. When we turned off the valley road shortly afterwards and climbed up to the tall arched gates set in high walls, I knew we'd reached Septempeda and hopefully a bath and soft bed for our aching limbs. We were to be disappointed. Asella and I were pointed towards a dormitory room where the maid shrugged and assigned us a bed between us which was lumpy even with our mattresses on top and Aegius had to be content with the floor.

The next morning, Aegius announced at breakfast – eaten standing at a street bar – that today could be a slower day as we'd be climbing over the highest part of the Apenninus Mons. None of us had slept well. Septempeda was brimming with people gathering for the Galilean festival of Pentecost when the Christos god's spirit descended on them, but the crowds pushing everywhere didn't seem particularly godly as we wound our way through them to the livery stable where our horses had been quartered overnight. Even they were squeezed in together. I was pleased to be back on my horse and out of the town gate.

'Ah, fresh air!' I said after taking a deep breath. Asella said nothing but scratched herself. I didn't think we'd had bedbugs, but you never knew until the itching started. The road was much better with firm paving for the most part and only giving into gravel in a few places. Aegius told us it was called (unoriginally, I thought) the Via Septempedana which would take us all the way to Nuceria.

We reached Prolaqueum within two hours and crossed its narrow bridge over the Flosis River in single file. Aegius insisted we stop for the horses to drink and graze by the roadside and for us to refill our water from the public fountain. Then we started climbing. I didn't really notice it at first. The hills became steeper, but were still covered in trees. The fields looked the same as they had for the past few days, but our horses started labouring a little. At only an hour out of Prolaqueum, we stopped at a *statio* where we fed and watered the horses again. The manager was a man of little words, but Aegius said his prices were fair enough. His wife gave us small cheese-flavoured pastries and *posca* while we waited.

'We don't have far to go in miles, but we'll have to take it gently with these beasts,' Aegius said as he patted his mount's neck.

'Will they make it?' I looked at mine who didn't seem out of breath now. I supposed they were lowland horses, but if they were ex-cavalry, they should be sturdy enough for these hills.

'They've probably had a hard life, but as we're not likely to be making any cavalry charges, they're perfectly capable of getting us to Nuceria well before the guards close the gates at sunset.'

The road rose up the side of the valley and back into trees as the passes between hills became higher. We'd seen a few travellers between Prolaqueum and the *mansio* at Dubios, but none since the *statio* where we'd fed the horses. I didn't worry as I was relishing the clarity of the air and the curving hills. Early June was a perfect time for riding through such beautiful countryside. Secure in my saddle and lulled by the scent of wild shrubs bordering the road, I sometimes even dozed in the warm air. We would be back in a proper town soon with all its bustle where I'd probably complain about the noise and smell. I smiled to myself. As long as we reached Rome before Turcilus could find us, I wouldn't care about any discomfort.

They fell on us when the sun was at its height, pouring through the trees and down the hillside and shouting incomprehensible war cries.

At first, the horses snorted, their ears back and eyes rolling at the surprise. Aegius reacted immediately and thrust his sword straight into the bearded face of the leader. The body dropped onto the ground, causing a cloud of dust to billow up.

Aegius twisted the *spatha* and wrenched it out of the body, then swung it to cut the next wild man. I had my gladius out by then and jabbed it into the side of the neck of one trying to unseat Asella. Blood spurted out in a fountain. Before I could do anything else, a blow to my middle almost knocked me off my horse.

Gods! My child. I gasped at the power of the anger that rolled up through me. They were attacking my babe. I wanted to destroy anybody, anything in front of me.

I swung round and slashed wildly. My arm jarred as my sword hit solid flesh. A grunt and he fell back. I gave my horse a hard kick with my heels. He sprang forward, knocking another man aside. The attacker fell, then screamed as my mount's hind foot caught him – somewhere fragile, I prayed. He deserved no less.

Back at Asella's side, a woman with long greasy hair had grabbed Asella's mount's saddlebags and was attempting to pull them off. I brought my sword down hard on the woman's forearm. She howled and covered the slash with her other hand. Asella had her knife out along with her fiercest stare. She gripped one of the front horns of her saddle with her other hand, drew her foot back and kicked the woman so hard that she fell as Asella shrieked a curse at her. The woman's eyes widened. She stared, terrified at Asella, then turned and ran off.

I caught my breath for a second. Then something stung my arm. The attacker's face and most of his head was covered, but I caught sight of a few strands of curling hair escaping from his bonnet. Eyes full of hatred. Instinctively, I jabbed hard and he fell back.

He shook his fist at me, shouted to the two others still standing and they fled into the woods.

'*Domina*?' Aegius, breathing hard, was by me. 'Is all well?' He studied my face.

'Yes, yes.' I looked up at him. 'No. I have killed. Oh gods, what have I done?' I shuddered, then burst into hysterical sobbing. All strength drained from me. Asella reached out from her saddle and put her arm round my shoulders.

'No, *domina*, you have acted as your father's daughter – full of fire and defending others. Weep now and gain release.' She held me tight until I calmed. Aegius passed me a leather bottle of water. I drank heartily, but just about remembered to pause now and again. Lucius had said it was a good way to survive and recover. Asella gave me a cloth to wipe the sweat from my face and blood from my arm. She fished in her satchel and brought out a long, thin cloth which she tied round my arm wound.

'Asella, will the babe be well?' I was afraid to ask her, but I had to know.

She glanced at Aegius for an instant then back at me.

'The child is but tiny and well protected by your body,' she said in a calm tone. 'You need to eat and rest. Then we will see.' I fixed my gaze on her, but she looked away and busied herself with packing up her cloths and tidying herself.

'Let's carry on to the next village as we are and find a safe spot to clean up properly,' Aegius said after a few minutes.

'What about the bodies?' I said. Five inert figures, arms and legs sprawled, lay across the road.

'I suppose we'll have to clear the road, but we'll just roll them into the side,' Aegius said. 'We're not going to waste time burying such rubbish. We'll take their weapons though.'

And that was how we rode into the next *statio* loaded with swords, knives and cudgels and looking as if we were a war band. Aegius gave the *statio* manager some coins and mentioned the five bodies as he also handed over most of the weapons we'd collected. He kept a couple of knives and one of the swords. He held it up in the sunlight.

'Well, that's interesting. This one is Noricum steel.'

'Are you sure?' I asked.

'I think I know one when I see one.' I frowned at him, but before I could say anything, he swiftly continued. 'I apologise, *domina*,' he said. 'I didn't mean to snap. But as you know, our blades are distinctive, expensive and the envy of the world. I have to ask myself how a group of ragged bandits came by such a thing.'

'Stolen, I'd think.'

'Yes, it must have been. Nobody who owned such a sword would let anybody take it off them easily, let alone give it away or sell it. This one has the mark of your father's foundry just under the handle guard.'

He said no more, just grunted and led his mount to the stable.

As I watered my own horse, and rested my hand on his warm flank, I marvelled how after the initial shock of the attack, he'd stayed calm yet responsive during the whole fight. He was indeed a champion of cavalry horses. As I rubbed the horse down and murmured words of reassurance to both of us and praise to him, I pushed Aegius's remark about the sword to the back of my mind.

Nuceria Camellaria, to give it its proper name, was noisy with narrow streets, but lay in the valley near a small river, the Tinia. At the gate, Aegius fended off nosy enquiries from a customs official who seemed happy to take a few coins instead of rummaging through our albeit meagre baggage. We were tired, sweaty and desperate to eat and sleep. My middle was sore and Asella's words after the fight had not reassured me one whit.

We found Mermelus's contact, Fulminius, and said goodbye to our horses. He promised to have fresh mounts for us in the morning and gave us a recommendation for accommodation for the night. As I stumbled after Aegius up the *decumanus maximus* to the inn with a silent Asella by my side, I didn't care at that moment if the stable owner gave us broken down mules.

When I came back from the baths, my arm started to bleed again. I tore the edge off one of my longer undertunics and wound the strip of cloth round my arm.

'We'll keep an eye on that, *domina*.' Asella fussed around me.

'It'll heal quickly enough,' I said. 'It's only a shallow cut.' It was starting to feel sore but all cuts and wounds did that. And I'd made sure to rinse it in the clear water of the fountain after we'd left the bath. It would be better in the morning. I flicked my fingers at her. She meant well, but she'd do better to keep her salves for Aegius's bruises. After our meal, I fell into bed and was asleep instantly.

Hours later, I woke, hot and dry. I threw the sheet and blanket off and grappled for my water bottle. The room was incredibly stuffy, but I felt too tired to get up and open the shutter. My arm was sore, but all I wanted was a drink. I must have dozed off because the next thing I saw was Asella's face hovering over me and a freezing cold cloth on my forehead. I tried to move my arms and legs, but they felt as heavy as lead. My heart was pounding and pouring pain into my arm.

'Asella,' I croaked.

'Lie still, *domina*.' She opened my lips with two fingers and poured a little liquid into my mouth. It was foul, bitter. I wanted to retch. She poured more, so I had to swallow, or drown.

'Your arm has become infected. I've tied a poultice on it of plantago and mallow I found by the roadside to draw out the poison, but I must go and find something to reduce your fever. The willow bark infusion will stop it hurting so much, but I must hurry.' She wiped my face and arms, then my ankles, with the wet cloth. 'Aegius will sit with you while I'm gone.'

All I heard after that was urgent whispering. I was too befuddled to work out what they were saying but I heard Asella say 'die'. Then everything went black.

22

Somebody was pulling my arm off. No, hacking it off with a blunt knife. I screamed. Then I smelt burning flesh. The cold cloth on my head. Vile drink forced down my throat again. Different, but vile. Something dripping down my face. Then I knew no more.

Humming, Asella humming as when I had been a child. I opened my eyes, blinked and turned my head. It was dark. Asella sat on a stool, chanting something as she twisted a string of beads. A candle flame flickered on a table at the side. A beaker by the candle holder. I reached for it and gasped when I rolled onto my arm.

'Thank the gods!' Asella bent over me. Her face was grey and she looked a hundred years old. She rolled me back onto my spine, then put her arm under my shoulders and brought the beaker to my lips. The liquid tasted mostly of honey but it didn't disguise the bitter taste from the previous drink.

'Asella,' I whispered, 'what happened?' I glanced round slowly.

'You're safe, *domina*. And now you've come back to us.'

Tears glistened on her cheeks. I marvelled at them. I couldn't recall I had ever seen her cry before. Another figure emerged from the darkness – Aegius.

'You have no idea how annoying this woman has been flapping around fussing over you.' He gave me a stern look. 'I thought for a while I was going to have to explain to Prince Bacausus that his darling daughter had expired in the middle of nowhere.' But his eyes were glistening. 'Welcome back,' he said, taking my good hand.

Aegius sent Asella to rest and settled himself on the bedside chair.

'I have to give you drink from the jug every four hours. It's some witches' brew Asella has made up from yarrow and calendula, she says, disguised with spoonfuls of honey. That wretched satchel she hugs to herself all the time turns out to be full of useful herbs. She says you can drink or eat whatever you feel like having now.'

'I could eat anything available, but first tell me what happened.'

'That wound of yours blew up like an unmilked goat's udder. Asella put a poultice on it, but in the end, I went up to the military *castra* and rousted out the *medicus*. Bit of a grumpy sod, but he was good. He lanced the wound, drained the pus and cauterised it. He even praised Asella's poultice and her brew, but you'll have to wear half a dozen fancy bracelets to cover the scar from now on.'

'Juno! Why did it swell so much? I've had cuts and scratches my whole life and nothing like that.'

'What was the water in the baths like?'

'Clear like a mountain stream. In fact, I asked why, and the slave said it had only been cleaned and refilled this morning.'

'Yesterday morning, you mean. You've been in bed a day and a night.'

I stared at him.

'Have I been very bad?' I asked in a quiet voice.

'Quite poorly.' Which I interpreted as being extremely ill.

'So what caused this?' I pointed to my bandaged arm.

'My best guess? Something nasty on the bandit's weapon.'

'You mean poison.'

'It could have been something simple like dog turd, but Asella said there was a funny smell coming off your breath. I'm sure she recognised it, but she won't say anything.'

I let that sink in.

'But that would mean it was deliberate and they weren't just ordinary bandits.' My stomach clenched. 'Turcilus wouldn't do that, however humiliated he felt. Would he?'

179

'No, I put him as the type who might whip you if he caught you, but he wouldn't do anything as underhand as try to poison you.'

The idea of Turcilus trying to whip me almost made me laugh. Almost. I tried to sit up, but Aegius caught me as I fell back.

'We must push on,' I said. 'We've lost a whole day.'

'Not until you can travel without the risk of falling off your horse.'

'Then tie me on it.'

He snorted.

'Rest now until morning,' he said. 'Then we'll see how you are.'

My arm was sore, but when I saw light coming from the edge of the shutters, not a candle, my overwhelming feeling was hunger. I reached over to the table by my bed and took a draught of Asella's honey-flavoured medicine which was refreshing, but not in any way sustaining.

After a minute, I swung my legs off the bed and stood up. My middle ached but my head was clear. Below the window was a small chest where I found a basin of clean water and a linen cloth, so I washed my face and uninjured arm. I stood still for a moment and caught my breath. Next, I changed my tunic and put on the rest of my riding clothes.

'*Domina*?' A voice from the bundle of blankets on the bed next to mine.

'Peace, Asella. Stay and rest. I'm going to look for something to eat.'

She struggled up.

'You shouldn't be out of your bed,' she said sharply, now fully awake.

'I'll be careful, but if I don't eat something soon, I *will* faint.'

'It's the baby pulling on you.'

'Gods, will it have been harmed?'

'I don't think so. You haven't bled, not even after that blow to your middle, so I don't think you've miscarried.' Her voice wasn't as assured as it could have been. But my stomach was growling now and I left the room and crept down the corridor to the inn's kitchen.

Aegius found me in the kitchen where I was devouring bread

dipped in olive oil, and cheese. I reached for an apple, then caught sight of him in the doorway.

He glanced at the kitchen maid who was stirring something in a pot on the fire then brought his gaze back to me.

'I'm delighted to see you well, *Daughter*,' he said. 'Perhaps you would like to take a walk around the town after your morning rest.'

'I'm very well, thank you, *Father*, but I would prefer to take a ride on my horse.' I glared at him.

'Understandable, but I don't think you are recovered sufficiently.'

Gods, now he was acting the pompous Roman father for the maid's benefit. I stood, apple in hand.

'I am returning to the room to see Mother.'

'I will accompany you,' he said. He turned to the maid and said in his most affable voice, 'Thank you for looking after my daughter.'

The maid opened her mouth, closed it then briefly bowed her head in acknowledgement. I stalked out to the courtyard.

'You are in no condition for a gruelling day's ride,' Aegius said as he caught up with me.

'Truly? And who are you to know how I'm feeling?'

'Because I am not an idiot, but somebody who's seen more battle wounds than you've eaten bowls of *puls*. You feel well for an hour and then the wound starts to throb, you run a fever, the wound inflames and you're out for a week.'

Why was it that these 'wise counsellors' were always right, but always so self-satisfied with it? I sighed.

'Can't we even go a short distance? We've lost a day already and back in Santicum you said we'd be only two days ahead of Turcilus. I promise on my honour that I will ask to stop if I can't go on.' I looked at him in the way I used to look at my true father when I wanted him to agree to a request.

'Don't try that look on me!' Aegius snorted. He rubbed the back of his neck. 'But you're right. We can't afford to waste any more time. But I don't want to deliver a corpse or near corpse to your tribune.' He gave me a steady look. 'Now we're joining the Via Flaminia proper we'll be on a better, faster road. We'll aim for Forum Flaminii today. It's where the road splits into western and eastern routes. The east is an easier road, especially for carts and carriages, but it's slower than the west which is hillier, but quicker for horses and mules.'

'We'll take the west,' I said.

'But only if you can go on.'

I nodded, then smiled to myself.

It was an easy ride on the fresh horses provided by Fulminius. He'd given us a token and letter for his correspondent in Rome itself. We followed the Tinia down its valley along a well-paved road which was busier than any we had seen for days. Even a troop of cavalry rode past us at full tilt, although the traffic was mostly merchants with mules or farmers in deathly slow ox-drawn wagons.

Aegius instructed Asella to bind my forearm to my body with a wide sash around my waist to stop the wound being jolted. I'm sure both of them thought riding with only one free hand would slow me down, but I had done that since I was a child. They meant the best for me, so I said nothing. Besides, resting my hand on my body where I could protect my growing babe reassured me as we jogged along.

We reached Forum Flaminii before midday and rested the horses. As he helped me down, Aegius studied my face. I gave him my best smile. My arm was sore but not throbbing, for which I was much relieved.

Asella went to buy provisions while we watered the animals. She came back with three peasants' straw hats.

'Don't laugh,' she said sternly. 'You'll be glad of them soon enough.'

As we continued on to Mevania, the hills had become a mere line on the horizon and the sun was indeed strong. I was sweating under my tunic. Gods, I hoped the fever wasn't returning but Asella's cheeks were red and even Aegius had a sheen of sweat on his forehead and dark patches on his tunic underarms. We stopped and ate in the square at Mevania – it could hardly be called a forum – but we could shelter in the shade of the houses for half an hour. All of them were shuttered against the sun, but some looked neglected to the point of crumbling roofs. A skinny dog crossed to us, but Asella shooed it away.

'Now you need to make a decision, *domina*,' Aegius said, sitting with his eyes shut on a stone bench and leaning back against a wall. 'The next stop I know about is Vicus Martis. It's a small settlement – one street of houses crossed by one other and that's it. It's mostly somewhere for the local farmers to quarrel about their pigs and get drunk, but it used to have an excellent *mansio* – clean and well run. It's several years ago so of course, it could have all changed.'

'How long will it take us?' I asked.

'Well, we have to go up and down some hills and the road winds round others…'

'Yes, but could we make it by sundown?'

'We could, if—'

I jumped up.

'Well, let's get on, then.'

When we eventually reached a hamlet which Aegius said was indeed Vicus Martis, I was almost falling off my horse with fatigue. And my arm had started to throb – something I would rather have died before admitting to Aegius. We'd been up and down so many hills they blurred into one. My head was full of the smell of olive flowers and leaves, my sight blurred by endless fields of growing wheat and spelt. To my relief, for the last few miles, the road had been flat and straight.

'Sorry, but there aren't any sleeping rooms. Had to close them down a couple of years ago as nobody wanted them any longer,' the middle-aged man behind the entrance said. We were standing in the street at a bar counter in front of a large building. The wide wooden shutter above it gave us shade but was held up by a length of fraying rope that looked as if it would break and crash down on us at any moment. To the side were a few tables under a vine-covered *pergula*, but only a man even older than the one in front of us was sitting there. His long tunic in coarse cloth was as worn as the barman's. He squinted at us from his corner. He lifted his hand and beckoned to us.

'Tie up your horses on the ring and talk to me,' his thin voice croaked.

I exchanged glances with Aegius who shrugged and did as he

was asked. Asella and I no choice but to follow but we sat at the next table. If Aegius wanted to gossip, then I was grateful to be off my horse. I signalled the first man to fetch us something to drink. He looked at the older man who nodded.

'Well, young man, what are you doing with two women travelling alone on the Flaminia?'

I suppressed a laugh, but I suppose that Aegius would have seemed like a young man to the ancient one.

'I'm travelling to Rome with my wife and daughter, sir. I am an artist, a painter of murals mostly, and hope to find work there.'

'Humph. Well, there are still enough rich men there to pay for it, but mosaics are more favoured. Good luck to you.' But I caught the cynical look in his eyes.

'Thank you. But for the moment, my women are exhausted, as are the horses. Can I persuade you to intervene with the barman to open up a room for us?'

Aegius slid some silver coins across the table. The ancient man covered them with his hand, skeletal with overlapping folds of skin on the back.

'He's my son.' He raised a hand and called, 'Cordus, find the key to the room along the corridor from mine. And three mattresses. And see to them horses and all.' He turned to Aegius. 'We sold the best beds and used the rest for firewood.'

'Has the passing trade been so poor, then?'

'We lost the imperial mandate to Carsulae, so we get no officials staying or eating here, and no income for providing hay and water for their animals. The commercial trade goes to Carsulae as well as the market there thrives. No merchant is going to stay here when he can be right on top of his potential customers there. In my young day, the legions marched here regularly, imperial post wagons thundered along and there were good pickings from other travellers. It's all finished now.'

The rabbit stew was well cooked, flavoured with herbs and wild mushrooms. Asella had noticed a vegetable garden and a chicken yard with a few scrawny hens from the window of our bare room when we'd dropped our things there. The stable block was empty apart from our three horses in a yard built for tens of wagons and their animals.

'They're managing, but only just,' she said to me when she came back with water for washing. 'There's only a single young woman in the kitchen – no other help. I reckon she's Cordus's daughter as she resembles the old man. She was perfectly happy for me to fill my bowl myself from the pot over the fire.'

'Not even a slave for the cleaning or outdoors?'

'Not that I could see.'

'Then they are indeed poor. I suppose it's not worth trying to sell this place and move to a smaller house where they could be more comfortable.'

'I don't know anything about selling inns, but I shouldn't think anybody would buy it with no prospect of guests.'

'That's so sad, Asella.'

'It's the times, *domina*. The rich become richer while the poor fall downwards, often thrown off land their family has farmed for generations. Or they turn to banditry in order to eat. People like Cordus's family, and Florus and Crispus back in Fons Timavi, are caught in the middle.'

'My father said that things were better now under Valentinian.'

'Not the roads, as you've seen. Nor the buildings.' She looked out of the window. Her eyes were unfocused as if she was seeing something in the distance. 'It's falling apart. Not quickly, but surely.' She closed her eyes and stayed completely still for several heartbeats.

'Asella?' I touched her shoulder. She spun round. Her face was white as a shroud. She shook herself.

'Great goddess, what on earth came over me?' she said. 'Come along now, *domina*. Let me look at your wound. I'm sure it needs a fresh dressing.'

I stretched out my arm, balancing my wrist on the edge of the window. She set about unwinding, examining and applying a clean bandage to my arm in her usual brisk manner, but she didn't say another word before we went to sleep on mattresses in an inn on the edge of its existence.

23

As we approached the great gate leading us into Carsulae, I realised how steeply we had climbed; the view was spectacular. We dismounted and led the animals under the arch of the gate where the Flaminia became the town's *cardo maximus*. At the forum, it crossed the main street, the *decumanus maximus*. I marvelled at the high buildings, the twin temples and the sheer numbers of people in the street. The *cardo maximus* itself was wide with gutters. With the raised pavements on both sides of the road, you could easily walk between shops without treading in slops or animal dung. Civilisation indeed. And those shops were alluring…

'We can't stop and gawk like fancy tourists, *domina*.' Aegius flattened my impulse to inspect the beautiful pottery, cloth and mouth-watering selections of fruit and olives. 'Nor visit the baths – sorry.'

'But we have to eat, surely?' I couldn't help it – I was ravenous all the time now. I wasn't starting to show. I calculated it wasn't quite three moons since my last courses – but the babe was making its presence known by emptying my stomach.

'Asella can buy some bread and sausage at one of the stalls on the way out of the town.' His answer was short, but he was busy finding a way through the crowded street. A porter with a handcart almost ran into Aegius and received a loud curse of military proportions in return. Two women, one in yellow embroidered in red, the other in green, with a servant trailing behind them, were so busy chattering that they stepped off the pavement and glared when they were faced with the solid presence of my horse.

'Oh,' one shrieked. 'Tribespeople! Out of our way, peasant.'

'You mistake yourselves,' I said in my best imperial Latin accent, then stuck my head in the air, ignoring their protests. At that precise moment, my horse chose to relieve his bowels at their feet accompanied by a noxious burst of wind.

When we reached a quieter part of the town, we stopped by a fountain and refilled our water bottles and let the horses drink at the trough. It was only the fourth hour and it was already warm. Well, it *was* near the ides of June.

'A pity about your encounter,' Aegius said, eying me as he drank. 'They'll remember it if anybody enquires about us. Not just the horses, but your perfect speech. You'd have done better to have lowered your eyes and spoken with a peasant's accent.'

'They were arrogant and had nothing to be arrogant about. Their clothes were cheap as was the paint on their faces. And no Bacausa apologises to that sort of woman.'

'Yes, I know, but we're trying to be inconspicuous, if you remember?'

Although I felt warmth growing on my face, I didn't lower my gaze from his.

'I apologise, but I think they are too empty-headed to remember.'

'You may have a point,' he replied. 'All the same…' He shrugged. 'Well, let's get on,' and he swung himself up on his horse.

When the sun was high above us, we entered a wide plain. The wooded hills and slopes brimming with olives were now far behind us. I was so grateful to Asella for the sun hat. Fields of vines stretched either side of us, alternating with fruit trees and hayfields, and we made good time. As we approached Narni, the hills loomed again in the distance and I could see a pair of steep inclines forming a high gorge. I was hot and tired.

'Don't tell me we're going to have to climb up there,' I said. 'I thought we were crossing a river.'

Aegius chuckled.

'Don't worry, we *will* be crossing the river, but on one of the highest bridges that the Divine Augustus built. Probably best not to look over the edge though.'

I glanced back at Asella, but I don't think she'd heard. I only hoped the Divine Augustus's bridge was still sound after hundreds of years. In the end, I need not have worried. Although patched up with a mix of stone and cement and interspersed with gaps, the parapet was sound. And we had much to occupy us as we negotiated the mule trains, other horse riders and wagons crossing at the same time. When we had all but stopped behind an ox-drawn wagon that plodded at the pace of one inch at a time, I glanced through the gap down towards the river. The Nar below was like a tiny grey ribbon. This bridge wasn't a mere bridge, but a viaduct for the strategically important Flaminia.

I blinked hard as I took a breath to steady that feeling of dizziness and attraction you felt when standing on top of a high place. Why did people have a fleeting desire to throw themselves off and see what happened? No one could survive a fall from here. Then the ox cart started moving again.

Inevitably, we started climbing again, this time through the town of Narni itself. The tall *insulae* blocks with their symmetrical windows gave way to a forum at the top of the town with a breathtaking view over the dark green hills to the south. We let the horses drink at the trough by the fountain. A few people drifted between the shops under the arches at the edge of the forum, but I was struck by the cluster of soldiers in one corner.

'Probably a *caupona* for drinking. It's a military town, after all.' Aegius swept his arm round the countryside in front of us. 'You can see anything and everything from here and guarding the Flaminia is crucial given the Goths' habit of using our roads to invade.'

'Surely not here in the heart of Italia?'

'Nobody and nothing is safe these days, *domina*.' He snorted. 'If it ever was. Our whole history is full of barbarians sacking our cities.'

'But we always fight back and punish them.'

'Not sure we have the power to do that now.'

'That's what Lucius told me in Virunum,' I replied in a low voice.

'Cheer up, *domina*. With the gods favouring us, we should reach

Rome itself and its high walls the day after tomorrow,' Aegius said. I was watching Asella buying food at one of the little shops while we talked, but his comment brought my attention back sharply.

Rome. And Lucius. My hand went to my stomach almost by instinct. There was no fluttering of new life yet – Asella said it would be several weeks yet – but my heart started beating faster as I took in Aegius's words.

We rested and ate our bread and cheese in a clearing at the side of the road just outside the town. We were still on the high ridge that Narni dominated, so it was relatively cool. The horses seemed content to graze on the short grass. As I sat and chewed the coarse brown bread, I studied the steep gorge of the Nar River in front of us. The dark, brooding green seemed both magnificent and malignant. I shook my head to clear it. I was tired, that was all.

An hour after we'd climbed on our horses, we were back on an open plain. Not long afterwards we were sweating up a hill, but it was a gentle climb and we made good time. Nevertheless, I would have given anything to have stepped down from my horse. Surely, we must be approaching Ocriculum, our next stop, soon.

'Look, *domina*.' Aegius was pointing westwards towards the path of the sun that had started to dip in the sky. Crossing the plain before us in grand curves was a wide river, shining in a patchwork of greens of every hue. I pulled the brim of my hat down and squinted into the distance. 'That's the Tiber, the great river of Rome.'

I stared at it. At its mouth lay my heart's love. I wanted to gallop straight to its banks and swim my way to Rome. Impossible, but for the first time, after trailing up and down the interminable hills and plains, it struck me that my journey's destination might truly have an end. The dream was going to become a reality.

Clean water, river-fresh, flowed over my skin. I looked up and round at the colourful, shining mosaics and paintings on the walls of the baths. Ocriculum truly was the gateway to Elysium. I closed my eyes for a moment and dipped under the surface again for a few seconds. When I re-emerged, Asella was waiting with a large linen towel.

'I've never seen anything like it,' she said. 'Especially the strange hexagonal room – it's almost decadent.'

I laughed, but she was right. An attendant told us the baths had not long been refurbished and extended with extra treatment rooms. Asella was proficient at massaging and oiling my skin, but the slave masseur here had the strongest and most effective fingers I'd experienced. He found every knot in every muscle in my body. I insisted Asella join me, but I noticed that the girl who massaged her was more lenient.

'At least we won't enter Rome stiff and limping like two filthy old crones,' I said as I dressed afterwards. My hair was still damp, but it would dry naturally in the warm evening air.

'Speak for yourself, *domina*,' Asella retorted. She made out she was old, plain and tired but she wasn't. She was in her fifty-first year, but her face was that of a woman in her late thirties and her hair was a mixture of brown and red as well as grey. After weeks in the fresh air and the exercise of riding each day, her skin had a healthy tone.

'Do you regret coming with me?' I asked and studied her face to gauge her reply.

'My old bones are sure it was a foolish idea—'

'Oh, Asella!' Juno, had I caused her real harm? I swallowed hard. I shouldn't have asked her.

'I was teasing, *domina*.' She gave me a broad smile. 'You should see your face.'

'You're impossible.'

'No, I stand in your mother's place and it would have indeed been impossible not to have come with you.' She rested her gaze on my face for a moment, then bent down and gathered up her things. 'We'd better get back to the inn or Aegius will think we've been abducted by slave traders.'

Next morning, we left the beautiful city of Ocriculum as dawn broke. Aegius was awake early and I was eager to ride as far as we could today. The sky was clear and I knew it was going to be another hot day. So the further on we could go before the sun reached its zenith the better. I leapt up to the top of the low wall to help me mount my horse and settled myself in the saddle.

'We can only go at the pace of the horses, *domina*. And Rome is a good day and a half, two days away.'

'I know, Aegius, but I want to get as near as possible and try to sniff the air of the great city.'

'Ha! You won't want to once you get there. I guarantee that,' he said as he wheeled his horse round to face the inn gates. 'Believe me, the smell will reach us soon enough.'

'Such a romantic optimist,' I said with a teasing grin. 'I can't wait to be there!'

'And it's not for the grand buildings or the sophisticated food.' He gave me a look that made me feel warm, even at this early hour.

'You keep your dirty thoughts to yourself, Aegius,' a caustic voice came from behind us.

'Morning, Asella.' He turned and grinned at her. He looked back, nodded to the porter who looked surly and yawned, showing gaps in his stained teeth as he opened the courtyard gates, and we made our way back onto the Flaminia. An hour later, we crossed the great river, the Tiber, on another of the Divine Augustus's bridges. Perhaps Lucius was looking at the same river. I imagined dropping a message over the bridge and asking the river goddess to deliver it to him saying I was on my way. Nonsense, of course. A tablet would sink and a piece of vellum would lose all its ink. But still…

By the third hour, the road climbed slowly but despite this it was heaving with farm wagons, groups of people on foot leading pack mules, and occasionally military. When two drivers of ox-drawn carts coming from opposite directions stopped to gossip, scratching their heads, exchanging baskets of vegetables, I was tempted to shout at them. But it would do no good. Thankfully, a troop of cavalry galloped up and their commander told them to clear the road or he'd order his men to push the carts into the ditches. The two farmers took their time, muttering about young upstarts who probably didn't know what to do with the swords they were carrying, but they complied. Aegius grinned and gave a salute to the commander who nodded back. Then we were back on our way.

Although we were climbing again, it was gentle and the road even and only occasionally missing stones.

We stopped for the horses at a *statio* way station called Aqua Viva. I knew they had to feed and be watered and I was desperate to find something to slake my own thirst. I walked from the courtyard into the bar and asked for a drink of *posca* for the three of us.

'Coming up, young man,' the barman said without looking at me. I knew my voice was deeper than many women's and my hair was bound up and stuffed under my cap, but this was ridiculous. He raised his eyes when he presented me with the beakers. 'Oh,' he said and pulled his hand back. 'You're a woman.'

'Yes, and a thirsty one. And with two similar companions.' I took a few small coins out of my drawstring purse. 'How much?'

'We don't serve women by themselves. Be off with you.'

'Do I look like a threat to you or attempting to start an immoral trade?'

'Where's your father or husband, then? Tell him to buy you a drink.'

Then he made a bad mistake. He leered at me. I dropped my purse on the counter and in the same movement drew out my knife. I thrust my left hand forward and grabbed his tunic at the neck, pulling hard. With the point of my blade in his neck, I repeated my question: 'How much?'

'On the house,' he whimpered, his eyes wide and bulging. He struggled to get free and the neck of his tunic ripped under the strain. I released my hand and resheathed my knife. I dropped the coins on the counter, picked up a tray from the side, placed the drinks and my purse on it and sent him the filthiest look I could muster. After that I strolled out into the courtyard, set the tray on a table and drank the weak wine in one beaker in two swallows. I sat on a bench at the shaded table while Asella and Aegius drank theirs, then he went and bought another round in a more conventional manner. He re-emerged from the bar with the barman in tow. As the barman set more drinks out on the table, Aegius raised an eyebrow at me then shook his head, but I saw his little smile.

Back on the horses, we continued to make good speed and I dared to wonder if we might reach Rome that evening, but when the daylight started to dim and the sky turned a pearlescent red and yellow, Aegius announced that we were still fifteen miles from the city. We passed one closed *mansio*, but the next was open and busy. There was no separate room available, so after a reasonable but lukewarm supper, Asella and I went to find our places in the women's dormitory. Aegius opted to sleep in a barn near the horses' stable. The *mansio* gates were locked and there was supposedly a nightwatchman, but Aegius said he preferred to be cautious rather than sorry.

Asella and I had the luxury of mattresses provided by the manager plus our own thin ones to roll out on top and our cloaks. We looked round the rows of women settling down for the night. A few oil lamps were still burning here and there but the low-level chatter and occasional giggle soon petered out. We exchanged glances.

'None of these women looks particularly dangerous,' I whispered, 'but we don't know any of them. Anybody could yield to temptation. We've come too far for some light-fingered madam to help herself.'

'Cynical, but yes.' Asella nodded her head.

'I'll loosen my breeches and take my boots off, but they and everything else goes into a bundle between the two of us.'

'Agreed.' But in the remaining dim light from a lamp nearby, I saw a sad look in her eyes. 'You've grown up during our journey, Julia Bacausa. Perhaps too much.'

I couldn't settle to sleep with all the snuffling, farting and snoring of over twenty women surrounding us. I must have dozed off eventually as I woke suddenly in the middle of the night with a jabbing pain in my arm. I must have turned over and jolted my wound. I couldn't go back to sleep, so I lay and waited for the dawn of the day.

PART III

ROME

24

'Juno, why are so many people going in the direction of Rome at this time of the morning?' Asella grumbled behind me. We'd left the *mansio* behind only under an hour ago and were now riding very slowly in single file. I relayed Asella's question to Aegius.

'It's more likely to be a customs post,' he said over his shoulder. 'We're passing from Etruria into Latium, or whatever they're calling the area this year. There'll be another one when we reach the Porta Flaminia at the wall.'

As suspected, it turned out to be exactly that. The post was set up in front of a tall, decorated portal spanning the road. When we edged nearer, I saw it had four arches, two for our road and two facing to our left and right.

'What in Hades is that?' I said to Aegius. 'Who's built this thing in the middle of nowhere?'

'It's a Christian thing, the arch of the Divine Constantine, they call it, supposedly where he said he experienced a vision from his god before his victory at the Pons Mulvius. Well, that's the legend.' He nodded towards it. 'Losing a bit of its marble cladding though.'

I said nothing and sat quietly, preferring to look round at the gently rolling open land in front of us. I turned in my saddle; the last of the hills were behind us. When our turn came to be inspected, the customs clerk cast his eyes over us quickly. He ignored our saddlebags, now scratched and faded, but demanded to see the proof of ownership of our horses. Animals were normally exempt from any taxes, but he peered at the token and tablet that Fulminius had given us in Nuceria for a good minute. He looked disappointed he could find nothing wrong with them, then jerked his head in a southerly direction and turned his attention to the merchant who had been behind us in the queue. As one, we urged our horses forward.

We spurted ahead, leaving the traffic dammed up at the customs post. Aegius slowed down to a trot.

'We got off lightly, ladies. We can't count on that when we reach the city.'

'But what glorious countryside in the meantime.' I wouldn't let Aegius depress my mood for anything.

'Yes, very pretty from here, but look closer, *domina*, and you will see a fair number of tumbledown farmhouses and neglected fields.' He pointed to a couple of intersecting soft hills. 'Those pastures should be full of sheep.'

'Why are they deserted?' In Noricum on my father's lands, every inch of land was cultivated or used for cattle. And the meanest peasant had a few goats.

'If there are no sons willing to continue farming or daughters to bring sons-in-law onto the land, the older ones sell up, usually to the bigger estates and not for much. Other tenants can't pay increasing rent or landlords push tenants into debt and foreclose. You don't need so many scattered farmhouses if it's all run from a big central one.'

'Then how is the city fed?'

'The rich have their big estates, their *latifundia,* which produce enormous levels of crops and thus profits, and the poor are fed by the dole – bread, olive oil, wine and pork if they're lucky – and menial jobs in the city. Or they turn to banditry.' He shrugged. 'There are, of course, still some of the middle-ranking estates left, but I reckon they're losing the battle. Then there's the big out-of-town villas where the rich still pretend they're country folk.' He pointed down to a shallow valley to our right where I could see a cluster of roofs just visible above the trees. 'That's the *Villa Ad Gallinas Albas* – the Villa of the White Chickens – which the first empress, Livia Drusilla, is said to have retreated to now and again.' He snorted. 'What did *she* know about raising chickens?'

He didn't say any more for the next hour as we rode past farms that were obviously inhabited and cultivated. Single dwellings became closer together with some smaller settlements clustered along the road, and then the tombs started. We came to a halt as we approached the Tiber again. The road had curved and was following the bank of the great river. Across the water I saw red-tiled buildings – my first glimpse of the beginning of Rome. My heart fluttered. At last. I was so near to Lucius.

'It's the bridge,' Aegius said, pulling me back into reality. 'Too much traffic going over it. The Via Cassia traffic's all pouring down to it as well.'

'And too many people jostling us,' Asella grumbled as a mule rider tried to edge past her.

'Is this the last one before we get into the city?' I asked. We'd been over too many bridges, all wonders, of course, but I'd be happy if I never had to cross another one.

'It's the big one – the Pons Mulvius,' Aegius replied, keeping his reins tight to stop his horse nudging forward. 'Supposed to be where two emperors, Constantine and Maxentius, slugged it out, they say, sixty, seventy years ago. Well, that's what my grandfather told me. Then they started pushing the story the Galilean god had given them victory and as you know personally, *domina*, that cult has been trouble ever since. Anyway, once we're over the Tiber, it's just a short ride to the gate.'

I shot him a look.

'You seem very conversant with all these details, Aegius,' I commented. 'Did you know the city well?'

'Ah, we're going forward. Stay close, ladies,' he said, looking ahead and seeming not to have heard my question. But I knew he had. We only advanced a few paces then stopped again. 'Now what?' he grumbled.

'I can't see anything from here,' I said, pressing my knees against my horse and stretching up as far as I could. 'Just wagons, mules and a litter or two.' And a mass of people that stretched for at least half a mile in front of us. I slumped down in my saddle, reached down and took a drink from my leather bottle. The sun was becoming fierce and I was more than ever grateful for Asella's straw hat. But my plait was like a wool scarf on my sweating neck. I took my hat off and wound my hair up on top of my head and jammed my hat back on with the brim shading the back of my neck. Aegius had dismounted and was chatting to the ox-cart driver in front of us. He sauntered back and stopped by my horse.

'Seems there's another check at the bridge. I'm going to take a look.'

'I'll come with you,' I said and slid down from my horse. 'I could do with stretching my legs.' I turned round, a little guilty that I hadn't considered Asella. 'Will you be all right staying here, Asella?'

'Don't mind me! No, just teasing. I'll look after the horses. There's a clump of trees just back there. We'll wait in the shade. I'll hobble them and they can graze.'

'We'll rejoin the queue when we get back,' Aegius said. 'Won't be a problem.' At this stage, I was beginning to think that nothing would be a problem for Aegius.

He and I set off at the edge of the road, walking just the other side of the gutter. He called out to drivers who grumbled at him for pushing forward that he wasn't, and that he was only going to recce. He'd be sure to pass any information back to them.

As we approached the arches of the bridge itself, the crowd was so dense we had to leave the road and scramble down the bank. Luckily, the sun was high and behind us. It glinted off the chain mail shirts of half a dozen helmeted guards with spears and fierce expressions. Standing beside them was a man in a long robe decorated with rich embroidery. He wore a gold cross on a chain round his neck. What in Hades was a Galilean priest doing there?

Then my heart froze.

Standing next to the priest and studying everybody who attempted to cross the bridge was that blond stranger from the ship and my father's chief guard, the one who was allegedly 'keeping me safe' – Musius. I started to tremble but couldn't move.

Aegius grabbed my good hand and pulled me away so hard I thought my arm was going to come away from my shoulder. I stumbled up the bank behind him, panting hard then burst into coughing as we merged back into the crowd. At last, he stopped. A wave of nausea rolled up my gullet. I sank to my knees and threw up my breakfast. I was trembling but managed to stand and stagger back down the road. All Aegius could utter was a string of expletives not entirely under his breath, most of which had every other word as 'fuck'.

Asella looked up as we approached the clump of trees under which she and the horses were sheltering.

'What is it? What's happened? You look as if the sky has fallen on us.'

'It has,' I replied. 'They're checking everybody going across the bridge.' I reached for my water bottle and rinsed out my mouth. Asella frowned at me, then understanding I had been sick, handed me a small cloth to wipe my face. She turned back to Aegius.

'But we have our story which has got us across half the empire. Why do you think it won't work now?'

'Because, my dear Asella,' Aegius drawled with a voice full of repressed fury, 'the delightful Musius is one of those checking along with that cheeky blond bastard from the ship. They've got half a dozen guards fully armed as well as a fancy priest with them, so I suspect they'll be able to call upon their church's cohort to back them up.'

'Great Mother! How has Musius got here?'

'Who knows?' I said. 'But he must have been sent by Turcilus.' I glanced at Aegius. 'And he has no love for any of us. But who is that blond man, the tribesman? Is he a spy employed by Turcilus? And how did he know what ship we would be sailing on? We were too far ahead of him for Turcilus to have commissioned him to follow us, surely?'

Asella looked away and bowed her head. She brought her head up after a minute. I was shocked by her frightened expression. She looked as if a ghost had appeared and frightened her witless. Aegius crossed his arms and stared down at her. She shook her head.

'We're going to look conspicuous here,' he said after a minute. He looked down the road to the bridge. 'We can't cross the bridge, so we join the next group of travellers going north and get out of this place and find somewhere we can work out what to do next.'

'But that means going away from Rome.' I could hardly hold back my tears.

'Yes, for the moment, but better than being caught by Musius and his mob. You, *domina*, would be forced back to Turcilus for a life of humiliation. Asella and I would likely be found dead in a ditch. Now let's mount up and get out of here.'

We rode for a miserable eternity which Aegius said in his crushing, practical way wasn't even an hour. We pulled up at a small way station with its *hospitium* built of red rock. I vaguely remembered it on our way earlier this morning, but I'd been so full of joy that I was going to see Lucius at last that I hadn't really taken it in. My stomach grumbled and I was hot and tired. Asella looked no better. Most of all, my dream looked as though it had dissolved into dust. I eased myself out of my saddle and stumbled onto the ground. My whole body felt limp.

'Come, *domina*, let's get out of the sun. We need food and drink.' She took my arm and guided me inside the building to a bench by a table. After a few minutes, Aegius stamped through the entrance lobby, nodded to the barman and gave an order. He dropped down onto the bench opposite but waited to speak until the waitress had set down a jug of *posca* and three beakers for us and left.

'Right,' he said. 'The horses are being fed and watered.' He looked round the room, but nobody was within earshot. Nevertheless, he continued in a low voice. 'We have to cross that bloody river somehow and there's no bridge around here that I know of.'

'Why not?' I said. 'We've crossed hundreds.'

'A slight exaggeration, I think, *domina*. It goes back to when the Latins and Etruscans were hurling insults and spears at each other. Nobody wanted a bridge. After that, nobody seemed bothered as the Flaminia crossed at the Mulvius bridge.'

I shrugged and concentrated on drinking my *posca*. It was light and cool – a blessed relief.

'But first,' he continued, 'I think Asella has something to tell us.' He glared at her.

'I'm not sure—' she said.

'Oh, I think you are,' he replied.

She swallowed so hard I thought her throat would rupture. Then I saw tears in her eyes. Gods, what was she going to say? Surely, she hadn't been acting as a spy again as she did for my father about my courses? If she had, then for whom?

'It's when I saw him on the ship, when you thought I'd seen a ghost, *domina*. I wasn't sure. But he looks so much like his grandfather,' she whispered.

'Who does?' I grabbed her hand. 'Who?'

'Siro.' Her eyes clouded for a moment, then cleared. 'Your half-brother.'

I blinked and jerked my head back.

'What are you talking about? I don't have any brothers, half or whole, not since Marcus died.' A dreadful thought struck me. 'Not my father's by-blow?'

'No, your mother's.'

'What!' I leapt up. My mother? I felt as if I'd been punched in the heart. 'Take that back, Asella. Take that back now.' I choked on my last word. My mother's honour was at stake. How dare Asella tell such lies? I swung my arm to slap the filthy words out of her mouth. An iron grip fastened on my wrist and stopped it mid-air. Aegius. I pulled against it, but his fingers refused to budge. My forearm started to throb around my wound.

'Peace, *domina*. Calm yourself.' Aegius pressed his fingers into my skin. 'I think we need to hear the rest of what Asella has to say.'

'If she is going to spout such obscenities, then I don't want to hear.' I looked at Aegius. 'It can't be true. My mother was completely faithful to my father.'

'At the risk of getting my head caved in, I venture to say that none of us knows what passes between our parents.'

'Aegius, I *know* she couldn't have been untrue.'

'In that case, then there must be more to it. Take some deep breaths and listen.'

Aegius had been my guide and protector, wise with his years, so I nodded, then sat down again. However, I fixed Asella with a cold stare.

'Proceed,' I snapped at her.

Asella wrapped her fingers round a fold of her tunic and worked the cloth between them.

'When she was living with the tribes, Suria was violated when she was fourteen. He was a young brute, handsome though, the younger brother of one of the junior chiefs of the Alamanni. His older brother had sought an alliance with your mother's father and suggested the young man as a husband for her. Your grandfather said she was too young. Suria took one look at the younger brother and said she'd rather throw herself in the Danuvius than accept him. But later, he came into her room. I was sleeping there on a truckle bed on the other side of the room – I'd been chosen as her body servant. I woke, he was looming over me, his hand raised holding his dagger by the top of the blade, then came the pain to my head and I blacked out. I came round to her screams and sobs. He said that now she had to marry him.'

Asella shuddered.

'Your grandfather killed him, and the older brother. Of course, there was a war. Nine moons later, despite her trying to abort him with my help, Siro was born. She got up from her bed afterwards, bathed herself and left the child on the bed. She told me to throw him in the river, but I couldn't.'

Asella looked away, her fingers folding and unfolding in the cloth.

'My mistress's aunt took the baby in. Suria never acknowledged him. She couldn't bear to look at him. The aunt loved him, but few of the other children would play with him. They said he was a sneak and a cheat, but that could just be children's tittle-tattle. Nobody wanted to wed Suria after that, chief's daughter or not. But she wanted no man either. When your father turned up as a Roman commander after defeating your grandfather's people, she knew she wanted him. She often wondered why – it wasn't just to save her tribe being sold. She told me it was an instant bond, a deep recognition. It turned into an abiding love.'

'What became of the child?' I asked.

'I don't know for certain. When we left with the Romans, Siro was twelve years old.' Asella lifted her head and looked at me. 'You know yourself she wasn't heartless. She showered both her Roman children with love, but that first child was the result of rape by a brutal man and she couldn't bear the reminder under her eyes every day.'

'Poor *Matir*,' I said. I couldn't help the tears. She must have been so angry and frightened. Nothing, nothing could have wounded her so deeply. And she was still a child herself at the time and then having to bear the result of that rape. I only remember her strong, passionate and always ready to stand up for us. I put my hand out and took one of Asella's. 'I am so sorry, Asella. I was too hasty. Please forgive me.' I dropped down to my knees beside her and pressed her hand to comfort her. 'I had no idea about any of this. You must have been terrified yourself and desperate to help her.'

'She sobbed her heart out at night when she thought nobody was listening,' Asella continued. 'In the day she was quiet and dignified, holding herself upright and fixing anybody who made a spiteful or even unkind remark with cold hard eyes. She refused to let anybody treat her as tainted. But she grew up quickly. Once the child was born, she turned to perfecting her reading and writing and knowing the laws. Along with learning to defend herself with her knife, she demanded she be taught how to heft a sword. She vowed she would never be vulnerable again.'

'So that was why she insisted I was trained to use weapons alongside Marcus.' I leant back. 'Then I will recommence practice to honour her spirit.' I stood. 'Now would be the time to start.'

25

Sometimes, I realised I was being overdramatic, but in that modest *hospitium* on the Via Flaminia, I was ready to avenge my mother against the whole world. Then I took one of Aegius's deep breaths and sat down again. He waved his hand at the barman and I drank most of the contents of another beaker of *posca* in one swallow.

'Very laudable, *domina*, and I'd be happy to accommodate you, but at this very moment we need to plan our next move.'

'You're right, but Asella's revelation upset me, to say the least. What is this supposed brother of mine doing here, interfering in my affairs? I presume he wants money. Well, he's going to be disappointed. He'd do better applying to my father, but he'd get short shrift there, I would think.'

'If that was it, he would have declared himself on the ship. It was the perfect place to approach you as you couldn't have escaped from him for a good two days,' Aegius replied. 'It must be something else.'

'What was he doing standing on the bridge with Musius? He can't have known him, surely?'

'That does seem strange.' Aegius drew his fingers across his mouth. 'Let's work it back. This Siro knows Musius and seemed at ease with him. That suggests he's known him for a while.'

'Even before we took the ship from Tergeste? Ah, I see. This… this brother joined the ship only at the very last minute. He ran up the gangplank just as they were about to lift it. Juno! He must have been following us since we left Turcilus at Meclaria.' I stared at Aegius. 'How?'

'Musius is the one who organised the guard accompanying us all from Virunum. This Siro must have been mixed in with them.'

'But Asella would have recognised him.' I turned and looked at her.

'I most certainly would have, *domina*,' she said, sitting up straight.

'Then he must have hidden himself well or not been in that guard.'

'People often don't see things if they have no idea they need to look,' Aegius said. 'I knew Musius wasn't a Vestal Virgin – he ran the illegal book on everything going – but I never thought he would get involved in something like this. The purse must have been a heavy one.'

'They can't stay watching forever – those guards on the bridge must be costing Siro a fortune,' I said.

'Agreed,' Aegius said. 'The best route from Ancona to Rome was going to be the Flaminia, so it's logical that we would have to cross at the Mulvius bridge. But I don't think they'd be able to run to guards at every bridge. They may have posted a description at the others.'

'I suppose they knew we were travelling fast in order to get here before anybody could prevent us. They must have driven their mounts like the Furies were after them. Poor beasts.' I touched my arm, still bandaged. 'But we lost a day and a half after we were attacked by those bandits.' I looked up. 'So now we must find another bridge.'

'Yes.' Aegius waved his hand to the barman for another drink. 'A bridge that leads directly to one of the gates. And fast. They'll expect us to take the next nearest way in, so the Porta Pinciana or the Porta Salaria. But that's a hell of a ride back up this road to find a bridge. The other option is to go west. The Pons Aelius is the obvious one, but it's near Peter's church that the Galileans venerate, so probably well maintained and guarded.' He looked me straight in the eye. 'There are other options, smaller and lesser used bridges, but I don't know if any of them are still being repaired, to be honest. Even when I was here last, Nero's bridge – the one the old generals used to enter the city on their triumphs – had crumbled.'

'So which one is safest? No, I mean, the quickest, from here?'

'We wouldn't know until we got there. It's only a best guess.'

'Oh, for Juno's sake, Aegius. Grow some balls and tell me.'

Both he and Asella stared at me. Her mouth fell open. Aegius recovered first.

'Ha, your father to the life.' He chuckled. 'Very well. This is what I propose…'

We rode back down the Flaminia until we reached the end of the queue which had grown considerably, but Aegius steered us towards a trackway to the right.

'Not crossing today, friend?' a bored looking mule rider asked.

'No, off to my sister's near the Cassia,' Aegius lied in a cheerful voice and waved at the man, who then shrugged. Asella and I exchanged a glance, then followed in single file down the track after our leader. Well-spaced substantial townhouses, some as big as villas, lined the track which was partly paved. We crossed the Via Cassia in a clatter of hooves on the stone paving shortly afterwards, then climbed uphill on a country track overhung with pine trees. In the afternoon heat, they smelt wonderful. After only a few minutes, we came upon a wider road and turned left onto it.

'You can't see it from here because of the trees, but this road leads us back to the Tiber, but a good way downstream from the Mulvius bridge. Then we follow the river south,' Aegius said.

'Then we can cross?' I said.

'With the gods behind us, yes, but we'll have to make our way through the side streets back up to the Porta Flaminia to return the horses.'

I would have preferred to ride through the very middle of the greatest city in the world, to see all the wonderful things I'd read about, but we had to be careful. But there was one thing I hadn't told Aegius and I was feeling guilty about it. I brushed it aside for the moment. We had to concentrate on getting into the city first.

There was no mistaking the high walls of Rome on the opposite bank ordered to be built by the Divine Aurelianus when the barbarians were threatening Rome. They loomed higher and higher as we approached. The wall sloped right down to the river on the other bank and then ran along it. I craned my neck to view the top; it must have been the height of nearly ten men.

'And that's why we need to find a gate. We'll head for the Septimiana and cross on Agrippa's bridge. Are we all ready?' He looked over our horses, their saddlebags and us. We'd packed everything securely and hidden our weapons. I'd shifted my knife sheath to the back of my waist belt.

I nodded in reply, but Asella looked terrified. I reached over and gave her hand a gentle squeeze.

'It will be well, Asella. You do not need to say or do anything. Just follow Aegius's lead.'

At the gate, a few people were leaving the city through the single archway. In front of us, also seeking entry, were a couple of mule riders and a family on foot who looked tired and hungry. The inevitable customs officer took his tax after a cursory look at our saddlebags, then we were inspected by the two guards who flipped them open then stopped at the dull coloured tunics we'd placed at the top. One even yawned. Aegius showed him his document with the imperial seal that had purported to be an invitation from the empress in Mediolanum – the one he'd shown in the port at Tergeste. I prayed to Juno the guard couldn't read. If he could, he'd see it was nothing to do with Rome and it would all be over. We would be arrested as forgers and thrown into a dark prison under the waterline never to emerge.

I held my breath so long I thought I would faint. Aegius had made a good job of the fake seal; it had fooled the customs clerk in Tergeste. Would the guard take it at its face value? After a long moment, he passed the vellum back to Aegius who thanked him and gave him some silver coins to share with his comrade.

'Thank the gods,' I muttered as we turned sharp left and crossed the wretched river.

'Indeed,' Aegius said. 'They say literacy is declining. I never thought it could save our lives.' He turned to me as we rode off the bridge into a small square lined with high *insulae*. 'Your fate might have been a bleak life with Turcilus, watched and guarded at every moment, or even with your ex-husband if that smarmy bishop

Eligius got in on the act. Asella and I would have been sent to the mines.'

I shuddered. The mines – a living death, but not for long. Nobody lasted long in those hells.

'I'm so grateful to you, Aegius, for guiding and protecting me on this journey. You must think I'm deranged. I—'

'Don't, *domina*. It's a pleasure to have cocked a snook at the bishop, Turcilus and that bastard Musius. A man must have a last adventure in his old age. Besides, I haven't seen Rome for twenty-five years.'

'Old age! You have only just reached the middle of your life. And you fight like a young man.'

He laughed.

'Well, let's try and get through the city without needing to.'

The city was enormous, high, with statues soaring over it on the top of every building. The red-tiled roofs stretched as far as I could see. In front of us was a grand theatre – Pompey Magnus's, Aegius said. Then we turned into a side street and Aegius led us through a maze of *insulae* that stank. Between the buildings, I glimpsed the hill of the great temple to Jupiter Best and Greatest.

'Close your mouth, *domina*,' Aegius said. 'And look where you're going. We can't afford any incidents or to be taken for tourists.'

He was right. There were people everywhere – hundreds of them, flitting in and out of shops and bars, or just standing in the middle of the street, or ambling along oblivious to the noise which deafened me. Some windows were shuttered and looked derelict; others had drying clothes hanging from balconies clinging onto buildings at uneven angles.

We passed by a long baths building which must have measured a hundred and fifty feet. I could only dream of what lay inside. We plunged back into smaller streets, then passed the largest temple I'd ever seen. The columns in front soared towards the sky and behind it was a gigantic dome. Across the front ran the inscription: M·AGRIPPA·L·F·COS·TERTIVM·FECIT.

'Is everything in Rome this big?' I asked, overawed.

'No, only the show-off places like this. Your man will take you there, no doubt.'

I said nothing more, still nagged internally by guilt that I had not confessed my secret to Aegius. We rode on slowly, weaving between all the people, jostled occasionally when the streets narrowed. Aegius slapped away beggars' hands and Asella and I kept close to him. At last, by the arches of an overhead aqueduct, we turned left into a wide street and rode through a triumphal arch.

'The Via Lata, ladies, the city part of our old friend, the Flaminia,' he announced. 'This is where we would have come to if it hadn't been for the hold-up at the Mulvius bridge. Now we must ride towards the gate and find Fulminius's correspondent. He said it was between Augustus's mausoleum and the Porta Flaminia and we should look for the sign of a green horse.'

'I hope it's not green because it's ill,' Asella said.

'No, just somebody's sense of humour, I expect.'

It was slightly less stuffy as we rode down the wide street past grand buildings and an extraordinary column of red stone.

'That's to the Divine Antoninius Pius,' Aegius said. 'But everything up the road and much else in Rome is outshone by the Mausoleum of the Divine Augustus.' He pointed at a large white circular building that dominated the skyline. On top stood a tall shining statue, the colour of molten gold in the late afternoon light. I was fascinated and hardly noticed anything else until we rode under another arch and emerged into an area of pine trees spreading their branches over the road. We rode by without another word. At last, we came within sight of the gate with two archways and a cylindrical tower on each side. It looked as if giants had built it. Clusters of buildings stretched along the street opposite the wall itself. Just to the left was a large, gated yard with a sign of a brightly painted green horse head nailed to the main building. We dismounted. Of course, Aegius stopped and stared at the painting rather than attempting to enter the yard.

'Hm, that's a good solid colour,' he said. 'Wonder where he got that from? It's not just *cretavitridis* – green earth – you know. I'd bet good money he's added malachite, and maybe a dash of Egyptian blue.'

'Very good!' We spun round to see a man in his forties, slim, with a smiling face. Grey hair touched his temples, but he was brown-haired and brown-skinned. He stretched out his hand. 'Leonius Mercator, known as Leo. You must be the painter and his family.'

Aegius handed over the letter and token and gave Leo a quizzical look. Leo smiled broadly. 'Fulminius's message arrived last night by courier from Nuceria. Come in. I expect you're tired.'

The yard was square and spacious with two sides taken up with stalls for horses, one other with a barn where the open door showed stacks of hay. In one corner was a well head. On the fourth side was a three-storied block, presumably Mercator's offices and home. A young blonde woman in a long blue tunic walked across the yard carefully avoiding the deposits of horse dung. She flicked her fingers and a young boy ran out from the stables with a shovel and two buckets. He scooped up the dung and dropped it in one bucket, then poured sand from the other to cover the patch left on the ground. He turned and ran off equally quickly.

'Ah, my wife, Clarita.'

'Tullius Ferrantius, painter and artist.' Aegius shook hands with her. 'And these are Serena, my wife, and daughter, Placida.'

She looked us up and down and then smiled. Not a hair of neat plaits wound round her head and coiled at her neck was out of place.

'Would the ladies like to come inside for refreshments while you men see to the horses?'

'Gladly,' I said. 'But should we not help with unloading our saddlebags first?'

'On no account,' Clarita said. 'The men can do that. The stable boys will help. Come.'

There was no argument to be made with such a firm invitation, so we followed. Clarita gave us a beaker each of *mulsum*; the honey in it tasted of mountain flowers. It was a delight after all the vinegary *posca* we'd had to drink over the past weeks. She disappeared into a back room for a few moments then returned and set a plate of small buns and pastries on the table. Each bite was delicious, especially as we had eaten little since breakfast and I'd lost most of mine. Then she brought out fruit tarts and fresh figs. I thanked her profusely. She shrugged.

'It's simple but I expect you'll be eating *cena* soon, so you won't want to spoil your appetite.'

Just at that moment Aegius and Leo entered the room carrying two of our sets of bags and followed by a stable boy balancing the third on his shoulder and our mattress rolls in his arms. Clarita gave the men a drink, then sat with a pleased smile on her lips. Were all the women in Rome so self-contained and confident?

'Well, we won't linger,' Aegius said as he set his cup down on the table. 'We want to get to my daughter's friends before the ungodly roam the streets at nightfall.' He turned to me. 'So, Daughter, where does your friend live in this splendid city?'

Oh, gods! Now I would have to confess. I felt heat creep up my neck to my face and I swallowed hard. I couldn't speak. Asella gave me a puzzled look. She wouldn't be able to help either. They both thought I knew.

'I—'

'Yes?' Aegius's smile became fixed, then faded.

'I don't know the exact address,' I blurted out.

'What? What do you mean? There are hundreds of thousands of people in this city. How in Hades did you expect to find him?'

'I don't know,' I whispered and bowed my head.

'Perhaps we could help?' Leo's voice interrupted my misery. 'We could post a notice on the wall in say the Septa Julia or somewhere more central advertising your friend's name.' Both he and Clarita tried not to look too interested.

Aegius stood, reached down and took my hand, forcing me up as well.

'Excuse us for a moment, Leo. I need to talk to my daughter in private. We'll go outside to the yard.'

'Of course,' Leo replied smoothly.

Outside, I recovered myself but I didn't know what to say.

'Well?' Aegius said.

I shook my head. A sour taste formed in my mouth and I thought I was going to be sick again. 'Lucius Apulius was dismissed so quickly, I didn't have the opportunity to ask for exact directions. When I wrote to him, I just addressed my letters to him at the Domus Apulia, Roma, trusting that would be enough.'

'But as we suspect, they were probably intercepted by your father.' He sighed impatiently. 'Very well, *domina*. But I, and Asella, would very much appreciate it if you could tell me how exactly we are going to find Lucius Apulius tonight so that we are not wandering around the streets as the prey of any and every group of criminal thugs. Or do you have a plan that you wish to divulge to me? As the sun will set within an hour, I trust you will be able to tell me now.'

He was becoming angrier by the minute. Tears welled in my eyes.

'I don't know!' I was so tired and upset after an anxious day that I could hardly stand, let alone think. I touched my middle, almost by instinct. Although I hadn't felt the child yet, I wanted to protect it against everything and anything.

Aegius stamped off, circling the yard, but when after a few minutes he came back to where I stood, he walked back in his usual calm way.

'Right, we're all exhausted. I'm going to ask Leo if he would mind if we bedded down in the barn,' he said. He raised his head and looked over the wall. 'We can't go chasing around the city now.' The sun was an orange ball hovering near the horizon. 'Main problem is that we can't ask him to help as it would set the rumour mill going and we might not get Apulius's location back before Musius, his guards and that bloody brother of yours get us, nor can we post a request on a public wall for the same reason. The gods alone know what the consequences of either would be.'

26

Leo insisted we use one of the rooms in the house. It was bare but for a single bed and a stool, but we'd slept in worst. I made Asella take the bed as she looked so tired. Aegius and I used our travelling mattresses on the floor. Aegius said Leo refused to take any money, but when I approached Clarita in the kitchen next morning, she happily accepted my silver. She studied the coins in her hand for a few moments before thanking me. Had she wanted more? She said nothing but slid the coins into her waist pouch.

After breakfast, Aegius, Asella and I went outside to find the gates open and the yard full of mules and carts, and very noisy people. Leo and two of his stable boys were busy corralling people and animals. Porters with baskets stood by as fruit, vegetables and amphorae were decanted. Another stable boy was hiring out handcarts. The smell of animal dung and sweaty people filled the air even at this first hour of the day.

'Over here,' Aegius said, nodding his head towards the corner furthest from the long stable block where stalls were filling up fast. 'It'll be chaotic for another hour, so nobody will take any notice of us.'

'I'm sorry I don't know where Lucius lives,' I began. 'It must be in one of the better quarters as his father is a senator.'

'Not necessarily so, I'm afraid, *domina*. Even the Divine Julius's family home lay in the Subura, but then I wouldn't think an old family like the Apulii would be down there.' He rubbed his cheek. 'Perhaps we *should* ask Leo for help. He's bound to know.'

'He seems sound enough, but I don't trust Clarita,' I said. 'She seems to measure everything up, assessing its value. Something warns me not to confide in her.'

'She'd sell her own mother, grandmother and throw in a neighbour into the deal for gold,' Asella snorted. 'Her type never wavers.'

'So sure, Asella?' Aegius raised one eyebrow.

'Yes,' she snapped back.

'Fair enough. We'll find some temporary lodgings today, then plan a way to find Apulius without making a noise.'

I pulled my lips together tightly. All I really wanted to do was to go through the gates, run into the main forum and shout Lucius's name. He would appear as if by magic and all would be well. But desperate as I was to be with him, I knew the sensible thing was to proceed cautiously. I skimmed my stomach with my fingers quickly, but Asella gave me such a look.

'You're not feeling anything yet, *domina*, are you?'

'No, no.' I looked around the yard, now less busy. A mule bearing a young man clattered into the yard. He wore a brown tunic and breeches, and a hat just like the bandit who had ambushed us between Prolaqueum and Nuceria. Curly hair escaped from the rim. I gasped. My hand flew to the base of my throat. Surely not. No, this man's hair was dark brown and his nose bulbous. I released my breath. In the next instant, a light seemed to flash in front of my eyes. Our attacker's hair had been curly and *blond*. I blinked hard, but the thought had pierced my mind. Suddenly, I knew.

'Oh, gods.' I could hardly breathe.

'*Domina*?' Asella put her arm round my shoulders. 'You're unwell. Come inside and sit down.'

'Wait. What is it?' Aegius said.

'She must go and rest,' Asella said. 'Out of my way, Aegius.' She went to move past him, but he blocked us.

'Peace, Asella,' I put my arm out and touched Aegius's. I swallowed hard. 'That man on the mule. In that hat, he looks similar to that bandit in the mountains. It isn't him, but I suddenly realised who the bandit was. He was also the man on the ship and the man at the Pons Mulvius. It was Siro, my not-so-dear brother, who attacked us.'

We made our farewells to Leo and Clarita and set off down the Via Flaminia past the great monuments but much more slowly without the advantage of being on horseback. At least our boots protected us from the hard stone and the unnameable things lying on their surface. Aegius had warned us to turn the buckled opening side of our saddlebags to the inside as a precaution against pickpockets and to keep as close together as possible.

'It's about a mile to the Arch of the Divine Claudius and the Virgo aqueduct, then we should be able to find some streets where ordinary people live. It might get more crowded then.'

We were being jostled on either side now. What on earth would it be like in narrower streets? I slapped away a child's hand near my waist. I'd tucked my pouch inside my breeches. My cloak was bundled up in a bag firmly attached by leather straps to each shoulder. Passing under the aqueduct arch, we turned left into a side street. It was like being surrounded by large wasps buzzing and pushing all around us. They were of every skin and hair colour, height, age and style of clothes one could imagine, with accents to match. I was catching my breath when we were flattened against the wall between two shops. I nearly tripped on the edge of a table full of copper and bronze pans and bowls in front of one.

'Watch it!' an angry man with a pinched face and few teeth said as he pushed me away. I was about to retort, but was stopped by the sight of a huge litter draped with yellow curtains hurrying by. Inside was a woman in a long deep red robe embroidered in gold. Her black hair was half covered in a gold net and from her ears dangled enormous gold earrings set with red stones. Immediately after she'd passed by, the crowd closed behind her.

Aegius pushed on with me directly behind him and Asella behind me. We two had linked hands and I was tempted to grab the back of Aegius's leather waist belt, but that would have been childish.

At last, the crowds lessened. The side street was narrower, lined with tall blocks of *insulae* but cleaner underfoot. A *caupona* barman shouted out an invitation to refresh ourselves but Aegius dismissed him with a pleasant 'Not now, friend.' A hundred paces further on, we stopped by a door with a light flickering in a lamp above. The plaque on the wall ran: *If you're clean and honest, Pia Afra welcomes you. If you're not, keep walking.* Underneath was written a list of prices.

'That's direct,' I said. 'Shall we go and see if Pia Afra considers us to be honest at least? As for clean, there are plenty of baths in the city, I understand.'

'Well said, *domina*,' Aegius replied. 'Glad to see you in better spirits.'

'We've travelled a long road, Aegius, and I'm damned to Tartarus if that bastard of my half-brother or Turcilus or even my father are going to stop me now.'

Pia Afra's inn was sparkling clean. The rooms were small but the beds were firm with plump mattresses, the pegs on the walls plentiful and each had a stool and small table on which stood a wide bowl and linen for washing. Asella and I shared a slightly larger room with a wider bed for two. Our lodgings gave onto a peristyle garden crammed with luxuriant planting. Basketweave chairs clustered around a dining table. Colourful birds flitted back and forth in a wide aviary across the back.

'They remind me of my childhood home,' Pia Afra explained. 'I came from Caesarea in Mauretania and married an ex-soldier turned purple dye merchant. He came from the city here and was homesick. I agreed to come here with him when he sold his business.'

'What a romantic story!' I said. 'And a long journey across the sea.'

'Unfortunately, he died a few years ago, but I decided to stay in Rome.' She looked away. 'I hope you will be comfortable here. The household eats *cena* at the ninth hour. You are welcome to join us.'

'Thank you, Pia Afra. But first, could you direct us to the nearest baths?'

Asella and I changed into our long tunics and as we were preparing to set off, Aegius took us aside.

'Make sure you cover your hair in the street, especially you, *domina*. While red hair isn't unusual, as you saw on your way here, yours is an unusually bright hue. Once in the baths, you should be safe. We must assume that Siro and Musius know we've managed to enter Rome by now and they'll be looking.'

'I do understand, Aegius.' I knew he was anxious to protect us, but neither Asella nor I was completely without wits. 'We'll be like Lucius's stories of his scouting when he went about disguised as an artisan or merchant. Asella and I will act like a couple of timid women.'

'Timid? Ha! You'll never succeed in that.'

At the baths, we entered the door Afra had described. She'd said the nearest women's baths were small and poky, but although not expansive, we found them perfectly adequate. Asella tipped a slave in the tiny *apodyterium* – more of an alcove – to watch over our clothes and gave her a dire warning of revenge if she felt tempted to filch them. The poor girl trembled under her fierce stare as she handed Asella a pair of wooden sandals.

'You were harsh, Asella,' I said as we seated ourselves in the *tepidarium* for a pause before going through to the hot room.

'Humph. You never know. Some can be tempted. Best to nip any tendencies in the bud.'

'You're so distrusting.'

'Yes, but I've survived that way.'

'A wise course, ladies.'

I spun round at the new voice. It was the woman from the yellow curtained litter.

'*Salve*. I'm Valeria Polia. First time in our little baths?'

'*Salve*. I'm Placida and this is my mother, Serena.'

'Oh, I thought I heard a different name.' She gave me a quizzing look. Hades.

'Just my silly pet name for my mother,' I said quickly. 'We're very close.'

'How quaint. I haven't spoken to mine for months.' She tittered. 'I thought I hadn't seen you before. Where have you come from? Your accent says here, but—'

'Shall we go through to the *caldarium*, Daughter?' Asella stood and pulled me up.

'Of course, Mother.' I turned to Valeria. 'Please excuse us. We'll chat another time perhaps.' What a nosy woman.

In the hot room, we sat in a little alcove for a few moments, sweating like donkeys, then plunged into the hot pool. Gods, it was near boiling. Every drop of dirt on my skin would have been pulled off by the heat. I only stayed for a few moments and gasped to catch my breath as I climbed out. Back in the *tepidarium*, there was no sign of the nosy Valeria. While Asella stayed in the *tepidarium* for a massage, I opted for a dip in the *frigidarium* to revive myself. It lived up to its name, but it *was* refreshing. Another young woman, very slim, with a heart-shaped face and dark brown hair bound up with cloth ribbons on top of her head, entered the room. I judged her to be younger than me. As she slowly inserted herself into the cold water, one inch at a time, I noticed she had a large birthmark on her right buttock. A pity, but at least it wasn't on her face. Her brown eyes widened and her lips formed a grimace, but she persisted.

'It's not too bad once you're in,' I said to encourage her.

'I'm such a coward.'

'No, I think you're brave to keep going despite your discomfort.'

At last, she was in the water up to her neck. She smiled at me then moved around the pool slowly.

'I've been in colder,' I said, remembering my own baths in Virunum.

'Oh, that must have been like ice.'

'I'm used to cold mountain streams.'

'Oh, how lovely to be surrounded by mountains. In the Alps?'

'No, in Noricum.' Hades. I shouldn't have said that. Aegius had told us to be discreet, but I didn't say which of the two Noricum provinces, and both were big. She was just a girl in the baths and in such a big city, I'd never meet her again. I smiled and extended my hand out of the water. 'I'm Placida, daughter of Tullius Ferrantius. We've only just arrived in Rome.'

'Oh, I hope you aren't too tired after your journey.'

'No, not at all. But I knew the first thing we needed was a trip to the baths.'

She laughed and I joined in. She left and swam round a circuit of the pool and came back to me. She looked embarrassed.

'I'm sorry, I'm being rude. My name's Lucilla Apulia.' I stared at her. Apulia? Was she related to Lucius? Juno.

Close your mouth, Julia.

'We have a proper bath at our country home in Latium,' she continued. 'I use this one when I'm in the city.'

'Oh?' I said. Now my heart was pounding, or perhaps it was the stimulation of the cold water. 'Is this your favourite or is it the nearest one to your city house?'

'The nearest. We live just off the Alta Semita on the Quirinal. Well, it's my uncle's house and I come to stay here when I get fed up with the country.'

'All that greenery?' I laughed, feeling like a traitor to my own beautiful Noricum.

'More the smell of the animals and the lack of conversation. My cousin's no use. He just mopes around after some girl he met on his last posting. You must come and visit me. I'm sorry I can't ask you to come back now. Mother said I had to go straight home after the baths as she has family visitors tonight. But shall we go and have a massage first?'

I could hardly wait to grab my clothes and run back to tell Aegius, but that would hardly have been polite, or even good tactics. Asella gave me a strange look when Lucilla and I entered the *tepidarium*, arms linked like lifelong friends. When I turned my head on the massage table in Asella's direction, I widened my eyes at her, praying she wouldn't say anything to betray us. But I should have known – Asella kept her face completely neutral.

'Mother,' I trilled at Asella, 'this is my new friend, Lucilla Apulia. She's invited us to visit her at her house on the Quirinal. Isn't it lovely to find a friend on our first day in Rome?'

27

It was only the knowledge that we had to try to be inconspicuous that prevented me from running back to our lodgings, but we didn't allow ourselves to be delayed by itinerant pie sellers or beggars. I gave Pia Afra a quick smile when we entered the vestibule then hurried across the brightly painted atrium towards our rooms. Aegius was lounging in one of the chairs in the peristyle.

'Ladies. Enjoy the baths?'

'Yes, yes,' I said, 'but never mind that. I know where Lucius lives.' I dropped into the chair opposite. His eyes narrowed.

'How did you find out?'

'I wasn't indiscreet, if that's what you're thinking.'

'Tell me.'

I gave him a word-by-word account. He sat up, attentive but passive as if he was used to receiving reports.

'And this Lucilla,' he said after I'd finished. 'She seemed genuine?'

'Yes, and quite sensible. When she referred to her cousin who was in Latium and "moping about a girl", I thought it had to be true.'

'It does sound like it.'

'Why are you hesitating, Aegius?'

'It strikes me as too much of a coincidence. On the other hand, the baths are the nearest to the Alta Semita or whatever they call it these days. When I left Rome, they were thinking of adopting a new name. But if your girl called it by its old name, that's probably what an old family would still call it.'

'So, shall we go there? Tomorrow morning?' I tried to sound casual but couldn't. 'Lucilla said they had something planned tonight, but nothing can stop us tomorrow.'

Aegius fixed his gaze on the back of the peristyle.

'I could go just with Asella if you don't want to come,' I added.

'No. I know I'm not your real father, *domina*, but I feel I must verify it. I owe it to the prince that your safety is absolute.'

'Oh, very well.' I looked away, over towards the caged birds in the aviary. I wasn't caged, but I felt as restrained as they were. But one more day would make no difference.

After *cena* was finished, Aegius excused himself and went out into the city. He dressed simply in tunic and sandals to look like any other ordinary citizen. I was sure he was going to the Alta Semita to check where the Apulius house lay. I opened the book that Pia Afra lent me from her reading cupboard, but when the letters started jumping up and down in front of my eyes in the dimming light, I had to put it back. I lit another lamp and brought it back to the table. Asella gave me a tunic to mend – our few clothes had become sadly worn – but I couldn't concentrate.

'There,' she said, holding up my best and in truth only spare long tunic. 'I've added a piece of embroidered ribbon to the neckline. It's not much, but it cheers it up.'

'Where did you get that from?'

'I didn't only buy bread and sausage at those markets on the way. When you and Aegius were watering the horses and enjoying the view from the square in Narni, I was replenishing my pins and threads as well as buying food. The little fabric shop had a tray of beautiful ribbons, made locally, he said. Anyway, I couldn't resist buying a few. And they were cheap.' Her face took on a mulish look.

'Peace, Asella.' I laughed, then examined the ribbon she'd stitched onto my tunic. It was wide with a blue and gold pattern of flowers and leaves. 'How beautiful. The gold thread work is unusual and very fine.'

'Yes, I wondered if the ribbons were taken in payment of a debt rather than woven by a local woman. Anyway, it wasn't money wasted.' She looked directly at me. 'You need to look your best when you meet Apulius again.'

I stood up and went over to her. I put my arms around her and kissed her cheek.

'Thank you. You are as a mother to me, Asella, and I am very grateful.'

'Just doing my duty,' she said gruffly and packed up her needles.

'You know that's not true. You've guided me since *Matir* died. I've been fortunate to have you.' I glanced at her. 'Would you tell me something?'

'What is it?'

'Did my father know about Siro?'

All I heard for a few moments was the chirruping and calls of Pia Afra's birds. Asella was looking into the distance. At last, she turned to me.

'I don't think so. He knew she was no virgin at her age, but she never told me if she had talked to him about that time.'

'Did she make you promise not to tell me?'

'Not as such. I think she'd closed that part of her life off. When we came south with your father, neither of us expected ever to encounter him again.'

'Is that why you never told me?'

'There didn't seem to be any reason to do so, either then or after Marcus's death.' Her voice was flat, leeched of any emotion. I wondered why she had spoken of Marcus's death, but she looked drained, beyond any further speech. I would ask her in the morning. I stretched out my hand and took hers and pressed it. We stayed like that as the moon rose, only stirring when Afra brought us a drink of watered wine.

The next morning, I washed thoroughly, and Asella dressed my hair elaborately, then I slipped on the now enhanced long blue tunic, my leather and gold belt that I'd concealed in the bottom of my saddlebag, and a pair of gold earrings. Asella stepped back and scrutinised me.

'Your skin looks as if you've been doing field work for a month, but the healthy glow enhances it and although you're breeding, you've lost some weight around your waist. Not that I think your Roman will notice any of that,' she added tartly.

'Oh, Asella, suppose… Suppose he doesn't want me? That he doesn't love me after all?'

'Now, what put that daft idea into your head? And after everything we've come through to get here.' She grimaced.

I didn't answer her, but looked down at the floor. If Lucius had given up on me, then that was the end. I saw nothing in front of me. I might as well go back to Virunum, submit to my father and agree to marry Turcilus. At least my child would have a name.

'Come and sit down while we wait for Aegius to emerge,' she said, giving me an encouraging smile. I couldn't, but walked up and down the peristyle.

'Where on earth is he?' I said. 'He didn't come to breakfast. Do you suppose he's gone out already?'

'No, I haven't.'

I spun round at Aegius's voice. He walked very carefully and slowly towards where we sat and lowered himself down on one of the chairs as if he was an infirm old man. I gasped. One of his eyes was half closed with crimson and purple skin circling it. It was accompanied by a cut on his lip, thankfully not bleeding. He took a slow breath in and out.

'Don't ask to see the other bruises. I'm too shy to show you.' He attempted a smile but winced. 'The other two men are in a much worse state – one's dead, the other has a cracked head and a broken arm.'

'What in Hades happened?'

Asella poured him a drink while he took another measured breath.

'I went out last night to find out exactly where the Apulius house was. I had no difficulty – it's old and big with a small name tablet on the wall outside. The house takes up the whole block so there's nothing built onto the back of it. A few groups of twos and threes were hurrying along the street and carrying torches, but interestingly, there were two men, built like wrestlers, who seemed to be loitering on the street opposite the entrance about fifty paces apart. They could be part of the Apulius house's security, but something told me they weren't.' He shrugged. 'Call it an old soldier's instinct. I carried on, then turned to go to the side and back of the house and found a service gate in the side wall. I perched behind a corner of a building opposite and waited.'

'What for?'

'Somebody was bound to come out after they'd finished for the evening. Not one of the slaves, obviously, but a house like that has a few freedmen among the servants and they won't all live in. Eventually, two men came out together. I tracked them to a bar on the edge of the Subura, Mars help me.' He took another sip of the *posca*. 'Anyway, I got them chatting, bought them some drinks. They didn't belong to the house, but had been brought in to help with labouring for some renovation work. Even better.'

'Why?'

'No loyalty beyond payment, so ripe for picking.'

'But how is this relevant to our visit to Lucius's house this morning?'

'I know you think I'm too mistrustful, but you've sacrificed so much for this – courageously so – that I don't want it to go wrong. In the event, my instincts were right.'

'How so?'

'Your Lucilla is nothing but one of the kitchen girls.'

'What! You must be mistaken.'

'Brown hair, skinny, pointy chin, about seventeen or eighteen and with a big mark on her bum?'

'Yes, but…'

'Apparently, she's a bit of a mimic and keeps them amused in the kitchen taking people off. I wouldn't like to say how my two drinking companions knew about that mark.' He smirked.

I dropped down into a chair.

'But why did she pretend to be one of the Apulii?' All my joy in the morning had vanished.

'That we don't know, but probably bought off by somebody to gain your confidence. Doesn't take a genius to work out who.'

'How could Siro possibly have had the time to do it? He was at the Mulvius bridge only the day before yesterday.'

Aegius drained his cup and spent a few moments looking at it.

'Yes, he obviously had some prior knowledge of that household. Bit of a worry, that. Of course, silver, or gold, has great attraction for a slave saving up against the day she is manumitted. Apparently, this Lucilla is a dab hand at pastry, so they won't let her go easily.'

If I ever became part of Lucius's family, she'd be sold as a priority.

'If we go there straight away and expose this… this sham—'

'That may be exactly what they intend us to do.' Aegius shifted in his seat and winced.

'Ah, a trap, you mean. But Lucius wouldn't stand for it.'

'No, of course not, but we may not even get to the front door. Even if we did, if he heard a fight outside, the porter might well be too terrified to open it.'

'We should at least try.'

'Naturally, but I think we should have another look first, but perhaps not today. I didn't like the look of those two heavies in the street. I need to catch my breath.'

'How did you get into a fight?'

'Well, I said farewell to my drinking companions last night and started back here. Although it's been twenty-five years, I can still remember most of the streets so I knew which ones to avoid. I walked with my hand on my knife handle like anybody sane does at night. I was two streets away from here when I was jumped.'

'Gods!'

'They gave me a good kicking, but I managed to roll away and stand, then one came at me with a cudgel and the other a knife. I felled the one with the cudgel, grabbed it and used it on his arm. It cracked and he screamed. But my head was ringing and I was staggering from the beating they'd given me. Then the knifeman grabbed my throat. I thought that was the last breath I'd take, when he collapsed in front of me, a blade pointing out of his chest. By the time I'd shaken my head to clear it, a grim-faced legionary had his foot on the knifeman's back and was pulling his sword out of the body. He helped me home.'

'Aegius, we must find that legionary and reward him.'

'I anticipated your permission, *domina*, and asked him to call here this morning.'

'You must go and rest until he arrives. Asella will treat your bruises and give you something for the pain.'

Aegius groaned, but I was having none of it.

'One last thing, *domina*,' he stopped and turned as Asella was leading him towards his room. 'I only remembered it this morning. Just as they jumped me, they said, "That's him."'

The young soldier presented himself two hours later. He was very correct when I received him and seemed not to wish to look directly at me for very long. I didn't think he meant to be discourteous. Perhaps he was merely reserved. Black-haired with sunburnt skin, his uniform was made from rich cloth and tooled leather and he wore a Galilean chi-rho badge on the strap that crossed his chest diagonally. From the soft lilt in his accent, he wasn't from Gaul or Italia, nor from anywhere north. Perhaps Hispania? He looked relieved when Aegius joined us and leapt up and took a step forward as if to help.

'Stand down, young man,' Aegius said. 'I'm not quite dead yet, although I *am* feeling my age this morning.'

'I was pleased to help, sir. Rome is not a safe place at night.'

'No change from when I was a young man, I'm afraid. Now, can we offer you some recompense for your trouble?' Aegius glanced at me and I nodded.

'No, it was my duty to help a citizen in difficulty,' he said stiffly and flushed.

'Then you are a very unusual and upright young man. I can only repeat my thanks.' He studied the younger man. 'Are you stationed here?'

'No, I'm carrying some dispatches for my father including one on a private matter here in Rome. I'm leaving tomorrow for the German frontier in the emperor's service and I'll be very glad to do so. This is a godless place, full of pagans.'

I stiffened. Lucius had told me in Virunum that many of his and his father's circles in Rome adhered to the true gods. To hear them called pagans so forthrightly was disturbing. Asella was standing in the background, but I heard her soft gasp. Aegius seemed not to react.

'Well,' he said, and rose slowly to his feet. He held out his hand.

'I wish you a safe journey as well as future prosperity.' The young man smiled politely and nodded. 'May your god protect you.'

The young soldier frowned at the 'your', but Aegius smiled back innocently.

'Oh, I should have asked earlier,' Aegius said as the younger man picked up his helmet. 'My apologies, but please tell me your name. I'd dearly like to know who rescued me.'

'Flavius Theodosius. My father is Count Theodosius, lately of Britannia and now promoted by our master, Emperor Valentinian, to be his *magister equitum.*'

28

'*Domina*?'

Asella's voice interrupted my scrambled mind. My body was still tense so I leant back into Afra's basketweave chair in an attempt to ease the stiffness.

'Sorry, Asella. I was trying to take in what that young man said. His father was the one who dismissed Lucius in Britannia which resulted in him being sent to us in Noricum. That dismissal wrecked Lucius's career. On the other hand, it meant that we met. However, the son undoubtedly saved Aegius from being murdered by street bandits.' I waved my hands in the air. 'I don't know whether to praise him or curse him.'

'Best not to do either, *domina*,' Aegius said as he returned from ushering Theodosius out of the inn. 'Keep it as a story to tell your man when he's in a good mood.'

'If I ever get to him,' I replied.

'You will. We need to work out how.'

'Do you think Siro knows where we are staying?'

'I don't think so, otherwise he'd have attacked us here. He sent Lucilla to the baths nearest the Apulius house, and those toughs are keeping a watch on the house. They assume you will eventually turn up there. Then they can pounce.'

'Curse them to Hades. What if we hire our own guards and attack them?'

'Oh, yes, and risk starting a brawl in a high-end quarter of the city and get arrested and thrown in a cell,' he said in a sarcastic voice. 'That would go down well with your future family.'

'Perhaps I can help, *domina*,' Asella said. 'They know Aegius, and I would think they have a good description of you. If they've bought Lucilla's services, she would recognise you instantly. She was concentrating on you at the baths, so she wouldn't have taken much notice of me. It's an advantage of being old – we're invisible. The street thugs won't know me either. I'll walk past with a basket and deliver a message to the house for Lucius Apulius. He will then come and escort you there.'

'Oh, Asella, that's an excellent idea.'

'I'm not so sure,' Aegius said. 'You'd have to be quick, or they'll try and stop you before you get to the door. If they're anything as brutal as the ones who had a go at me, you could get badly hurt.'

'I'll be careful. I'll wait until a group of others is passing by and join them, then divert to the door.'

'A sound stratagem,' Aegius said, but his face took on a solemn expression. 'Don't hesitate to leave if there's the slightest risk. The goddess Fortuna go with you.'

When Asella returned, I pounced on her as she was laying her *palla* aside. Her face said it all.

'Here's not here in Rome.'

'Oh, gods.' I seized her hand. 'Who did you speak to? What exactly did they say?'

'I only got as far as the porter – not the brightest spark in the hearth. I said I had a message for Lucius Apulius from my mistress. He asked who that was and I said it was a discreet matter.' She shrugged. 'Perhaps that was the wrong thing to say as he then made a rude gesture. I repeated that it was urgent, and Lucius Apulius would be angry if he didn't receive the message. His reply was that the young master, if he was here, would not want to be importuned – he said unportuned, ignoramus – by a tart's slave. Then he slammed the service window shut on me.'

I stared at her, willing her answer to be different. But it wasn't, of course. I paced once round the peristyle, then came back to her. 'Let me think. Lucilla in her play-acting didn't say where her supposed cousin was. Perhaps he's at the farm in Latium.' I turned to Aegius. 'Is it possible to find him there?'

'Latium is huge and part of the Campaniae. We could be months wandering around it.'

'But surely the city authorities will know who owns what land?'

'If it's an old holding, perhaps, but if the Apulii acquired it in the past hundred years the records may be inaccurate,' Aegius replied. 'The city Tabularium isn't what it used to be in ancient times.'

'For Juno's sake, Aegius! You are so depressing. Go and rest. You must still be feeling the effect of your wounds.'

Asella murmured that she would give him a draught to ease the bruising and went to the kitchen to prepare her brew. I sat and tapped my fingers on the table and stared at the exotic birds flitting back and forth.

'Placida? Did you want something?' Afra had appeared in front of me. I blinked.

'Oh, no, thank you. I'm sorry. I didn't mean to disturb you.' I glanced up at her. 'I'm trying to work out a problem.'

'Can I help?'

'That's very kind of you, but I don't think so.'

'Very well. I need to go out for a short while. A new consignment of olives from Latium was promised for today by my favourite stallholder and I want to ensure that I have some before he's sold out.'

'Oh. From Latium? I don't know much about it. Are there many farms there?'

She laughed at my ignorance, but warmly.

'Indeed. Some very large ones, stretching for miles, and some older estates which are family run which specialise. The small tenant farmers have all gone.' She looked pensive. 'My husband's brother had one in Sabina, in the hills, but the competition from the big *latifundia* killed his production. He called it a day before he got into debt and came and lived with us here, working as a porter in the markets. I felt sorry for him – a poor end after twenty years. Well, I'd better get on.'

'Would you mind if I came with you?'

She looked me up and down.

'Perhaps if you left your jewellery here and wore a plainer gown. You look too glamorous to go shopping in the market.'

We left ten minutes later, each carrying a basket. I'd changed into my other tunic and wound my thin *palla* round my body then my head to hide my hair completely and looped the end tightly over my shoulder. I adjusted the knife sheath attached to my belt so that I could easily reach between the folds of my skirt if I needed too. I hated having to hide myself like this the first time in this magnificent city and to think of carrying my knife, but too much was at stake to do anything else.

Afra's market brimmed with scents and colour as well as noise. Two men were arguing over a horse next to a cart full of yellow and purple blooms and herb plants fussed over by a woman in a tawny *palla.* Further on, stalls lined with straw held eggs and early vegetables. At the side were stacked small cages of chickens. Afra walked determinedly past fruit stalls and a cloth merchant and eventually stopped by a large cart with a drop-down side. Bowls of shining olives, oil and pots of honey filled the table in front of it. Behind it stood a middle-aged man with brown and grey hair, accompanied by a spotty-faced boy. The man hailed Afra in a friendly way and they began a bargaining conversation about prices and quantities. I looked round carefully at the forest of columns, the ornate doors, even at the gaggle of schoolboys being herded by a schoolmaster. Here was life, busy and colourful, not at all a city in decline in my eyes.

'There now, I have finished,' Afra said smiling. 'Can you take these four pots in your basket?'

'Oh, of course,' I said. 'I'm sorry, I was just taking in everything around me. It's so different from my home in the north.'

'Well, shall we walk a while and you could see more?'

'That's very kind of you, Afra.' I had been secretly hoping she would agree to come with me, so I was delighted with her offer. Although Asella had reported that Lucius wasn't here in the city, I had to find out for myself. Perhaps I could discover when he was likely to return.

'Would you mind if we walked up the Quirinal? I understand the view from there is exceptional.'

'Of course. Good thing you have your boots on,' she said, laughing.

Afra was an excellent guide and told me about the buildings as we walked. My basket was starting to weigh my arm down by the time we reached the crossroads past the old Temple of Serapis and the *thermae* of Constantine, but my excitement pushed out the tiredness in my arms as we continued up the road. We stopped for a moment to look at the ancient Quirinal temple. The view across the roofs of Rome *was* impressive, but I was looking for the Apulius *domus* as Aegius had described it.

We walked on for another fifty paces. I spotted the first watcher. He was obvious from his muscular build, wide leather belt and matching wristbands. His hands were thick-fingered and he exuded menace. He was trying to look as if he wasn't watching, but this was not the area where he could have hidden in a street *caupona*; there were none. I looped my free arm through Afra's and bent my head.

'Please don't think I have been inflicted by the gods with madness, but I need to call at the big house over there,' I whispered. 'Could we pretend to be selling our olives?'

'Why can't you just knock at the door?'

'Please trust me, Afra. There are ill-wishers who are trying to stop me contacting my friends, so I must do this secretly.'

She gave me a long look, then nodded. We marched up to the door and I saw another movement further up the street. Another watcher, I presumed. He was marching towards us. I caught my breath. Afra let her *palla* slip from her head, showing her dark hair and skin, and the watcher stopped. She put her basket down and thumped on the door.

'Olives,' she shouted. 'The best from Latium.'

The crossbarred window within the door opened and a bearded face appeared.

'Yes?' the gravelly voice said.

'Is Lucius Apulius at home? I have an urgent message for him,' I said.

'The young master doesn't take messages from itinerant olive sellers. Clear off.'

'Wait!'

'What?'

'Tell him it's a message from Noricum.'

'Humph.'

'Please.'

'Wait here.'

The window slammed shut. I glanced round very slowly, moving my head as little as possible. The two watchers were now looking at us. One was frowning. Gods! The window opened again and a younger face appeared. Not Lucius.

'I'm the steward here. What's your message?'

'It's for Lucius Apulius himself. I must deliver it personally.'

'There is nothing he would wish to hear from an olive seller, even from Noricum. He's not here in any case. Now go away and don't bother us again or I shall be obliged to set the *urbanae* on you.' He slammed the window shut.

I stared at the door.

'Come,' Afra whispered in my ear. 'We're attracting attention.' She pulled me down the road. I glanced back once to see the two watchers standing together, legs braced and arms crossed staring after us. A third one was walking towards us, his hand on his knife handle and smiling unpleasantly. Afra gripped my arm and hurried us down the hill. I couldn't stop the tears flowing.

29

One look from Aegius's face as we entered the inn prompted Afra to reach for my basket and retreat to the kitchen with both. Aegius was frowning and his eyes were like hard stones.

'A moment of your time, if you please, *domina*,' he spat out, then turned his back on me and limped towards the peristyle. He presumed I would follow him like a meek subject. Instead, I made my way round the far side to my room where I removed and folded my *palla*, detached the knife sheath from my belt and tidied my hair. Well, Aegius was probably going to shout about the dangers of my little expedition with Afra, but I would sit and listen politely until he had spent his fury. He meant well and had been my faithful guide, but he had no authority over me. However, I did admit to a feeling of guilt...

I opened my door and walked towards the group of basketweave chairs where he was standing glowering into the garden. Asella was sitting, fiddling with some threads and fabric. Both turned towards me as I approached. I sat and waited for the tirade.

'It's time for me to leave, *domina*,' he said in the coldest voice I'd ever heard. 'My services are no longer of any interest or use to you. I shall go back to Virunum and continue painting.'

'If that is your wish, Aegius,' I replied in my own mountain ice tone.

Asella opened her mouth and looked at me, then shook her head.

'You have no need of my counsel and seem perfectly happy to wander around Rome unescorted,' he continued.

'Not entirely unescorted. Afra was kind enough to come with me.'

'And was thus exposed to Siro's thugs. Very considerate of you towards her.'

'You are being dramatic, Aegius, but I realise it's out of concern for my well-being,'

'I leave the drama to you,' he retorted. 'What in Hades were you thinking of?'

'I'm not entirely incompetent in defending myself,' I shot back. 'I needed to find out for myself that Lucius was truly not there,' I added in a quieter tone. 'And try to discover if he was ever coming back to the city.' All I could hear were the birds in the aviary, but in the dreadful pause when Asella said not a word and Aegius stood silent as a stone statue, even they seemed to chirp more softly. I bent my head and blinked hard. 'Perhaps it's a lost cause and I *should* give up and come back with you to Virunum.' I brought my hands up to cover my face.

'Oh, for Jupiter's sake, stop feeling sorry for yourself, girl, and have a bit of confidence,' he said roughly. 'Are you really going to let yourself be defeated after a couple of tries?'

I looked up and glared at him.

'When I learnt you'd gone gallivanting off with just Afra, I was ready to strangle you and put us all out of our misery. Naive isn't the word. If you're going to live in Rome as a member of a senatorial family, you'd better sharpen up.'

'As that seems increasingly unlikely, I don't think I will need to,' I flashed back.

'Humph. I thought you had more spirit in you than that.'

'I have plenty, but if our journey has taught me one thing, it's that I must be a realist.' I felt exhausted, as though I'd fought a season of hard campaigns against countless barbarians.

'Very well,' he said. He took a deep breath and blew it out. 'If you forgive me saying so, *domina*, you are the most exasperating girl at the moment. It must be your condition. But I'll tell you this – you'll regret it your whole life if you don't give it one more try.'

He was right. I was being weak. And as my father the soldier would have said, I had already burnt my bridges. Even Turcilus wouldn't want me back. I needed to pull my courage back into my soul, but at this very moment, tiredness overwhelmed me, and my head was aching.

'I am sorry I'm causing you and Asella such trouble.' I stood and stumbled, catching my finger on a loose wicker strand on the back of the chair as I steadied myself. 'I must go and rest now. Forgive me.' As soon as I reached my room, I dropped onto the mattress and fell asleep within a moment.

The birds were calling and screeching. I saw shadows flitting across the gaps between the louvres of the shutters. Perhaps it was from the plants waving in the breeze. Miraculously, my headache had gone so I sat up, but my stomach growled. I hadn't eaten since the second hour. But first, I had to speak to Asella and Aegius.

She smiled at me, a little nervously, I thought, as I walked along the peristyle towards them. He looked up, flushed then stood. He bowed and drew the third chair away from the table for me.

'Please, sit,' he said. 'I wish to present my apologies to you, *domina*. I should not have spoken to you as I did. You are the daughter of the prince who gave me shelter and asked for very little in return.'

'No, it's I who am to blame. As you rightly said, I needed to find my backbone. I cannot think what came over me that I acted like a wilting flower. I could not have made this journey without you and Asella and I had no right to weaken in that way given everything you have done for me.'

'If I may say so, I think you are being harsh on yourself,' he replied in a gentler voice than I had ever heard from him.

'I think we're all tired,' Asella said. 'You, *domina*, will be feeling it worst as the child within you is pulling on your strength.'

'Yes, I think you must be right, Asella.' I looked from one to the other. 'I feel calmer and refreshed from my sleep. Now we must have a council of war and plan our campaign. But first I want to work out why this Siro hates me so much. I haven't wronged him in any way.'

'Perhaps your very existence is the trouble, *domina*,' Aegius said.

'That's nonsensical. I can't help who my mother was, and my father is.'

'Agreed, but it's what you symbolise for him.'

'Siro was mostly brought up by his great-aunt and had little contact with his mother,' Asella said. 'A pity, but he must have resented it when he saw others had them and all they represented. You are the child he should have been and have taken the place of what he considers he's lost.' She sighed. 'But he never had it in the first place.'

'So, Asella, you think he's out for revenge?' Aegius said. 'Could he be bought off?'

'Unlikely,' she said in a huffy voice. 'Not all tribespeople see money as you Romans do. Their honour counts more.'

'Really? So that's why they keep raiding across the Danuvius?' Aegius's look of contempt was hard to misinterpret. 'You're being romantic, Asella. Gold *solidi* is what they're after.'

Asella grasped the edges of the table, half rose and shot a fierce look at him.

'A true tribesman would kill you for those words.'

'He could try.' Aegius shrugged.

'Peace!' I shouted. 'For the gods' sake, let's not act like barbarians. Sit down, Asella.' I gave them both a fierce look. 'Now, we must try to think up a proper plan to get past these bullies on the gate. Who do you think they are, Aegius?'

'Most likely street thugs, possibly ex-gladiators. Locals, I'd think.'

'Why?'

'Siro travelled alone on the boat, and before you say it, I don't think that chancer Carpus and his roughnecks on the boat were anything to do with him. As for when he and the bandits who attacked us in the mountains fell on us, I'm sure they were also locals to the area. He's finding people desperate to earn some silver, so I reckon the ones outside the Apulius house are a similar type.'

'It would stick in my gullet to waste our money on bribing them,' I said. 'But let's keep that in reserve. We only need to get the porter to open the door to us properly, then we'd be safe.'

'You have two options – force or deception,' Aegius said. 'I could go and ask Leo where we could hire some similar muscle, but that would inevitably result in a vicious street brawl and possibly a dead body. Not what we want, as we decided earlier.'

'The three this morning looked capable of anything. I imagine three or four more like them clashing in an open street battle would make that inevitable. That leaves us with deception. Afra and I didn't do at all well today. What do you suggest?'

Aegius gave me a very strange look, then turned to look at the splashes of colour made by the caged birds.

'It will have to be deception and on a grand scale,' he said, but his voice was flat, almost fateful. After a minute or two, he roused himself and went to find Afra. He said he needed to use her kitchen boy to send a message.

The next morning, Aegius was already sitting at the table dipping bread in olive oil and eating heartily when Asella and I went for breakfast. It was only the first hour and I thought *we* were early.

'Ladies. I hope you are prepared for today.' He looked me up and down. I was only wearing my old tunic and had tied my hair back loosely.

'We will be ready at the third hour,' I said huffily. My stomach was bubbling, so I poured a beaker of *posca* in the hope of settling it. We ate in silence after that. After breakfast, Aegius asked us to stay in our room. He asked politely but his eyes were half closed and he looked as solemn as if he was about to commit suicide.

Shortly after, I heard voices – Aegius's and a deep one, loud, almost bellowing. We couldn't avoid hearing. They argued, the deep one laughed, but it was mocking, then became hard. Aegius's voice became subdued. It was too much to bear. I opened the door to my bedroom carefully to half an inch so I could catch at least a glimpse of who had reduced Aegius to supplicant status.

Through the leaves swaying in the breeze, I saw a toga with a broad purple stripe. Somebody important then. But so few men wore togas now – it was archaic. My father only used his on formal occasions or when he wanted to impress or squash pretension in others. Who was this man? I eased the door open a little further. Thank the gods it didn't squeak. I almost let go of the door ring in surprise. The other man was a mirror reflection of Aegius. No, he was burlier, rounder in the face with heavy jowls; a looser, less solid form of Aegius. He looked like one of Afra's exotic birds; his dark red robe decorated with a deep collar of gold embroidery shimmered as he moved.

'If I do this for you, Aulus, then that's the end of it,' the deeper voice blustered at Aegius.

'I have no intention of asking you for anything else,' Aegius replied flatly.

'I should hope not,' the other replied. 'You've brought enough disgrace on the family with all your artistic flimflam. Father never mentioned your name again when you ran away from the legion.' He sniffed loudly and looked as if he had rotting animal flesh under his nose. 'Not that that wasn't a poor choice in the first place. And now you're acting as a servant to some barbarian woman.'

'We're all servants, Primus,' Aegius said in a flat tone. 'Some serve a master or mistress, others the empire or the gods. Sadly, some only serve themselves.'

The other man sent Aegius a puzzled look.

'You're trying to tie me up in your stupid rhetorical knots,' he said. 'You could have used your talents if you'd tried. Your life has been a wasted one,' he blustered on.

'I see my sins are unforgivable,' Aegius replied.

'Don't take that clever, cutting tone with me. I'm still the elder.'

'Only by twenty minutes.'

'There you are again. I've a good mind to withdraw the favour.'

'I apologise for my lack of respect, I'm sure.'

'Humph. Very well. But if anything comes back damaged, I expect full compensation.'

'I wouldn't do anything less, my dear brother,' Aegius said smoothly.

'I have to go to an *important* meeting at the Senate now,' the other man said in a pompous tone. He nodded, turned and waddled in the direction of the vestibule. I opened my door and slipped out to watch him wave imperiously at Afra to open the entrance door.

Aegius brought his hand up to cover his face and rubbed his forehead with his fingers. He gave a great sigh, but didn't move. He let his hand fall, then looked up to the heavens and moved his lips as if in silent prayer. I shrank back against the wall to leave him to what must be an intense and private moment, but he turned in my direction.

'Come and join me, *domina*. I know you're there. I need a drink and you probably need an explanation.'

I waited until we were sitting at the table.

'You don't have to tell me anything, Aegius. Or should I call you Aulus now?'

'No, stick to Aegius. I've called myself that since I left home at seventeen.'

'That man… he's your brother, isn't he?'

'Alas, yes. My elder twin by twenty minutes as he always reminds me.'

'And a powerful man?'

He snorted.

'He likes to think so, but the imperial court in Mediolanum no longer takes any notice of the Senate in Rome. It's more like a glorified town council. And the emperor in Constantinople couldn't care less about their bleatings.'

'But your brother – he's going to help us?'

'Only after I reminded him of an incident in his youth that would bring him down if it was known. I have a letter from the young man involved.'

'Would that be enough?' I wasn't such a provincial that I was ignorant of how common it was for older men to frequent young men.

'Oh, yes. It's not merely about sexual behaviour but blackmail and attempted murder.'

'Juno!'

'Indeed,' he said drily. 'I never intended to use it as I never thought I'd see him again. I nearly threw it away. But this is the time.'

'I cannot thank you enough, Aegius. It must have been painful for you.'

'Oh, I don't know.' He looked up. 'Yes, it brought back the way my family didn't approve of me, and my feeling of rejection by them. But that was years ago.' He tipped his cup up to his lips, drank then set the empty beaker down on the table. 'My twin doesn't have an ounce of brotherly feeling.' His eyes gleamed. 'But he never knew when he was being played – too stupid and too full of himself. I found it dirty using the letter just now, but it was very satisfactory putting one over on him again.'

Dressed again in my blue finery and gold jewellery, I waited with Asella in the atrium. In truth, I was walking round in order to contain my nerves. Asella was sitting patiently, my folded *palla* on her lap.

'How is Aegius going to get us past those thugs without causing a scene?' I asked again.

'*Domina*, I don't know, but it's something to do with that basket his brother sent.'

'How is a basket going to help us?'

She sighed but said nothing.

'I know you got the impression from that dim-witted porter that Lucius may not even be in Rome, but at least we'll get into his house to find out. And we can leave a message with his family. Father said he'd been forbidden to travel out of Latium, so he can't go *that* far away. Always supposing he wants—'

'*Domina*, stop pacing around and worrying yourself. It's no good for the baby either. We won't know anything until we go there. This visit may only be a step, but it will be a step forward.'

'You're right, Asella.' I came back and sat in the chair opposite her, but kept looking for Aegius.

No sooner had I settled myself than a vision appeared in front of me. I blinked. The figure was dressed in a long deep green tunic embroidered with gold and blue strips falling from the shoulders and a gold roundel high on each sleeve. Around his waist was a heavy military-style belt. Draped over the whole was a rich saffron *pallium* edged with a broad purple stripe. Most surprising above all the gaudy colour was Aegius's face wearing a haughty expression. His grey hair was now entirely black and by a miracle, the bruising on his face had disappeared.

Asella's mouth opened and I was sure mine did the same. Then the familiar Aegius smile appeared.

'Ha! Surprised you, didn't I?' He grinned. 'The togs were sent by my brother. A bit flash for my taste, but just what we need. And his wife's dresser sent some cosmetics to cover up the effects of my beating.' He waved his hand in front of himself. 'Behold Senator Primus Sempronius Tuditanus.'

'Great Mother! I hardly recognised you, Aegius.'

'Hopefully it will get us past those thugs without incident.'

'We'll walk by with our noses in the air and to Tartarus with them,' I said.

'All of that, *domina*. But there's one more little surprise. Come.'

He still limped as we walked towards the front door of the inn. Outside, we found an even more striking vision; a large litter with crimson curtains, gold finials at the corners and four men waiting who were built like professional wrestlers. A fifth man with a long staff topped with a silver ball was fussing about placing and replacing silk cushions inside the extravagant litter.

'That snotty woman riding in the yellow curtained job the day we arrived – the one who rammed through the street – gave me the idea,' Aegius whispered to me as he handed me into the litter. 'I'll be walking in front with Primus's understeward, clearing the way.'

Asella climbed in beside me and we released the plaited silk ties to let the curtains fall and conceal us. I caught my breath as we were lifted, and we moved forward. The litter tilted slightly as we climbed, and only the faster breath of the bearers told me of their effort. We must have been ascending the Quirinal. I would have loved to have seen Aegius strutting along like a self-important senator, but we had to remain hidden or the whole effort would have been wasted. The understeward's shout sounded pompous enough. I had counted just over a thousand paces from the bearers' footsteps when the litter slowed. The understeward's voice became louder.

'Out of my way, fellow. You impede the most noble senator!' he cried out.

'Just doing our job, your honour,' a gruff voice replied.

'Impudence!' the understeward replied.

A few paces further on we stopped. A loud thump. My heart set up a similar pounding. Had Aegius and Primus's understeward been attacked? Despite Asella's anxious eyes, I pulled the curtain back a few inches. No, he was knocking on the wide door of

Lucius's house with the silver ball at the top of his staff striking the metal studs of the door. We had arrived. I grasped Asella's hand. She covered it with her other one and pressed it. Aegius stood directly behind the understeward, his arms crossed and a frown on his face as if he really were his brother.

The porter opened his window.

'Yes?'

'Open the door, porter, for the noble senator Sempronius Tuditanus and his lady calling on Lucius Apulius. Hurry up, the senator is waiting.'

Gods! This steward was as pompous as his real master, but effective as the porter nodded and touched his forehead with his finger. The door that had been stubbornly closed to me before now opened. Aegius's hand appeared at the edge of the litter curtain and pulled it back fully. The porter took one look at me then hurried back into the house. Was that normal behaviour for the porter of a grand *domus*? I stepped out and across the threshold of the house. I felt rather than heard Asella behind me. Then everything else faded. At the end of the vestibule, only a few paces away, was Lucius.

He stood sideways to me, his full attention wrapped up in listening to the porter. My heart nearly burst with equal parts of relief and love.

'Well, do what the steward says,' he was saying as he gestured towards the door. 'I can't delay. I have an important meeting.'

I stepped forward, covering the short distance between us.

'And what, pray, is more important than meeting me?' I said. My heart pounded. I caught my breath. His head whipped round. Frozen as a Greek statue, he stared at me. Oh gods, he'd forgotten me. He didn't want me. His mouth opened, but no words came out. It was unbearable. My throat tightened and became dry.

'Julia,' he croaked, his face pale. 'How are you here?'

'I've been travelling for nearly four weeks by ship, horse and litter,' I replied. 'I'm parched. You may no longer want me, Lucius, but you could at least ask me in.'

He raised his arms and took my hands. He searched my face as if seeing me for the first time.

'It really *is* you,' he said. 'Dear gods, how I have missed you.' He released my left hand and ran his fingers over my cheekbone and jaw. I closed my eyes and trembled at his touch. His fingers touched my mouth and my lips parted. 'My love, oh, my love,' he whispered. I leant into him and he brought his arms up to surround me in his warm embrace. With his lips close to my ear, he murmured, 'We will never be parted again.'

'No, never,' I said. 'And now we can be married, Lucius, according to your gods.'

'Tomorrow, or sooner,' he said, smiling.

I chuckled.

'Oh no, sooner than that.'

He bent his head back and laughed. Then he brought those peat lake brown eyes back to meet mine. They were full of love.

30

A discreet cough behind me interrupted us. Aegius. I blinked and with great reluctance stepped back from Lucius's gaze. Around us were Aegius grinning, Asella smiling, the porter with goggling eyes, the Apulius steward with a raised eyebrow, and a middle-aged man with brown and grey hair, a similar beard and Lucius's eyes. He was frowning.

'Well, Lucius?' the older man said. He flicked his fingers backwards and the steward and porter vanished. Aegius and Asella became stiff as statues with solemn faces. This must be Lucius's father, the one who'd been a senior officer with Emperor Julian at Samarra. His commanding air and upright figure radiated authority. He nodded briefly and turned, saying, 'Come.'

Lucius took my hand and looped my arm through his.

'Gods, I'm overjoyed at seeing you,' he whispered. 'I can't believe you're truly here.' He lifted my wrist. 'And you're wearing my bracelet.'

'Ever since I received it.'

'Ah, Julia,' He bent his head and kissed my wrist, just by the bracelet. We'll talk later.' He pressed my hand as we entered the atrium, the heart of the house. It was tall and wide with a square *impluvium* in the centre directly below a circular opening in the roof. Around the painted walls ran vivid hunting scenes, then towards the back, garden scenes with graceful trees and an image of gods feasting. I imagined Aegius would wish to look at them more closely. But for the moment, he stood back.

Lucius's father ignored us and studied Aegius.

'You're not that oaf Sempronius.'

'No, sir, but I have the misfortune to be related to him,' Aegius replied.

'Then what are you doing here?'

I opened my mouth to answer, but Lucius pressed my hand again and shook his head.

'I've been escorting my prince's daughter on her journey to Rome.'

'Ah.' He looked at us. 'Present the lady to me, Lucius,' he commanded.

'Father, this is Lady Julia, daughter of Prince Bacausus of Virunum in Noricum Mediterraneum.' Lucius smiled at me. 'And this is my father Senator Quintus Apulius Pius.'

The senator looked me up and down, in a guarded, but not unfriendly way, then slightly frowning, he studied my face. I kept my eyes on his. I would not drop my eyes like a good little Roman woman was supposed to do – I wasn't such a creature – but I studied his face in turn. Firm lines, a long prominent nose set in sun-weathered skin, he was a very different creature from Aegius's senator brother. Quintus wore no jewellery, and his long tunic was plain, off white with only simple embroidery, unlike the majority of men I'd seen since we'd arrived in Italia. Eventually, he turned to Lucius.

'Well, Lucius, she has courage enough not to be cowed. Take her to your mother.' He turned to Aegius. 'Come with me to my *tablinum*. I presume that as one of the Sempronii you are literate. Firstly, I want to know the woman's situation, then I suppose I will need to write to her father.'

'I am hardly in a position to speak for the prince,' Aegius said.

'Well, of course not, but you can at least take him a message that will be delivered without being garbled.'

The senator stalked off towards the other side of the atrium. Aegius cast a pleading look at me, but I tipped my head at him to follow. He would not betray me and he would guide Quintus Apulius in how to approach my father and my father in how to answer the senator. Perhaps I would forgive my father for betrothing me to Turcilus if he would forgive me for running from that betrothal to find Lucius.

We were left standing in the middle of the large atrium surrounded by silence.

'Your father speaks his mind,' I said to Lucius. I felt bruised by being referred to as 'woman' and dismissed so peremptorily. My own father, although he'd treated me recently in a high-handed way, talked to me about our house, our land and our people and I had run a large household since my mother's death. We discussed the latest books and even his business ventures. Well, this old-fashioned Roman would soon learn that we 'barbarians' were more enlightened than he was.

'He's a traditionalist, I admit,' Lucius said. 'But a good man. However strict he appears, he does take a great deal of notice of my mother. She usually does what she wants to do without him noticing.' He smiled to himself as if at an inner thought or a memory.

'Will your mother accept me?'

'I know she will, but you'll see for yourself. She's kind as well as clever.'

He led me across the atrium to an ornately painted entrance. I stopped and swallowed hard. His mother. Most men adored their mothers. Perhaps Lucius was biased. Would she be like the snooty Valeria at the baths or those tittering women in Carsulae? A woven silk cord tied back an embroidered curtain and I could see a couch, a side table and two inlaid stools. An unlit brazier stood in the corner between two painted panels of rural scenes, the colours highlighted by the strong sunlight through a glazed window.

On the couch, reading a codex with a cover covered in tiny metal studs, was a large woman, her fine brown hair escaping from a crown of curls which then fell to her neck. She was dressed in a dark red *dalmatica* with the sleeves of an ivory underdress covering her forearms. She looked up.

'Lucius. I thought you were going out.' Her gaze turned to me and she smiled. 'And who is this?'

Unless she was afflicted with deafness, she must have heard everything.

'Mother, this is Julia, daughter of Prince Bacausus in Noricum. Julia, this is my mother, Constantia of the Flavii.' He spoke softly and gave his mother a loving smile which was returned. The couch creaked as Constantia sat up. She waved us to the two stools.

'Welcome, Julia. You've made a long journey which must have been tiring. Are you staying long in Rome?'

'Mother, Julia is to be my wife.'

'Ah, I see I have erred.'

Instinctively, I knew she hadn't done any such thing. Like her husband, she was testing me. I sighed inwardly. Perhaps it was going to be harder to settle in Rome than the journey to reach here. I supposed that as Lucius was their only son his parents were concerned about this wild, northern woman whom they didn't know.

Lucius fidgeted on his stool. I heard Asella, who was standing by the wall, sniff loudly.

'We would welcome a gathering of friends and a blessing by a priest as soon as possible, but not the whole fuss of a *confarreatio*.' He glanced at me.

Following my father's insistence, I'd gone through a day-long dreary ceremony with special hair and dress stipulations and endless sprinkling and chanting when I'd married Deodatus. As a Galilean, he'd looked down his nose at the whole day's proceeding which had made me exceedingly uncomfortable. I had no wish to repeat it. I nodded vigorously at Lucius.

'I'm sure you will be happy to arrange it, Mother.' He gave her a steady look. Then he took my hand. 'But from this moment, Julia is my declared wife. She has consented to live with me as my wife and will be treated as such by the whole household.'

'But of course, my son,' Constantia said. 'Now, you may leave us. I'm sure you should attend on your father at this moment.'

Knowing he was dismissed, Lucius bent and kissed his mother on her cheek, smiled at me then left.

'Now, Julia, tell me about your long journey,' Constantia said. 'And about your home in the mountains.'

. . .

Lucius returned an hour later, a thunderous look on his face. I put my hand out to him. He took it and kissed the back, but turned to Constantia.

'I know it is your domestic concern, Mother, but I have an urgent request about one of the slaves here.' Constantia raised an eyebrow. 'Father has agreed, subject to your consent, but I really must insist.'

'Calm yourself, Lucius. Whatever is it?'

'Julia may have told you already, but she could not approach our house for fear of being abducted by her enemy's thugs and was even tricked with the connivance of a member of this household.'

'Great Juno! She hinted at some difficulty but did not elaborate. Julia?'

'I haven't had time to tell you. I didn't want it to interfere on my first day with you as I was nervous enough.' I looked at Lucius. 'Aegius told you, I suppose?'

'Yes. The words "poisonous little snake" were in his account. He has a very protective regard for you, *cara*,' Lucius said.

I gave them the full details of my dealings with Lucilla at the baths. Constantia frowned, then rang a silver handbell on her table. A girl, no more than ten or twelve, appeared almost instantly and bowed.

'Go and fetch the steward. Interrupt him if necessary.' Constantia said nothing until the steward presented himself very shortly afterwards.

'*Domina*?' He bowed to Constantia who gestured towards me.

'This is Lady Julia, my new daughter, Master Lucius's wife. Please inform the household that she will be treated with utmost respect.'

The steward bowed to me, his face completely expressionless as if he had forgotten our previous encounter. I gave him a steady look so there would be no ambiguity in the future. He looked away first, as I had intended.

'Another matter,' Constantia continued. 'Please bring the young pastry cook to me, whatever she is doing.'

He blinked but hurried off. Constantia had been abrupt which didn't seem to be her natural manner. But I was only starting to know her. Perhaps she kept a firm divide between herself and her servants.

A slim young woman, dark brown hair tied back simply which emphasised her pointed chin, and a flour smudge on the skirt of her tunic, entered the room with an assured air. It was 'Lucilla'. She gave a minimal bow to Constantia, raised her head, then saw me. Her brown eyes widened. Realisation spread over her face and then terror. She shrank back. Her eyes darted round to the door, but the steward grabbed her arm before she could move.

'Well, Daughter,' Constantia said, glancing at me. 'Is this the person who accosted you at the baths and claimed to be a relation of your husband, my son?'

'It is, Mother,' I replied equally formally. The girl had stopped struggling and to my amazement tried to stare me out with insolence shining from her eyes.

'Well, girl, you may speak,' Constantia said.

'*Domina*, with respect, I have not met this lady at any baths or anywhere else.'

Lucius stepped forward with anger plain on his face. I shook my head, then replied in my coldest voice.

'Not only is she a deceptive creature who takes bribes from a criminal wishing to harm me and pretends to be a freeborn member of a noble family, but she also lies,' I said. All my anger of discovering she had taken silver to act as bait to trap me returned. 'If you inspect her buttock, you will see she has a large brown birthmark. I could not know that if I had not seen it at the baths.'

Constantia nodded to the steward who grasped the girl's tunic and pulled it off her. And there was the mark. Lucilla fell to her knees and started crying. She prostrated herself at Constantia's feet, sobbing that she had served her mistress well. And had made only one mistake.

'Get her up, steward. You, girl, make yourself decent.'

Lucilla wiped the snot from her nose with her forearm and took her tunic from the steward, giving him a hate-filled look as she pulled it on.

'After a good whipping, you will be sold,' Constantia said. 'Steward, make sure she is fitted with a collar and tablet saying that she makes heavenly pastry, but has a corrupt soul, and lies.'

'One moment. If I may, Mother?'

'Yes, Julia?'

'I would like to question Lucilla, if that is her true name.' Constantia nodded. I turned a hard stare on the girl. 'You may be spared the whipping if you answer willingly. Who gave you the money?'

'A man,' she said to the mosaics on the floor.

'Describe him.'

'Good-looking with curly blond hair.'

'Accent?'

She looked up at me, startled.

'Yes,' she replied sullenly. 'Northern.'

'And when did he give you the money?'

'Can't remember.'

The steward slapped her face. She flinched away from him. I felt sorry for her as he raised his hand again. I looked at him and shook my head.

'Make an effort to remember,' I said. 'It will go better for you if you tell the truth.'

'He was here a few weeks ago. Took me out to a private room several times and we had fun.'

'Fun?' Constantia frowned.

'He fucked her,' Lucius said, flatly. He looked at me then flushed. Perhaps he remembered our first meeting. Constantia frowned at her son's crude words but didn't say anything further as I continued my questioning.

'And when did he give you money?'

'Every time. Then a big bonus for at the baths. I was saving up. We were going to run away together.' She stuck her chin out at Constantia.

'But you knew what you were doing was wrong, didn't you?' I continued.

Lucilla shrugged.

'You were an easy victim,' she said, looking at me.

'Perhaps so,' I said, 'but the man has made *you* a victim of your own greed and lies. He is not going to lift a finger to save you, nor will you ever see him again.'

Tears ran down Lucilla's face.

'You have been duped, Lucilla, and as Lady Constantia says, you cannot stay here now. You will be punished and then sold, but if she agrees, and only then, I suggest no tablet. You will have a chance to redeem yourself in a new household. Make sure you use it wisely.'

Asella had prepared a tisane to relieve the headache that ambushed me after questioning Lucilla. I had to concede. She made me lie down with the shutters closed in the room Constantia had instructed Lucius to show me to, then she shooed him out, insisting as only a favourite servant can.

'You must rest now, *domina*. All this anxiety has drained you and the child. I have spoken to the cook. They eat *cena* at the twelfth hour, so you can stay here for at least two hours.' She pointed to a dish on the side table. 'There are some figs, cheese and small pastries. It would be wise to eat them.' She drew a linen sheet over me. 'I will come back at the appropriate time with a bowl of warm water and ensure your robe is refreshed.'

'Thank you, Asella,' I murmured and fell asleep.

I woke with a warm hand holding mine. Toughened skin. Then strong fingers pressed mine. The smell of lemongrass and cypress. Lucius. I opened my eyes. His were shining in the light of a lamp. He stretched over me and kissed my forehead.

'Are you well?' he said. The light showed tiny shadows from creases in his forehead above his nose.

'Yes, just tired. And relieved. I thought I would never find you, Lucius. I wept when we couldn't even reach the door. And those thugs—'

'Shh.' He kissed the corner of my mouth. 'Don't concern yourself now. Aegius told me all about them. They've disappeared, but I've sent out an enquiry to a friend – well, an acquaintance – of mine who commands one of the urban cohorts. Father knows the urban prefect, so we'll approach him if we don't get far with my contact.'

'Did Aegius tell you who we think is behind them?'

'He said you'd tell me all about it when you're ready.'

'Lucius…'

'Yes, *cara*?'

'I have something much more important to tell you.'

'More than your life being threatened and you fighting bandits to save it?'

'Yes.' I brushed his face and the side of his neck with the tips of my fingers. 'A new life, created by our love. And our passion.' I watched his face. A spark lit in his eyes.

'A child?' he whispered.

'Yes.'

He lay against me, his head in the round dip at the base of my throat. I stroked his hair. He gave a sound, somewhere between a sob, a grunt and a laugh. It reverberated through my body.

'Julia, I cannot find good enough words to say how I feel. This will be the most precious child in the world. This is the happiest day of my life. I thought I would go mad when I thought I had to endure life without you. I was ready to convert to the Galileans if that meant I could marry you. I was on the point of going to their temple when you arrived.'

'Oh, my dear,' I said. 'You should never have thought of perjuring yourself like that.' I couldn't tell him that even then he couldn't have married me because the Christians forbade divorce from each other. Bishop Eligius was hypocritical enough to have enjoyed telling Lucius that.

'I belong to Mars and always will,' he said. 'I will honour the gods every day in my heart until the day I die, but I ached for your loss. And I didn't have any letter from you.'

'Nor I from you. I suspect my father intercepted them.'

'He seemed too honourable to do that.'

'I think he was trying to make me forget by cutting off all contact with you. If I didn't hear from you again, he thought my memories of you would fade.'

Lucius bent over me and kissed my forehead, then sighed.

'And you have fought in your own battles to get here.' He kissed the scar on my arm. 'I itched to travel to Virunum and just fetch you,' he said, 'but I was forbidden to go beyond Latium on pain of execution.'

'No!' I grasped the base of my throat. 'How could they threaten you with that?'

Lucius shrugged. 'What the emperor wishes, his court will carry out.'

'It's Eligius, curse him.' I lay back and stared up at the ceiling. 'I know he's behind it. He would stop at nothing to prevent me marrying another man, losing my wealth and jeopardising his quest for power over the region.'

'Why do you think that?'

'He told me as much – that he had powerful and influential connections – when I went to visit him to beg him for a Christian annulment.' I waved my hand in the air. 'I wondered at the time if it was boasting, but Father said afterwards that Eligius's tentacles even reached into the imperial court. Gods, I could thrust a knife through his neck for threatening you like that. It's a good thing I came here instead.'

'Oh, my Julia. You are like a burst of fresh mountain air – heady and clear. You lift my spirits.'

'Be careful, Lucius, you are becoming poetic. Love me instead.'

He kissed me on my lips, softly, and several times. His hands went to my hair and he pulled the pins out urgently, destroying Asella's careful work. He buried his face in it.

'Such fire,' he murmured, his voice low and on the edge of roughness. 'I only want it to spread through me and consume me.'

I shed my tunic and we consumed each other.

31

I was sure that over the next few days both Constantia and Quintus were watching me, each in their own way. She seemed all complaisance when we sat in her private room, sewing and talking, she probing and me fending off the nosiest questions. I thought it strange that a woman of Constantia's rank undertook needlework, but her eyes twinkled when she assured me that it was a female tradition she was happy to follow.

'I know you modern young women leave it to your servants,' she said, 'but it gives me thinking time. And there is always sewing to do. There'll be even more when children come.'

I bowed my head over my own work so she couldn't see the flush I knew was creeping up my face. Luckily, Asella entered the room carrying her plain cloak and my fur-lined green one which she laid on the table beside me. She'd also brought a large earthenware bowl lined with a double-folded piece of linen.

Constantia reached over and touched my cloak.

'This is beautiful weaving and such fine wool.'

Aegius had told the town guard at Caporetum it was a gift from his patroness at the imperial court, but in truth it was made from a length of cloth I'd purchased from a Saxon trader.

'It's from Britannia where the finest wool is bred and woven, but it contains a secret.' I smiled. 'Do you have any small shears or scissors?'

She gestured towards a leather roll. I unwound it to find three beautiful pairs of pivoted scissors, the largest decorated with a pattern of whorls, the other two plain. I picked up the tiniest ones and snipped at the stitching below the hood. Asella held the bowl under my hands. Gold *solidi* slipped out of the gap created by my unpicking, followed by precious stones, rings, brooches and earrings. My amber and gold necklace followed.

'Great gods, Julia, this is hidden treasure.' Constantia looked at the heaped bowl.

I smiled to myself, but said nothing. I started unpicking the hem and two more gold necklaces, a series of belt plaques, a shower of gemstones, linked bracelets and gold *solidi* fell out. Asella took another pair of scissors and set about unpicking the hem on her own cloak. Silver *miliarensia* and gold *solidi* tumbled out adding to the pile in the bowl.

'We could only bring this amount with us, but if my father releases my possessions, there is much more.' I looked over at her. She said nothing, but gazed at the shining pile as if she were seeing a mirage.

Asella picked up my cloak and selected a thread to start repairing it. I doubted I would need it with the warm spring weather, but she liked to keep everything in good order. I picked up a handful of the coins, slipped them in my waist pouch, excused myself to Constantia and went to look for Aegius. He'd been hiding himself exceptionally well these last few days and I needed to thank him properly. But I couldn't find him. I stood in the corridor leading to the peristyle and tried to think through where he could be. He wouldn't have gone back to Virunum without saying farewell. A movement in the peristyle. One of the doors of the rooms on the east side opened. I drew back against the wall into the shadow so I could watch without being seen. A familiar figure came out. Aegius. So that was where he was.

His hair was starting to show grey again and he was dressed in a simple tunic and sandals. He walked slowly along between the pillars and I could hear him humming. He turned into the corridor and stopped when he saw me.

'Well, Aegius, where have you been hiding?'

'*Domina,*' he said and bowed.

'Don't. You have been revealed as a senator's brother and your family is an ancient one. No wonder you have that authoritative air. Does my father know?'

'No, I didn't think it worth telling him.'

'You are a complete mystery.'

'Not really. I have followed my own road – that's all.'

'Where have you been?'

'Your father-in-law grilled me into the night about you, your family, your father's position, your divorce – everything – but I fear he was unsatisfied with my answers. He is going to prepare contracts for your marriage, but I suggested he consult me before sending them. I hinted that Prince Bacausus would just laugh and tear them up if they in any way disadvantaged you. He wasn't pleased.' He gestured to the garden. 'Shall we sit? I may need a little time for the rest of my story.'

He told me how he ran from home to join the legions although his father had forbidden it. He'd been fascinated by paintings and mosaics he'd seen during his service and taught himself to paint as a relaxation. In the legions, he'd risen to centurion, acted as a trusted imperial messenger, then one day after an order to slaughter natives, he'd had enough. He deserted, travelled north supporting himself by taking on painting commissions, studying techniques when he found teachers, finding rare pigments.

He'd crossed the Adriatic and worked his way up the Illyrian coast from villa to villa, but never settling, especially after the affair with Stella near Fons Timavi. Then he saw his name on a deserters' list in Aquileia, so he headed up the old amber road and ended up in Virunum where he found peace at my father's palace.

'Did you not fear coming back to Rome, with me?'

He shook his head.

'I'd changed my name, become old and thought that everybody I knew before would have forgotten about me.'

'Then asking your brother to help was very dangerous.'

'Not really. He had no choice since I had that letter.' He smiled at me. 'On the day we managed to gain access to this house, I sent the litter back with the understeward and told him I would return the basket later. Although I felt duty bound to restore the fancy dress outfit Primus had lent me to him, I wasn't going to strip off then and there.' He grinned. 'In the end, I went back with it myself. Primus was icy at first, but we sat down over a cup of wine or two and he thawed out. We even laughed together about some of the things we did when we were young. I stayed to supper, and we talked again the next day and the next. He's been caught in the career course outlined for him by our father. I have a sneaking suspicion he envies me, although he'd die before admitting it.'

'Are you reconciled, then?'

'That's a bit strong, but I'd say we are probably on the way to an understanding.'

'I'm so glad. Truly, Aegius. Will you stay here then?'

'Gods, no! I'll go back to Virunum to my daughter and my grandson. But not until I'm sure you are well settled here.'

'Will you arrange something for me?'

'What is it?'

'Can you find a safe way to send a letter to my father?'

'Of course. Shall I take it with me or is it more urgent?'

'If you can, I'd like to send it now. I must tell him I'm safe and that he should not worry about me. Although I would like to have my marriage portion for Lucius's sake, I want to tell Father that if it helps to settle Turcilus's ruffled feathers, he can give it all to him.'

The next morning, as Lucius belted his tunic and prepared to go to Diocletian's Baths, his eyes shone with a teasing light.

'I really need to exercise some of my other muscles.' I said nothing but raised one eyebrow and he chuckled. 'When I returned to Rome,' he continued, 'my father kicked me out of the house for being moody and sent me into the country to the family estate. I tried to drown my longing for you with the hard routine of managing and working on the farm.' He sat on the bed and took my hand. 'It didn't work, of course.'

I didn't reply but wondered if he'd wished to find some young male company and catch up with some of his city friends. It was strange living a domestic life together now when we'd had to snatch time for our meetings in Virunum.

Asella came in a few minutes after he left and we prepared to go to the bath suite towards the back of the house. Although small, it had everything; *caldarium* with wooden slatted seats, a *tepidarium* with just about enough space for two massage couches and a *frigidarium* where you could just swim four strokes. After the episode with Lucilla, I was slightly wary of public baths. I hadn't been out of the house since I'd arrived. It was nearly a week, but I'd been luxuriating in my reunion with Lucius. Constantia said she would introduce me to some of her friends, but there had been no visits yet. Nor any mention of even the simplest marriage ceremony.

We emerged from my room and were walking a few steps along the mosaic floor of the corridor when I heard an argument in full swing. I stopped. It was bad manners to eavesdrop, but the voices were raised so high that we couldn't help but hear. Asella and I exchanged glances.

'She's little more than a barbarian. I spent much of my military career knocking Hades out of them. Your family and mine would be mired by such an alliance. I won't have it, despite what Sempronius says about the father's wealth and supposed status.'

Sempronius? Oh, of course, he meant Aegius.

'You're being unreasonable, Quintus.' Constantia's voice was conciliatory. 'She's a lovely girl, well mannered and well read. She speaks, reads and writes Latin and Greek and there is obviously money.'

'But a tribeswoman for a mother – I ask you!'

I gripped Asella's hand. How dared he disparage *Matir*?

'You exaggerate, Quintus,' came Constantia's voice. 'She's the daughter of a prince and Noricum is an old, well-established province, not a wild place like Britannia.'

I spun round. I'd heard enough. Asella tried to grab my forearm, but I shook it off.

'No, *domina*, don't,' she cried out.

The voices stopped, but I marched in the direction of where they'd come from. I found Lucius's parents just by the entrance to his father's *tablinum*. Constantia's eyes were blazing, and Quintus's face was red and angry. They both turned. I glared at them. Quintus looked defiant. Constantia glanced away, then back at her husband. I took a massive breath in.

'I appreciate you don't know me very well yet, and are unfamiliar with my background. Rome is, after all, its own small world,' I said in my iciest tone. 'Perhaps you don't realise that the royal house was ruling in the *regnum Noricum* since before Hannibal the Carthaginian destroyed the Romans at Cannae. My father is a member of that house.' Neither said anything, so I continued. 'If my memory is correct, both the Apulii and the Flavii families are of plebian stock, farmers and tax-gatherers, I believe?' I half closed my eyes and lifted my chin. 'As for my mother, she was a chief's daughter, a lawgiver and counsellor – hardly a peasant barely out of the forest.'

'We didn't mean—' Constantia began. I gave her a tight smile then turned to Lucius's father.

'I think you spoke from ignorance, Quintus Apulius. That is my charitable interpretation. I am going to take my bath now. We will speak more fully of this later.'

Now I was starting to tremble addressing Lucius's parents like this, but I turned and walked away with as much dignity as I could muster. Round the corner in the narrow corridor, I stumbled, and Asella put her arm round my waist.

'Well played, daughter of Noricum,' she whispered and helped me along to the baths.

Later that morning, I sat in an alcove in the atrium absorbed with reading the latest of Ausonius's works. Even though Ausonius was much older, he was apparently a great friend of Symmachus, a young man on the rise, according to Lucius, and whose father was an equally great friend of Lucius's father. Rome was indeed a small world.

Ausonius's writings always soothed me. His style was easy and fluent, and he wrote about country life and the concerns of real people. And it reminded me always of that poetry evening at Quietus's house in Virunum when his daughter Priscilla read Ausonius's love poem to his German slave, Bissula, with so much passion. That was the evening I started to fall in love with Lucius.

I first sensed Lucius near me before I saw him. Over the last few days, our bond had intensified to become instinctive, and not merely physically. When he wasn't with me, I felt colder. When he was with me, I was complete.

'Julia,' was all he said. I watched him walk towards me, confident, vital, his mouth smiling and eyes wide. 'Come with me, if you're not otherwise occupied.'

'What is it?'

'More a question of *who* it is.'

I put the book back on the shelf, careful to find the correct pigeonhole. Quintus was as strict about keeping his library in order as was my father. Lucius took my hand and led me to the back of the house to the peristyle where through the trees and shrubs, I saw a young man lounging on a bench and sipping from a silver cup.

'Sit up, you lazy toad,' Lucius shouted.

'Only when you manage to beat me in a fight.' He let out a hearty laugh.

As we came nearer, the young man not only sat up, but stood and placed his cup on the bench. He was tall, even taller than Lucius, and wiry. He was dressed in military uniform complete with decorated buckles and plaques but uncovered legs below the knee hem of his ornate tunic. He bowed, then straightened up. Although brown-haired like many Romans, his piercing blue eyes were the colour of high summer.

'This is my friend, Gaius Mitelus. Gaius, the Lady Julia Bacausa, my wife,' Lucius said, still holding on to my hand. I extended my other hand.

'I am pleased to meet you, Gaius Mitelus,' I said formally, but gave him a friendly smile.

'Let me assure you, lady, that the pleasure is all mine.' He took my hand and winked at me. 'I have been longing to meet the mysterious enchantress who has captured my comrade's heart. You have no idea how tiresome he's been.'

Was he joking?

'I am no enchantress, Mitelus, merely a woman who loves a man,' I replied.

'Ha! And knows her own mind, by the sound of it.'

'I think it best to be unambiguous.'

He flung up his free hand and grinned.

'*Pax*, lady. I surrender.'

'And I accept,' and I laughed. His eyes half closed as he chuckled.

'Then I shall tread carefully.' He kissed the back of my hand before he released it, and winked again. I think I was going to like Gaius Mitelus.

Lucius pressed my other hand and automatically, I turned and smiled at him. He led me to the opposite bench, one in the shade.

'Gaius is on leave. I met him at the baths,' Lucius said. 'He serves in the *comitatus* and has managed to circumnavigate the religious problem.'

'A polite way of putting it,' Mitelus said. 'My commander suspects I am no true follower of the Christos, but he never asks so I don't need to answer. I mumble their prayers and do what's necessary.' He glanced at Lucius. 'I'm not as stiff-necked as Lucius. He has much higher principles, something I admire, but I won't sacrifice my career.' He sighed. 'But it's getting harder and harder, and Mercury knows one day I'll get rumbled.'

'How were you granted leave?' Lucius asked. 'I thought you said your commander was having trouble with desertion.'

'He is. We're about a third understrength. But he says he trusts me as I'm from an old military family and know my duty.' He rolled his eyes.

'So how long have you got?'

'Only a few weeks, then back up to the Rhine. The emperor is in a temper that he failed to grab Macrian – the German king that's been causing trouble by trying to bring together the tribes to challenge us. He's deposed Macrian and put his own man in, much good that'll do him, but he's determined to go after Macrian again. So it's back to the forests of Germania again for me.'

'Well, you can make yourself useful by helping me,' Lucius said.

'Oh? Now what have you done?' Mitelus glanced at me then back to Lucius.

'Nothing. It's what's been done to Julia.' He turned to me. 'May I tell him your story? Only the relevant parts?'

'If you think he can help,' I replied. Mitelus seemed lightweight in his manner, jokey even, but he listened intently to Lucius and without blinking. Afterwards, he leant back, clasped both hands around his knee and gazed into the distance. After a moment, he unwound his hands.

'The first level is your contact in the urban cohorts, but another approach is via the underworld. Let me make a few enquiries. Of course, grabbing this half-brother would be the best result. I'll add him to my tasks list.'

32

The next day, an invitation came from an Honorina Mitela to visit her in the afternoon. I read the note again, but it seemed straightforward.

'Who is this, Lucius?' I said, handing it to him. I realised it must be a member of his friend's family.

'Mars alive! It's the old lady. She's Gaius's aunt and rules the household with a rod of iron. Gaius's father just does what he's told when she's in full flow. She also runs the social life of most of Rome. Shall I come with you?'

'The invitation says to come alone. I shall take Asella, of course.'

'I'll escort your litter. We can't be too careful.'

'Because of Honorina or Siro?'

'Ha! Well, you never know. The Apulius livery should protect you and our bearers are no delicate flowers.'

Constantia looked taken aback when I advised I would be going to visit Honorina. She'd been intensely, almost over-polite since I'd confronted her and Quintus.

'Please give Honorina my best respects and affection,' she said. 'Would you like me to come with you as this is the first time you would be meeting a member of Roman society?'

'No, thank you. I have moved in society since I was sixteen and run my father's household from that time.' I affected a thinking pose. 'It's high time I met some other ladies, don't you think?'

She flushed. Normally, a mother-in-law would introduce her new daughter to her female acquaintances as soon as she could, but Constantia had not lifted a finger in this respect. Or perhaps Quintus had forbidden her. I was sure he was still antagonistic towards me.

I picked up my new silk *palla* and wound it round my shoulders and over my hair and stepped out of the entrance door with Asella in my wake.

'A moment!' Aegius's voice called from the vestibule. 'I'll come with you for the walk.'

Lucius looked him up and down.

'Do you feel we need an additional escort, Aegius?' he said in a cool tone.

'Oh, I'll just amble along a bit behind you. Just ignore me.' He gave Lucius a genial smile.

My skin prickled. Despite the warmth of the day, Aegius was wearing a short plain cloak over his tunic so I knew he was concealing a knife.

'Let us go, Lucius,' I said. 'Aegius will go his own way. And it may not harm to have him watch. It's *his* time he's frittering away.'

'Oh, very well,' Lucius said, but he looked affronted.

We soon plunged into the noise and smell of Roman streets lined with tall buildings which loomed above us and cut out most of the light. I didn't know how the litter bearers avoided multiple stray dogs and boys, people carrying enormous loads, workshop goods spilling out into the road and crowds of people in front of shops and street bars, let alone people just standing around in the middle of the street.

We had to grip the sides of the litter once when they swerved to avoid being hit by a man pushing a handcart and gossiping with his neighbour, not looking where he was going. Then we climbed up another hill where the crowds and giant buildings lessened, and the view improved immensely.

Lucius told me the Mitelus *domus* sat on the summit of the Cispius Mons, part of the Esquiline, so it wasn't too far away. We arrived shortly afterwards at a large door in between a shop selling fine pottery and one smelling heavenly with piles of spices in large bowls. Lucius knocked and the porter opened immediately. Asella and I climbed down and entered the narrow vestibule. I glanced back at the street. Aegius was nowhere to be seen. Ah, well. Perhaps he had found an agreeable companion to drink or gamble with in some dark corner.

A servant led us to the atrium, but Lucius strode along with the confidence of knowing where he was going. In the atrium to one side sat Juno's twin sister. Dressed in an embroidered sleeved tunic with a dark blue *palla* draped from her shoulder about her body in the old way, her hair fell in waves from a parting in the middle of her head and was bound under a tiara. It wasn't a tiara – it was just the style – but that was the effect. Her face *did* resemble the old statues of the goddess – sculpted lines complete with a haughty expression. A woman with authority – no doubt of that.

She frowned and fixed a sharp gaze on Lucius.

'What are you doing here, Apulius? It was your wife I invited. Go away and find my rascal of a nephew.'

He bowed and fled towards the back of the house.

'Now let me look at you,' she continued. She studied me so intently that I felt as if I'd been turned inside out. She gestured me to the padded stool set at an angle to her chair. 'You *are* as handsome as my nephew reported. And you have none of those dreadful freckles Celtic women have in Britannia.'

I blinked at her directness.

'No, *domina*,' I said. 'But they sometimes try to appear on my nose in high summer if I've been up in the mountains too long. They usually fade quickly as I've inherited my mother's skin.'

'Ah, the hillwoman,' she said, and waited.

'I do not wish to be disrespectful, but I think you are trying to provoke me,' I replied, holding her gaze.

'Ha! You stand your ground well, also as my nephew reported. I like that. The simpering misses these days are too scared to disagree with even their servants. Now, you must call me Honorina. As you are a blood daughter of a prince, I think we are all several stages below you.'

'Thank you, Honorina. I am content to be the wife of Lucius Apulius.'

'I doubt you'll be able to keep your northern freshness confined to that.' She glanced at the top of my head. 'Nor the temper that no doubt resides in all that red hair.'

I laughed and she joined in.

'No, probably not, but I am determined to at least attempt to be a good Roman wife.'

'Humph. Just make sure you keep young Apulius in line. They get out of hand so quickly if you let them. Now, who have you met so far here in Rome?'

'You are my first acquaintance, Honorina.'

'Indeed? Then what in Hades has Constantia been doing? Or is it that fool she married?'

'I cannot say. Perhaps they are letting me settle in.'

'Very loyal of you, Julia.' Her eyes narrowed. 'Gaius tells me there has been no priest called in yet to make a sacrifice and bless your union. Is that true?'

I looked away. She said a word that even my father would shrink from uttering. She raised her hand and a young boy ran to her side.

'Wine and cakes, then my town litter.' The child ran off as if Tartarus himself was after him. Within a few minutes, a young man with a silver tray appeared with a platter of pastries and small cakes, a blue glass flagon of wine and a clay jug of water. He mixed the drinks, handed one to Honorina, then one to me and left as silently as he'd come.

'Now, we will revictual ourselves as my late husband the general would have said, then take the fight to the enemy.'

Her eyes were indeed shining with a martial spirit. These Miteli seemed to be a fighting race.

When my mother-in-law saw who had descended on her house, she paled, then flushed and stood in her atrium shocked into silence. I thought her heart would fail. She collected herself after a minute and invited her formidable visitor in.

'Well, Constantia,' Honorina began when she had been seated in the best chair, the one normally used by Lucius's father. 'I'm surprised I haven't received an invitation to the marriage blessing. I do hope you haven't held it without me.'

'No, no, of course not.' Constantia shot a look at me, but I returned it with a passive expression on my face. 'Julia has endured a long journey,' she continued, 'so we were waiting until she had recovered. Julia and Lucius have asked that it be kept simple. We're on the point of drawing up the list. But then there are the contracts—'

'Don't treat me as a fool, Constantia. The girl's divorced and the only child of a wealthy man of high status. How complicated can it be? If writing contracts is beyond Quintus and his secretary, I'll send my brother to help him. He's an idiot, but at least knows his law. In the meantime, you can at least give the girl a ceremony. Now, what date have you in mind?'

Constantia and I stood side by side as we said farewell to Honorina; she relieved, and I still amused at how the formidable presence had reduced Constantia to witless schoolgirl. Constantia said nothing but gestured towards the peristyle garden and the seat in the shade.

'Julia, I—'

'I know, Constantia. These things are hard.'

'It's Quintus. He thinks it may be a passing fancy for Lucius. That you're exotic and Lucius will revert to a Roman woman.'

'I see. What do you believe?'

She took my hand.

'It's as plain as it can be, my dear. But Quintus is hard to move. He forbade me to introduce you to our friends, but to wait it out.'

'I rather think Honorina has thrust a spear into the wheel to that. She has invited Lucius and me to join them tomorrow at *cena* and afterwards a poetry evening to which she's invited the great and the good. I doubt few will refuse her invitation,' I added drily.

'Gods, no.'

'You will come with us?'

She hesitated for a moment.

'Yes,' she said. 'Yes, I will.'

Constantia hurried off – to draw up a list, she said. Honorina had put the fear of the *lemures* into her. I would not mention this to Lucius as he would not wish to see his beloved mother distressed. She and I would work together on his father. I took a deep breath in. Perhaps my future here was starting to become more established, in my mind if not yet in fact. Perhaps it would become even more solid once the babe was born. I picked a leaf from the nearest shrub and twisted it between my fingers. Perhaps—

'Julia Bacausa?' I looked up, broken out of my daydream. Aegius stood there.

'You called me by my name.'

'Well, you said I was not to use *domina*, now I had been fingered as belonging to a senatorial family. I can't address you as "Hey, you".' He grinned briefly. I laughed, but stopped when I saw the expression on his face.

'What is it, Aegius?'

'I followed you to the Domus Mitela but hung back about fifty paces. I'm sorry to report that you were followed.'

'All the way?'

'The whole route.'

'Perhaps it was coincidence.'

'You really believe that?'

'No,' I said, dully.

'Was it Siro?'

'The hair was brown, but curly, so he's dyed it, and he had a light beard, same colour. He was dressed like a workman, but his gait was what gave him away. He glanced at the Domus Mitela door, then walked on.' Aegius scratched the side of his head. 'I'm embarrassed to admit that I lost him in the Subura. Must be getting old.'

'Oh, no. Aegius. I'm very grateful you spotted that he's still around. It's bad news, but I suppose it would be foolish to think that he's just given up.'

33

The next morning I was up early, but even then Lucius was missing. I dressed in a breast band, tunic, belt and tied on linen *bracae* Asella had made for me, then strapped on my reinforced sandals to prepare for some exercise.

The peristyle garden was spacious, and I was exhilarated by the sensation of the fresh morning air entering my body. But it was tedious running round and round, even dodging in and out of the columns for some variety. But I had nowhere else to exercise. Rome might be the highly sophisticated city, but in a way, I was less free than I had been in Virunum.

Perhaps the public baths would have a women's exercise room with ball games and weights, though probably not sword practice. However, until the threat of Siro was eliminated, I felt inhibited about leaving the safety of the *domus* without adequate escort and I would feel foolish asking either Lucius or Aegius to accompany me every time to the public baths.

But I had to keep healthy for my own sake as well as the baby's. By my calculation, I was nearing the end of the third month. Asella said that if I didn't bleed in the next week, then the baby was safe despite the journey and I would likely carry to term. I was thrilled at the thought, although anxious about the birth itself. Other women seemed to relish tales of pain, suffering and death, but Asella told me to ignore them. She would be there to ease the baby's passage into the world.

I paused in my running to catch a few breaths, but saw something from the corner of my eye that moved. The steward appeared at the opposite wall. Where on earth had he come from? Then I saw it – a door so carefully fitted into the side wall it was barely noticeable. When the steward had disappeared into the kitchen area, I trotted over to the door. The edge followed a straight line of decoration in the wall and the handle was disguised as a twig with a little bird perched on it as part of a mosaic panel. Clever. I heard voices from the other side – shouting and calling. I grasped the handle and pulled.

In front of me was a walled area open to the sky which ran down the whole side of the house. And in the middle were Aegius and Lucius engaged in sword fighting with wooden practice gladii – panting, lunging and shifting, feet stirring up clouds of dust. At the side, under a shallow tiled roof, were benches and a store chest with an open lid. Around the perimeter of the enclosure three men were running round on a marked-out track. Towards the far end, two pairs of men were wrestling. A group of young house servants were throwing a damned hard looking ball between them.

A second later, that ball was flying in my direction. I jumped left, caught it and threw it back with a grunt into the group. Then every single man stopped and stared at me. The ball dropped to the ground. Weapons paused in mid-thrust. Incredulity marked the face of every man.

'Julia.' Lucius was the first to recover. He stepped forward. 'Let me escort you back to the house.'

'Why?'

'It's not seemly for you to be here.'

'Really? Why is that?'

'We are exercising.'

'Yes, I have enough wit to see that.' I gestured at my clothes. 'I am doing the same, but for some reason I have been left ignorant of this place which looks perfect for such activity.'

'You cannot exercise here with the men of the household.'

'Why not? Are they afraid they may look weak against me?'

Aegius burst out laughing and came over to me.

'I think your husband finds it unmaidenly.'

'He knows very well I'm no simpering maiden.'

One of the young men gave an audible snigger. Lucius turned towards the youngster who blenched at his furious expression. I reached out and grabbed the practice sword from Lucius's hand. Then stretched out my other hand to Aegius. He shrugged and gave me his sword. He grasped Lucius's arm.

'Let her settle it her way,' he murmured.

I marched over to the sniggerer, all of seventeen if that, and threw one of the wooden swords at him. He didn't catch it. He stumbled back.

'Pick it up,' I commanded and braced my legs, knees bent, ready. Some of his companions jeered at him. He flushed bright scarlet. He still didn't move. 'Scared?' I said in a loud voice. 'Better run home to mother, then.'

He bent down, grabbed the sword and ran at me. I feinted, let him through, spun round and hit him in the kidneys. He cried out and turned, fury in his eyes and the sword aimed at my stomach. I swept my arm up, knocking the sword out of his hand. He looked dumbfounded, unbelieving.

'More?' I said.

He bent down and snatched the sword up. He approached me more carefully this time, jabbing much more scientifically.

'Much better,' I panted, moving, almost dancing in the dust. I parried his strokes, although he landed one on my shoulder. Then I remembered the trick I'd played on Musius after the games in Virunum. I feinted at my opponent's head. He went to parry and I jabbed him full in the stomach. He collapsed, clutching his middle and crying out. I waited, flexing my fingers on the sword handle, but nevertheless holding it firmly. The young man's friend helped him up.

'I believe you owe me an apology,' I said.

'*Domina*,' he gasped and dropped to his knees and bowed his head. 'I beg your forgiveness for my rude and ignorant behaviour. I am truly sorry.'

'Nicely done. Now go and rest. You'll need a poultice for your stomach. My woman, Asella, is a gifted healer. You have my permission to ask her for help.' With that I picked up the other practice sword, turned my back and marched back to Lucius and Aegius. I handed them the swords. Lucius looked stunned and said nothing, but Aegius smiled and nodded at me.

'Nobody will make that mistake again,' he said. 'That's a good trick you used there, but I can show you a better one, slightly dirtier, but nearly always effective.'

'I'd like that, thank you,' I said. I daren't look at Lucius. I could feel his anger from here. 'Perhaps you have time now, or I could wait until you two have finished.'

'As you wish,' Aegius said.

'Let us proceed.' I looked sideways as if to adjust my belt. Lucius stood with his legs braced and arms crossed and a tight line of a mouth. Aegius went through the move slowly, then I practised it back at him. He speeded up, and I did the same. Then we started practising properly. I failed to parry once, and nearly succeeded the next time. I think he let me succeed the third time.

'It takes practice, Julia. Don't despair,' Aegius said.

'I'll try again tomorrow. But yes, a good move.'

I wiped the sword with a rag and placed both on the bench. I threw one look at Lucius and left the practice ground without looking back.

He caught me after I came back from my bath. He grabbed my wrist and pulled me into our room. I shook his hand off and sat at my table, picked up a comb and drew it through my damp hair.

'Say it and give yourself release,' I said.

'Are you being deliberately crude?' he thundered.

'No, but you obviously want to rage at me, so please go ahead. You will feel a great deal better when you have.'

'You are impossible, immodest and make yourself ridiculous.'

'Please continue. I'm sure there's more.'

'That was intensely embarrassing.'

'Who for?'

'For you, of course. You cheapened yourself in front of the household. You acted like a gladiatrix, an actress, a—'

'Don't say that word or you will regret it.' I laid my comb down. 'Lucius, you knew that I practised sword skills when I lived in

Virunum. We even fought. If you remember you nearly strangled me.'

'That was in private.'

'Not really. The whole household knew and respected me for my skill.' I turned round to face him. 'My mother insisted both Marcus and I knew how to defend ourselves. She was raped at fourteen despite being within her father's house where there were guards everywhere. From that day, she practised and swore no man would ever touch her again without her consent.'

'This is Rome and I will defend you.'

'I know you will protect me, but I cannot turn into a fat and lazy city woman. It's not in my nature. I have fought off bandits. I carry a knife to protect myself and I know how to use it. With Siro still around, I need to keep my skills on a fine edge.'

34

The *cena* at Honorina's was lavish with meats so fine and vegetables so subtly spiced and flavoured, I wasn't entirely sure what I was eating. I took a little of everything but balked at the tiny stuffed cygnets. The Syrian musicians were perfectly pitched and the dancers acrobatic and beautifully costumed. Why did I feel a little uneasy?

Lucius was polite and caring, helping me in and then out of my litter, holding my hand when we met Honorina, but he went to join his friend Mitelus when eating and through the poetry reading. He had obviously not forgiven me.

'Lovers' tiff?' Honorina asked as we went through to the hall for the poetry.

'A slight disagreement,' I replied.

She chuckled.

'I heard you'd been waving a sword around and piercing a few egos with it.'

Hades, the rumours flew here even faster than at home. I didn't want to lose this formidable woman's friendship.

'Honorina, I—'

'No, I commend you, my dear. There are a few I would like to take a sword to. Do not be discouraged. My own niece, Maelia, itches to do more than merely swim and play ball. Perhaps you would take her under your wing.'

'Of course. Though would she be comfortable exercising with men present?'

'Maelia has scrapped since she could toddle with her brothers until her mother insisted that she sit down with her sewing and learnt decorum. In the country, she hardly keeps off her horse all day and loves to hunt with the men. Let me introduce her to you.' She beckoned to a girl around my own age with curly brown hair and sparkling eyes. As she walked towards us with a sure and energetic step, I knew almost instantly that Maelia Mitela would become my friend.

Seven days later, she attended me for the priest's blessing on our marriage. In law, we didn't need it. We were of age, we weren't related, we were both *nobiles* and citizens. Living together by mutual consent as husband and wife was now all that was required. Lucius had discovered that under recent laws neither Quintus nor my father could legally withhold their consent without good reason. We would leave them to argue about contracts at their leisure.

Turcilus had made me no betrothal gift – he'd said marrying me was gift enough from him – so everything in the baggage train that set off from Virunum – all of which were my possessions – would hopefully come back to me. I would gladly give Lucius everything I owned. However, I knew that a public confirmation meant a great deal to Lucius. Constantia managed to keep the number to under thirty which was a blessing in itself.

Aegius stood *in loco patris.* I was divorced and no virgin, but I wore a long white tunic and a yellow *palla* which I draped over my head while the priest intoned his prayers. He made the sacrifice of a young female pig and the seedy looking haruspex he had brought along peered at the entrails and declared the omens were of a fruitful future. He hardly looked at me, but as I slid my hand to my middle I wondered if he did after all have some talent in his profession.

Lucius had thawed by this date, thank the gods, reconciled to my sword fighting, not a little helped by Maelia having joined me for practice in the exercise yard every other day. In this house, in this city, he showed his more traditional nature, but he looked at me with his peat-coloured eyes full of love and expectation as the ceremony was ending, waiting for my formal words.

'*Ubi tu Gaius, ego Gaia*,' I said, smiling at him.

'*Ubi tu Gaia, ego Gaius*,' he replied in a voice so full of emotion I thought he would be overcome. He held my hand for a little longer and slipped a gold ring with a cut-out motto onto my Venus finger.

'What does it say?' I whispered.

'ANIMA DVLCIS VIVAS MECVM. And I hope you will live with me always, my sweet soul.'

'To the end of my days,' I replied.

Despite us wishing not to have the usual patrician fuss of a full *confarreatio* lasting the whole day, Constantia had produced the traditional loaf made from emmer – a *panis farreus* – not the most tasty thing to eat at a feast. We ate it with due solemnity, but I spotted Lucius's friend Gaius Mitelus rolling his eyes. I tried not to laugh, but nearly choked on the crumbs. I swallowed all my portion as I didn't wish to hurt Constantia's feelings.

Quintus stood by Lucius, his shoulders taut and a tight smile on his lips throughout the ceremony. After we sat down to the meal that followed, Aegius diverted Quintus with stories and wine to the extent that we hardly saw him.

After several hours, when the light was fading, Lucius and I rose and made a small prayer at the family shrine containing the *lares* and *penates* statuettes and the *genius* image. I laid a piece of the *farreus* loaf and a few flowers from my garland there.

Lucius leant over and whispered:

'Escape to our room?'

'Yes.'

But Mitelus spotted us and gave us away. Ignoring the dubious catcalls and crude sexual remarks, we walked with as much dignity as we could muster. Maelia softened it all by organising flower petals to be showered over us, causing a rainbow of floating colour around us. Lucius pushed open the door of our room and shut it behind us, pushing the latch down firmly. I dropped onto the bed, overcome with tiredness. He pulled me into his arms and kissed me.

'Now we are as one in the gods' eyes, Julia, and will face the world together.'

'I have a feeling the world had better look to itself then.'

. . .

We lay together in a lazy mood the next morning, a heap of clothes on the floor which was spattered with flower petals. Lucius reached for a beaker of water and drank deeply.

'I think my mother would like to know about the baby, although we don't need to make any announcement to the world.'

'Would you mind very much if we kept it to ourselves for a few days?'

'Of course, if that's what you'd like. But I think we should tell her soon. Even my father can't complain about that.'

'Why is he unhappy about me, Lucius?'

'I really don't know. Perhaps it's because you stand up to him. My mother doesn't, you see.'

'Well, he'll have plenty of time over the next few years to get used to me.'

He laughed, then kissed my forehead, eyelids and lips. His hands ran over my breasts and stomach. I sighed with pleasure that became ecstasy as he loved me.

Later, after bathing, we settled in the peristyle lying on a summer couch. We attempted to read, but even in the soft spring breeze I felt warm as his hand lay on my thigh. I was almost dozing off when a shout came from inside the house. I blinked. Gaius Mitelus and his sister Maelia bounced out of the atrium into the garden.

'Haven't you had enough of fondling each other by now?' Gaius teased.

Maelia threw a look at her brother that should have felled him to the ground.

'Envy doesn't suit you, Gaius,' Lucius shot back. 'What do you want?'

'That's nice, isn't it? Not only have we come to add our further congratulations, but I have some interesting news about the person you're looking for.'

I sat up. Lucius sighed and pulled himself up by me. We exchanged glances. Could we talk in front of Maelia?

'As you're such big friends with my sister, I hope you didn't mind me sharing some of your story with her, Julia.'

Did I have a choice? But I gestured him to continue while Maelia drew up one of the stools.

'This Siro hired a troop of retired gladiators who usually work as debt collectors. Apparently, he's here fairly regularly, usually spring, summer and often in early winter. He supplies things that can't be bought or sold on the open market – stolen no doubt – and sells them through covert channels. He also trades in information. My informant tells me your Siro—'

'Never *my* Siro!'

'Of course. My apologies.' He gave me a half-bow. 'Well, our enemy, then, has a network of contacts of the unsavoury kind in Rome. So when he came to act against you, he already had the men he needed. Apparently, he spun them some story about family quarrels, but to be honest, they probably didn't care as long as they were being paid.'

'Where did you get this from, Gaius?' I was curious about how he, the son of a noble house, had such connections.

'I ran a little wild when I was young. Too much time and a love of gambling on the races. And taking too many risks.' He flushed, then grinned. 'I didn't make the most genteel of friends, but I had fun.'

'Yes, so much fun your father had to bribe a senior magistrate with the promise he would thrash you and send you to the wilds of Britannia to serve in a hard legion,' Lucius said.

'But then I ran into you again, my dear tentmate, and became an upright member of the community.'

'And I ask myself what I have done to deserve such a fate.' Lucius mock-groaned.

This was threatening to become a meandering conversation of reminiscences, so I stepped in.

'Did you learn anything else from your unsavoury friends?'

'I know where he's staying – in a scrotty, half-dilapidated *insula* in the Subura. Not the best part of the city.'

'Then can't the urbans go and drag him out of there?' I asked.

Three faces looked at me as if I'd asked for the moon, the stars and Jupiter's beard.

'*Cara*.' Lucius spoke first. 'It's impossible. First of all, he hasn't actually broken any law here. Gaius's, er, friends won't go anywhere near a court of law to testify about him. Secondly, even if the urbans went in fifty strong, it would cause a riot that would last for days, if not weeks. They just won't go into some parts unless it's a matter of high treason or insurrection. That area runs on its own codes and rough justice. As long as it doesn't spill out into the public parts and the better quarters, the authorities leave the Subura alone.'

'That's ridiculous.' How could a great city run like this? Then I remembered Aegius's discomfort at having to go even to the edge of that district with the two labourers when he was investigating Lucilla. All the pleasure of my morning with Lucius was ebbing away. We had returned to the real world where Siro was stalking me as his prey. I looked at each one in turn. 'Then we will have to tempt him out of it.'

35

No!' Aegius and Lucius spoke together like a Greek chorus.

We'd brought Aegius into our discussion as he had both knowledge and experience of clandestine matters. Lucius was too straightforward and principled, Mitelus too much of a risk-taker, and I wouldn't dream of letting Maelia become involved.

'Don't give me that mulish look, Julia,' Aegius said. 'I know how courageous you are and you have the sharpest and strongest knife Noricum can produce, but Siro is an exceedingly dangerous man, as we have seen. You acting as bait is going too far.'

Lucius put his arm round my shoulder with a firm grip.

'We've only just found each other again and I'm not losing you now.'

'You won't. I'm not proposing doing anything rash or extraordinary, just live a normal life. He's tried to attack me before several times, so we cannot imagine he'll give up now. He can't get inside this house and his one connection, Lucilla, has gone. So we must act as if we believe he has given up.'

'But if somebody is with you all the time, how is he going to get near you?' Lucius asked.

'That's the problem,' I replied.

'I suggest you go about your normal business,' Aegius said. 'Your husband can accompany you sometimes – that would seem normal. Other times, you should go out with Asella and perhaps Maelia here with you—'

'No, Maelia must not be drawn in,' I replied.

'Oh no, Julia, you're not leaving me out,' she said. 'Of course I want to help.'

'Your aunt would never forgive me if you were hurt.'

'Do you believe I'm not capable of striking somebody down?' Her voice was distinctly icy.

'Gods! You're as bad as your brother. This is not a little adventure for a joke. This is trying to draw out a very capable and completely mad assassin.'

'Then all the better that we're as cunning as he is,' Maelia retorted.

That afternoon, Lucius and I set off, I in the litter and he walking beside me. I'd drawn the curtains back so I was fully visible.

'I don't like this,' he muttered.

I put my hand out to join his.

'I know. Let's hope it works. Anyway, I'm looking forward to seeing something of Rome.' I pointed at the enormous temple with two myrtle shrubs, one each side of wide steps leading up to the entrance. Its pediment frieze showed heroic characters, Victory with her palm, birds flying over the tall principal figure and other forms brandishing swords or branches each side. 'You can tell me about this great temple to start with.'

'Ah, the Temple of Quirinus...' he began.

Soon my beloved and knowledgeable husband had become absorbed in showing me his city. I wondered at it all, but occasionally glanced sideways and once or twice backwards but I couldn't see anyone even resembling Siro. Nor did I know whether it was Aegius or Gaius Mitelus who was following us at a distance. We returned after two hours. I'd had enough of the hot sun, the noise and the smells.

Next day, Asella and I went to the nearest market with both Aegius and Gaius trailing us separately at distance. The stalls and carts with flowers were a heavenly respite from the animal dung and dubious cooking smells. Asella bought some small pots of growing herbs and I a beautiful woven red, yellow and blue fringed *palla* the merchant swore came from the land of the Seres, beyond India, at the eastern edge of the world. Although I managed to bargain him down a third, I certainly thought I'd paid the ship's voyage as well. But it was very beautiful.

'It suits you, *domina*, and will go with any of your robes.' Asella stood completely still, closed her eyes for a moment, then opened them and looked into the far distance without saying a word. I waited for a few heartbeats, then became concerned.

'Are you well, Asella?'

'This city is a strange place, full of noise and perpetual movement, overwhelming in every aspect. But I have found a grove in the gardens near the Apulius house where I can be at peace. The young girl who serves Lady Constantia, Diacu, is an Alamanna captive and she showed me. She is straight out of the woods and seems happy to have found somebody who knows the rituals. Even if she was manumitted, though, I think she would be lost.'

'Poor child. Would you like to have her as your particular assistant? I'm sure Constantia would agree.'

'Perhaps, but you and I are still relative newcomers here, and you are only just finding your place. We have plenty of time, now that you are here and with your Apulius.'

'And I have you to thank for being my staunch supporter, Asella.' I placed my hands on her shoulders then pulled her to me in a close embrace. 'You have been as a mother to me since *Matir* died.' I rested my chin on the top of her shoulder, catching the scent of rosemary from her hair. 'I can't think why I haven't done it before, but as soon as we return to the house, I will draft your writ of manumission.'

'All in good time, *domina*. But I hope you are not going to make me have to earn my keep afterwards.' She gave me a mock-serious look, but I saw the laughter in her eyes.

'You see, you're always teasing me,' I said, 'when you're not scolding me.' She knew I would never turn her out. She was my link to my dead mother and too large a part of my own life. I linked her arm through mine, closer to her than ever.

We were wandering back along the street to the turning for the Domus Apulia when I had the sensation of being watched. I was very tempted to turn, but Aegius had instructed me never to do that. It was better to appear as if you hadn't noticed, he'd said.

'Have you noticed that somebody—'

'Yes,' Asella replied. 'Let's keep going. Hopefully one of ours will spot whoever it is.'

We reached the *domus* without incident, but I was grateful for the protection of being inside the house and behind its stout wood door. I let out a long breath. I knew I had talked Lucius and Aegius round to my scheme, but I was still trembling at its execution. After a beaker of refreshing *posca*, I hurried off to speak to Constantia about arranging a household ceremony for Asella's manumission. At present, that seemed more important than anything.

'But surely, that's for Lucius to decide, my dear,' Constantia said. 'Or your father.'

'No, Asella was my mother's body slave and I inherited her under her will.'

'Oh, I see.' But she still looked puzzled. Hades take these old-fashioned ideas! But I said nothing more as I didn't want to upset her. I was still the junior wife whatever I might want to think, and she was Lucius's mother after all. But I was determined we would do this as soon as we could.

Aegius appeared a short while afterwards from the back of the house with his hooded cloak slung across his arm and boots dusty from the street. I stood and went towards him. He held his hand up.

'Before you ask, it *was* Siro following you. He's a clever bastard. This time he's shaved off his moustache and put something in his hair to make it greyer. But it's his slightly bowed walk that gives him away. Too much time on a horse, or more likely, a mule when he was younger, I'd suspect.' He paused. 'But he's still here and he's still watching. Now we have to corner him.'

Quintus ordered Lucius to go to the farm estate out in the country with the quarterly stipend for the free workers and to check with Zolcius, the overseer, that all was well. There had been a shortfall with the last consignment of produce.

'I'll only be away for one night, *cara*, two at the most.'

'I think I'll survive,' I said. 'But you will be back in time for Asella's ceremony?'

'Of course.'

'Mercury keep you,' I said as he set off the next morning. But I had to admit to some anxiety. Even though the god protected travellers, he was also the trickster and patron of thieves.

Eating *cena* with Quintus, Constantia and Aegius that evening, I was surprised when Quintus asked how I was settling in. I finished eating my piece of spiced chicken before answering. Aegius shot me a warning look.

'I find the city completely fascinating, thank you, Quintus. Lucius has been escorting me round some of the important public buildings and I've been visiting the markets with Asella and making a few social contacts. Maelia Mitela is taking me to the women's rooms at Diocletian's Baths tomorrow – I gather it's magnificent.'

'Humph.'

Constantia glanced at him. 'And in the house with us?' she said.

'You could not have been kinder,' I said looking at her. I thought her too subservient, but her relationship with Quintus was not my concern.

'Very well,' Quintus said with a resigned air. 'Then there is no need for Sempronius here to dally. He should set off to your father with my letters tomorrow.'

I looked at him with horror. We needed Aegius here to help catch Siro. I cleared my throat.

'I would like him to stay for a few more days, in particular for my maid Asella's manumission ceremony. Lucius said he wished to be here as well.'

'For an old slave, a tribeswoman, who doesn't belong to the *familia*?' Quintus snorted. 'That's no reason. He goes tomorrow.'

'I regret, Father-in-law, that I will have to decline,' I said in a frosty tone. 'Aegius Sempronius will stay with me as long as I require him. His actions are my responsibility and at my orders, as set down by my father, his patron.'

I thought Quintus was going to have a seizure. Why did he always need to make everything a battle?

'And Asella is not merely an old slave, as you charmingly put it,' I continued. 'She is my beloved body slave who cared for my mother and, since I was a child, for me. I have been negligent in not considering her manumission before.'

'You'll do as I say, my girl, while you're under my roof!'

I sat up and signalled to the house servant to bring my sandals.

'Then I will remove my unbearable presence. Please excuse me while I instruct Asella to pack my belongings.' I sent Aegius a look which I hoped conveyed my unambiguous message. He finished eating immediately and rose from the *triclinium*. He bowed to Quintus and Constantia and walked by my side to the corridor leading to the row of bedrooms. Round the corner, he seized my arm.

'What in Hades was that about?'

'The gods know. Lucius's father doesn't like me. I think he sees me as a threat to his authority and somebody who has taken his son away from his control.'

'That's Italian Romans for you.'

'I don't think it's geography, Aegius. That's how he is.'

'Yes, but where are we going? Here at least you're safe. And Siro can't get you.'

'We'll go to Honorina, of course.'

'And how in Tartarus will Lucius Apulius take it?'

'You remember the ancients' accounts of the volcano eruption at Pompeii in the reign of Titus?' I raised an eyebrow at him. 'Lucius's reaction will be as explosive.'

Aegius said he only had a few tunics and sundries to stuff in a bag, so I sent him to Domus Mitela with a begging letter. Just over an hour later, he returned with Honorina's litter and a note for me.

Greetings to Julia Bacausa ux. Apulia at Domus Apulia from Honorina Mitela.

Of course, you must come and then tell me all about it!

Maelia will be ecstatic.

H

36

When I turned in the vestibule to take one last look, Constantia held her hand out to me.

'Oh, my dear, won't you change your mind?'

'I'm sorry, Constantia, truly I am for your sake, but I will not be dictated to about my own people nor live under a cloud of continuous resentment. Please inform Lucius that I am staying temporarily with Honorina Mitela who is welcoming me into her home. He is also welcome. Thank you for your personal kindness to me. Goodbye.' I turned quickly to face the entrance door so that she wouldn't see my tears.

Half an hour later, Honorina Mitela was welcoming me into her arms and her brother's *domus*. Maclia embraced me and showed me to a room which was enormous with colourful vivid frescoes. Asella followed me and even she gaped at the luxury of the furnishings.

'Come along, Julia,' Maelia said. 'I'm sure Asella will organise it all perfectly.' She nodded to a tall woman who had followed us in. 'Marcia here can help her. Aunt Honorina is agog to hear your news. I expect she won't get anything out of Aegius. He's far too fly.' I just wanted to sit quietly for a while to think over what I had just done. Had I sabotaged my life with Lucius before it had really begun?

In the atrium, Honorina was holding court. The fact that Aegius was the only courtier present made no difference. She must have been formidable as the general's wife. She lifted her hand and a servant was there with a tray moments later. He set the tray down, mixed me a beaker of wine and water and vanished.

'Now, I'm delighted to see you, my dear Julia, but I confess to deep curiosity about your removal from Domus Apulia.'

After I'd finished relaying the events, she raised both hands and her eyes towards the *compluvium* gap in the high roof.

'Juno Sospita! Quintus is even more of an idiot than my brother. He seems to think he's living in Republican times. And Constantia needs to buck her ideas up. Not that she will.' She sighed. 'When is your husband back from the country?'

'Tomorrow, or possibly the day after.'

'I hope his father is ready for the tempest.'

The next morning, Maelia persuaded me to continue our plan to visit Diocletian's Baths. We set off early, with Marcia and Asella trailing behind. It was further away than Trajan's, but nearest to Domus Apulia. If Siro was trying to follow me, it was there that he would expect me to go. I'd seen it from the outside – an enormous stone building built by giants – but inside it was as magnificent as Maelia promised. Blue and red overlaid with mosaics and paintings of gods and nymphs soaring over us. Statues looked down on us from every angle.

'However did they haul so much stone to build this?' I waved my hand around.

'It's brick, covered with stucco. Well, so Gaius says. A bit like some people – beautiful outside and clay inside.'

'But it's so high. I'm amazed it hasn't collapsed under its own weight.' I couldn't take my eyes off the huge vaults. The roof was the height of twenty men. Now I did feel like a provincial.

'Never mind that. Let's go and choose some oils. My favourite's calendula. What's yours?'

I selected a rose one, almost at random, from the hundreds of coloured vials on display. The noise of talking, music, calling, splashing in the main swimming pool and grunting from exercise echoed round the walls. Maelia led me away from the main hall to a small room where we undressed and went into a *caldarium* where half a dozen women were sitting or lying elegantly but sweating like anybody else. It was only after we'd dipped in the cold water of the *frigidarium* and were being massaged by bath slaves with our chosen oils that Maelia spoke in confidence. She looked round first, but no other client was near us.

'I know this is one of the women's rooms, but I couldn't see any sign of you-know-who as we walked here and then through the hall. Aegius told me and Gaius about his distinctive walk. Gaius is shadowing us today so maybe he'll see him.'

Relaxed after the massage, we strolled back through the enormous hall, glancing round, but seeing no sign of Siro we left and returned to Maelia's house. We were eating a light lunch with cheese and spiced vegetables when Gaius strode into the room and threw himself into a chair near us.

'No show, I'm afraid. But at least we're all clean and it cleared my hangover.' He grinned at me. But I didn't feel very cheerful, so I gave him only a polite smile back. I worried about Lucius who had no idea of what was waiting for him when he arrived home and I worried equally about our inability to trap Siro.

When Aegius appeared, I invited him to walk round the peristyle at the rear of the Mitelus house, where I confided in him. He listened without commenting as we completed the circuit several times.

'Leave Lucius to sort things out with his father. I think Senator Apulius will already be regretting his high-handedness.'

'I know I must respect Lucius's parents, but his father keeps trying to oppose me or order me about as if I were fifteen or trespass on my personal concerns. I know I'm not the wife he wanted for his son, but I'm not entirely unacceptable.'

'Think of it this way – you're the daughter of a royal house, a confident and wealthy young woman in her own right and one who comes from a long line of independent and fierce fighting women. You probably scare him to death!'

'Oh, that can't be right.'

'Believe me, insecurity takes many forms,' he said. 'Give the old man time.'

'Perhaps. I will think about it and discuss it with Lucius when he returns.'

'Now, about Siro…'

'We need to drop our guard and invite his attack or we're never going to come to an end of it,' I said.

'Agreed, but I dislike making you more open to possible harm.' He sighed. 'But I would like to return to Virunum, to my daughter and grandson. She's patient, but I promised him I'd let him help on the next panel in your father's atrium.'

'I'm sorry to keep you here, Aegius. You must go when you want to.'

'We'll try a few more times to get this wretched half-brother of yours first. But yes, I think I must go very soon.'

I couldn't help but feel depressed about Aegius leaving. He'd supported me steadfastly from the beginning. Nobody could have asked for a more competent and wise counsellor, or one with humour and courage. It would be like losing a second father. But he had his own life and family and I had to forget my personal wishes. The heat was becoming stifling, so I went to rest in my room with the shutters closed. But all I did was turn everything over in my mind as I lay in the semi-dark.

After my rest, I couldn't find Asella. I tracked her down eventually to a secluded part of the peristyle garden. She was muttering about the fates and the goddess of retribution and holding her arms to the sky in supplication. I waited until she'd finished her prayers. When she turned, her face was deathly white.

'Asella? Are you well? Here, sit with me in the shade.'

'I was lost in the veil between the worlds, *domina*.' She sat up straight and took several deep breaths. I hadn't ever questioned her beliefs or practices, which she observed sincerely and intensely. She wasn't a witch – she cast no spells nor pretended to have the sight – but sometimes she seemed to be somewhere other than with us. She turned and searched my face, her eyes dark and large.

'Yes, it is important for those who will come after you that you are safe. The wild one must be destroyed.'

Then she fainted into my arms.

I spoke her name, trying to rouse her, and patted her cheeks, but she was too far gone in a trance. If I was honest, it was frightening that her body was so limp. I could hardly detect her breath. She was truly with the goddess. Helpless to do anything but guard her, I sat with her, my arms folded round her body to support her, and found myself humming a formless tune. After a while, I realised it was one she had sung to me as a child. The late afternoon breeze had started, refreshing us both and the colour returned to her skin. She blinked and a moment later sat up straight.

'What happened? Why are you holding me as if I were a child, *domina*?'

I let my arms drop.

'You were overcome, Asella. Possibly by the heat? You were standing right in the sun.'

'Nonsense. I never faint. Except…' Her voice trailed off. She glanced at me. 'Well, never mind that. We must get you changed for *cena*.' She stood, completely balanced, with a determined look on her face. She wasn't going to talk about what had just occurred, so I didn't insist. But something significant had happened.

It was high time I made my own spiritual observance and I chose the Temple of Juno Licina on the Esquiline. Apart from being the queen among the gods, Juno represented all aspects of the life of women, particularly married life. Although she never answered me, I found contemplating her soothing, and a connection with all women. As Licina, she was the goddess of women in childbirth. I hadn't felt any sign of the babe when I put my hand on my belly, but Asella said it was too soon, even at the end of the third month.

Asella and I walked up the short flight of steps through the portico and into the *cella*, the central part of the temple. The walls had been freshly painted and tables along the side gleamed with many hours of hard polishing. A statue of Juno sitting with two babes in her lap on a shallow dais greeted us. Nearby were braziers and small dishes in the centre of each with oils sending out the scents of dittany, catmint and verbena.

We both bowed our heads, lost in our own thoughts. A priestess approached us and we made our sacrifice. Asella stared at the rising smoke for a long time while I prayed for a safe delivery. Next year, I would come to the Matronalia in March to celebrate with other mothers.

As we left, I felt calmer. Perhaps it was merely having a quiet time of reflection in a cool and serene place. We started back to Honorina's house which wasn't far. For once, the street with its tall blocks of *insulae* wasn't crowded and we strolled along, arms linked, almost without hindrance.

'Lucius should return today, so we'll hold your manumission ceremony tonight. I have the writ prepared.' I gave Asella my warmest smile.

'I've never told you this, but I expect you know that I have always seen you as the daughter I never had.' She returned the smile.

'Well, you're as strict as any mother could be,' I said.

She laughed and I joined in, content with the world.

I looked to make sure we were on the right street that led to Domus Mitela. I was confident enough with the area now to have taken a shortcut that would bring us to the house within a few minutes. Then I saw him walking towards us.

Hair short and grey in some places, but blond growing through, no moustache, but it was him. His swinging walk betrayed him. He was looking straight at us, a knowing smile on his lips.

I gripped Asella's arm.

'Siro,' I whispered.

'Goddess protect us.' Her eyes widened in panic.

I briefly touched my robe in the place where my knife was hidden. He was twenty paces away from us. The gap between him and us was closing fast.

'Steady,' I whispered to her. 'Aegius will strike him down.' Then it flashed into my mind. Aegius was somewhere behind us. He wouldn't have seen Siro coming from the opposite direction. Siro would reach us before Aegius even knew about the danger we were in. I looked round but couldn't spot him. Minerva help us. We were on our own.

37

Siro came to a halt three paces in front of us. In his right hand he held a *pugio* dagger with a wicked, shining blade that reflected the sunlight. He stood, legs flexed at the knee and head held high. He was ready for battle.

'Well met again, little sister.' His voice was as mellow as it had been on the ship when his hair had been fully blond and curling. The lines on his face were deeper than before.

'What do you want, Siro?' I said and tried to keep calm. Asella's arm still on mine trembled.

'And I thought you were supposed to be a clever woman, Julia.' He snorted. 'To kill you, of course.'

Asella whimpered and her fingers brushed my skin as she withdrew her arm. A stab of fear struck my middle. The baby. I pulled myself up to my tallest height.

'Why? I have done nothing to you.'

'No? Your father stole my mother. I'm going to deprive him of his daughter in retaliation. Permanently.'

'My mother went voluntarily with my father. She loved him until the day she died. Asella told me of her rape, of her anger and shame.' I stretched out my hand towards him. 'I'm sorry you suffered in your childhood from her violation.'

'Suffered? My life was blighted. I was a non-thing for her.'

'But her aunt brought you up and cared for you.'

He pointed to Asella.

'I see the witch has been busy with her tongue.'

'Asella has told me the whole story.'

'Not all of it, I warrant. How I was shunned, left to be bullied, made to carry out a slave's tasks. And my grandfather was one of the most powerful chiefs of the Alamanni, a war leader.'

'You were fed and sheltered.' Asella had found her voice. 'Many wanted you left in the woods for the gods, but you were spared. And we all had to work.' She gave him a hard look. 'You were lucky not to have been cast out when you were discovered thieving and trying to make others take the blame.'

Siro took another step forward and raised his dagger in Asella's direction.

'Peace!' I shouted. He switched his gaze to me. 'You were on the ship from Tergeste. Would you have killed me there in front of all those people?'

'I could have thrown you overboard, but your tame gorilla protected you too well. Still, I made sure he got a good beating here in Rome. Pity that damned soldier interfered.'

'You could have declared yourself and we could have talked together,' I said.

'You are so naive,' he replied. 'What would I want to talk to you about? No, it's twenty years too late.'

'You were the one who led the attack in the mountains.'

'Of course. I allow you put up a good defence.'

'And you tried to stop us at the Mulvius bridge?'

'Yes, the Christos followers were easy to convince to help me stop my young Christian sister being abducted to make forced marriage to a pagan.'

'How dare you? I was *not* being abducted and my marriage was my heart's desire.'

'I know that, and you know that, but the facts could easily be moulded into that story.'

'You unspeakable liar.'

'Is that the worst name you can call me?' he said with a smirk.

'How did Musius fall for your manipulation? I saw him standing next to you at the bridge.'

'You did, did you?' He snorted. 'That so-called soldier of your father's was so cheaply bribed it was embarrassing. After a few drinks, he maundered on about the deep shit he would be in with your father having lost you. He was sure he'd lose his place as soon as he returned to Virunum. So for a small bag of silver, he threw in his lot with me.'

'Well, it didn't work,' I retorted. 'We entered the city despite your manipulations.'

'Your lumpen servant – the old centurion – must be cleverer than I thought.'

'Aegius is loyal and clever – a hundred times your worth.'

'Dear me, do you have feelings for him, Sister? Your husband would be upset.'

'Keep your filthy thoughts to yourself. He is my father's age and his loyal client,' I shouted at him.

Where in Hades was *Aegius?*

I caught my breath. The heat was so oppressive and I was starting to feel faint. Out of the corner of my eye, I noticed two women had stopped and were looking at us curiously. An old man was walking by slowly, helped by a stick and watching us. A murmur of voices came from the other side of the street and a man shouted out, 'Are you all right, darlin'?' I ignored him. Siro shouted out, telling him to mind his own business. But I kept my eyes firmly on Siro. Now my skin was crawling and not because of the heat.

'You know nothing of decent friendship and comradeship,' I said. 'You even suborned a slave in my husband's household.'

'Ah, Lucilla – she was a tasty piece in every sense. Nice buns.'

Would he ever wipe that supercilious smile off his mouth? Now he was shifting from foot to foot, as if excited in the worst way. I had to keep him talking, praying Aegius would appear.

'Lucilla confessed you'd visited her several times here in Rome.'

He laughed with a sharp and bitter tone.

'I've been watching you for months, Julia. And planning. You didn't take much notice of the brooch seller in the Virunum market, did you? I was just one of many tradespeople under your nose.' He jabbed a finger at Asella. 'Even the witch didn't see me for all her supposed talents.' He laughed, then his face took on a smug expression. 'I couldn't get to your father, although I managed to filch one of his prized swords. A fine blade until I lost it. But you… you made yourself so vulnerable when you fucked that Roman. I learnt about you – your temper and your waywardness. I watched you waiting in the street for him – pathetic. So I knew you wouldn't let him go.'

'How did you know which ship I'd be on?'

'Ha! Your father buggered my first plan when he sent you off to be married.' He gave me a curious look. 'Why was that?' He stared at my face, then my middle. I tried to stop my face going red by taking slow breaths, but I couldn't.

'You're breeding.' His eyes gleamed. 'Two for one when I push you into the shades. Even better.'

I swallowed hard, then took a deep breath to calm my pulse and rising anger. It would do no good for him to see how furious I was. And how frightened. My heart was pounding. I squeezed Asella's hand hard. Siro grasped his dagger tighter, oblivious to the passers-by who had stopped to watch us. I put my hand back and grasped the handle of my knife whose sheath was concealed by the full skirts of my robe.

'What would killing me achieve?' I rasped.

'You are the last of your line. It will be eradicated when you die. And your brat. I will have had my vengeance on your bastard father and our whore mother.'

'My mother was no whore.'

'She was also a killer.'

'What?' I croaked. What in Pluto was he saying?

'After her other whelp died, she set her brother, my uncle Ittu, on me. To dispose of me.' His face flushed and tightened. 'He nearly succeeded. For some reason, she thought I'd had something to do with your precious little Marcus's death.'

'You poisoned him,' Asella cried out. 'I could smell it on his breath, the poor mite. It had to be somebody from our village – that plant grows few places elsewhere.'

I stared from one to another. What was Asella talking about? What other secrets did she have?

'I couldn't help it if that greedy little turd ate the sweetmeats I sent to my dear mother,' Siro said and smirked.

'You bastard!' I saw a red mist before my eyes and flew at him, but Asella grabbed my wrist and held me back. Then she shouted at him in a language I couldn't completely follow, although I recognised the words burn, curse and eternity.

'The gods' pity that Ittu didn't succeed in killing you,' she shouted, shaking her other hand clenched in a fist at him.

He raised his dagger above his head and launched himself at me. A flash of green came between us. Asella's scent of rosemary flooded around me. She screamed. Her body hovered, then collapsed in front of me. Siro bent over her, his dagger now gleaming bright red with her lifeblood. A dark stain gathered in a patch on her chest.

'No,' I shrieked. 'Asella!' I dropped to a crouch beside her lifeless body. Then I looked up. Siro's face was contorted. His eyes were bulging in their sockets and brimming with hatred. He raised his dagger again and lunged at me. The point of his dagger, still dripping Asella's blood, came within inches of my eye.

As if by instinct, I leant back then sprang up and I thrust my dagger into the side of his neck. His eyes flickered as he grunted. His mouth opened and a loud gurgle came from his throat. Blood spurted out of his neck over me. He fell on me, a dead weight, his breath still warm on my face. As I fell, I knocked my head on the hard slabs of the street. Then nothing.

38

'Stand back, for Mars' sake, stand back!' a man shouted. A voice I knew.

My head was spinning. I blinked. Then I remembered. I burst into sobs.

'Gods, oh gods,' I cried out. Tears ran down my face. I started trembling as I struggled to sit up.

'No, stay where you are.' Aegius.

My head hurt as if Vulcan himself was pounding at it. I closed my eyes.

Booted, hobnailed feet thumped by, then stopped. Aegius shouted at somebody. The smell of sweat. More shouting. Then arms underneath my body and I was lifted onto something soft. Curtains around me and I opened my eyes to see cloth flapping in the breeze. I was in a litter being carried along at speed.

More arms lifted me. I was laid down on a soft surface that didn't move. Somebody was wiping my face with lavender water, then removed my robe and bathed my body.

'Asella?' I murmured.

Silence.

'Sleep now, Julia,' a young voice said after a few moments.

• • •

Stone beaker on my lips. A bitter infusion. Warm arm around my shoulders. I smell him. I know him. Lucius. I open my eyes. The peat-brown eyes, the smile. I drink. I'm safe now. I close my eyes. Sleep.

'You will not bleed her. Her maid – a renowned healer – thought it barbaric.'

'But sir, the humours must be drawn from her.'

'My final word. Now get out.'

I heard somebody humph, then leave the room.

'Are you sure, Lucius?' Maelia.

'Yes. Nobody will touch her.' Lucius sounded angry and determined.

'Lucius,' I murmured.

My hand was grasped in a warm one. The weathered skin along the back and the soft palm. I opened my eyes and saw two anxious faces, eyes reflecting the dim light from a pottery lamp at the side.

'Oh, you are back.' I smiled.

'And so are you, *cara*.'

I looked at his dear face, now lined with ridges and shadows that hadn't been there before. He looked exhausted. Maelia stood the other side of the bed. I realised I was in my room at Honorina's house, Domus Mitela. But it was dark apart from the oil lamp.

'Is it night-time?' I asked.

'No, the late afternoon,' Maelia said. 'We thought you would find it more restful to lie quietly in the dark. Aegius said you had struck your head when you… fell.'

'Please open the shutters. I would like to see the light.'

Maelia pushed them back and the soft afternoon light lit up Lucius's face. Most of the shadows disappeared, but not the solemn expression or the intense look in his eyes. I turned away and gulped.

'What is it?' he asked.

'Asella. Is she…'

'She has crossed the Styx,' Lucius said in a gentle voice and turned my chin back so I faced him. 'She died quickly and with very little pain, nobly defending you. We will honour her memory with every observance.'

'Oh, gods, Lucius, I feel so guilty. She sacrificed herself for me. I cannot live with the guilt.'

'Now, listen, Julia,' he said. 'She would have been the first to chide you for such thoughts.' I stared at him. 'I did not know her as you did, but I realise your bond was strong. Talk to Aegius who knew her so much better.' He stood, then bent and kissed my forehead. 'I am going to leave you to rest now but I will return this evening. I have some words to say to my father.' His face became grim. 'You will never be so slighted again. I can assure you of that.'

I insisted on sitting up later but gave in to half lying on a couch in Honorina's favourite alcove in the atrium. Maelia had hovered over me as I made my way there.

'I am well, Maelia, and I can assure you that my headache has nearly gone. I promise you I will be careful for the remainder of the day. But I make no promises for tomorrow.' I gave her what I hoped was a reassuring smile.

'Very well, but you're not going to fob me off so easily. The first stumble and I shall make you go back to your bed.'

'Hm. You can try.'

She laughed, and left me with her aunt, but not before wrapping a *palla* around my shoulders.

'She means well, Julia,' Honorina said. 'She's so strong and energetic that she doesn't know how to cope with illness or injury and so overcompensates and fusses. She'll learn.' She handed me a steaming beaker. 'Now, my woman has prepared this for you. Apparently, it's fortifying and good for the blood.' I sipped it and made a face at the bitterness.

'Why do all medicine drinks taste vile? Even Asella's and she—'

I looked away.

'Now, my dear, you must let your grief come out but not to the detriment of the child growing within you. Although I saw only a little of her, I think Asella would have supported you in your mourning – the sacrifices, prayers to the gods and lighting her pyre – but she would, I feel, have told you to carry on with your life afterwards.'

'I don't know, I feel numb. I keep expecting her to come round the corner ready to tell me it's time to change or my hair is a mess and must be combed. But she doesn't.'

'Well, the men will be back soon and I expect Aegius will have something to say on that as well as reporting your brother's death.'

Perhaps it was the herbal drink, the warm June evening, the rhythmic rippling of water in the reservoir below the *impluvium* or even the soft lyre music that Honorina had commanded, but I dozed off. I was rudely awakened by several series of footsteps.

'All this lying down is not good for you, Julia. You'll become lazy then you'll despise yourself.' Aegius.

'Hush, my wife is resting. She has been gravely injured.' My beloved Lucius.

'Come off it, Lucius, she's made of tougher meat than that. You haven't married a soft flower.' That could only be Maelia's brother, Gaius.

I decided to open my eyes.

'And what do you all mean by clattering in here like a horde of barbarians?' I said.

Aegius and Gaius laughed and dropped onto stools. Lucius came to sit by my side.

'Well, you'll want to know our news,' Aegius started. 'I've made a witness statement and I grabbed two of the bystanders to say their piece as well. The urbans arrived just as you were injured, so they were useless. My brother will ensure that there's no blame of any sort attaching to you in connection with your half-brother's demise.' He looked at me steadily. 'I regret infinitely that I could not arrive earlier to help. A donkey-brain had spilled the contents of his cart over the road and caused another to smash up against it and shed his load of furniture over the rest of the road which completely blocked it. The gods know why they allow drivers to stack their wagons so high.' He looked down at the mosaic floor. 'By the time I found you, Asella was gone.' He held out a hand. 'I would feel greatly honoured if I could join you by the pyre.'

'Oh, Aegius, the world is such a bleaker place without her.' A tear rolled down my cheek. I looked at him. 'Of course, you must be with me at the funeral.'

Lucius brought his warm arm round my shoulders and I rested my head on his.

'I've made a statement on your behalf, *cara*, although I know you are still in the guardianship of your father. I did not wish you to be subjected to questioning.'

'I appreciate your thoughtfulness, Lucius, but I will comply with any request from the magistrates. I feel a great deal better now.' I knew he had my best interests at heart and would protect me with his life, but he would learn in our life together that I would order my own affairs. But I turned and smiled at him.

Later in my room, we were able to talk privately.

'Did you see your father?'

'Yes,' he said in a terse voice. 'I gave him the choice. He must apologise to you and mind his manners, or we leave his household and set up our own. I am fully emancipated, and I have my grandmother's property, so we would not be paupers. Would you like living by the sea?'

'Oh, Lucius, the last thing in the world I want is to be the cause of division between you and your father. And your mother who was kind to me. She will be embarrassed by the scandal.'

'Well, I've told him that I will be staying here with you until I hear from him.'

39

With all the rest I'd been having, I couldn't sleep beyond dawn the next day. My head was clear and I went for a brisk walk several times round the peristyle in the fresh white light of the morning. It also banished the nausea I'd experienced on waking.

I was eating my breakfast of bread and cheese when Honorina's housekeeper who would normally be supervising her staff at this time, hurried up to me. She looked flustered.

'It's the Lady Constantia of the Flavii. From Domus Apulia, *domina*. The porter was on his break, and I was passing by the vestibule when I heard knocking at the door.'

'This early? Show her in immediately, please, and bring some refreshments for her.' The housekeeper nodded and disappeared.

Moments later, my mother-in-law walked across the atrium. She was simply dressed with only a plain necklet and earrings enhancing her long tunic and *palla*. She looked tired with the skin below her eyes drooping. I stood up to receive her.

'Mother,' I said as I kissed her cheek. 'Please, sit and join me.'

She glanced around the richly painted walls.

'We are quite alone and can speak freely,' I reassured her.

'I'm sorry to disturb you so early, Julia, but I had to come and see how you were. Lucius said you were badly injured after your half-brother attacked you in the street. Is this true? The attack, I mean.'

'Unfortunately, yes. It's a very long story but I hope I will be able to recount it in full later when we are all settled.'

'Ah! That is the other matter. Lucius was quite plain with his speech yesterday to his father and I agree with him. I am embarrassed about how Quintus has behaved. But he is the head of our household…'

'Then we will go and live at Lucius's grandmother's house and bring our child up playing in the sand and swimming in the sea.'

'Child? You are breeding already?' Her eyes widened in shock, then she gave a broad smile. She stood and waving aside the housekeeper's offer of food, she looked at me. 'That settles it. I shall talk to Quintus again, but I can assure you that we will be welcoming you back to our house – your house – very soon.'

'Ha!' Honorina said later with a gleam in her eye. 'Nothing like news of a child to continue the bloodline to bring an old-fashioned *paterfamilias* like Quintus Apulius into line.' I went to speak, but she continued, 'Never underestimate the thirst for heirs with these old families.'

'I'd rather be accepted for myself.'

'Times are changing, Julia, but not that fast. However, I never thought Constantia would be the rebel of her circle. Well, we are all surprised from time to time.'

And so it was that later that day I crossed the threshold of Domus Apulia on Lucius's arm, Aegius following and Asella's body on a wheeled bier. Quintus stood beside Constantia to welcome us. He and Lucius nodded at each other, but exchanged no word. Constantia gave me a warm hug and took me off to her room.

The following day, we prepared Asella's body for her pyre. We carried out these rituals in a room at the back of the Apulius house, given the widespread Galilean distaste for traditional public funeral processions. I laid one of the *solidi* I'd brought from Virunum in her mouth to pay the ferryman. Constantia's young serving girl, Diacu, the Alamanna who had prayed and carried out the rituals of the tribes with Asella in their private grove, begged to help. She stayed in the corner, almost hugging the walls of the cold room while the family priest said his prayers, read the signs in the pig sacrificed in Asella's name and gave his blessings.

When the door closed, the young woman came forward and sprinkled oil smelling of pine over the body. She laid a branch of rosemary over the place where Siro had stabbed Asella and started chanting in a high, rhythmic, almost other-worldly voice. At first, it was melancholy and I wept, then the song seemed to be calling to something or somebody. It ended with the girl raising her arms up to their full height and making three short, high-pitched shouts. Perhaps it was only the cold of the room, but at that point I shivered.

Aegius and I held the torch together that evening at the private burning ground near the Apulius mausoleum along the Appian Way. Lucius insisted that Asella's ashes be placed within his family *columbarium*. Dusk had just fallen, the time when spirits start to stir. As we bent the torch down to light the pyre, I whispered my last farewell to her, hoping she would hear me.

'Goodbye, my dear beloved companion, my other mother who gave me so much. May your journey be a smooth one wherever your gods take you.'

Asella was my last connection with my mother. That bond was now broken. Perhaps weeping for her, I also wept for my mother. Lucius held me as we watched for the hours it took. Afterwards, we sprinkled wine on the ashes, and Aegius gathered them with the few fragments of bone remaining into an urn which we placed in an empty niche in the mausoleum. The priest gave a final blessing, then hurried away in the darkness. He didn't return for the *novendialis* nine days later, but we said our own prayers then and carried out the rituals of fire and water before eating and drinking in Asella's memory.

Although I gave Aegius some silver to defray any possible expenses, I didn't ask him how he'd disposed of Siro's body. He, Lucius and Gaius ventured into the Subura a week later in daylight and examined Siro's room. They brought everything back with them, not that it was much – some tunics, breeches, a pair of boots and a travelling cloak and a roll of cloth containing two stoppered vials of brown liquids, one half empty, another dagger and a purse with a significant amount of *miliarensia* and *solidi*. I told them to give the money to a charity to help educate children of poor parents. The clothes they could offer to the servants.

The contents of the two vials which Aegius thought were noxious should, he said, be discarded well away from any house. I wondered if that was the substance Siro had coated his sword with that had caused the grave infection in my arm when he attacked us in the mountains. Aegius poured them away on the spoil heap of amphorae shards near the Horrea Galbae warehouses and reported to me that the nearest shards sizzled when the liquid fell on them and burnt a hole in the pottery.

A month after Asella had passed into the shades, and Aegius had parted to make his way back to his family in Virunum, I woke one morning to a stomach spasm. Then another. They were faint but definite.

'What?' Lucius murmured, still dozing. I guided his hand to my stomach. His eyes widened. 'Gods, it's the baby.'

'Yes, she's still alive.'

'She?'

'To have survived this year, it must be a girl. They're more robust than boys.'

'Ha! I'm not sure about that. Perhaps *my son* is a natural fighter.'

I laughed and tapped him on his chest with the back of my hand. He grasped it and kissed it.

'We truly are a family now.'

Our baby was born just over four months later, ten days before Saturnalia began. A fuzz of red brown covered her scalp and her good lungs gave the whole *familia* no doubt of her vitality. Eight days later in front of family and friends, I watched as Lucius laid her down on a cushion at the feet of his father. She wasn't crying, but mewing like a kitten. Maelia Mitela stared at her as if she was a miracle. Honorina and Constantia looked on as if the baby had been

308

all their own work. Gaius looked slightly bored, but hovered by Lucius to support him.

Quintus took his time looking at us one by one with a stern expression. Juno, he wasn't going to refuse the child, was he? He had made me a formal apology when Lucius and I had returned to Domus Apulia, although it hadn't been a very enthusiastic one. If he didn't acknowledge my child, she would never be part of the family. We had agreed with Quintus that he headed the Apulii, but that Lucius and I would have control over ourselves, any children we had and any property. Lucius's hand sought mine, but he glared at his father. If Asella had been here, I wouldn't have put it past her to have eaten Quintus alive.

People began to fidget. Honorina now looked daggers at Quintus and Constantia's cheeks became flushed. Eventually, Quintus raised his hand. From it dangled a leather strap with a moon-shaped gold locket. I closed my eyes for a heartbeat in relief. When I opened them, he was bending down. He scooped the baby up in his large hands.

'Her names?' he asked his son.

'Galla Julia Apulia Prima.'

'Humph. That's a lot of names for a tiny mite,' Quintus said. 'She might not live long enough to learn how to say them all.'

Lucius gripped my hand hard so I could not move. I would never like Quintus Apulius and I liked him a little less in this moment. My child had been in danger of never being born. I was determined she *would* grow to adulthood whatever Quintus said.

EPILOGUE

Rome, summer AD 371

Galla was six months old when I had a strange visitor. It was June and I was nursing her in the peristyle. I'd fed her myself since her birth despite Constantia hinting heavily that it was inelegant and would ruin my figure. I loved the sensation of the tiny warm lips on my breast, her eyes closed in concentration and the dribbles that fell down her chin as she dozed when she was full.

I was absorbed in gazing at Galla's contented face, when I had a tingling feeling I was being watched. I looked up and gasped. In front of me was Asella's cousin, the wild tribeswoman, the shaman. Talusia.

She still wore a boldly patterned dress with bells and fringes at the edges of an overtunic. The fibula holding her cloak at the shoulder was silver with the same fantastic and frightening animal shapes as before, but the metal had tarnished. The intricate twisted gold torc round her neck was the same as six years ago when she came to my mother's deathbed. And her belt of plaques resembling skulls seemed to be more crowded. But now her hair was grey instead of black, and sparser. And she seemed shorter, shrunken somehow.

Diacu, Constantia's body servant, was hovering nervously behind her, the fingers on her hands twisting together.

'Talusia,' I said and stood, clutching Galla to my chest.

The tribeswoman fixed me with dark grey eyes buried deep in her face.

'You remember my name,' she replied in a wavering voice barely above a whisper and in my mother's language. Some of her teeth were missing and others stained.

I nodded and waited.

'I came to see that my cousin has truly passed into the next world.'

'She has, and I grieve for her every day. To my great sorrow she never saw the child I was carrying.'

'She sees her.'

I shivered.

'Yes, you know it. You are your mother Suria's true daughter.' She half turned and waved her hand in Diacu's direction. 'This child will show me Asella's resting place so I may purify it, but first I have something to say to you.' She looked at me, but in a strange way, she gazed straight through me into the distance. 'This is the first of your daughters and she will wear the purple, but not here. She will return to the mountains, but not with you. You and the man in your bed have founded a long line that will struggle through time, but preserve the things you hold dear.' She blinked then swayed. Diacu came forward to support her. Talusia turned without a further word and limped towards the vestibule, Diacu in her wake. The porter opened the door without being asked and bowed as they left.

I blinked and shook my head. What on earth had she meant? I heard footsteps behind me.

'Who was that?' Lucius's arms folded round me. I leant back against him, reassured by his warm physical presence after an encounter with the messenger from the spiritual world.

'An old cousin of Asella's come to pay her respects. She made some confused remarks about Galla's future but mumbled so I'm not sure I heard correctly.' I turned slowly and smiled at him. 'Our future is here, together, and so is Galla's and that of any other children the gods may give us.'

WOULD YOU LEAVE A REVIEW?

I hope you enjoyed *JULIA PRIMA* which is the tenth in the Roma Nova series, but the first in time.
If you did, I'd really appreciate it if you would write a few words of review on the site where you purchased this book.

Reviews will help JULIA PRIMA feature more prominently on retailer sites and invite more readers to find out about Roma Nova. Thank you so much!

You can meet Julia's descendant, Silvia, in *INCEPTIO,* the first of the 21st century Roma Nova adventures.

GLOSSARY

Actuariolum – Small ferry boat

Arrhae – Marriage portion

Aurora – Goddess of the dawn

Balteus – Balustrade running round the front edge of seating in an amphitheatre

Basilica – Large hall for for legal matters to be carried out and a place for business transactions

Cardo maximus – North – south street in cities and camps

Caupona – Scruffy bar

Cena – Dinner

Chi-rho – Symbol widely used by Christians

Comitatus/comitatensis – Late Antiquity mobile field army

Confarreatio – Formal patrician marriage ceremony

Curiales class – Merchants, businessmen, and mid-level landowners who served in their local *curia* as local magistrates and decurions

Dalmatica – Late Antiquity robe worn by men and women

Decumanus maximus – East-west street in cities and camps

Decurion – City councillor

Diocesis – Late Antiquity regional governance district

Equites – Property-based class of ancient Rome, ranking below the senatorial class

Familia – Blood family plus household members

Galileans – Name given to early Christians by non-Christians

Illustris (pl. *illustres*) – Member(s) of the highest ranks within the senates of Rome and Constantinople

Insula (pl. *insulae*) – High rise city apartment block(s)

Limes – Roman border defence or delimiting system

Limitanei – Professional border troops

Mansio – Rest and refreshment establishment on a Roman road for the use of officials and those on official business

Milites – Soldiers/sailors

Miliarense (pl. *Miliarensia*) – Large silver coin, 4th century

Oneraria – Sea going merchant ship

Palla – Roman woman's mantle, secured by brooches

Pallium – Roman cloak. Had replaced the toga by Late Antiquity

Paterfamilias – Male head of household

Porta libitinensis – Door of the dead

Porta sanavivaria – Door of the living

Salutatio – Greeting ceremony

Solidus (pl. *solidi*) – Late Roman gold coin

Spatha – Long (later) Roman sword

Statio – Basic way station on Roman roads

Stibadium – Semi-circular dining couch of Late Antiquity that replace the three couches of the Classical period

Tablinum – Office in a house

Tabularium – Public records office

Urbanae (cohortes urbanae) – Gendarmerie or militarised city police (Also called 'urbans')

PLACE NAMES ANCIENT AND MODERN

Latin name – **Current name and location**

Aesontius fl. – River Soča or Isonzo, Italy/Slovenia
Ancona – Ancona, Italy
Aqua Viva – South of Città Castellana, Italy
Aquileia – Aquileia, Italy
Argentoratum – Strasbourg, France
Asculum – Ascoli Piceno, Italy
Augusta Raurica – Augst/Kaiseraugst, Switzerland
Auximum – Osimo, Italy
Caporetum – Kobarid, Slovenia
Carsulae – Abandoned, near Terni, Italy
Castra Regina – Regensburg, Germany
Danuvius fl. – River Danube, Europe
Dravus fl. – River Drava, Austria and Slovenia
Flosis fl. – River Potenza, Italy
Fons Timavi – San Giovanni, Duino, Italy
Forum Flaminii – San Giovanni Profiamma, Italy
Forum Iulii – Cividale del Friuli, Italy
Iulium Carnicum – Zuglio, Italy
Lauriacum – Lorch/Enns, Austria
Mare Adriaticum – Adriatic Sea, Mediterranean Sea
Meclaria – Arnoldstein, Austria/Italy/Slovenia border

Mediolanum – Milan, Italy
Mevania – Bevagna, Italy
Narni – Narni, Italy (see last section in the Historical Note)
Nar fl. – River Nera, Italy
Noricum – Austria & part of Slovenia,
Nuceria Camellaria – Nocera Umbra, Italy
Ocriculum – Otricoli, Italy
Ovilava – Wels, Austria
Pucinum/Castellum Pucinum – Prosecco, Italy
Pletium – Bovec, Slovenia
Pola (Pietas Iuila) – Pula, Italy
Pons Mulvius – Milvian Bridge, Rome, Italy
Pons Sonti – Mainizza, Italy
Prolaqueum – Pioraco, Italy
Saloca – Krumpendorf am Wörther See, Austria
Santicum – Villach, Austria
Septempeda – San Severino Marche, Italy
Seres – Cathay / China,
Spoletium – Spoleto, Italy
Tarvisium – Tarvisio, Italy
Tergeste – Trieste, Italy
Teurnia – St. Peter-in-Holz, near Spittal an der Drau, Austria
Tinia fl. – River Topino, Italy
Tricesimum – Tricesimo, Italy
Vallicula – Barcola, Italy
Vicus Martis – Massa Martana, Italy
Virunum – Zollfeld, Maria Saal near Klagenfurt, Austria

Note: fl. = fluvius (river)

HISTORICAL NOTE

The story of Julia and Lucius is a personal one, although implanted in the brink of a momentous transition in the Roman world. However, few people like a history lesson when they're immersed in reading a story! But if you're interested in background about Virunum, Noricum, the state of the Roman Empire, the famous Noricum steel, emperors, religious conflict, marriage laws in the late fourth century, Roman timekeeping and why Narnia isn't called that in this story, read on…

Virunum

Julia Bacausa's home city of Virunum, or more formally, Municipium Claudium Virunum, was founded under Emperor Claudius (AD 41–54) as the capital of the province of Noricum which covered more or less today's Austria and northern Slovenia. It's gone, but there are some fascinating ruins you can visit today.

Virunum lay in the valley below Magdalensberg, widely believed to have been the earlier royal capital city of the pre-Roman Celtic kingdom of Noricum. The Roman new town was built on the main route from the Adriatic to the Danube, with a branch of that route running through south-eastern Carinthia connecting Virunum with the Amber Road (hence the amber traders in Chapter 1).

The city enjoyed Latin Rights, a series of privileges roughly equivalent to those of the citizens of Rome itself, and was the seat of the provincial governor (*procurator Augusti provinciae Norici*) until the middle of the second century. After the Marcomannic Wars (AD 166 until 180), the centre of civil government for Noricum moved north to Ovilava, but the administration of the province's finances remained in Virunum. When Emperor Diocletian later split Noricum in two, Virunum became the capital of the southern province of Noricum Mediterraneum.

A note about a legendary capital

The kingdom of Noricum was formed, albeit it loosely with many sub-chiefs, hundreds of years before, around 400 BC, complete with royal residence in a city called Noreia which, unfortunately, nobody has been able to locate conclusively.

Many (rather romantic) theories float about even today concerning its location. As a result of excavations in the 1920s at Sankt-Margarethen am (or bei) Silberberg (west of Graz in Austria), much excitement and campaigning led to the village's name being changed to Noreia. After further examination, the ruins and finds proved to be those of a medieval settlement. But the name of Noreia stuck. You can even find it today on online digital maps.

According to Julius Caesar, Noreia was known to have been the capital of the Celtic kingdom of Noricum, but it was already referred to as a lost city by Pliny the Elder (AD 23–79). We'll leave it in the romantic legend category for now…

Later Virunum

From AD 343 at least, the city is known to have been a bishop's see (hence the character of Bishop Eligius). Virunum (*Virunensis*) is still a titular see of the Roman Catholic Church today.

Little is known about the decline of the city. However, being unfortified and lying in an open, flat valley and unable to be defended, Virunum was probably partially or probably completely evacuated by its inhabitants during the Migration Period of the fifth to seventh centuries. They would have left for more secure walled settlements on the surrounding hills such as Ulrichsberg or Grazerkogel.

Perhaps some might even have gone back up to the safety of their ancestors' Magdalensberg.

The famous Noricum steel

Noricum was mountainous but like many Alpine regions well endowed with wide fertile valleys for cattle breeding and agriculture. The plant *saliunca* (wild or Celtic nard) grew in abundance, was exported and used for perfume according to Pliny the Elder. But its core source of wealth were metal-bearing deposits, especially iron ore, gold and silver. The famous Noric steel was widely used in making Roman weapons. Even Horace (*Odes*, i.16.9–10) mentions *Noricus ensis*, 'a Noric sword'.

The strength of any steel is determined by its composition and heat treatment. Most wrought iron produced in the Greco-Roman world was too soft for tools and weapons. Ore from Noricum, by contrast, yielded a superior product.

The best ore needs to be rich in manganese (an element still essential in modern steelmaking processes) and contain little or no phosphorus, which weakens steel. Ore mined in Noricum fulfilled both criteria particularly well. The Celts of Noricum had discovered around 500 BC that their ore made superior steel, so they built up a major metalworking industry. Traces have been found on the Magdalensberg (the pre-Virunum settlement on the hill) of a major production and trading centre where specialised blacksmiths crafted metal products, including sophisticated tools and weapons.

Once the military authorities of the Roman Republic discovered this, they were not slow in setting up a robust supply agreement with Noricum which consequently became a major provider of weaponry for the Roman armies from the mid-Republic (290 BC–90 BC) onwards.

Dealing with Rome

By 200 BC, the tribes of Noricum had united into one kingdom, the Regnum Noricum, which became a key ally of the Roman Republic, providing high-quality products in exchange for military protection. This was demonstrated in 113 BC, when the German tribes Teutones and Cimbri invaded Noricum. In response, the Roman consul Gnaeus Papirius Carbo led an army over the Alps to repel these Germanic tribes. He ambushed them near Noreia (wherever that was). Although Carbo had the advantage in terrain and surprise, his forces were overwhelmed by the sheer number of tribal warriors and roundly defeated. He was afterwards accused by Marcus Antonius (yes, that one) for losing the battle through incompetence. Convicted, Carbo committed suicide rather than go into exile.

Roman rule

For a long time, the Noricans enjoyed independence under princes of their own while continuing to trade profitably with the Romans. In 48 BC, they took the side of Julius Caesar in the civil war against Pompey – a savvy move.

In 16 BC, they joined with the neighbouring Pannonians in invading Histria and were defeated by Publius Silius Nerva, proconsul of Illyricum – not such a good move.

As a result, Noricum was annexed by the Roman Empire and, although called a province, it was not organised as such but remained a kingdom with the title of Regnum Noricum, yet under the supervision of an imperial procurator.

When Noricum was fully integrated into the Roman Empire during the reign of Claudius, apparently the Noricans offered little resistance. It was only in the time of Antoninus Pius (AD 138–161) that troops in the form of the Second Legion Pia (later renamed Italica) were stationed in Noricum; their commander became the governor of the province.

Under Diocletian (AD 245–313), Noricum was divided into Noricum Ripense (Noricum along the right bank of the Danube, the northernmost part of the original province), and Noricum Mediterraneum (landlocked Noricum, the southern, more mountainous area).

Each division was administered by a civilian governor called a *praeses*, and both belonged to the diocese of Illyricum in the Praetorian prefecture of Italy. But pragmatism often led to a *praeses* leaving fully Romanised local community leaders like Julia's father to manage local affairs.

Noricum and Christianity

Rome's many nationalities practised widely different forms of religion, but all priests and communities recognised the overarching authority of the emperor, especially as he was the *pontifex maximus* (chief priest) for the whole empire. Diocletian and his immediate successors strongly promoted the traditional Roman pantheon of gods. When members of the Christian cult refused to make sacrifice to the established gods, which included deified past emperors, they were deemed by the emperor to have rejected imperial rule, i.e. committed treason. And treason tended to have only one outcome.

In AD 304, Florianus, a Christian serving as a high-ranking imperial military commander in Noricum who had amongst other achievements set up an extremely effective firefighting unit, refused to sacrifice and was executed. He was later canonised as Saint Florian and to this day is the patron of firefighters in the German-speaking world.

Traditional religion still flourished in Noricum and a new temple to the god Mithras, especially revered by the military, was dedicated in Virunum around AD 311.

Only when Constantine (reigned AD 306–337) became emperor, and in practice only from AD 312, did Christianity begin to take hold in Noricum. By AD 343, there were at least five bishops with well-established circuits of congregations. By the end of the fourth century, statues of gods in the Virunum baths quarter had been destroyed.

In the fifth century, enthusiastic Christian mobs smashed the most important shrines and traditional temples throughout Noricum. Pagan cults survived in patches as late as the second half of the fifth century, but those practising the rites were officially shunned and courting death.

Knowledge of Roman Noricum has been extensively documented by Géza Alföldy in his work *Noricum* (Routledge, 1974, rev. 2014) to which I am much indebted.

Roman emperors

At the time of JULIA PRIMA, which takes place between AD 369 and 371, the emperor was Valentinian I, sometimes called Valentinian the Great, who reigned from AD 364 to 375. He named his brother Valens as co-emperor, giving him rule of the eastern provinces while Valentinian retained the west.

During his reign, Valentinian fought successfully against German tribes – Alamanni, Quadi and Sarmatians. Most notable was his victory over the Alamanni in 367 at the Battle of Solicinium. His general Count Theodosius defeated a revolt in Africa and next routed the Great Conspiracy, a coordinated assault on Roman Britain by Picts, Scots and Saxons, in which our character Lucius Apulius fought, but which led to life-changing consequences for Lucius.

Valentinian was also the last emperor to conduct campaigns across both the Rhine and Danube rivers. He rebuilt and improved the fortifications along the frontiers, even building fortresses in enemy territory – something which, unsurprisingly, was strongly resented by the tribes. Unfortunately, his sons Gratian and Valentinian II who succeeded him in the western half of the empire were neither as tough nor successful, but that's for another story.

The state of the Roman Empire in AD 370

The empire had evolved significantly since the classic time of Augustus and Marcus Aurelius (first and second centuries AD). It was in transition; fewer public buildings were maintained, more cities built defensive walls, enormous landholdings for some opposed a dispossessed urban proletariat, more barbarian incursions and/or settlements became normal, civil and military organisations changed significantly.

Gone was the 'one of the people' rulers of the Principate and in its place were the remote and 'godlike' emperors of the Dominate. Power had shifted from Rome to Constantinople, Milan, Trier and Antioch as Eastern and Western Empires drifted apart.

Yet people still saw themselves as intrinsically Roman. Not only was Roman law in the late empire universally valid, but it's also now broadly accepted that the late Roman administration was more effective and responsible than once believed. Looking back, it appears that the quality of legal training, the judicial competence of Roman officials and the strong interaction between law and society in the late empire still flourished, particularly in the towns and cities. Sharp awareness of Roman law and its impact is highlighted throughout literary sources of the period.

However, as in the Classical period and in every time period since, there were limits of law as an influence on social habits. And the Roman concern with property was still to the fore. The principal function of the state's law was to regulate, to provide publicly enforceable rules for transactions between parties that might result in dispute. And in family law, private contracts were fundamental.

But the power and influence of, and respect for, the Senate in Rome was diminishing further during the fourth century. The senatorial order expanded precipitously from around 600 members to in excess of 3,000, slowly displacing the equestrian ranks and requiring from the late fourth century ever finer gradations of status within the order.

This expansion was fuelled both by the rise of local elites, principally decurions, and by the admission of an ever-increasing proportion of 'new men', principally through imperial service. Thus, the status of the fourth-century Roman aristocracy became more fluid and weaker.

On the positive side, the Mediterranean in the middle to third quarter of the fourth century was nevertheless home to an exceptionally wealthy, urbanised society ruled by a single state, integrated economically and socially. In a high-fertility, high-mortality society dominated by the basic needs of feeding and reproducing itself, the structure of the family, its concerns and activities had changed little in the late empire.

Although roads and bridges were not always repaired – local funding through taxation dwindled and some routes were abandoned – trade still flourished along those remaining in use. Roman society was complex, defined by legal and economic relationships, and although not as robust as in the high empire, those relationships were still strong. Being Roman and acting like one was still an ingrained habit, acquired over centuries.

By AD 370, the traditional founding of Rome in 753 BC was 1,123 years in the past, equivalent for us today of AD 900, the year after the death of Alfred the Great. Did the Romans see themselves as lasting forever? Unknown to them, the process of continuous evolution and adaptation that had saved them over the centuries would grind to a halt and the colossus, weakened over decades, would soon disintegrate completely.

Within a bare hundred years, the last Western emperor would abdicate, having surrendered his last small landholding around Ravenna with a sigh.

Roman families, marriage and divorce in Late Antiquity

Our heroine Julia Bacausa's problem is that she is caught between Roman law and Christian dogma; divorced legally under the first, but bound to her unpleasant (ex-)husband under the second. The late Roman family inherited its basic form from the high empire. Monogamy was a strong cultural value, whatever the personal sexual behaviour of the spouses.

Late Roman law, following social practice, tended to recognise the nuclear family unit when considering the rules for marriage, guardianship and succession. Christianity reinforced this but introduced two distinctive and revolutionary ideas: the doctrine of indissolubility of marriage and the ideal of sexually exclusive marriage.

Familia in the Roman sense meant the legal group under the power of a *paterfamilias*, not only of biological descendants, but extended family including cousins, sometimes brothers, sisters, sons- and daughters-in-law, protégés and slaves. It was a complex organism, but the conjugal bond and parent–child relationships were at its core.

The marriage bond in classical Roman law was only lightly regulated by the state. Marriage was a relationship formed *procreandorum liberorum causa* (for the purpose of producing children); it required no formal ceremony or even property exchanges, only marital intent, consent from all those who were a party to the marriage (including the *patres familias*), and legal capacity to marry (age, degrees of separation, status and citizenship). Because mutual intent defined marriage in classical law, a marriage could be dissolved by either one of the spouses.

By Late Antiquity, things had changed. Betrothals became increasingly formalised and enforced by public law; moreover, men began making a contribution similar to the dowry, the *donatio ante nuptias*, allotting part of their property as a donation to a conjugal fund.

Already in the imperial period, men were known to have made engagement gifts to cement the process of contracting a marriage. Third-century texts show that these gifts could be reclaimed by the man if the engagement was broken, unless he was responsible for breaking it off. At some point before AD 380, Roman legislators instituted a system in which betrothals were ensured by the exchange of earnest payments, called *arrhae*. Breaking the engagement entailed repayment of four times the *arrhae*.

Whatever its origins, the practice of the *donatio ante nuptias*, the gift from groom to bride, extended rapidly over the fourth and fifth centuries. These gifts, which joined the dowry as part of the conjugal fund in the wife's ownership, would be considered a form of insurance that was especially useful in situations where the man's social position or social intentions were less than fully defined.

The *donatio* functioned more like a safety deposit than a true exchange, since the property went to the wife rather than her natal family, thus remaining under the husband's control unless he ended the marriage.

Constantine, abandoning law and practice of centuries, issued his own regressive law restricting the grounds for divorce to the most heinous crimes. If a woman repudiated her husband for any other cause, she not only lost her dowry, but she was also deported. Nevertheless, women could breathe a sigh of relief when during the later reign of Julian (AD 361–363), the classical regime of free, unilateral divorce was re-established. This is how Julia was able to divorce her unsatisfactory husband perfectly legally under Roman law.

However, the doctrine of indissolubility which prevailed in late Roman Christianity held that a marriage was the joining of two into one flesh which meant the early Christian Church strongly opposed both divorce and remarriage. Moreover, to discourage remarriage further, bishops could evoke the belief in an afterlife and insist that a couple joined on earth continued to exist after death. Divorce was therefore impossible, and remarriage would be considered bigamous, even for a widow or widower.

Elements of the traditional Roman marriage would go on to blend with Christian dogma, leading to the purpose of marriage being defined from Late Antiquity as 'procreation, partnership, and preventing fornication' (Isadore of Seville, *Etymologiae* c. 600-625). But easy divorce and the lack of need to have a blessing or sanction from the state or religious authorities vanished until the twentieth century.

Roman timekeeping

Initially, the day was divided into two parts: the *ante meridiem* (before noon) and the *post meridiem* (after noon). With the advent of the sundial circa 263 BC, the period of the natural day from sunrise to sunset was divided into twelve hours.

An hour was defined as one twelfth of the daytime, or the time elapsed between sunset and sunrise. Since the duration varied with the seasons, this also meant that the length of the hour changed. Winter days being shorter, the hours were correspondingly shorter and vice versa in summer. At Mediterranean latitude, one hour was about forty-five minutes at the winter solstice, and seventy-five minutes at summer solstice.

The natural day (*dies naturalis*) ran from sunrise to sunset. The hours were numbered from one to twelve as *hora prima*, *hora secunda*, *hora tertia*, etc. To indicate that it is a day or night hour Romans used expressions such as for example *prima diei hora* (first hour of the day), and *prima noctis hora* (first hour of the night).

Just as a point of interest, the Roman day starting at dawn survives today in the Spanish word *siesta*, literally the sixth hour of the day (*sexta hora*) and in Church services such as prime, terce, sext and none, and of course, a.m. and p.m. in the 12-hour clock.

And finally, a confession

Around the start of the first millennium an Osco-Umbrian people settled on a high hill in Umbria above the River Nar and called their town Nequinum. Records mention the name as early as 600 BC. Along came the Romans in the fourth century BC and promptly conquered it. In 299 BC it became a Roman municipality and took the name Narnia. Yes, Narnia.

When looking at a map of Roman towns in *Murray's Small Classical Atlas*, C S Lewis came across the name of a little town in central Italy called Narnia. He never visited it but took the name for the imaginary country in his books for children simply because he liked the sound of it. Not sure what the Romans would have thought of that...

It's not entirely certain when the city of Narnia changed its name to Narni, but likely from around the thirteenth century onwards, although until the end of the nineteenth century tombstones and in official documents still used inscriptions with the ancient name of Narnia.

To avoid readers making unworthy connections, giggling over the name and making fruitless searches for fauns and talking lions, I decided to use the more modern name of Narni. Apologies for any lacerated feelings.

ACKNOWLEDGEMENTS

I firmly believe that writing a book is a team effort. No writer can achieve much in isolation. The plot, characters, themes, message and prose is theirs, but when it comes out of the forge, it's a bit of rough pig iron. The honing and tempering is so vital to producing a shiny end product. So sincere thanks to my fellow smiths:

The indefatigable Denise Barnes (a.k.a. novelist Molly Green), my critique writing partner of ten years, for casting her eagle eyes over the first version and giving it her usual 'brutal love'.

Helen Hollick for her invaluable help with horses, their characteristics and their care, and for generally making sure I didn't make a horse of myself.

Ruth Downie for guiding me through Roman travel, kindly providing me with excerpts from Lionel Casson's *Travel in the Ancient World* (which I went and bought).

Gordon Doherty who put together a list of late Roman Empire texts for me. Some I knew about, but others were undiscovered treasure.

Anna Belfrage for straight talking, especially for romantic matters.

Jessica Bell Design for her patience and professionalism for designing the cover and fending off my wackier ideas.

Carol Turner, who has copy-edited several Roma Nova stories with firmness but friendliness, pinpointing repetitions, mis-spellings and preventing me from mixing up Pliny and Livy. She has more than knocked my commas into line.

THE ROMA NOVA THRILLER SERIES

The Carina Mitela adventures

INCEPTIO

Early 21st century. Terrified after a kidnap attempt, New Yorker Karen Brown, has a harsh choice – being terminated by government enforcer Renschman or fleeing to Roma Nova, her dead mother's homeland in Europe. Founded sixteen hundred years ago by Roman exiles and ruled by women, it gives Karen safety – at a price. But Renschman follows and sets a trap she has no option but to enter.

CARINA – A novella

Carina Mitela is a new officer in the Praetorian Guard Special Forces. Disgraced for a disciplinary offence, she is sent out of everybody's way to bring back a traitor from the Republic of Quebec. But the conspiracy reaches into the highest levels of Roma Nova…

PERFIDITAS

Falsely accused of conspiracy, 21st century Praetorian Carina Mitela flees into the criminal underworld. Hunted by both security services and traitors she struggles to save her beloved Roma Nova as well as her own life. Who is her ally and who her enemy? But the ultimate betrayal is waiting for her.

SUCCESSIO

21st century Praetorian Carina Mitela's attempt to resolve a past family indiscretion is spiralling into a nightmare of blackmail and terror. Convinced her beloved husband has deserted her and her children, and with her enemy holding a gun to the imperial heir's head, Carina has to make the hardest decision of her life.

The Aurelia Mitela adventures

AURELIA

Late 1960s. Sent to Berlin to investigate silver smuggling, former Praetorian Aurelia Mitela barely escapes a near-lethal trap. Her old enemy is at the heart of all her troubles and she pursues him back home to Roma Nova but he strikes at her most vulnerable point – her young daughter.

NEXUS – *A novella*

Mid 1970s. Aurelia Mitela is serving as ambassador in London. Helping a British colleague to find his missing son, Aurelia is sure he'll turn up.

But a spate of high-level killings pulls Aurelia away into a pan-European investigation and the killers threaten to terminate her life companion.

But Aurelia is a Roma Novan – they never give up…

INSURRECTIO

Early 1980s. Caius Tellus, the charismatic leader of a rising nationalist movement, threatens to destroy Roma Nova.

Aurelia Mitela, ex-Praetorian and imperial councillor, attempts to counter the growing fear and instability. But it may be too late to save Roma Nova from meltdown and herself from destruction by her lifelong enemy….

RETALIO

1980s Vienna. Aurelia Mitela chafes at enforced exile. She barely escaped from her nemesis, Caius Tellus, who grabbed power in Roma Nova.

Aurelia is determined to liberate her homeland. But Caius's manipulations have ensured that she is ostracised by her fellow exiles.

Powerless and vulnerable, she fears she will never see Roma Nova again.

―――

ROMA NOVA EXTRA

A collection of short stories

Four historical and four present day and a little beyond

A young tribune is sent to a backwater in 370 AD for practising the wrong religion – his lonely sixty-fifth descendant labours in the 1980s to reconstruct her country. A Roma Novan imperial councillor attempting to stop the Norman invasion of England in 1066 – her 21st century Praetorian descendant flounders as she searches for her own happiness.

Some are love stories, some lessons learned, some resolve tensions or unrealistic visions, some are adventures. Above all, they tell of people with dilemmas and in conflict, and of their courage and effort to resolve them.

Printed in Great Britain
by Amazon

58396468R00199